PETER CORRIS was born [...] worked as a lecturer a[...] freelance writer and jour......., specialising in sports writing and personality profiles. In the late 1960s and early 1970s he travelled in the Pacific Islands, including Papua New Guinea, the Solomon Islands and Fiji. The author of many books about the Sydney-based private eye Cliff Hardy, he has also written spy novels, historical novels, a social history of prizefighting in Australia, quiz books and radio and television scripts. His best-selling historical novel, *The Gulliver Fortune*, was published by Bantam Books in 1989.

Peter Corris has three daughters and lives in Sydney.

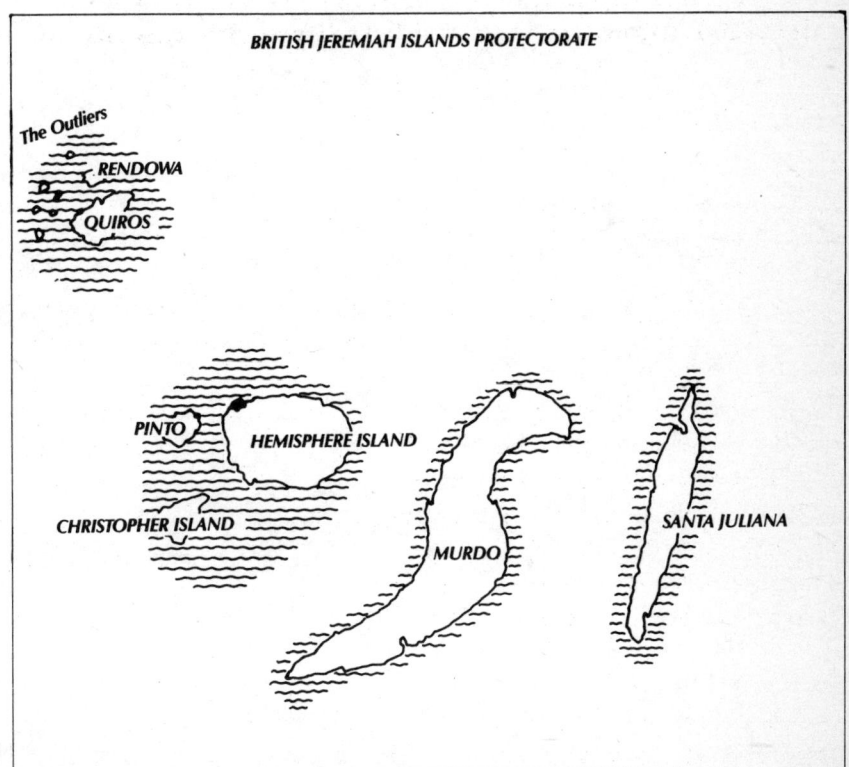

BRITISH JEREMIAH ISLANDS PROTECTORATE

The Outliers

RENDOWA

QUIROS

PINTO

HEMISPHERE ISLAND

CHRISTOPHER ISLAND

MURDO

SANTA JULIANA

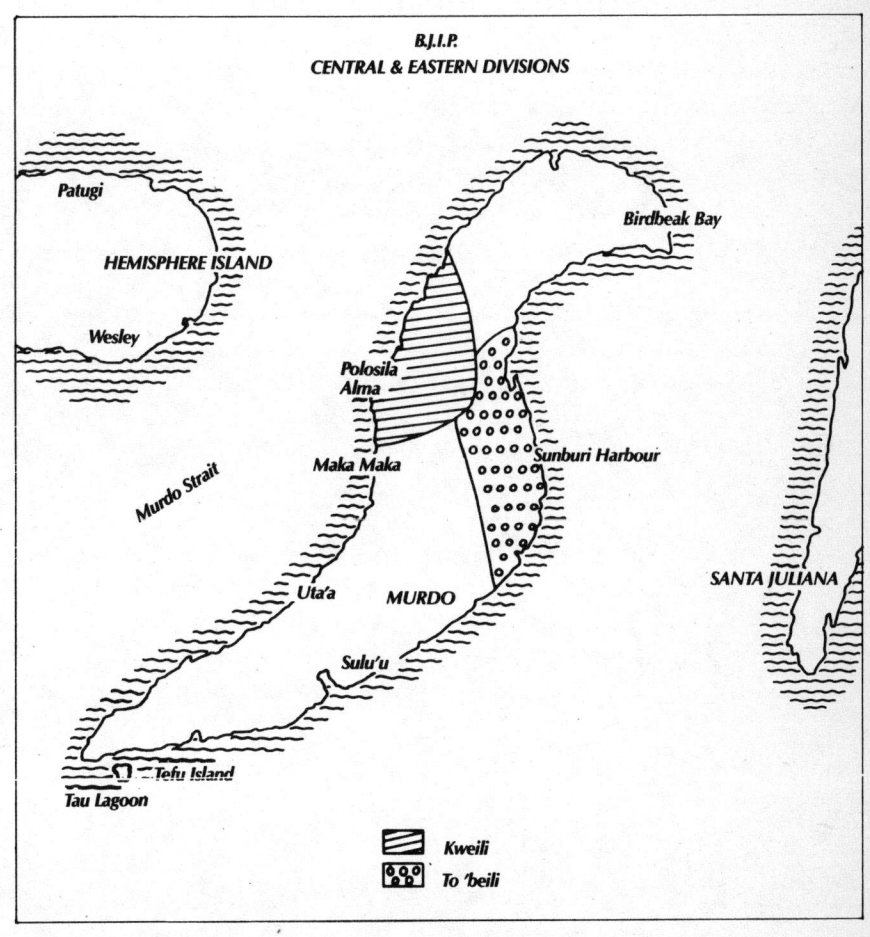

B.J.I.P.
CENTRAL & EASTERN DIVISIONS

Patugi

HEMISPHERE ISLAND

Wesley

Birdbeak Bay

Polosila
Alma

Murdo Strait

Maka Maka

Sunburi Harbour

Uta'a

MURDO

SANTA JULIANA

Sulu'u

Tefu Island

Tau Lagoon

Kweili

To 'beili

NAISMITH'S DOMINION

PETER CORRIS

BANTAM BOOKS
SYDNEY • AUCKLAND • TORONTO • NEW YORK • LONDON

For Warwick Richards

NAISMITH'S DOMINION

A BANTAM BOOK

Printing History
Bantam edition published 1990

National Library of Australia
Cataloguing-in-Publication entry

Corris, Peter, 1942–
    Naismith's dominion.

    ISBN 1 86359 017 x

    I. Title.

A823.3

Bantam Books are published in Australia by
Transworld Publishers (Australia) Pty Limited,
15–25 Helles Ave, Moorebank NSW 2170
and in New Zealand by Transworld Publishers (NZ) Limited,
Cnr Moselle and Waipareira Aves, Henderson, Auckland
and in the United Kingdom by Transworld Publishers (UK) Limited,
61–63 Uxbridge Road, Ealing London W5 5SA
and in the United States by Bantam Books,
666 Fifth Avenue, New York, New York 10103.

Front cover illustration by Mike Worrall
Back cover illustration by Peter Bollinger
Cover design by Lizardesque

Typeset by Excel Imaging
Printed by The Book Printer

CONTENTS

Thanks to Jean Bedford, Rosemary Creswell, Heather Falkner, Richard Hall, Mandie Johnson (for maps), Roger Keesing, Jacquie Kent.

PROLOGUE

Patugi, British Jeremiah Islands Protectorate, 1 February 1908

The resident commissioner mopped his face with a linen handkerchief. The sweat was threatening to drip into his eyes and he intended to be very dry-eyed indeed for this event, his first hanging. The gaol building at Patugi, the tiny capital of the Protectorate, had little ventilation and a lot of galvanised iron in its construction, and was stifling. The temperature outside was climbing rapidly as another torrid tropical day evolved. Everyone was sweating. The execution was running late.

The RC fretted at the delay. He'd been standing up stiffly for much longer than was comfortable; the native prison officers, held at attention, would soon be shuffling their feet. The fat chief of constabulary looked ready to collapse; the medical officer was fidgeting. Only the boy, held firmly by two native policemen, seemed unaffected by the heat. The RC glanced down at him. The boy, whom he judged to be about fourteen years old, was nuggety and strong. He wore canvas shorts and a white shirt buttoned at the neck and wrists. He held his dark, shaved head rigidly, slightly tilted up and his eyes were fixed on the timber scaffold twenty feet in front of him.

Suddenly the airless room was a scene of swift, unhesitating action. A door opened and two policemen entered, propelling ahead of them a small, slight man who walked with quick, certain steps. His hands were manacled in front of him and he looked neither to left nor right. Before the prisoner and his guards reached the ten high steps that led to the platform, a figure moved smoothly from behind the structure and glided up ahead of them. The executioner made his preparations quickly and efficiently: the noose was ready to be slipped over the condemned man's head as soon as his bare feet reached the chalk marks on the rough boards; the hood was raised and lowered, covering the man's proud features, intercepting his burning gaze which had been fixed on the perspiring face of the RC.

The executioner bent and fastened straps around his subject's ankles and chest. He stepped back and pulled the lever. The mechanism operated smoothly and almost without noise. The tightly lashed, hooded figure dropped from the sight of the watchers and appeared under the platform as a twitching, twisting thing. But only for three seconds. Then it hung slack and limp and the stench from the involuntarily vacated bowels cut through the smell of alcohol, tobacco and perspiration from the living bodies and assailed the nostrils of the witnesses.

The RC was glad he had resisted the temptation of a stiff whisky before coming across from the residency to the gaol in the dawn light to perform his duty. His stomach was in turmoil and he could feel a blinding headache building inside his skull; he needed all the control he could muster.

Turning slightly, he addressed himself to the rigid, trance-bound boy. "Eglito, you have witnessed the death of your father." He paused to allow the young native policeman to perform the translation into To'beili, one of the many languages of Murdo Island. "He broke the law of His Majesty the King of England and in so doing he broke the laws of this Protectorate. He became the enemy of the government and of the people and he has paid the price for his crimes. You have seen what retribution such crimes bring. You are young enough to learn this lesson and to take it back with you to your people. Do not fail to do so. That is all."

Neither by word nor gesture did Eglito respond to the RC's words. It was as if he was alone in the hot space, or almost alone. His eyes were fixed unblinkingly on the bundle that was being cut down and rolled in a plaited grass mat. His guards could feel the slight tremor that ran through his limbs and hear the grinding of his teeth. But to other observers, and he was the centre of a good deal of attention, some of it shamefaced, Eglito was immobile and emotionless.

The RC wiped his face again and addressed himself to the medical officer who had shuffled forward. Without thinking, the MO inspected Eglito's head which he had ordered to be shaven to prevent lice while the boy was being held in custody for three months as his father's trial and sentencing proceeded. The head, he noted, was clean and the boy's nose was free of the yellow-green mucus common among prisoners held in the stifling, unhygenic gaol.

"Take the little brute away, Morgan," the RC said, "give him a decent meal and . . . two shillings and put him on a boat back to his bloody island."

Three hours later, Eglito slipped into the water before the government motor launch had cleared Patugi harbour. Several Murdo men, members of the government marine service, watched him go. He swam to shore and hid in the scrub behind the gaol. Then he waited for six hours until the light had almost gone and the worst day of his life was nearly over. He felt different — stronger despite his loss, older because of the way he had been treated. He was sure the man who wore the white suit and the strange hat with feathers in it like a bird's tail feared him. This was right and good.

The sun sank and three men joined Eglito. All four climbed a wall and walked across gravel and grass to where a mound of earth rose above the blank flatness of the prison burial ground. The earth was still moist from the afternoon rain, still warm from the sun. Eglito and his To'beili clansmen disinterred the body and restored the mound to its exact shape using sticks and rocks they gathered around the sites of other graves. They wrapped it in lengths of trade cloth and carried it over the wall, through the bush and down to the beach, where they placed it in an outrigger canoe.

As he paddled away from Hemisphere Island, the small, near-circular upthrust of sand and rock and soil on which Patugi stood, Eglito's mind was numbed with pain and hate. His father would lie in an honoured place and he would be honoured himself for having caused this to happen. He knew his youth would be overlooked — he would be instructed by powerful men and accounted a powerful man himself. Rituals would be performed, pigs would be sacrificed and omens read. His future as a man of influence was assured.

But his experience had shaken him to the roots of his being. He had seen the power of the *gafamanu*, the white men, with their money to buy people and their guns and places that smelled overwhelmingly of death. He sensed that his destiny was to test To'beili power against *gafamanu* power, and he did not know which was the greater.

After paddling for six hours Eglito fell asleep. One of the other men covered him with a blanket and the canoe continued its journey to Murdo.

The Jeremiah Islands, which lie some three thousand kilometres off the north-east coast of Australia, were discovered in the sixteenth century by a Spanish expedition seeking gold and human souls. There is no gold to speak of in the islands, and the disappointment over that probably made the Spaniards rougher in their proselytising than was wise. They kidnapped women and children and burned villages when the warriors retaliated. The children and adult hostages, taken aboard the ships and held under restraint in the fort the Spaniards constructed on Hemisphere Island, rapidly sickened and died on a regime of salt meat and Christianity. Many of the Spaniards died also, some from spear and arrow wounds, but more from fevers contracted on the swampy beaches and sweltering coastal plains. The islanders managed to burn one ship to the waterline and kill the entire crew; another ship was lost on the reef off the east coast of Murdo. The Spaniards gave the islands their mournful name and left, never to return.

Over the next three hundred years Europeans steered clear of the Jeremiahs, where they knew they could expect neither profit nor hospitality. After the settlement of New South Wales in 1788, ships bound for China passed through the group. Most avoided landing but when this was necessary to carry out repairs or to obtain food and water, the Jeremians invariably signified their displeasure. The whalers who entered the group in the 1820s were the first to gain any footing in the islands. As ruthless killers of the biggest beasts on earth, they had no fear of spears and arrows. They marched ashore, took the food and water they wanted and shot anyone who opposed them. Inevitably they dropped, lost, or discarded the knives and axes they used to carve up the whales. These things changed the Jeremians' attitude to the visitors; with a steel axe one man could clear a garden site faster then six using stone tools. A steel knife made the manufacture of weapons and other tools easier and faster, leaving more time for sex and ceremonials. For the first time in their history, the Jeremians welcomed intruders, giving them food and water and lending them women in exchange for steel.

In the early 1870s the whales were on the decline; the Jeremiahs had never been a source for sandalwood or *bêche-de-mer* but, paradoxically, the very thing which had created the group's fearsome reputation now attracted ardent interest — the strength and resilience of Jeremian men. The Murdoans were most in demand but men, a very few women and a handful of children were also drawn from Hemisphere and the small islands nearby, as well as from Santa Juliana east of Murdo and the outliers to the north.

The demand for labour on the sugar farms of Queensland and the copra plantations of Fiji brought hundreds of recruiting vessels to the islands. For a wage of six pounds per year thousands of islanders indentured themselves for three years. Many died, but most returned to their islands equipped with guns, axes, knives and tobacco — the islanders had joined the world economy.

The recruiting era was a violent one. Many recruiters regretted the passing of the blackbirding days and got tough at the wrong times. For their part, the islanders often attacked the ships, sometimes in revenge for deaths of kinsmen overseas, sometimes out of impatience to acquire the cargoes. They killed the crews, looted the ships and fled in terror when the warships arrived to shell their villages and burn their canoes.

In 1890, in response to requests from the Queensland and Fiji governments and to forestall the colonial aspirations of France and Germany, Great Britain declared a protectorate over the Jeremiahs.

The Great War scarcely touched the islands. An off-course German cruiser hit a reef near Quiros and was lost with all hands; a couple of German planters were interned on Hemisphere, but this amounted to little more than the loosest form of house arrest. After the war administration was tightened. The group was divided into three districts — east, west and the reefs — each with a district officer supported by a native police force. The British district officers were tax collectors, licence issuers, magistrates, gaolers and census takers, among other things. Colonial Office policy in respect of the British Jeremiah Islands Protectorate was simple — keep the peace and make the place pay its own way. Responsibility for enforcing this policy lay with the resident commissioner, who delegated the duty to the district officers. These delegated in turn, partly to their native police sergeants, but essentially the district officers had to get things done themselves. If this meant an occasional hanging, a twenty-year prison sentence or a fine in native currency so heavy that a wealthy, powerful chief was reduced to beggary, then so be it.

Conventional wisdom in the Patugi Club, where British officials, planters, traders and others with white skins gathered to drink, was that a DO should be respected; failing that, feared. Failing that, he should find another job.

HEMISPHERE ISLAND

1

Patugi, British Jeremiah Islands Protectorate, 10 February 1928

Will Naismith wiped sweat from his eyes and lined up the putt. Hunched over the tiny white ball, his heavy body made an incongruous picture — his physique was built for power and endurance, not for the trifling task of knocking a ball into a hole a mere eight feet away. But Naismith took the matter seriously, as he did everything. He squinted against the intense light from the tropical sun, reading the slope of the green, and wriggled his toes for a firmer grip. He eased back the putter, held it until the bamboo shaft was utterly steady and brought it forward with precise deliberation. The ball, struck dead centre, rolled quickly at first, slowed on the close-cropped grass and dropped into the hole.

There was a round of applause from the dozen or so people gathered around the ninth green of the Patugi golf course. Naismith looked up and smiled — he loved to compete, loved still more to win. Major Ashley Price-Kane, Resident Commissioner of the British Jeremiah Islands Protectorate, stepped forward and shook Naismith's hand. "Well done, partner. The drinks are on me."

Naismith shouldered his putter. "Thank you, sir."

Price-Kane released Naismith's hand, ostensibly to wave in the direction of the Patugi club, adjacent to the golf course, but in fact with relief. *Bloody nuisance,* he thought. *Bloody colonial. Stiff as a board and the bugger won't even drink.*

But Naismith looked affable enough as he handed his putter and a shilling to the islander who shouldered his golf bag. The young caddy muttered, "Thank you, masta," but Naismith was already giving his attention to the two men he and the RC had defeated.

"You've done it again, Will," said Bruce Rixton, a red-faced New Zealander who ran a copra and coffee plantation on Quiros, one of the outer islands in the group. "Nineteen-twenty-bloody-eight and another clean sweep for Naismith. *And* you've carried another RC to the pairs championship."

Rixton's partner, Colin Clements, was a 'commercial', a servant of the Burns Philp Company. He was a tall, thin Englishman whose frequent failures as an independent operator had not soured him. He clapped Naismith's broad, meaty shoulder. "What're you going to do when you become RC yourself, Will? Looks bad for the boss to have the lowest handicap in the history of the club."

Naismith, as was the custom for the player with the best individual score, tipped the caddies of his partner and the defeated pair sixpence each. Again, he ignored their thanks and attended to Clements' comment. "No colonial'll ever be RC here," he said. "Britain'd sooner let the natives run their own affairs."

Rixton guffawed. "That day'll never come, but you're right, Will, and saving your presence, Colin, we colonials'll go on getting the short end of the stick as long as the British Empire shall last."

"Amen," Clements said, "the natural order of things, like a stiff gin and tonic after a hard round of golf."

"Stiff and warm," Rixton said, "if I know the club barman. Hey, that's not bad — stiff and warm, if you see what I mean."

Naismith didn't see, or perhaps chose not to. He turned

and stumped away in his white shirt with rolled sleeves, cricket creams tucked into long socks and cleated shoes, up the track towards the club. His sun helmet, which he had removed to play each of the eighteen drives and thirty-six fairway shots in his round, was now firmly on his head, covering his still-thick thatch of greying fair hair. He was forty-eight years old, a bachelor and district officer of Murdo Island, the most populous and volatile in the Jeremiah group. He knew he could remain individual and pairs gold champion of the Protectorate for as long as he chose, and that he would never be married and never be resident commissioner. In a way, the closing off of these options was a blessing. It enabled him to ignore the nonsense that passed for social life in the capital, Patugi — a tiny, sweltering township on Hemisphere Island, and concentrate on his job — bringing the fifty thousand Murdoans under the sway of British law.

Few of the men who climbed the rocky path from the golf course, crossed the bridge over the creek and entered the gardens of the Patugi Club handled the heat or the gradient well. Ashley Price-Kane, who had distinguished himself in the Great War, had suffered a mild gassing which left him short of breath after exertion. A good many of the other men, planters, government officials and commercials were, like Rixton, noticeably overweight. On one of the islands lived a planter who was rumoured to weigh one hundred and ninety kilograms and to be carried everywhere by a team of islanders. In Patugi were no such mammoths, but some of the desk sitters and gin drinkers appeared to be going the same way. But Clements strolled along comfortably and Naismith, toughened by years of trekking in the rugged interior of Murdo, found the walk easy.

"Heading back to that hellhole you run soon, Will?" Clements asked.

"Quick as I can," Naismith replied. "Go now if I could. No offence, Colin."

Clements laughed. "None taken. You're a round peg in a round hole. There's no better way to be. Look at me, I was cut out to be a scholar and here I am a ... what? Salesman, ledger keeper ..."

"And salary drawer, don't forget," Naismith said. "There's a depression on and not much of a market for scholars. Besides, you can always be a scholar in your own time. You read a lot, don't you?"

"Yes."

"I love music. Used to play the piano pretty fairly and sing a bit. Now I play phonograph records at night when I've finished work. Opera mostly."

This was a side of Naismith the legendary golfer, cricketer and tough, efficient administrator that Clements rarely heard of and was curious about. He had found the district officer prickly about the status of Australians in the Protectorate, over-competitive and a bit inclined to be pompous. Feeling warmer now towards Naismith, Clements wondered whether the district officer might indeed possess the quality he found essential in a friend — a sense of humour. "And sing?" he ventured.

Naismith's laugh was a harsh roar. "Damn badly. The boys laugh at me and I give them curry. See this?" He stretched his head up, and Clements saw a white scar running across the right side of Naismith's thick neck. "Got that in South Africa. Boer bullet. Ruined my voice, or at least that's my excuse. Here we are. Let's get this nonsense over with. You blokes can get on with poisoning yourselves with alcohol, and I can get back to work."

Naismith and Clements had reached the steps to the club, a white-painted timber building surrounded by a wide verandah, yards ahead of anyone else. Naismith's hand touched Clements' arm. "Wait for the boss," he said.

Clements took off his hat and fanned himself. "Christ, Will, you're the hero of the hour. You should stroll in when you feel like it."

Naismith shook his head. "Have to set an example for the natives. We defer to Price-Kane, they defer to us. Part of the system."

As on several past occasions, Colin Clements was not sure whether Will Naismith had passed his friendship test.

Several hours later the noise of celebration in the club had reached the level at which Price-Kane, the president, usually asked the secretary to advise the rowdier members to tone it down. This was always done discreetly, and soon afterwards the RC took his leave. Then the evening could drag on in a maudlin fashion with a few old soaks outsitting the rest, or it could flare into life around the billiards or card tables before fizzling or ending in a brief, quickly suppressed fist fight. Monday and Friday were ladies' nights, when the very few women in the islands were admitted to the club. Usually quieter, these nights were much appreciated by the club servants, who could count on being back in their quarters by midnight. But this was a Saturday night and likely to be a long one.

There was the golf tournament to celebrate and also the arrival of the steamer from Australia. The four-monthly visit of the 8000-tonne Burns Philp ship *Moresby* was an occasion. The sight of the big white vessel with the black and white chequered funnel, Australian flag and company thistle emblem gladdened homesick hearts. The steamer brought supplies, mail and people; not all in the last category were welcome. Planters who had been expelled from the Protectorate for infringements of the many government regulations sometimes risked an early return; accountants arrived periodically to oversee the liquidation of plantations and trading companies; Chinese and Indians, apparently with legitimate papers, posed problems for officials. The Asian population was small and policy was to keep it that way. This provided another reason for the resident commissioner's early departure from the Patugi Club — the *Moresby* might bring people whom it would be unseemly for him to meet socially.

Will Naismith had drunk all the lemon squash he could stomach and had verbally replayed various shots in his round until he was thoroughly bored. He had talked with Clements most of the time but also, out of politeness, to planters, other district officers, Father Jean Bondil of the Marist mission and to Barnett Campbell, the deputy resident commissioner. Naismith was the most senior of the

DOs and, in a different context, might have aspired to Campbell's job and the one above it. Price-Kane's health was suspect, and it was widely known that concern for his pension entitlements kept him in the service, rather than imperial zeal. Naismith knew better than to aspire to promotion, but he found it hard to tolerate Campbell, whom he thought a fool whose only advantage was to have been born in Edinburgh. No one in the Colonial Office would have heard of Naismith's birthplace, the Victorian coastal town of Warrnambool.

He smiled at some inanity of Campbell's and was gratified to see Price-Kane depart. He could leave himself in a few minutes, but first he wanted to say goodbye to Clements and to renew his invitation to the Englishman to visit him at his post in Alma on the east coast of Murdo. Just thinking of Alma made Naismith feel better. His patrol launch, tied up at the Patugi wharf with the crew standing by, would get him across to Murdo in less than two hours. Then he could have a bath and a late meal and listen to *Don Giovanni*.

He had to wait to catch the attention of Clements, who was deep in an apparently friendly argument with Father Bondil. The plump priest wiped his sweating bald head with a white handkerchief.

"Aha," said Clements, "*le drapeau blanc. Je suis le vainqueur.*"

"*Jamais*," said Bondil. "*Athée!*"

"Agnostic," Clements said, "*vive la différence.*"

Naismith, who knew no French, grew impatient. "Colin," he said, "excuse me for interrupting. What about coming over next week? There's a market on. You might pick up a few nice things."

Clements was a keen collector of Jeremian artefacts and, as a somewhat solitary and altogether kindly man, he sensed the need for company in Naismith's invitation. He nodded. "Right ho, next week it is."

"Good, I'll crank up the Victrola."

A sudden hush fell in the hot room so that the ceiling fans could be heard whirring and the tail ends of conversations sounded unnaturally loud. Clements looked over Naismith's shoulder in the direction of the door. "Hello," he said, "here's trouble."

"What in hell do you mean, she can't come in? We're just off the goddamn boat and she needs a drink. *I* need a drink."

"I'm sorry, sir. No ladies are permitted in the club on Saturday nights." The club secretary was barring the way to a stocky man with a broad face and a head of thick, wavy, black hair. He wore a crumpled tropical suit and a soft-collared shirt. Instead of a tie, a light cotton scarf was carelessly knotted around his neck.

"Do you know who I am?" The newcomer spoke with a twangy American accent. Behind him, a young blonde woman in a blue linen frock leaned against the wooden rail. She was very pretty and her figure was good. Looking cool and fresh despite the steamy heat of the evening, she opened a white clutch bag, took out a gold case, extracted a cigarette and lit it.

"It doesn't matter who you are, sir. His Majesty the King couldn't bring Her Majesty the Queen into the Patugi Club tonight."

The American gaped and half turned to the woman. "Christ, honey, I think he means it."

"I don't need a drink, Tom," the woman said, "but if you must have one there has to be someplace else. I would like to know how come that guy directed us here if we can't get a drink?"

The secretary disliked the sight of a woman smoking. He aimed his remark at a point some distance above her head. "Anyone who directed you here tonight, madam, was having a joke at your expense."

The woman smiled and blew smoke. "Not a very funny joke. Maybe we'd be laughing if we had a drink."

"Look," the American said, "we don't want to be hard to get along with. I respect local customs, but maybe you can make an exception. I'm Tom Birmingham, and this is my wife, Louise. That make any difference?"

The secretary stared at Birmingham's outstretched hand uncomprehendingly. "I'm afraid . . . "

The Protectorate's chief medical officer, a stout figure with a drooping, tobacco-stained moustache, stepped forward and gripped Birmingham's hand. "Mr Birmingham," he said, "what a pleasure. Mrs Birmingham, how do you do? I've read all your books, sir. I can't say how happy I am to meet you. I'm Ian Herbert, medical officer, you know."

Birmingham pumped Herbert's hand. "Great to meet you, doc. Now, what about a drink?"

Interest in the newcomers had waned with the intervention of Herbert and the mention of books. Herbert, despite his liking for drink and heavy-handed humour, was one of the most efficient administrators in the government; the club secretary and others could rely on him to set the interlopers straight quickly and without fuss. Herbert took Birmingham's arm and steered him back down the steps. He managed to draw the woman along with him and also to signal to one of the club servants. "Tell my boy to bring the car round," he said.

Birmingham had taken a cigarette from his wife's case and Herbert smoothly produced a light. "I'm terribly sorry about this. I'll run you down to the hotel."

"We've checked in," Birmingham said. "Bar's closed."

"Then we'll jolly well open it. The club will be delighted to have you as a visiting member and to welcome Mrs Birmingham on Monday night. Ah, here's the car. The boy'll drive. I've just finished *Adams up the Amazon*. Tell me, do you drink whiskies with salt water like your hero?"

"Sure," Birmingham said.

"Nonsense, Tom," said Louise Birmingham.

The car's headlights picked up the figure of a man walking in the direction of the club. Richard Webb blinked as the lights caught him, but he moved quickly and gracefully clear of the car without breaking his stride. As he got nearer the club he heard the sounds of men's voices and the clink of glasses. The pitch and quality of the noise reminded Webb sharply of an officers' mess and triggered memories that confused and almost angered him. He stopped in his tracks, all grace of movement gone. A bulky man striding towards him failed to anticipate the sudden stop; his shoulder bumped heavily and painfully into Webb's upper right arm, near the spot where a German bullet had hit him ten years before.

"I'm sorry," Will Naismith said. "No damage, I trust?"

"My fault," Webb said. "No damage. Is this the Patugi Club?"

Naismith wedged his helmet, which had been a little dislodged by the bump, firmly on his head. "That's it. Goodnight."

"Goodnight." Webb didn't know why, but he had an impulse to salute. He continued up the drive and climbed the steps to the open door. Colin Clements was leaning in the doorway, nursing a drink and trying to breathe fresh air. The air inside the club was grey with smoke.

"Good evening," Clements said. He took in Webb's new linen suit, close-cropped brown hair and slightly peeling nose. "I'd say you were just off the steamer."

"That's right." Webb mounted the stairs, and the two men shook hands. Webb was a little under six feet and of medium build. His face was thin with an olive complexion. "Richard Webb. How did you know that?"

Clements introduced himself and took a sip of his drink. "Clothes are new, you've been told to keep your hair short in the tropics because it's so bloody hot, and you've had a case of windburn. Well, what are you, government or commercial? Not missionary, I hope."

Webb smiled. "No. Academic, I suppose you'd say. I've come to do a study of the natives on Murdo. For my doctorate."

A pang of envy made Clements speak more sharply than he intended. "Bit old for a student, aren't you?"

"Slowed down by the war and one thing and another," Webb said. "I was hoping to meet a chap named Naismith, the district officer. I'm told I need his say-so. Is he here tonight?"

Clements laughed. "You just missed him, or rather, you didn't miss him. That was Naismith you bumped into just now. The way Will Naismith walks he'll be halfway to the wharf by now, and he's got his boys trained to get ready when they see him coming over the rise. He's on his way back to Murdo right now, so you really have missed him."

"Damn," Webb said.

Clements drained his glass. "Doesn't matter. There's other ways to get to Murdo, God help you. Come inside. I'll sign you up and you can buy me a drink."

2

Envy struck Colin Clements again as he saw Richard Webb enter 'Balliol College, Oxford' as his address in the visitors' book. He let Webb buy him a whisky and noticed Webb's heavy hand on the soda siphon when dealing with his own drink.

"You'll learn to take it straight or with water on Murdo," he observed, shepherding Webb towards a quiet corner.

Webb slumped into a cane chair. "I've done that often enough," he said. "Cheers."

Clements lifted his glass. "Ah, yes, in the war. Tell me about yourself, Webb, while I try to remember everything I know about anthropology."

"I'd rather you told me about Naismith."

"We'll trade. You first."

Webb felt for a no longer existing lock of hair above his right eyebrow. "Not much to it. Born in London, father a doctor, mother a nurse. Dulwich College, lots of Latin and cricket. You're English, you know the sort of thing."

Clements did know; his father had been a solicitor before he went to gaol for embezzlement, thus ending his son's sojourn at Cambridge. "Will Naismith's an Australian. Going on for fifty, I suppose. His people were farmers, I believe. No idea where he went to school. He speaks some Fijian and one of the Murdo languages. I doubt he has any Latin. On a good day I'd say his batting was about county standard, but old hands say he's stiffened up a bit. He's the club's golf champion. Look behind you."

Webb screwed his head around to peer through the fug of smoke at the teak board that carried a list of names in gold. W.E. Naismith appeared as champion for eleven out of the twelve past years.

"What happened in 1920?"

"Extended leave," Clements said, "some kind of crisis. Don't know the details."

"Is he a friend of yours?"

"I wouldn't say that. I'm not sure that anyone in the Protectorate could claim him as a friend. I've played golf with him, talked to him a good deal, but he's a diffident chap. For example, I only found out tonight that he likes opera and was wounded in South Africa." He explained to Webb how the two facts were related.

"I don't care for opera, I'm afraid," Webb said. "Tone deaf."

"Well, you're not much of a drinker," Clements pointed to Webb's barely touched glass, "you don't smoke and you survived a war. That should give you a fair bit in common with Naismith. How *was* your war?"

"Bloody awful. I got a touch of gas in France. That's why I don't smoke."

"I noticed you rub your arm after you bumped into Will. Touch of lead as well?"

Webb nodded. "And some shell shock. I was a thousand times luckier than most. I'd really rather not talk about it. What's Naismith's position on the native question?"

Clements smiled. "What's the question?"

"Using the head tax revenue to improve health and education services for the people, surely."

"As against . . . ?"

"Using it to defray the costs of colonial administration."

"Is this what they talk about at Oxford?"

"Well, no. At the London School of Economics. I'm getting some supervision from a man at London."

Clements leaned forward across the table so that he could speak quietly but still be heard. "Let me give you a few words of advice. First, don't talk about the head tax. There's no such thing in the Jeremiahs."

"I thought there was an annual levy on every able-bodied man."

"There is — three pounds per year. It's called the rate."

"The rate?"

"Exactly, the rate. That's what it's called, officially and unofficially. Nothing else. Secondly, I wouldn't go about spouting about reform of the system of government, if I were you. The people who run the system are perfectly happy with it. It's all they know, and they don't want to learn anything new."

Webb took his second sip of whisky and soda. "And what about the others, the people who don't run the system? I take it you're not a government official yourself?"

"No, I'm one of the people who're subject to it. I work for Burns Philp." Clements relaxed and leaned back. "Most of us think the system's too easy on the natives. Most of the chaps here tonight'd tell you the rate should be higher, double perhaps."

"Why?"

"*Not* to raise more money for schools and clinics. To make the lazy sods work, old boy, to make 'em work."

"Is that what you think?"

Clements smiled. "Sometimes, when I can't get a shipment together, and I know that if I just had a few more boys on the job I could do it easily. Then I do."

"And at other times?"

"I have read a bit of anthropology, you know. Malinowski, that sort of thing. And I collect string bags and carvings. When I see some of the things the people make here and consider the time and skill they put into them, I don't see why they should cut copra or pick coffee at all. Mind you, I'm mad, anyone'll tell you that."

"And Naismith, what does he think?"

"That you'll have to find out for yourself. Where are you putting up?"

"I'm booked in at Parkinson's Hotel."

"That'll do you. Look, you'll need to see his nibs and a few others in the Secretariat, I expect — permits and so on?"

Webb nodded.

"That'll take a few days. You'll want to acclimatise, get some gear together. Will's invited me over to Murdo next weekend. You can come along if you like."

"That's very kind, Mr Clements, but wouldn't I be imposing?"

Clements snorted. "Call me Colin. You have to impose around here. Place runs on favours done and reciprocated. Finish your drink, and I'll walk back down with you. First, I have to collect ten bob from a chap."

Webb raised his eyebrows. "Bet?"

"Mmm, got him to put it on Naismith and the RC against Bruce Rixton and me in the pairs playoff. Two to one on we didn't get eight holes. Just to make it interesting."

"You bet against yourself?"

"When Will Naismith's in the field, that's the prudent thing to do."

Louise Birmingham leaned over the balcony at Parkinson's Hotel and looked up at the clear, dark sky and out over the inky waters of Murdo Strait. Behind her, in the smallish room, Tom Birmingham lay in bed under a mosquito net. A ceiling fan stirred the gauze of the net, and the slight breeze it created travelled to the balcony and ruffled Louise's nightgown.

"Come to bed," Birmingham said.

"In a minute. It's great out here. It's wonderful to be able to look at the sky and the water and not feel a damn ship moving under you."

Birmingham sighed. He was still deeply in love with

his young wife (he had loved all three of his wives), but he had begun to notice that she complained a good deal. He fancied that he had never heard her complain about anything when they first met six months ago in New York. Her father was Hiram Waldeck of Waldeck & Marsh, the firm that very profitably published Birmingham's books and those of many other popular writers. Louise was beautiful, had been to exclusive schools and completed four semesters at Smith College. She had a job in the firm, mostly consisting of meeting interesting people, one of whom had been the handsome adventure writer Tom Birmingham, and he had fallen in love with her. What would she have to complain about? The honeymoon in Mexico had been perfect and Louise had been fine in San Francisco while he was polishing the final draft of *Adams in Acapulco*. Her complaining had started back in New York when he had begun planning this Pacific trip.

"You should come out here, Tom, and taste the air. It's like a fruit cocktail."

That was more like the old Louise, enthusiastic. Birmingham slipped out of bed, pulled on his undershorts and walked across the rush mat to the balcony. He took a breath of the clear air, admitted that it was good and swept a professional eye across the sky and water. *The southern stars were unfamiliar to Adams,* Birmingham jotted mentally, *but he would soon know them as well as any antipodean and be able to tell the time and weather by them and to navigate across trackless seas.* He put his arms around Louise's slim, firm body and pressed against her.

"Want to start a baby?"

Louise recoiled violently. "No!"

Birmingham was strong, and he held her easily. "Hey, hey, don't get upset. Just bringing the subject up."

Louise could feel his erection; in Mexico or San Francisco, or New York even, she would have laughed at the joke and they would have made love. Now she felt she needed something other than her husband's good nature and frank lust, and it wasn't a baby. "You've already got four children. Isn't that enough?"

The associated subjects of alimony and child support could be relied upon to cool Birmingham off. "It's enough to support," he said glumly. He released Louise and went back into the room for cigarettes. Husband and wife leaned on the balcony and smoked. Below and to the left were the Patugi wharves where the *Moresby* was tied up, a whale among minnows — fishing boats, trading cutters, government vessels, all showing lights. A clutch of masted outrigger canoes and double-hulled canoes with platform decks were moored in the shelter of a breakwater. The native craft carried no lights, but cooking fires winked on the decks and fires on the stony beach cast light out over the water.

Birmingham extended his right hand with the cigarette held in the fingers, cocked his head and squinted along the line of his arm.

"What're you doing?"

"Drawing a bead on that guy on the deck of the steamer. It'd be a tough shot in this light, but it could be done."

"But why? Who is he?"

"Hell, I don't know, just some guy. I was thinking of the book."

Louise flicked her cigarette butt into the dusty street below. "What book?"

"*Adams in the Antipodes*. I'm sort of writing it in my head. That's the way I work, honey. You'll see me grinning from time to time, taking a swipe at things, trying out insults even. I'm writing, I'm working. Take that business at the club tonight. Now that was real interesting. Could make a great scene in a book. And that doctor, quite a character. I was right. You can keep your Samoa and Tahiti, they're all played out. This is where the real Pacific characters are nowadays!"

Louise recalled Birmingham's bluster and the slow way he had responded to Ian Herbert's frank admiration. One stiff scotch had been enough for Louise. The drink had relaxed her and enabled her to consider as exotic the stuffy little hotel bar with its potted palms, bone-biting wicker furniture and broken-bladed fan. Herbert and Birmingham had had a few more drinks and talked about crocodile shooting. "Then you weren't really mad? You didn't think they were a bunch of stuffed shirts?"

Birmingham drew on his cigarette and dropped the glowing butt into the pot plant beside him. "Just people, honey. All good material."

Louise stared at him. *God almighty,* she thought. *I've married a child.* She recalled how appealing Birmingham's devil-may-care attitude had appeared in New York, how open and unassuming he was after all the egotistical writers, devious publishers, scheming agents and paranoid editors. *A thirty-nine-year-old child.* She lit another cigarette.

"Think I'll make a few notes if you're not coming to bed yet," Birmingham said. "A croc hunt's a great idea. Wonder if you need some kind of permit for that?"

"I wonder," Louise said. She grew tired of looking at the harbour and shifted her gaze to the township. Tin roofs gleamed under the starlight. The hotel stood at the end of Patugi's single street, on one side of which were half a dozen Chinese trade stores, a church and the police barracks. The other side was dominated by the Secretariat building, a long, low structure with a verandah across the front. The Union Jack hung slackly from a tall flagpole outside. On both sides of the building was a garden, and between them and the wharf was a ships' chandler, a fuel depot, and a slipway. A large flat area of beaten earth provided a site for the native market held once a month.

As Louise watched, a man stepped from the shadows and stood motionless on the starlit strip of beach, looking out over the water. After he and Colin Clements had walked amicably back to the hotel together, Richard Webb had spent some time attempting to talk in his textbook pidgin English to the Jeremian boatmen clustered around one of the campfires on the beach. He had found them not exactly hostile, but wary. Although he didn't smoke he had taken a packet of Players with him to the beach, and the cigarettes were now all gone. He considered that they had bought him valuable information.

"To'beili," Webb spoke aloud, trying out the sound of

the word. He liked it. One of his informants, a chain-smoking boatman from the north of the group, declared the To'beili the worst people in the Jeremiahs. Webb suspected that meant the most interesting.

Webb climbed the wooden steps from the beach to the road, and for a moment Louise lost sight of him. When he was in view again, standing with his back to the water and looking towards the jungle-covered escarpment a mile back from the coast, Louise recognised him as the man she had seen in the car's headlights as they'd left the club. Something about the calm way he had stepped aside had impressed her then, although she had immediately forgotten the movement. Now the impression created by that graceful, easy sidestep came back forcefully and was reinforced by the image of the tall, lean man standing motionless under the stars.

A sound from behind her made her turn abruptly. Tom Birmingham's notepad dropped from the bed to the floor, dragging down a section of the mosquito net. Birmingham lay on his back, holding a sharpened pencil. A loud snore escaped him, and he dropped the pencil. Louise turned quickly back to look again at Webb, but he had gone. Her forgotten cigarette burned her fingers.

"Goddamnit!" She threw the butt over the balcony.

"What? What?" Birmingham muttered.

Louise did not reply. She heard footsteps below and the door to the hotel's guest entrance open and close. She stood, breathing shallowly, until she heard footsteps on the stairs outside the room. Feet scuffed on the rush mat, and there was the sound of a key being located among a pocketful of coins. The footsteps retreated to the right, and Louise judged that they stopped at the end of the corridor, one room away. *If he comes out onto the balcony I'll be able to see him,* she thought. She drew back from the rail and waited, but he didn't come.

3

Ashley Price-Kane was the sixth resident commissioner appointed since the Crown established the BJIP, and in his third year of office he had inherited certain problems. Some of his predecessors had compromised themselves by giving large land grants and favourable trading concessions to large commercial enterprises. One had sanctioned a scheme for importing Japanese labour, which had to be quickly snuffed out by the home authorities and the erring RC recalled. His legacy was a small, troubled Japanese community in the Jeremiahs, clinging precariously to tiny leaseholds or squatting on disputed land near Patugi.

Until recently, the Jeremiahs had been a backwater, a mere fragment of the empire, and it suited the mandarins of Whitehall to have a time server in office there. But no longer. Whitehall and Washington had grown alarmed at the increasing Japanese naval presence in the Pacific and the extension of Japan's commercial interests. The Jeremiahs had suddenly become of strategic importance — mere specks in the ocean, far distant from Singapore and Hawaii, but red specks, possible coaling stations, supply depots and, some said, important to future aviation and communications. Price-Kane's brief was to keep a firm hand on things. Watch for subversion among the Japanese: preserve the status quo but, if an opportunity arose to demonstrate to Nippon that the Empire still had teeth, to seize it and act decisively. It was his habit to do a few hours' work following the obligatory church attendance which, he had discovered, had a pacifying effect and enhanced clear thought. Price-Kane needed pacifying: he held in his hand a letter from the manager of Jeremiah Plantations Limited's operations on Murdo. The manager accused DO Will Naismith of having obstructed him in recruiting natives, undermining his authority as an employer and improperly using government regulations to frustrate his legitimate commercial operations. And on the desk lay a letter from Pastor Karl Stoltenberg of Murdo's Maryborough Evangelical Mission describing Naismith as 'an opponent of Christianity, sympathetic to heathenism and devoted to furthering his own personal power at the expense of the legitimate spiritual and temporal authority of the churches and the Empire'.

Naismith was the most effective district administrator in the Protectorate. Price-Kane shuddered to think of the mess some of the other DOs he had known would make of the eastern district.

As he reread the letter, parts of his last official conversation with Naismith ran through his mind. Price-Kane had put his finger on a paragraph in Naismith's report. "Six murders?"

Naismith had nodded. "Down fifty per cent on last year. I've got three times as many people in my district as in the rest of the group. If I get fewer than double the murder total for the other two districts, I'm doing better than they are. What are the figures for west and reefs, sir?"

"Fifteen," Price-Kane said.

"And the apprehension rate?"

The RC consulted his summaries. "Sixty per cent, just about."

"I caught five of mine, and I know where the other one is."

"Why haven't you caught him, then?"

"I'm waiting for the bushmen to hand him over to Tefu, the saltwater chief in the Tau lagoon. He's my man. If he's got the influence to get that blighter out of the bush, it'll mean my authority will extend into the mountains for the first time."

Price-Kane sighed. He was very little interested in Melanesian ethnology and had never mastered more than a few halting words of pidgin, but somehow what Naismith was saying smacked of unorthodoxy. "What's involved?" he persisted.

Naismith shrugged. "Sacrifices of pigs, casting of omens, payments in shell money."

It was as bad as the RC had feared. Shell money — the barbaric, tawdry baubles the natives toiled over and used for their murderous blood feud bounties and cattle market dowry payments. He shuddered. "You're behaving like some kind of white rajah."

Naismith stiffened, insulted. He took the RC to mean that he had, in Australian terms, 'gone combo', relaxed all European sexual and moral standards. In fact Price-Kane simply referred to the practice of grafting native authority onto colonial systems. The two men glared at each other.

"I stand on my record," Naismith said.

Price-Kane jerked his mind back to the present. *This* was different; administrative efficiency was all very well, but to antagonise the most powerful planting interest and most influential mission on Murdo looked like poor judgment and future trouble. He jotted a few notes towards replies to the planter and Pastor Stoltenberg and took another paper from his in tray. Naismith had renewed his request for an assistant. Using a needle-sharp pencil and writing in a crabbed Sandhurst script, the RC minuted the document in the negative. The next paper was a list of arrivals on the steamer, sent by wireless message twelve hours before the vessel arrived. Price-Kane ran his eye down the short list: a missionary; a Burns Philp trainee;

travellers Mr and Mrs Thomas Birmingham; student Mr
Richard Webb; cadet officer Mr Keith Larke.

Alone in his office on Sunday, with the windows propped
open to catch the breeze, his tie and belt loosened and no
one around to hear him, Price-Kane sometimes indulged
in speaking aloud to himself. "Suppose I'll have every one
of them on the doorstep on Monday morning," he said.

He lit a cigar and considered a gin before lunch. He
picked up the passenger list, intending to leave it on his
secretary's desk for him to use as the requests for interviews
came in. The name of Keith Larke arrested him. He'd had
a subaltern by that name in France. *Good chap*, he thought.
*Did his duty . . . killed at Verdun. Wonder if this fellow's any
relation?* The RC drew on his cigar as an idea dawned on
him. "Naismith wants an assistant," he said softly. "It could
be damn useful to have someone to keep tabs on him." He
retrieved the paper bearing Naismith's request from the out
tray and erased the minute. Then he underlined Larke's
name on the passenger list.

Sunday lunch at Parkinson's Hotel was tinned tomato soup,
corned beef and vegetables, trifle and custard. Tea and tap
water were available to be drunk throughout the meal.
Bottles of beer could be brought from the bar and there
was also a sweetish Portuguese wine which appeared on
the bill of fare as 'white whine'. Louise Birmingham
looked idly around the room for the man she had seen by
headlight and starlight, but Richard Webb had accepted
Colin Clements' invitation to lunch. The other guests in
the dining room, some of whom she recognised as fellow
passengers on the *Moresby*, were of no interest to her. A few
florid long-term residents hogged the tables near the fans,
while the new arrivals diffidently occupied separate tables.

Louise and Tom took a table near a window and
Birmingham ordered beer and wine. The soup arrived;
Louise tasted it and put her spoon down.

"Christ," she said. "It's foul."

"Have some wine."

Louise tasted the wine. "It's warm. I guess I'll have some beer."

"Beer's good," Birmingham said. He poured a glass for his wife and lapped up his soup. Tom Birmingham could eat anything.

Feeling disloyal and guilty, Louise looked at her husband with distaste. He was getting fleshy around the neck. Protectively, she stroked her own slender neck and then she felt vain and dropped her hand.

A young man, slightly built and of about middle height, entered the dining room. He was wearing dazzlingly white, stiffly starched clothes, and he was flustered at being late for lunch. His fair hair was plastered down flat and his round face was red and sweaty. Louise had seen him board the steamer at Brisbane, but he had apparently kept to his cabin throughout the voyage. She half rose from her seat and beckoned.

"Hey, honey. What're you doing?"

"Getting us some company," Louise said. "I want to *talk* to someone."

The young man approached the Birminghams' table. "Hello," he said. "I'm afraid I'm late."

"Please sit down. I'm Louise Birmingham and this is my husband, Tom. You've only missed the soup, and believe me, you haven't missed anything."

Birmingham extended his hairy paw. "Take a pew, son. What's your name?"

"Keith Larke. Thanks awfully." Larke pulled out a chair and sat down. The Indian waiter hurried towards the table, carrying two plates; he spun around, retreated to the sideboard and returned with three.

"Smart boy," Birmingham said. "Another beer, pronto."

"You were on the ship, Keith," Louise said, "but we never saw you."

"Seasickness, I'm sorry to say."

"Never been seasick in my life," Birmingham said. He filled his mouth with corned beef and potato and chewed enthusiastically.

Louise pushed her plate aside and lit a cigarette. Heads

turned disapprovingly in the room. Louise blew the smoke towards the window and gave Larke her full attention. "What brings you to this strange place?"

"Listen to her," Birmingham said. "Hasn't been outside the hotel and she already calls the place strange. Looks like a regular place to me."

"You haven't been outside any more than I have. It's not a matter of walking the streets to get a feel for a place. What about what happened at the club? That was curious."

"What?" Larke said. "I got off the boat and went to bed. I was so glad to feel solid ground under me. Did you go to the club?" Louise gave an account of the incident at the club while Birmingham finished his food. Larke ate sparingly and drank one glass of beer to Birmingham's three. The trifle arrived and Louise, who had a sweet tooth, ate half of it before lighting another cigarette.

"What you have to understand, Mrs Birmingham," Larke said, "is that governing these places is a very ticklish matter. The natives far outnumber us and could run us into the sea if they chose."

"What's that got to do with keeping women out of a club?"

"It's a question of standards." Larke looked to Birmingham for support.

Birmingham swallowed the last of his trifle, took a pipe from the pocket of his expensively tailored but creased bush jacket and began to stuff it. "From what I've read about the Jeremiahs and other places in the Pacific, the natives'd completely approve of keeping women out of the club. They do the same — they have men's houses and women's houses. Damn good idea."

Larke recoiled as a cloud of dense, sweet-smelling smoke wafted across the table. "That's not exactly what I meant . . ."

"What'd puzzle the natives," Birmingham went on, "is why you let 'em in on Mondays and Wednesdays or whatever the hell it is."

Larke coughed and cleared his throat. "We have to show the subject peoples that we have rules and codes of conduct.

These may be puzzling to them, but they represent an ideal to which they can aspire in time and with the proper guidance."

"That sounds like something you've learned off by heart," Louise said. "Going to work in the government here, are you?"

"I did a course at the Administrative Training College. Yes, I'm a cadet in the Colonial Service. It's a wonderful career. What do you do, Mr Birmingham?"

This was a question that always displeased Birmingham. He puffed smoke. "Writer," he grunted. "Not so sure about your wonderful career. Times're changing. Colonies could be on the way out."

"Oh, I don't think so," Larke said. "There'll be changes of course, but just look at India. Still as loyal as ever."

"Been there, have you?"

"No."

Louise leaned forward; she was more interested in her husband when he was showing some aggression.

"I have," Birmingham said. "Wrote a book about it called *Adams in Assam*."

Larke, not a reader, nodded politely.

"Place is a goddamn mess, bound to split apart along religious lines. Britain won't be in India in twenty years' time."

"I say, I couldn't agree with you there."

"Well, what the hell. Twenty years is a lifetime, or should be. I plan to pack a lotta living in, myself. What about you? Where will you be stationed?"

"I really don't know. It'll be up to the RC. In the field, I hope. I had a brother in the army. He was killed in France. I want to . . . see some action, I suppose."

Birmingham pointed his pipe stem at Larke's snub nose. "Murdo's the place for you. Missionary got speared there last year. Did you know that?"

"No."

"Yep." Birmingham changed his grip on the pipe and made a spear-launching motion. "Read about it in one of the Frisco papers. Length of steel reinforcing rod right through him. Excuse me, got to go to the bathroom."

Thoroughly bored, Louise yawned as Birmingham lumbered off. She stared out the window. The thick, damp-looking bush seemed to threaten to spill down from the hills and engulf the township. "Were you the only government man on the boat?" she asked.

Larke nodded. "Yes, why?"

"Oh, nothing. I thought there was another man who might be in the same line. British-looking, but a tall, thin type."

"No, he's some kind of anthropologist. Come to study the natives. Oxford man, I believe. His name's Richard Webb."

"Oh," Louise said.

4

Will Naismith nodded as Baekani, his chief house servant, placed the tea things on the table by his arm. Naismith was sitting on the verandah of his house at Alma. Before him was the rugged, bush-shrouded mountain spine that left only a narrow coastal plain along the western side of the island. Naismith would have preferred a view of the bay, but the first DO on Murdo, a determined landsman, had chosen the site. It was a large, comfortable dwelling with windows that propped open to let in breezes and light, and a high pitched iron roof under which Naismith had had rush matting installed for insulation. His servants had laughed at the notion of putting floor covering in the roof, but the resulting coolness had silenced the mirth.

Naismith sipped strong black tea with two spoonsful of sugar and nibbled at a scone. Baekani was a ruthless household administrator. He oversaw the buying of supplies and prevented pilfering by deliverers and servants; he ensured that Naismith's official and non-official clothes were always clean and in good repair; he was responsible for the security of the house by day and night. Baekani could keep a cook up to the mark, but he was an indifferent supervisor of house cleaning. Naismith irritably put up with this deficiency because Baekani was such an excellent shot. Naismith's house stood in the centre of the government compound, a cleared area of one and a half acres which also accommodated the gaol, police barracks, courtroom and administrative office. When Naismith arrived at Alma one of the first things he did was to have the high croton hedges which ran around three sides of the DO's house cut down. It was from the shelter of this hedge that a sniper had put a bullet through the previous DO's head. Now there was a clear field of fire for a hundred metres around the house, and everyone knew that, as a result of hours of patient training and practice supervised by Naismith, the best shot on Murdo was Baekani and that his Mannlicher rifle was the best weapon in the Jeremiahs.

Naismith reviewed the work of the week ahead: a two-day launch patrol around the north end of Murdo into Birdbeak Bay, court on Wednesday, an inspection of the road being constructed to the south of Alma on Thursday, followed by a day of office work. He was acutely aware that he did not do enough patrolling; he hadn't visited the southern sector of the island in three months, for example. If Price-Kane gave him an assistant he could be three times as effective, but Naismith held out little hope of that. He finished his tea and realised that he didn't want another cup and had no appetite. His stomach was sour and he was bothered by rheumatism in the knees and ankles, a legacy of sleeping in the cold rain on the veldt in earlier days and later of travelling in canoes and climbing mountains in tropical downpours. *At least there's Colin Clements' visit to look forward to,* he thought. *He seems to be able to get through an evening without getting drunk, and with any luck he plays cribbage.* Naismith pushed the tea tray aside, wound the portable gramophone and selected a record. He leaned back in his chair as the opening bars of the overture from *The Pirates of Penzance* swelled up and drifted out over the dry red earth of the drilling ground, the soft green lawn of the compound, crossed by precisely aligned gravel paths, and the still blue waters of Alma lagoon.

"Got something lined up that could be useful for you," Clements said as he finished sucking on the rind of a slice of pineapple. "Little boating exercise. Like boating, do you?"

"I have done," Webb said, "but not in recent years."

"More punting lately, eh?"

Over lunch at Clements' house in one of Patugi's residential compounds, Clements had thrown in a few of these sallies, and Webb was beginning to tire of them. He pushed aside his plate and swilled the last few inches of beer in his glass. "Look, Colin, I wish you'd drop this notion that I've spent the last three years among the dreaming spires gazing from an ivory tower and all that bloody rot. I was in a bad way when the war ended, and I went farm labouring for a time, to put myself back together again. Then my father died and he left me enough, *just* enough, if I lived like a monk and worked every holidays, to go to Oxford. I spent the last year working for a gunsmith in a filthy factory while I tried to convince someone to fund me to come out and do this study. It hasn't been a bed of roses."

It was the longest speech Webb had made to Clements, and it took Clements by surprise. He nodded to the houseboy to take plates and watched Webb pass the plate rather than wait for it to be picked up. "I'm sorry, Dick. I get jealous of people who seem to be making a go of things. I had some bad luck when I was young, as I've told you, and I've had a tendency to feel sorry for myself since. I was a shade too old for the war. Maybe that would've toughened me up."

"Laid you out, more likely," Webb said. "Mark my words, the people who're going to do things, I mean in government and moneymaking and philosophy if you like, are the ones who *didn't* get their brains scrambled in that bloody mess. There'll be exceptions, but generally speaking the survivors will have exhausted themselves surviving. Listen to me, hobby-horsing."

"Why did you work for a gunsmith?"

"That's part of what I mean. Guns were what I knew best, machine guns particularly, but guns in general. But I was gun-shy and it wasn't to do with being wounded. I . . ." Webb mimed squeezing a trigger several times, "had the twitches about them. I got over it. But the war's left a lot of people damaged or only able to do one thing, often destructive. Damn the war. Where're we sailing to?"

"Just round the island. The doctor's got a few calls to make, and he said we could come along. Point is, only Murdo men will work the boat today. Know why?"

Webb shook his head.

Clements laughed. "It's Sunday, you bloody pagan. The missionaries've brainwashed the Hemisphere people and most of the others, but your Murdoans aren't interested in the good news."

"What are they interested in?"

Clements stood. "Time to go. They're concerned with money, pigs, women and fighting."

"In what order?"

"Any order."

The government launch *Equator* was waiting for them at the dock with Ian Herbert, one of his Fiji-trained native assistants and seven Murdoan sailors aboard. Herbert greeted them with a bottle of beer in his hand.

"God rot you, Colin, you've kept me waiting." Herbert held up his bottle. "Had to take some medicine for my impatience." He waved his hand at the bosun, a short, chunky man with a blue handkerchief tied over his tight black curls. Like the other sailors the bosun wore blue shorts and a grey singlet; his only apparent badge of office was the silver whistle on a cord around his neck.

"Cast off, or weigh anchor or whatever the hell it is you do."

The engines growled and the water at the stern of the launch boiled as she edged away from the dock and out into the channel. Marked by a line of buoys, the channel led through the reef that ran along this part of the coast out to the open sea. Clements introduced Webb to the doctor, refused the offer of a beer and settled down to sleep on a shady part of the deck. The launch was a twenty-footer, quite stylish and superbly maintained by the Marine Department. White with green trim, carrying red life preservers and with its brass gleaming, the *Equator* made a brave showing. The small Union Jack mounted at the bow would be stiffened by the breeze. Herbert drained his bottle and tossed it into the green water. He wiped his moustache with the back of his hand and lit a cigar.

"Anthropologist, eh?"

"That's right, doctor," Webb said, "the first one to work in these parts."

"That why you're here? To be first? Make a name for yourself?"

"Anything wrong with that?"

"No. Makes you a bit of an odd man out. Can't think of anyone else in the Jeremiahs who's hoping to make a name for himself. Gave that up long ago myself."

Webb didn't reply and the two men stood by the starboard rail as the launch threaded through the reef and stood out into the Murdo Strait. Murdo itself, dark, high-backed, was twenty miles to the west, but Webb could see the irregular shape of its mountainous interior. Dark clouds boiled up over the highest peaks. By contrast, Hemisphere was a soft island; its surrounding reef was broken only in four places and protected lagoons and bays lay within. The almost-circular island had a wide plain on the east coast and its interior, though rugged, was penetrable — crossed by many footpaths a fit European could negotiate. The air was warm and moist and the clouds were gathering for the early afternoon rainstorm, which would last a few minutes and then clear to leave a steamy heat.

"I tell a lie," Herbert said.

Webb, occupied with thoughts of kinship groupings and initiation ceremonials, was startled. "I beg your pardon?"

"There *is* someone else who intends to make a bigger name for himself, fellow named Birmingham. Writer chappie. D'you know him at all?"

"No. I've read a couple of his books. I heard he was on the steamer but, well, I was third class and he was first."

Herbert rubbed the side of his nose. The organ was redder than it should have been, with a few broken blood vessels beginning to show. "I'll tell you one thing that's first class about him. His wife. What a corker!"

Webb struggled to recall the couple of Birmingham books he had leafed idly through at Blackwells. Large, glossy affairs, handsomely produced and illustrated. About India and Afghanistan, or was it Ceylon and Madagascar? The bold, flamboyant writing hadn't attracted him.

"I didn't think much of the books," he said.

"I like them. Great stuff. I don't know what he expects to find around here, though. Place is deadly dull. Sure you won't have a beer?"

Though his days as an infantry captain were long behind him, Richard Webb sometimes could not resist falling back into some of the attitudes that had been second nature. "Forgive me for saying this," he said slowly, "but should you be drinking now? Haven't you got some sort of medical duty to perform?"

Herbert chortled. "You've got a damn cheek, but you don't know how things work around here, so I suppose you can't be blamed. Look, Colin there's asleep in the shade, I'm about to have another beer and you're leaning on the rail. Who's working around here?"

Webb looked forward to where a sailor was sitting in the bow gazing into the water and shouting his information to the helmsman. In the stern a thin youth was baiting a heavy hook at the end of a trawling line. At his feet were a gaff and a long bushknife. "The locals," he said.

"Exactly. Great trick to running colonies is to never let the natives see you working. They're amazed that everything gets done while we sit about. Doesn't seem to occur to them that they're doing all the work. Same with me. Young Aliki'll do the work, and he'll do a damn fine job of it."

Webb struggled to conceal his distaste. "Who's he?"

"My assistant. Hemisphere boy, good Methodist. He was trained in Fiji, and giving a few smallpox inoculations is child's play to him. But the point is this — *we* arrive on this smart ship, flag flying and all that rot, and the bush people'll come down and get their jabs. If Aliki just came strolling into the village with his medicine chest and bare feet, he'd be lucky to get two old women to listen to him."

"I see," Webb said, "I'll have to keep an open mind on that."

The *Equator* bucked and rolled as she passed through a long, rough swell set up by inter-island currents. Clements muttered in his sleep and Herbert swore as he spilt some of his beer. The vessel entered calmer water and Webb went to the stern to watch the bait, a lump of fish and a few strands of white cotton, leaping around in the spreading wake, six metres behind. The sailors paused in their work to glance at the line from time to time, but there was no one watching except Webb when the line tightened and he saw a large fish plunging and turning in the turbulent water.

"Hey!" Webb yelled. "Hey, we've got a bite!" There was no reply so he took a tentative pull on the line. He could feel the strength of the fish, and as he tugged in an unthinking, competitive response, he saw it — a large, silver-bellied creature, firmly caught but fighting, leaping and twisting, trying to throw the hook. Farm work and long hours at a gunsmith's machine bench had toughened Webb's hands and, although he favoured his left arm a little, he had strength in his shoulders and wrists. He wasted no more breath in shouting, but hauled on the line to keep a firm pressure and avoid the slack in the line that would enable the fish to tear the hook through its flesh. He spread his feet, gripped the deck with his rubber-soled plimsolls, and fought the fish. Luckily the launch was on a straight course in calm water, and Webb could pull smoothly and let the line drop behind him. He felt the sweat break out

on his forehead and realised that he badly wanted to land
the fish. As he drew it closer he saw the cotton turn red
as the fish's blood soaked it. Then it was clear of the water
and a flapping, jerking nine-kilogram weight at the end
of the line. He wound the cord around his left arm and
took the weight while he reached with his right for the
long-handled gaff. A quick, well-directed thrust had the
fish impaled at the gill. He stepped back, keeping the line
taut and lifted the fish over the stern onto the deck, where
it throbbed and bled in its death throes.

"*Nambawan, masta.*"* The young sailor killed the fish
with a heavy blow from the bushknife. Webb let go the
line and gaff and leaned back against the rail, panting and
feeling triumph surge through him. He watched as a sailor
approached quickly with a bucket; the bushknife was used
to hack the fish into pieces; the deck was quickly doused
and swabbed and the fish went into the bucket. The sailors
grinned quickly at Webb as they energetically cleaned the
deck.

"They'll catch it if the bosun sees blood on the deck."
Clements touched Webb's shoulder. "Not a bad effort,
Dick. Fish for dinner."

Webb was embarrassed by his exultation and was
grateful for Clements' laconic reaction. "How will they
cook it?"

"Don't get any fancy ideas. This is the Jeremiahs, not
Paris. They'll boil it and we'll eat it with rice. Done
yourself some good with the Murdoans, though. They
admire a good killer."

"What kind of fish is it?"

"God, don't ask me. As far as I know they call them all
kingfish."

Herbert, Clements and Webb all had a beer on the
strength of Webb's catch, and the doctor sent a bottle below
for his assistant. "Why doesn't he come up?" Webb said.
"I'd like to meet him."

Herbert tilted his bottle and took a deep draught. "He's

---

* "Terrific, master."

studying. Poor little blighter never does anything else. He's sitting for the London externals. Wants to do a medical degree, God help him."

"Will he make it?"

Herbert shrugged. "Perhaps. He's bright enough, and it has to happen someday. He'd be the first."

The young sailor who had dealt with Webb's fish hung about close to the white men, shuffled his feet and waited to be noticed. Eventually Webb responded. "Is there something I can do for you?"

"*Please masta, yu wantim boy?*"

Webb's pidgin was equal to this. "You mean an assistant? Yes, I will need someone from the To'beili district. Are you To'beili?"

"Yes, *masta.*"

"But you work in the marine?"

"*Brother bilong me, masta.*"

"I see. Well . . . "

Clements lowered his beer and moved to Webb's side. "Sorry to interfere, Dick, but no can do."

"What d'you mean?"

"Will Naismith'll get you a boy."

"What if I want to make my own choice?"

"Wouldn't be wise."

Webb felt anger rise inside him, the sort of anger he had felt for years after the end of the war when he saw disabled soldiers living in poverty in the London slums while the politicians and generals rode about in Daimlers. He turned to the sailor, who had retreated a step at Clements' intervention. "Tell your brother to come and see me when I get to Murdo."

The sailor ducked his head in acknowledgment and moved away.

"Mistake," Clements said.

"We'll see," Webb said. "Hullo, what's this?"

A canoe had shot out of nowhere and was on a collision course with the launch. The breeze was stiff and the sail of the canoe was full, even straining. The bosun held his course and the man in the canoe adjusted the sail setting so the two vessels would come within a few metres of each other. When this happened the canoeist stood and shouted. Webb's head whipped round to see where the call had been directed. What he saw was instant consternation: on the deck, towards the bow, the bosun was shouting at one of the sailors who was shaking his head and looking dumbly at his feet. The bosun's voice was shrill with anger, and when one of the crew appeared to take the other sailor's part, the bosun let go the wheel and struck him with a savage backhander.

"Stop that!" Herbert shouted. "Or I'll put the lot of you on report."

The bosun glared at the two men who had incurred his displeasure and manhandled the first offender out of sight of the Europeans.

Webb watched the canoe's sail subside as the small craft changed direction. Then the sail filled again and the canoe headed back the way it had come. "What's the trouble?" he said.

Herbert snorted. "God knows. Best to make them keep their quarrels to themselves. Anyway, they'll have to look lively now, we're approaching the break in the reef."

The *Equator*'s engines slowed and the vessel came about to head towards the lighter-coloured, shallower water above the reef. The crew performed their tasks briskly, but Webb noticed that the knees of the sailor who had reacted to the shout from the canoe were shaking violently as he made preparations to lower the dinghy.

"That boy's frightened," he said to Clements.

"None of our business," Clements said. "I didn't bring you along to get you embroiled in native disputes. Take a look around you, this is a beautiful spot."

The passage through the reef was a twisting, treacherous channel expertly read by the sailors, but the coral formations, growing close to the surface and threatening to rip the bottom out of any boat, were weird and magical shapes. Their beauty was matched by the scene that spread out in front of the new arrivals as the *Equator* entered the shelter of the lagoon. Here, in contrast to the other side of the island, the beach was yellow, almost white. The hills behind the coastal plain were gently undulating, with none of the threatening abruptness of the western escarpment of Hemisphere or the mountains of Murdo. The broad, shallow lagoon was tranquil, and the clusters of moored canoes moved gently on its surface. Behind the beach and its fringe of palm trees could be seen the roofs of huts raised high off the ground, and the smoke of cooking fires. The sun had broken through the clearing clouds and the scene was bathed in intense light. The soft greens of the trees and hills seemed to mute the glare, and the clear blue water appeared to absorb the sunshine rather than reflect it. People young and old gathered on the beach to greet the launch. They seemed oddly sober to Webb, and then he remembered that this was a Methodist village on Sunday.

"You're right, Colin," Webb said, "it *is* beautiful. Why didn't they build the capital here instead of at Patugi?"

"Look over the side," Clements said, "see the bottom? Too shallow here for a deep draught vessel, and the reef passage is too narrow. No, we're stuck with Patugi. Besides, this place is too much like paradise for an administrative centre. Who'd ever get any work done?"

"What is it called?"

Clements shot him a sideways look. "Wesley," he said.

5

A pleasant lunch of tinned ham and fresh salad, with a gin before and a small brandy afterwards, had failed to compose Ashley Price-Kane's mind. On Sundays he missed England — the Cotswolds specifically, the misty afternoon walks with the smell of honest oaks and birches on the air. There it was possible to forget one's cares, even the demands of soldiering, for a time at least. But here, in his hot sitting room with the whirring fans getting on his nerves, there seemed to be no escape from the preoccupations of his high office. He put aside his book — Buchan's *The Three Hostages* — and poured himself a glass of water from the carafe on the table beside him. He took a long time to drink the water, and while he did so he made up his mind. He picked up the hand bell that sat beside the carafe and rang it sharply.

"*Masta*?" The head houseboy, dressed in clean white shirt and long laplap, stood almost to attention the way he had been taught.

"Send someone to the hotel to find Mr Larke. I'd like him to come to tea this afternoon. Tea, savvy?"

"Yes, *masta*. Mr Larke?"

"Arrived on the steamer last night." Having to explain anything to a native always irritated Price-Kane. "Larke, like the bird."

"Bird, *masta*?"

The RC waved him away and picked up his book.

Keith Larke almost panicked when he received the invitation. His clothes were creased, he was aware that he needed a haircut, and he had cut himself that morning shaving in front of the stained, cracked hotel mirror. And he had only one hour to prepare. He lit a Players and sat on his bed, forcing himself to be calm. *This is an honour,* he thought. *A good CO will always give you marks for trying — that's what Jeffrey used to say.* He located a housemaid and persuaded her, with the aid of a sixpence, to press his tropical kit. He fretted about a dust streak on his white shoes and attempted unsuccessfully with cream and brush to make a rebellious crest of hair lie flat. He dressed quickly and far too early in his expertly ironed kit and sat sweating in his room, not noticing the spot of blood that had dripped from his shaving cut onto his stiff white collar.

He arrived at the Residency, set in a spacious garden behind the Secretariat, ten minutes early but too nervous to care. The head houseboy ushered him down a passage that carried photographs of military gentlemen, singly and in groups, and ushered him into the presence of the resident commissioner.

"K . . . Keith Larke, sir. At your service."

"My dear fellow." Price-Kane shook Larke's hand warmly and waved him into a cane chair. "Tea'll be along shortly. You're perspiring a little, I see. Secret is a close-fitting undervest. Might feel hot but it solves the problem. That's my first piece of advice to you. Won't be the last."

Larke was acutely aware of the damp patches spreading from his armpits and had an impulse to flap his arms in the air. "Thank you, sir," he said. "It's all very new to me."

"Of course it is, of course it is. Your first posting?"

"Yes, sir."

Can't be much chop if they send him here, Price-Kane thought. *Doesn't look a bit like Jeffrey Larke. Still . . .* "I had a chap named Larke serving under me in France. He . . ."

Excited, Larke so far forgot himself that he interrupted. "My brother, sir. I didn't know you were his CO."

"Well, just for a time. He was a very gallant officer. You should be proud of him."

"I am, sir. I am indeed. I hope I can acquit myself equally well, if required."

"Do you? Ah, here's the tea."

The two men drank tea and ate sandwiches made of thinly sliced bread and tinned cucumbers. Larke slowly relaxed as the RC continued to exhibit a rather schoolmasterly friendliness. He was vastly relieved, for Price-Kane had a reputation as something of a martinet. For his part, the RC continued to be unimpressed by the cadet. Larke's minor public school was unknown to him and he seemed to have no important family connections in the service. *A dull young man,* he concluded, *but possibly all the more useful for that.*

When the tea things had been cleared away, Price-Kane suggested they sit on the verandah and smoke. "Can't stand the smell of cigarettes in the house," he said.

Larke agreed, thankful he hadn't asked permission to smoke. Sitting companionably side by side under the verandah, the two men lit up, Price-Kane a cigar and Larke his Players.

"I'm thinking of posting you to Murdo," the RC said.

"Really, sir? There's nothing I'd like better."

"Heard anything about the place?"

"A little, sir." Larke determined to practise the clipped delivery that seemed to mark the man of authority. "Rough."

Price-Kane puffed smoke into the heavy, moist air. "Yes. But it's slowly coming under control. DO Naismith is doing a first-class job, in most respects."

"I'll look forward to meeting him, sir."

"He's an Australian. Bit raw perhaps, but an excellent chap. Went to the war in South Africa and won some gong or other. His brother won a VC in France."

"Did Mr Naismith serve in the Great War, sir?"

"No. Not sure why. Bit of a mystery man, Will Naismith, in some ways. Are you much of a reader, Larke?"

"No, sir."

Price-Kane grunted. "Haven't read Buchan?"

"No, sir, but I did see a play of *The Thirty-Nine Steps* in Bradford once. Jolly good."

"Then you know the form. You know what intelligence work is? That's what Hannay did before he got into that spot of bother."

"Like spying, sir?"

"Not exactly, nothing underhand. More to do with compiling information and passing it on. All completely above board." The RC laughed. "Sure, it's happened to me in Africa and other places. DO Naismith will compile reports on you that you won't see."

Nothing could have been calculated to alarm Keith Larke more. He was desperately short of self-confidence and the notion of confidential reports being written about him was enough to make his teeth chatter. He drew on his cigarette and choked on the smoke. When Larke had finished coughing, Price-Kane turned his face towards him. The short grey hairs of his military moustache were like pig bristles.

Larke's voice was thin and wavering. "He would be fulfilling his role as the superior officer, sir."

"Exactly. And so am I in instructing you to prepare reports, for my eyes only, on Mr Naismith."

Larke was just imaginative enough to be excited by the order. "Report on what, sir?"

"Everything," the RC said.

Tom Birmingham had gone on drinking beer after lunch and moved to whisky by mid-afternoon. Louise lay down for a nap, annoyed at his tipsiness, and found him deeply drunk when she awoke. She sat up in the narrow bed and pushed the mosquito net aside. Birmingham was squatting on the other bed; his face was red and sweating and there was a fug of pipe smoke in the room. He lifted a half-full tumbler of whisky to his mouth and gulped.

"Tom, what do you think you're doing?" she said sharply.

"Oh, hi, honey. You're awake. Good nap?"

"Put that glass down! You're drunk."

Birmingham took another gulp. "Practising, m'dear. All the chaps out here drink a lot, don't y'know. What about the doc the other night? Some drinker."

Louise Birmingham had had a moderate amount of minor sexual experience in her college years and subsequently in New York, but she had been a virgin when she married, technically, at least. Tom had approached her gently and expertly, and she had enjoyed their wedding night and many nights that followed. She remained grateful to Tom for the manner of this initiation, because she knew enough from reading and talking with other women to be aware that a bad sexual start was a big handicap. If her feelings for her husband had shrunk to gratitude and affection, that was still a strong enough bond to make her concerned when he seemed to be jumping the tracks. She scrambled onto the other bed and sat beside him.

"What's the matter?"

"Nothin', hon."

"Don't say nothing. You're sitting here in this hot box, getting drunk and smoking yourself sick. There must be a reason."

Birmingham made a clumsy attempt to touch her breasts inside the low neck of her nightgown. "Frustration. Need some loving."

She pushed him off. "You smell like a spittoon. Get yourself cleaned up, Tom, and we'll have a talk. If you don't, I swear to God I'll be back on that ship and out of here tonight."

Birmingham looked stricken. "You wouldn't!"

"Don't try me. The bathroom's at the end of the hall. There's a towel on the back of the door. I'm going to open the windows and clear this goddamn stink. You do as I say, Tom, or I'll do as I say."

Birmingham pushed himself up from the bed and wavered towards the door. He wore only his undershorts, and flesh around his waist bulged. His bulky shoulders were padded with fat. Louise watched him as he drunkenly draped the towel over his shoulder and opened the door. She threw back the doors to the verandah and propped up the windows. The grey smoke swirled and drifted towards the openings. She emptied butts and pipe dottles from the ashtray onto a sheet of newspaper, wrapped it up and placed it in the waste bin. She poured some water from the stoppered bottle on the chest of drawers onto a handker-chief and sponged her face and neck.

Louise leaned against the balcony rail and felt a thrilling and frightening surge of power. This was the first time she had attempted to impose her will on her husband, and she had been totally successful. That was a thrill. She was frightened by the thought that having done it once, she would want to do it again, and not just to Tom Birmingham.

When he returned Birmingham's face was scrubbed clean, though still bristly. His thick hair was wet and slicked down. He smelled of tooth powder and soap with just a touch of Johnnie Walker scotch whisky. He unwrapped the towel from around his waist and pulled on a pair of trousers. He took a clean shirt from a drawer and put it on, leaving the collarless neck open. Louise thought he looked like a butcher about to go to the neighbourhood speakeasy for a beer. She watched him as he sat on the bed, bent forward and fumbled on the floor for his shoes. His face was red when he straightened up.

He looked across the second bed out to the balcony. "I'm sorry," he said.

"That won't do." Louise spoke quietly, and Birmingham had to go out onto the balcony himself to hear her. "It's not good enough to say you're sorry. I want to know why you got yourself in that state. What's troubling you?" She knew she should say that she'd help him, but she didn't.

"Hell, honey. It was just being out here, where there's no prohibition an' all. I just got to drinking a bit fast, that's all."

Louise was enraged. "You must think I'm an idiot! Prohibition's never worried you. You knew a thousand places to drink as much as you liked in New York and San Francisco. And the boat was wet. But I never saw you like that before. Don't insult my intelligence, Tom."

"Intelligence," Birmingham muttered.

"What was that?"

"I was just wondering how important intelligence is, compared to courage, say."

"Don't change the subject."

"I'm not, not really, hon. You're right. I've got a bit of a problem. You see, the last two books haven't sold very well."

"I don't see why not. They were just the same as the others."

Birmingham smiled at her tone. It was the first time he'd heard from Louise a note he'd detected in the reaction of many others to his books — a condescension, slight but detectable. "That could be the problem. Also there's a legal matter, but I don't want to go into that."

Louise decided instantly to see if she could exert the power again. She held herself stiffly. "Tell me about it!"

"A guy's talking about suing for defamation. Says I called him a coward in my last book."

"Did you?"

Birmingham shrugged. "Depends how you look at it."

"How does my father look at it?"

"He isn't happy." Birmingham drew a deep breath, as if he was about to plunge into a pool and attempt a long swim underwater. "It wouldn't look good, a lawsuit involving cowardice and me and this guy."

"Why not?"

"He went to the war and I didn't." Birmingham's face flamed red again.

Louise was startled. She had been fifteen years old when

the war ended. She knew no one who talked about it. How could it matter?

"I tried to go!" Birmingham exclaimed. "I did my training and I was on the ship all set to sail to France. And then the goddamn war ended and we never left New York. Just got off the boat and went back to camp and waited to be demobbed." He put both hands to his head and burst into tears, rocking back and forward on his heels.

Louise watched him in horror. She had never seen her father weep, nor any other man. It was as impossible as seeing her mother urinate in public. She was rooted to the spot, unable to move to help him. She wanted to be back in New York or back on the boat, anywhere but here with this eighty-five-kilogram weeping baby. But she was not thinking only of herself. *Thank God I can't be pregnant. This is no father.* Waldeck & Marsh had published a revised edition of Marie Stopes' *Married Love* which Louise had read avidly. She had absorbed the information on contraception and put it into practice assiduously, starting on her wedding night. Her fingers shook as she took a Lucky Strike from the packet and lit it. Birmingham stopped crying and joined her at the rail. Louise handed him her cigarette and lit another for herself. "I'm not a coward," he said.

"I thought you'd proved that all over the world."

"Sure. I'm very sorry, Lou. Things just seemed to bear down on me there for a while. I'm all right now. This book has to be good, that's what it comes down to."

Although she hated to be called Lou, Louise could not bear to apply any pressure to him now. "I'm sure it will be."

"Right." He puffed on the cigarette, stuck it jauntily in his mouth and thumped his fist into his open palm. "Right. It'll be good, damn good. And you won't leave me, will you?"

Louise Birmingham looked down at the *Moresby* riding high on the full tide in the harbour. The rust stains on the hull, which had ill disposed her towards the vessel when she first saw it, did not trouble her now. One part of her yearned to be on it and to be leaving this place, another was responsive to the sights and scents of the island. She wanted to see more. She put her hand on her husband's shoulder and stroked him tentatively, as if he was a stray cat in need of comfort. "No, Tom," she said, "I won't leave you."

On an impulse, Naismith spent the afternoon supervising the cleaning up of the garden; a severe storm the previous week had brought down branches and uprooted small trees. The workers were To'beili prisoners, pagans, the only men he could legitimately employ on Sunday. They would enjoy a generous respite later in the week and jeer at their fellow prisoners for their foolish adoption of the white man's religion. The To'beili worked well and cheerfully; Naismith issued extra tobacco and went off to bathe before dinner.

After eating he read some back issues of the Melbourne *Argus*, noting with satisfaction the statement made by the Australian prime minister, Stanley Bruce, at the London Imperial conference. Yielding to habit, Naismith read the words aloud: " 'Each dominion in the future, as hitherto, while it remains a member of the Empire, must be the sole judge of its obligations; and I believe that under these conditions our co-operation in any common cause will be such that no part of the Empire will be imperilled.' That's the stuff!" He nodded approvingly over the successes of the Warrnambool cricket team in the country competition and read with alarm of the inflammatory, revolutionary-sounding activities of Jack Lang, the premier of New South Wales.

He put the papers aside and was about to select a phonograph record when Baekani coughed at the doorway.

"Yes, Baekani?"

"Sir, Eglito has escaped." Baekani spoke in the Kweili language of the area around Alma. He also spoke several other Murdoan languages, including To'beili, as well as several of the Santa Juliana dialects. Kweili, however, was Naismith's only local tongue. It was sufficiently close to several of the other east coast languages to allow the DO to get by in those districts, but the languages of the west and the interior were a closed book to him.

"The fool," Naismith said. "When?"

"Sir, in the night, but he was not discovered to be missing until sunset."

"His canoe?"

"The police say it is gone, sir."

Naismith sighed. *More work*, he thought, *and dirty work at that.* He asked Baekani to fetch the station logbook. As he replaced the record in its paper sleeve, he marshalled his thoughts about Eglito: son of a *lemo* who had murdered a missionary and been hanged for it, Eglito was a *lemo* himself, a bounty killer. Naismith searched his memory for a picture of the man. Yes, he had him now. Jaw like an ox and a stubbornness to match. A consistent evader of the rate; a throwback to the time of unchecked feuds.

When the heavy bound volume arrived, he settled down in his sitting room close to the kerosene lamp to read the entries regarding the case of Eglito. The To'beili clan leader had a long history of refusing to pay the rate, which occasioned fines, seldom paid, and periods of imprisonment. A recent entry recorded Eglito's latest sentence — ten years' hard labour for manslaughter. A member of a clan group involved in a bitter feud with Eglito's clan had been shot in the back while gardening. Some evidence of provocation had been produced that had reduced the charge from murder. Remembering the trial, Naismith recalled a sneaking admiration for the stocky, composed figure who had paid the proceedings no attention whatever. Eglito had been lucky — a decade before, he would have swung.

Naismith's eyes rested on a later notation. 'Eglito, convicted last month of manslaughter, has sworn to kill Waimasu, a To'beili who informed on him and is a member of the clan against which Eglito has directed his aggression. I am informed by Baekani that a sizable bounty of shell money has been placed on Waimasu's head by Eglito, who is the ceremonial and war chief of his clan.'

Naismith walked through the house to the boxroom

adjacent to his bedroom, where the hand-operated station radio was installed. He switched on and called Patugi.

"Patugi receiving, Alma. Over."

Naismith spoke crisply and quickly, "This is DO Naismith, Patugi. I wish to inform the head of the constabulary on Hemisphere that the To'beili prisoner Eglito escaped custody, possibly ten hours ago. His canoe is missing. There is reason to believe that he will have gone to Hemisphere to pursue further vengeance killing. Seaman Henry Waimasu of the Marine is a likely target. I suggest a close watch be kept for this escapee, he is a desperate and dangerous man. Further information tomorrow. Have you anything to report on this matter, Patugi? Over."

"Message received and understood, Alma. Nothing to report. Over."

"Thank you, Patugi. Over and out."

6

Wesley, 11 February 1928

The jetty at Wesley, constructed of rocks, lumps of coral and bracing timbers, could be used by vessels other than canoes only at high tide. At other times, all goods and personnel were landed by dinghy. So it was as the *Equator* arrived. Herbert the medical officer and his assistant went ashore first. The sailor who took them did not row the dinghy, but stood in the stern and propelled the boat by manipulating a single oar.

"Pretty smart, don't you think?" Clements said.

Webb nodded. "I'll say."

"Of course he's showing off. Only works in still water like this. If the waves were up he'd be rowing like any other blighter. Still, have to admit it, they're great boatmen."

"I can't help wondering what that business with the canoe was all about."

"Forget it. Want to go ashore? The dinghy'll be back soon."

Webb and Clements took the dinghy to the beach, where they jumped from the bow onto the dry, bone-coloured sand. A group of villagers stood about as the sailor heaved, trying to push the boat off. Webb added some weight to the push and the dinghy floated free.

"Just branded yourself a pagan," Clements observed, "working on Sunday."

They strolled about the quiet village in which the most imposing building was a large, open-sided, iron-roofed church. A Sunday school class was in progress, and Webb watched and listened briefly before turning away to look at the people sitting listlessly in the shade under their houses.

"Not quite what you came to see, eh?" Clements said. "Don't worry. It's very different on Murdo."

"I wonder how the doctor's getting on," Webb said. "Couldn't presenting yourself for an injection be considered work?"

Clements smiled. "I imagine there's a passage in the scriptures to justify it. Christ probably cured a few lepers on the Sabbath or something. Besides, the Methodists aren't as rabid as some of the sects. Did you see the water tank to collect runoff from the church roof?"

Webb nodded.

"Couldn't have that with the Seventh-day Adventists, for example. I know of a small offshore island where the people have to paddle a mile to get water from the mainland. Island's dry. They could get all they need from the church roof but it's not permitted, using the house of the Lord for practical purposes."

Webb shook his head. "I saw a few men die in France who could've been saved if they'd agreed to blood transfusions. Germans and English both."

Clements nodded. "Jehovah's Witnesses. Madness. Come on, let's see what the quack's doing."

They found Herbert sitting comfortably in the shade while Aliki attended to a long, patiently waiting line of men, women and children. Richard Webb's eye was beginning to distinguish differences in physical type among the Jeremians. The Hemisphere Island people were generally taller and more slender than the Murdoans he had encountered. Among the people in line, however, were several who resembled the Murdoans in build: well-proportioned but noticeably deep in the chest, and wide-shouldered. Webb commented on this to Herbert.

"Very observant of you," the doctor said. "You're learning; in fact, these chaps *are* Murdoans. They belong to a community that was established here after the repatriation of the islanders from Queensland. You've heard about that, I suppose?"

Webb had. After Australia federated, non-European migration was legislated against, and thousands of the Melanesian labourers who had served their indentures in the colony and contrived to remain there were repatriated. Only a few hundred — those who had married or acquired land or influential patrons among the clergy — avoided this mass exodus.

"Quite a few of the recruits went to Queensland to escape punishments and feuds back here," Herbert said. "It was a death sentence to put them back on Murdo, so the all-wise, all-loving Protectorate government allowed some of 'em to settle on Hemisphere. They bash their Bibles like the rest and give no trouble."

Webb tried to remember what the man who had hailed the *Equator* from his canoe looked like. Stocky. "What about that chap in the canoe?" he asked Clements. "Was he a Murdoan?"

"Still harping on that, Dick? Very likely — he came from the right direction. How's Aliki doing, Ian?"

"Bit slow," Herbert said, "you need to get into a rhythm with this sort of work. Bit like cricket really. But he's coping. I'd say he's got about an hour ahead of him. Then there's a few individuals to attend to. Have to have a cup of tea with the deacon, I'm afraid. Then we can hop back on the boat and rinse the tonsils."

"Have I got time to take a look at this Murdoan village?" Webb asked. "It interests me."

"So it should." Clements pointed to his right. "It's about a half-hour walk that way. Easy track. Don't worry if you don't get back in time. You can walk out along the reef and give us a hoy. We'll come in close and you can swim out, that's if you don't mind the sharks."

Webb grinned. "I'll be back."

"It's still pretty warm," the doctor said. "Have a swig of water before you go, and watch you don't cut your feet. An infected cut is the very devil here, and those plimsolls are pretty thin."

Webb took a few healthy mouthfuls of water from the jug on the medical assistant's table. Aliki, a tallish, serious young man, was working with deep concentration. He took hold of the recipient's upper arm gently but firmly, swabbed, used the hypodermic deftly and pressed cottonwool to the spot. He talked quietly to the next in line as he cleaned the syringe and drew up the next dose. A child whimpered; Aliki said something and several people in the line laughed. *Bedside manner's all right,* Webb thought.

He crossed a clearing in front of what looked like the village meeting place and took the track Herbert had indicated into the light bush. Webb was not alone on the track; he was passed by people returning from the medical post and he encountered others hurrying towards Wesley. The track had a steady incline, and it was hot and hard going where there was no tree cover. On cooler sections, where a canopy of vines and leaves grew above head height, Webb enjoyed the walk. The bush was full of unfamiliar smells and, even after the time spent on the ship and a brief stay in Sydney, he still found arresting the intense light and the deep green of the sea, which he glimpsed at odd turns in the track.

He reached the village to find it in an uproar. Several men ran towards him, shouting in a pidgin too rapid and excited for Webb to understand. They indicated that he should follow them and he did, moving fast between the huts and stone rockeries to a point on the beach where a spindly jetty, roughly thatched and walled at its end, jutted out several metres into a deep tidal pool. Webb knew from his wide reading that these structures were latrines, flushed by the tide.

A group of people were gathered around at the edge of the pool and they parted to allow Webb through. A naked man lay on his back on the sand, his throat deeply cut from one end of the jawbone to the other. His head lolled back, exposing the depth and width of the wound, which was white and pink. There was no blood.

"*Him stap long pool, masta,*" one of the villagers said. "*Mi pullim long bis.*"

Webb understood. The dead man had been pulled from the pool onto the beach.

"When?" Webb said. He tapped his wristwatch.

The man shook his head.

"Who is he? *Wannim?*"

"*Name belong him Sampson. Him belong Equator.*"

With a shock, Webb recognised the dead man as one of the sailors — the man who had so skilfully brought the dinghy to shore using a single oar. "Where's his uniform?" he asked.

Colin Clements became bored watching the injections and conversing with Herbert. He decided to go back to the launch, where he had a readable book waiting and could get a cup of tea. The dinghy was drawn up on the beach, but there was no sign of the boatman. Irritated at this interference with his plans, Clements considered rowing the dinghy himself but gratefully abandoned the idea when he saw a sailor hurrying across the clearing. He strolled to the dinghy and stood ready to help to push it into the water, thinking as he did so that Webb's catching a fish himself had set a very bad example. The boatman grasped Clements' intention and pushed until the dinghy was almost into the water; he signalled for Clements to jump in and completed the job himself, driving the boat into the water without apparent effort.

Clements sat in the dinghy and drowsily watched the boatman wielding the oars. It occurred to him that the rowing was somewhat clumsy, but Clements hardly registered the thought. They drew closer to the launch, and Clements waited for the dinghy to come alongside, near the rope ladder slung from the *Equator*'s rail. He stood, expecting the boatman to steady the dinghy and allow him

to climb the ladder first. Instead, the man knocked him
aside and went up the ladder in three easy movements.
Puzzled, Clements gathered himself and began to climb
the ladder. He stopped when his head cleared the rail and
he had a clear view of the deck.

The man who had rowed the dinghy was pulling a knife
from the chest of a sailor. He drove the blade in again and
jerked it free; a plume of blood spurted across the scrubbed
deck. Another member of the crew appeared on the deck
and the assailant picked up the fishing gaff and slashed at
him, catching him a solid blow on the head and knocking
him down. Clements opened his mouth to shout but no
sound emerged. Slipping on the blood, the murderer bent
and carefully cut the throat of his first victim. He
straightened, took two long strides and dived into the
water.

Clements clung to the rail and watched the man swim
quickly to a canoe moored twenty yards from the launch.
He flipped from the water into the canoe and within
seconds was paddling fast towards a long spit of land at
the easternmost end of the lagoon. Clements gripped the
rail and pulled himself up.

"Hey!" he shouted. "Someone help!"

Blood flowed across the deck from the body of the dead
man and from the gaping wound on the head of the man
who had taken the blow from the gaff, and who lay still
with one leg twisted under him. The bosun stepped onto
the deck and immediately ducked back, to reappear with
a heavy military pistol in his hand.

"Too late for that," Clements said. "He's gone."

The bosun looked wildly about him. He swallowed as
he saw the throat wound. "Waimasu," he said.

Clements collected himself. "Get the doctor for the
other man. He's alive. The doctor. Go!"

The bosun moved to the rail and saw the dinghy floating
three metres away from the launch. The tide was turning
and the boat moved rapidly towards the reef. The bosun
handed the pistol to Clements, jumped into the water and
swam to the dinghy. He climbed aboard and began to

propel himself rapidly towards the beach, using the one-oar method. Clements knelt close to the wounded sailor, who was breathing shallowly; blood leaked from his mouth and his eyes fluttered. Clements was afraid to touch him. He went to the rail and looked in the direction of the spit — the canoe was nowhere in sight.

Richard Webb ran the whole distance from the Murdoan settlement to Wesley. He arrived just as Herbert and Aliki were boarding the dinghy.

"Doctor," he shouted, " a man's been killed."

"On the launch, I know. Get out of the way, man. There's another one wounded."

"But . . ."

"Get in if you must, and grab an oar."

Webb and the bosun rowed to the *Equator* and Herbert climbed the ladder. Clements sat on the blood-soaked deck beside the wounded man. Herbert knelt and examined him quickly.

"Dead," he said. "Christ, what a bloody mess. What happened?"

Webb, Aliki and the bosun climbed aboard. Webb paled as he saw the third murder victim, killed in the same fashion as the man he'd seen. He recognised the young sailor who had exhibited such fright as the launch was nearing the lagoon. The bosun leaned against the rail and sobbed. Aliki spoke rapidly to him; the bosun replied, his voice shaking with emotion. The Europeans waited.

"This man's name is Waimasu," Aliki said. "He is a To'beili man from Murdo. A man named Eglito had sworn to kill him, and now he has done it."

"How did this Eglito bastard get aboard?" the doctor asked.

7

The bodies of Eglito's victims were wrapped in canvas for transportation back to Patugi and thence to Murdo, where the appropriate mortuary ceremonies would be performed. Herbert, Clements, Webb and the bosun conferred briefly to establish an understanding of events. Distressed, the bosun confessed that the shout from the canoe they had encountered before reaching Wesley had been a warning.

"What sort of warning?" Herbert said.

"*Wanpela say Eglito, him stap long Hemisphere.*"

"He was very frightened," Webb said.

The bosun nodded.

"You were lucky, Colin," Webb observed. "He could've done for you while he had you in the dinghy."

Herbert was shocked. "He wouldn't kill a white man."

Aliki made enquiries on shore, but he could learn nothing about the identity of the man who had warned Waimasu.

"We should try to get hold of him," Webb said. "The coroner'll want to know all he can about the circumstances."

Herbert and Clements exchanged glances. "There won't be a coronial enquiry, Dick," the doctor said. "We'll make statements and that'll be it."

"Would it be different if he'd attacked Colin?"

The doctor nodded as he watched the bosun, the remaining crew member and a Seventh-day Adventist visiting relatives on Hemisphere and not observing Sunday as the day of rest, at work. They hoisted the dinghy and fastened it at the stern.

"And what'll happen to this Eglito if they catch him? Will he get a trial?"

"Yes," Herbert said, "and then he'll be hanged."

The *Equator* got under way as the last of the light died. Herbert sent a brief radio message to the capital and then returned to his beer. Aliki resumed his studies. Clements took his book to a chair under a flickering lantern suspended above the forward deck, and settled down to read. The sailors swabbed the bloodstained deck with sea water and mops. The bosun picked up a knife that had been half concealed by a coil of rope. He bent to wash the blood from it by dipping it in a bucket.

"Don't do that!" Webb said sharply. "That's important evidence."

Clements glanced up from his book. "Keep out of it, Dick."

Webb wrapped the knife in his handkerchief. "Look, Colin, you didn't mention anything about what happened to the knife so far. He must have thrown it down there."

"When he picked up the gaff, I suppose. I don't recall."

"It might be interesting to know whose knife it is, and how Eglito got hold of it."

"I thought you were an anthropologist, not a lawyer."

"I'm not an anthropologist yet. Not until I do this study."

"All the more reason to stay out of this business."

"What do you mean?"

"What I've said before. You'll need every ounce of Will Naismith's co-operation if you hope to do your research on Murdo, and the last thing he'll want from you is interference. Eglito was *his* prisoner."

"That shouldn't affect the course of justice."

Clements sighed. "Go and get us a couple of beers from Ian, there's a good chap. The boys should have the fish ready soon. You'll feel better after a drink and a meal."

Eglito dug the paddle into the water savagely, using all his strength to drive the canoe. It was an action he could perform for hours, tirelessly, once he struck the right rhythm and his mind and muscles fell into a co-ordinated pattern. He was a small man among Murdoans, about five feet five inches tall, but with immense strength in his deep chest, sinewy arms and bunch-muscled legs. He had a singularly pronounced jaw, almost a deformity. It jutted forcefully, particularly when he spoke, which was rarely. Eglito had worked hard during his time in gaol; he had cut grass, cut timber and carried rocks and sacks of cement. There was no spare fat on his body.

He found the rhythm and dropped into it so that the action of paddling seemed not like a fight against the water but an entering into it, a co-operation. The canoe moved steadily, lightly laden, perfectly balanced by the outrigger. Eglito read the wave patterns and currents as a scholar reads a book, making minute adjustments, altering his stroke, allowing for surges of power in the wind and water. As Hemisphere Island fell away behind him, he allowed his mind to run over the tumultuous experiences of the past few days. But not idly; Eglito's thoughts were always purposeful, always directed towards the next action.

The escape from the Alma lockup had been easy, merely a matter of waiting for the right time once the arrangements had been made and the signs — the pig entrails, the drift of smoke from the fire on which the bones had been placed — had been interpreted. Securing a passage to Hemisphere had been planned long before — the swim from the jetty to the dinghy, the quick, silent row to the stern of the copra boat, the quiet burrow into the pile of coconuts and the stinking journey. Eglito ignored the discomforts, focussed as he was on the next stage of his plan — killing the Murdoans, which would earn him bounty and renown and his return to Murdo as a *lemo*, killer and leader, of unassailable authority. It had all gone well, but Eglito, the long-range plotter and revenge-taker, had been unprepared for one part of his experience.

Patugi. He had not been in the place for almost twenty years, not since they had killed his father in front of him and treated him as a beggar, a nothing. As he had grown in stature, knowledge and authority, Eglito had cherished a dream of burning the white man's village to the ground. He had seen it happen inside his mind — the tin-roofed houses exploding, the glass windows breaking and the afternoon rains turning the ashy ruins into blackened slush. But as he poked his head into the fresh air while the copra boat anchored briefly in Patugi Harbour, he was astonished at how the town had grown. These roads, buildings, gardens, all were new. He squinted at the hill where the gaol had been, straining to see the rusted iron and rough timber construction. It had gone. In its place was a solid-looking construction — an affair of white-washed cement with a high gate.

Eglito paddled on, stopping at long intervals to drink from the water bottle placed in the canoe by his Murdoan clansman on Hemisphere. The killings, by no means his first, had briefly filled him with power and confidence, but he was aware of limits that surely the old *lemo* had never confronted. Had his father felt fear as he thrust the spear through the body of the missionary who had polluted the ancestral shrine? Eglito could recall his father's face at the moment before the hood had concealed it forever. There had been no fear, no sign that his father had not believed utterly in the rightness of everthing he had done. A true *lemo*!

Was I afraid to kill the white man in the dinghy? Eglito thought. *Why did I not burn the ship the way the old warriors did? Was I afraid?* He did not allow himself to be diminished by the questions. He set them aside for later consideration.

The first indications that Murdo was close were matters of tide and current; the island itself was shrouded in dark mist. Eglito adjusted his course and paddled hard. He knew he could not burn Patugi or kill the man who now wore the white helmet with the bird feathers. Eglito had kept the two shillings he had been given that day and he had forgotten nothing. Murdo was not Hemisphere, Alma was not Patugi and District Officer Naismith was not the same as the red-faced man in the white uniform who had killed his father and buried him like a dog. But the old *lemo* did not always kill the man who had committed the crime. To kill a substitute, to devastate the garden of a kinsman, to lay a curse on a clan, were honourable acts ...

The killings at Wesley brought about a degree of activity in Patugi unusual on a Monday morning. A platoon of police drilled long and hard on the parade ground before the sun climbed over the trees; a thorough cleaning of the the *Equator*'s deck was ordered and another launch despatched to Wesley with a native police sergeant aboard, whose object was the arrest of the person who had shouted the warning to Waimasu. Ashley Price-Kane, told of the murders the night before, was early at his desk, reading Dr Herbert's brief report on the event, issuing orders, familiarising himself with the Eglito case and drafting a cable to the western Pacific high commissioner in Fiji. His secretary had made up a list of appointments at staggered times through the morning, but the RC's workload caused him to cancel some of these and to fit others in as best he could.

So it was that Tom and Louise Birmingham and Richard Webb, who had arrived at the Secretariat half an hour apart, found themselves waiting outside the RC's office at the same time. The secretary asked them to wait and indicated a small anteroom containing a table, a bowl of wilting flowers and four straight-backed chairs. Webb stood aside to allow the Birminghams to enter first.

"Good morning," he said. "You must be Mr and Mrs Birmingham."

"Right," Birmingham said. "Read my books, eh?"

Louise looked embarrassed; she sat nearest the window and adjusted her long, loose skirt. Webb watched her nervous, jerky movements and could sense her discomfort. "One or two," he said, "but Dr Herbert told me you were here."

"Just arrived yourself, haven't you? How come you know Herbert?" Birmingham was hung over and blustery. Quinine and alcohol were warring in his system.

"I was on a boat with him yesterday."

"Were you?" Louise's head jerked around. She was nervous, partly because she was in Webb's presence. Often since girlhood, her fantasies about particular men had seemed ridiculous after she had actually made contact with them. But she found Webb attractively tall and well formed, and his calm, British voice soothed her jangled nerves. "Then you saw the murders?"

Webb sat on the chair next to her, although he could easily have taken another chair further away. He shook his head. "I didn't actually see them, just the aftermath, which was bad enough."

"Bloody, eh?" Birmingham said.

"Very."

"Yeah. I remember when I . . ."

Louise extended her gloved hand. "Louise Birmingham, and you are . . . ?"

Webb expected the glove to be damp, but it was dry. "Richard Webb. What time's your appointment?"

Louise pushed back the sleeve of her white cotton blouse and looked at the small gold watch on her slim wrist. "Now."

Webb smiled. "Likewise."

"Desk drivers," Birmingham said, "all the same. What about this killing, then? A story in it, would you say?"

Webb was more interested in watching Louise remove her gloves. Her fingers were long, and the index and third finger on her right hand were tobacco-stained. Webb made a mental note to look at her teeth if she smiled. *I'm assessing her like a prize animal*, he thought. He refused Birmingham's extended cigarette case. "No thanks. A story? I don't know, depends on what you want. It's a very local matter as I understand it. A blood feud. Of course, that's of great interest to me."

"As an anthropologist?"

"Yes."

Birmingham seemed not to notice Louise's knowledge of Webb's business. He was more interested in her refusal of a cigarette. "Sure you won't have a smoke, hon?"

"I'm sure," Louise said. "What part of the islands are you going to study, Mr Webb? I mean, what people? God, I don't know what I mean. The only anthropology I've ever read is *The Golden Bough*."

"You've read that?"

"Parts of it only. Fascinating. I worked for a publisher in New York and we did some anthropology. Some of it sold very well."

Webb laughed. "I'm not writing a book, at least not yet. I'm doing a thesis for my doctorate, that's all. I'm planning to study the To'beili people on Murdo." He gestured in the direction of the RC's office. "That's if his nibs will give me permission."

"We're going to Murdo, aren't we, Tom?"

Birmingham nodded. "That's it, eh, Webb? You're not doing a book?"

"No, I assure you."

Birmingham dropped his cigarette end into the vase that held the flowers. A patch of the polished floor at his feet was already covered with ashes. "Maybe we can team up. You planning on any crocodile shooting?"

"God, no. I plan to sit on a log, learn the language and make a lot of notes. Photographs too, of course."

Birmingham grunted. Mentally Louise compared images — sitting in a canoe up a crocodile-infested creek with the dark jungle closing in all around, or strolling along a sunlit beach while the natives fished and sang and wove baskets.

The secretary appeared at the door. "Major Price-Kane will see you now, Mr Birmingham."

Webb rose fractionally from his chair as the Birminghams got up and moved towards the door. Louise looked back and nodded. Webb raised his hand and smiled. He realised that the throbbing in his arm, which had troubled him through the night and early part of the morning, had ceased.

An hour later, several arrangements had been made. The Birminghams, Webb and Keith Larke were to travel to Murdo that afternoon aboard the Protectorate's flagship *Braidwood*, named for an earlier resident commissioner. Also aboard would be the bodies of Waimasu and Eglito's other two victims. Price-Kane had signed the necessary documents with a flourish. His reasoning had been that the Eglito case would be a headache in itself for Naismith. With the added responsibility of an anthropologist and an American writer, plus wife (the RC had not been favourably impressed by the Birminghams), he was likely to make mistakes. And Keith Larke had been well briefed. Price-Kane sensed that the moment for the symbolic display of Imperial strength might be at hand. Naismith would certainly oppose such a demonstration. Therefore it could be time to reduce Naismith's influence . . .

Webb's pidgin had improved quickly as a result of his conversations with sailors and other islanders. Shopping for equipment in the Chinese stores, he found himself able to describe what he wanted, even to haggle. He intended to travel light, but he needed such things as a bushknife, lantern, enamel mugs and plates and a camp bed. He deliberated whether or not to buy rice and ships' biscuits. He had been unable to find out what the stores on Murdo stocked, or even whether stores existed. In Patugi there was a determined reluctance among all ranks to talk about the dark island.

"I wonder if you could help me, Mr Webb?"

"Mrs Birmingham, hello." Webb pulled off his hat; he realised that he was holding a large, wickedly hooked bushknife in his other hand. He put it down quickly.

Louise laughed. "I expect Tom'll buy half a dozen of those."

"Is there something I can do for you?"

"Yes. Tom's up the street buying . . . God, things, I don't

know. I was told to come in here and buy a couple of soo-loos. But I don't even know what they are."

"I'm glad you reminded me. I must do the same. A sulu's just a length of cotton trade cloth, a yard and a half or so. You wrap it around yourself." Webb mimed the action of wrapping a cloth around his waist. He was suddenly aware of Louise's slim figure, how little cloth would be needed to envelop her. He had a bright compelling image of her naked and slowly wrapping the brightly printed cloth around her breasts. The vision staggered him.

"What's the matter? Are you all right?"

"Yes. Yes, I'm fine. Here's the cloth. It's a matter of what colours you like. It's dirt cheap."

The Chinese storekeeper hovered behind the counter on which a dozen or more bolts of metre-wide cloth were laid out. The light was dim in the store and Louise squinted, trying to assess the colours. She rejected several bolts quickly and exhibited a preference for a deep blue with yellow Chinese designs and a red with white markings. "I can't decide."

"Take a look in the light." Webb carried the cloth to the door and almost hit Tom Birmingham in the face with the heavy rolls. Birmingham reeled back and steadied himself against the door jamb.

Webb said, "I beg your pardon."

"Tom, Mr Webb's helping me choose some cloth."

"Good," Birmingham said. He turned to three islanders who were walking behind him. "Take 'em to the . . . what's the name of the ship?"

"The *Braidwood*," Webb said.

"Right." Birmingham put a half-crown into the pocket of the shorts of one of three islanders who were carrying boxes, wrapped packages and half-gallon tins. The porters set off for the wharf and Birmingham, who was carrying a bushknife, took out a handkerchief and wiped his sweating face. "Cloth, eh? I like the red. You buying cloth too, Webb?"

Webb smiled. "And a few other things. Malinowski says the anthropologist's main tool is his notebook."

"Malinowski. He a Russian?"

"A Pole."

"Can you help me deal with the storekeeper, please, Mr Webb?" Louise asked. "I want four lengths."

"I'll do it," Birmingham said. "Lookee, John, me wantee four pieces of this red stuff."

The storekeeper looked blank.

"I want the blue," Louise said.

Webb held up four fingers. *"Fuwa fela sulu long missus, Mr Wong. Blu olsem. An tu fela red."*

8

New York, 12 February 1928

William Cavendish, the publisher at Waldeck & Marsh, sat at the large polished desk in the company conference room and chain-smoked Camel cigarettes. Some of the firm's more successful titles were displayed in glass cabinets standing around the room. A number of plaques — awards for production design and quality of colour reproduction — hung on walls that featured a muted, gold-flecked wallpaper. Despite the Volstead Act there was a bar in one corner of the room beside a window that looked out onto busy 10th Street.

Cavendish usually enjoyed these opulent surroundings and found them relaxing. But today he had arrived anxiously before all other parties with business at the regular weekly meeting to give himself time to think. And worry. Sales of Tom Birmingham's latest title, the most expensive in terms of the money expended on the author's travels and high-quality production of the book, were catastrophically low. Secondly, the lawsuit threatened by Nigel Burton, a safari guide whom Birmingham had described in one passage as 'less than courageous' and as 'a coward' in another, was becoming a reality. Burton had sold his trekking and big game hunting business and come to New York. He had hired Tom Cloud, the foremost defamation lawyer in the city, and the preliminary documents Cloud had posted were most disconcerting. The amount sought in the defamation action would severely strain the publishing budget, at least in the short term. Even if a settlement of half the amount was reached, that would wipe out the profits of almost all Birmingham's books. Waldeck & Marsh's lawyers were advising quiet compromise. The nature of the case was such that there wasn't even any publicity value to offset a payout.

The most serious problem of all was the matter of informing Hiram Waldeck, the proprietor and founder of the firm. Now an old man, Hiram Waldeck was known to dislike his wife and to love his publishing house more than his daughter Louise. But Waldeck was an intensely private man and Cavendish, recently appointed from outside the firm to his senior post, scarcely knew him. He did not know whether the proprietor viewed his son-in-law's affairs as business or family matters. Cavendish's impulse was to placate Burton with a money settlement and by dumping Birmingham. A tentative discussion with Tom Cloud led him to believe that Burton's chief concern was to destroy Birmingham's reputation. And there were other considerations. Cavendish was a skilled meeting manager; today's editorial and budget planning meeting would test those skills.

They filed into the room — the accountant, the editors responsible for commissioning titles in the fiction, non-fiction and technical fields, the head of marketing, the newly created director of publicity, the production manager — and last of all, Hiram B. Waldeck himself. Over seventy years of age and more than six feet tall, Waldeck held himself tautly erect. Unlike the others present, who had been at work for several hours, he had come straight from home. There were melting snowflakes on his thick hair, still more dark than grey. The eight men and one woman — Valerie Benson was the fiction editor — had the typed agenda in front of them — twelve items of business. Cavendish had taken the precaution of separating the questions of Birmingham's falling sales and current expense account and the legal matter. This way, he could judge the wind of Waldeck's reaction to Birmingham's case in two stages.

"Gentlemen and Miss Benson," Cavendish began smoothly, "we have a lot of business to get through so I suggest we move straight into it and try to finish before lunch. That way we may finish before afternoon coffee break."

Cavendish got the laugh he'd hoped for and proceeded to steer the meeting through the early, innocuous items about perceived gaps in the list, new commissionings and a slightly contentious proposal to change printers. These were disposed of without difficulty. The next item was the sales record of the firm's three leading writers — satisfactory in all but one case.

"Mr Chairman, I suggest we amalgamate items six and nine, those relating to Tom Birmingham." The speaker was Maxwell Peters, head of marketing. Peters had a Harvard law degree and behaved as if he had done Waldeck & Marsh a favour by joining it. He made veiled references to offers from other employers and gave the impression he wished to convey — that he had nothing to lose by being aggressive at meetings.

"That's not fair." Valerie Benson, New-England-accented, a handsome dark-haired woman with twenty years' experience in publishing behind her, was a staunch Birmingham supporter. "The two issues aren't related."

Right away, Cavendish found himself having to take a position. He looked quickly at Waldeck. Nothing. Neutrality. "In the interests of efficiency we'll take them together," he said. "Maxwell?"

"The sales are lousy," Peters said, "and getting worse. The back titles stopped selling years ago, and . . ."

"That's not true!"

"Wait, Valerie," Cavendish said, "you'll get your turn."

"There's something called buyer resistance . . ."

Waldeck spoke for the first time. "What's that?"

"It's stronger than lack of interest, sir. It means, well, a positive aversion to Birmingham's books."

"That's absurd." Valerie Benson was close to rage; she had accepted the first Adams book as a tattered, much travelled manuscript and had commissioned the subsequent ten. She had been entranced with Tom Birmingham's exotic settings from the beginning. She detested American parochialism and would have made it mandatory for everyone in an executive publishing position to travel overseas at least once a year. She was herself, as far as her budget permitted, a great traveller. She had briefly considered Birmingham in a romantic light but, as he had married three other women, she transferred her feelings to his books.

Collins, the accountant spoke. "The figures can't be quarrelled with. My projection is that there is no means of recovering the present outlay on Mr Birmingham from his next book. If he sat at home and wrote another three that didn't cost us anything, maybe."

"Tom Birmingham doesn't sit at home," Valerie Benson exclaimed. "He *lives* his books, and his readers live them too!"

Peters snorted. "What readers? You're out of touch, Miss Benson. Have you ever heard of Ernest Hemingway?"

"Of course."

"His stuff's going to put an end to Birmingham's. It's got all the exotic places and strange customs, and it's beautifully and sensitively written."

"It's barbaric and filthy, full of obscenities. The grammar is atrocious. The locations are simply brothels and barrooms, barely described."

"He's going to win a Nobel Prize some day."

"Nonsense!"

"This shouting match isn't going to get us anywhere," Cavendish said. "The position is that Tom Birmingham has a contract for his present book, and . . . "

"I've looked at the contract," Peters said. "It's not

watertight. We can get out of it. He's at the end of a three-book deal. We can drop him."

Cavendish said, "I don't think we ought to make any decisions about that here."

"Why not?" Waldeck said. "These sales figures are terrible. And the reviews are worse." He held up a bunch of clippings.

"Where did you get those?" Valerie Benson said sharply. Then she remembered whom she was addressing. Her employer, her paymaster, and she was booked to go to Marrakesh in her vacation. "I'm sorry, sir. I . . . "

"I circulated them," Peters said. "I won't beat about the bush. Let's have the lawyer in so we can talk about Birmingham's contract and the libel suit at the same time."

Cavendish caught Waldeck's slight nod. "Very well," he said.

Anthony Lacava was the son of immigrants who had put themselves into early graves working to pay for their son's education. Now a graduate of Columbia and Chicago, he saw his success as the only way of repaying the debt. He was intelligent and industrious, hated to lose, and consequently regarded courts as places to be avoided. He gave it as his opinion that Birmingham was already in breach of his contract, not having submitted a manuscript by the date specified.

"But we've never held Tom to those dates," Valerie Benson said.

Lacava smoothed his dark, close-clipped moustache. "That was your prerogative. It doesn't change the legal position."

"How do we stand on the libel?" Peters said.

Cavendish sat back in his chair, knowing he had lost control of the proceedings.

"Defamation, to be exact," Lacava said. "Very bad. I have to tell you that Mr Burton has a very good case. The author calls him a coward more than once."

"No," Valerie Benson said.

Lacava was firm. "Yes. This is a man whose courage is his stock-in-trade. No one wants to go tiger shooting with a coward. He also won medals fighting in France during the war. Very damaging, professionally and personally. It's the worst kind of defamation."

Cavendish saw his opportunity and seized it. "My understanding is that there's never been a big damages award for this kind of thing in America. Our laws protect publishers and writers."

"That's the point," Lacava said. "Burton will proceed against the British publisher, not Waldeck & Marsh, and they've got watertight protection. Anything Burton got from the British they'd recover from us. And believe me, his attorney, Tom Cloud, would be devastating in a British court. And expensive, very expensive."

"How expensive?" Hiram Waldeck said.

"Hard to say, sir. That's why it's such a dangerous case."

Waldeck took a cigar case from his pocket and extracted a panatella. He unwrapped it and lit it with a gold lighter. He pointed the cigar at the lawyer. "Why the hell did Birmingham call him a coward? Doesn't make sense."

Valerie Benson's wide, generous mouth was set in a hard line. Peters shot a look at her before speaking. "I . . . ah, heard Tom talking a bit about it at a party. He'd had a few highballs at the time. Said the guy insulted him. Something about the war and his honour. I didn't understand it myself."

"That isn't surprising," said Valerie Benson.

Waldeck grunted impatiently. "We must have some kind of a case."

"Not much. The problem lies in the use of the guy's real name."

"How did that happen?" Waldeck said.

It was the moment Valerie Benson had dreaded. She interpreted the question as *Whose fault was that?* and she answered, "Mine. I mean . . . a mistake occurred. Tom used the real name in his typescript on the top copy and changed it on a carbon second draft he submitted later. He assumed we were working from the carbon. There were a lot of technical problems with the manuscript, and . . ."

Waldeck puffed smoke at the ceiling. "Didn't Birming-ham read his proofs?"

The silence around the table was broken by Lacava. "You see where we stand, gentlemen. Excuse me . . . and Miss Benson. We've got multiple responsibility."

"Why is Burton here in New York if he's going to sue in the British courts?" Waldeck asked. His pale complexion had taken on a slight flush, an indication, to those who knew him, of a rare, rising anger.

Lacava expelled a slow breath. They were moving into his territory now. He lifted his briefcase from the floor, opened it and took out a notebook. "Because he wants to do a deal."

Hiram Waldeck pushed back his chair. "Mr Lacava, I'd like to meet with you now in my office. William, perhaps you can join us when you've concluded the other business. Say in an hour?"

Cavendish nodded and only just managed to restrain himself from getting respectfully to his feet as Waldeck left the room.

An hour and ten minutes later, the outline of a deal was on the table. Lacava was instructed to make an offer on behalf of Waldeck & Marsh to Nigel Burton of a five-figure sum on condition that no details of the arrangement be made public. The contract for Tom Birmingham's current book was to be cancelled and no further funds were to be forwarded to him. Valerie Benson's employment was to be terminated.

Waldeck's office had a view down 10th Street and across the East River. Snow was falling and the old man wished he was back in his warm house in Connecticut. His pleasure in direct participation in the running of the firm was diminishing rapidly and he was aware of it. *But I really enjoyed screwing that bastard Birmingham,* he thought. He had disliked the writer from the moment he met him, as he disliked all easy-going, women-attracting men. He turned away from the window and felt a twinge of sciatica in his leg. "Will he go for it?" he asked Lacava.

"Tom Cloud'll put up the ante so Burton can cover his costs."

Waldeck smiled grimly. "And we'll have to pay you. No matter. Get us out of it as cheap as you can."

"Yes, sir."

"Peters talked to you about his big idea, William?"

Cavendish was still feeling shock at the brutality of the deal. He shook his head.

"Wants to make an offer to Hemingway. That young man thinks big. I want you to go into it. Peters thinks this Hemingway has a big future. Do you?"

"I don't know, sir."

"For what it's worth," Lacava said. "I agree with Mr Peters. But there could be an obscenity problem."

"Christ help us," Waldeck said, "this used to be a business for gentlemen."

The words touched a rebellious nerve in Cavendish. "Are you aware, sir, that your daughter is out in the Jeremiah Islands and her husband has just recently cabled us for five hundred dollars?"

"Louise has her own money," Waldeck said.

MURDO ISLAND

9

Alma, British Jeremiah Islands Protectorate, 13 February 1928

Naismith stood on the jetty watching the *Braidwood* enter the Alma lagoon. Behind him was a party of native police, *solodia*, dressed in blue shirts and lavalavas with white webbing belts. The oiled stocks of their Lee Enfield .303 carbines gleamed in the late afternoon sun. Sweat darkened the collars of their shirts. Naismith brushed away flies and fanned himself, but the *solodia* remained rigidly still. Also waiting, in a small flotilla of canoes poised near the jetty, were a dozen or so To'beili — clansmen of the murdered sailors. Naismith had not informed the To'beili of the murders, but somehow they knew, and the canoes had arrived early that morning to transport the bodies back to their ancestral lands. Naismith could see a few old Snider rifles and at least one .303 in the canoes. He was supposed to confiscate these weapons, many relics of the Queensland labour trade and a danger to anyone who fired them. He confiscated selectively, when he thought there would be no resistance, or he could offer an inducement. This was not such a time.

Almost nothing about the situation pleased Naismith.

Recapturing Eglito, placating the outraged To'beili, restraining hotheads among his police force, would all take time and energy that could be better spent. And as for foisting on him an anthropologist and a married American scribbler . . . Naismith felt an anger that almost caused him to swear. Almost; his army experience in South Africa had cured him of swearing, drinking and smoking tobacco. He had seen men wasting their breath on all three, sometimes the last of their breath, and his own iron self-control had been forged at that time. He attributed his survival of the Eland's River siege, and the scourges of fever and pestilence which had swept through the ranks, to his capacity for unemotional, clear-sighted judgment. Tin hat at all times, personal hygiene likewise, boiled water. And his subsequent success in government service, he believed, was a product of the same qualities.

The only comfort was the appointment of the cadet, Keith Larke. Naismith expected the worst — a puppy-dog type most likely, product of the English public school system, a grownup head prefect. But at least he could turn him loose on the paperwork and be freed to patrol and bring his personal influence to bear where it counted.

His thoughts turned to Eglito as the *Braidwood* drew closer; it stopped and began to reverse towards the dock. Its wake set the To'beili canoes bobbing and rocking. The waves splashed against the stones of the jetty which had been constructed by the forced labour of tax avoiders from the artificial islands — the people who really knew how to build in the water.

The vessel edged towards the pylons. *Eglito,* Naismith thought. *Always troublesome. A traditionalist, a would-be shaman and war chief, except that these functions were fast falling into disuse. Even his own people are afraid of him. An outlaw, almost.* Among any people but the To'beili, Eglito would have been considered more trouble than he was worth. But most of the To'beili adhered to the old ways, and among them there were prophecies about great leaders, great killers, great magic-makers. Only that morning Baekani had told him that Eglito had ambitions to fulfil these prophecies.

"I should have known this when I sentenced him," Naismith said. "I should have hanged him or exiled him to another district."

"Sir, the evidence was not strong enough. The people were afraid."

"They'll be more afraid now."

"Some will rejoice, sir."

"Not for long," Naismith said grimly. "We will take Eglito and this time we will hang him."

"Yes, sir."

It was Naismith's opinion that that was what he should be doing now, instead of preparing to be polite to tourists. The *Braidwood* bumped against the jetty and sent a shudder through it. Ten years before, the fractious Maka Maka people who occupied coastal and mountain land to the south of Alma had threatened to destroy the structure. But they were pacified now, and the jetty had withstood storms and stress. The sailors tied the vessel up, and a hinged section of the rail was swung open to allow the four Europeans to step onto the wharf. As they walked towards where Naismith was waiting, a shout went up from the To'beili sitting in their canoes.

The police platoon stiffened, and the sergeant barked an order.

"Arms, ready!"

Three canvas-wrapped bundles were carried from the deck of the *Braidwood*. Six strapping, oiled and decorated To'beili sprang from their canoes up the short ladder onto the wharf, received the bodies and lowered them into the canoes. Naismith watched in disgust as the oldest and stockiest of the new arrivals took a series of photographs of the To'beili laying the bodies in the canoes, lifting their paddles and digging hard into the water in short, chopping strokes full of anger and pride. *Not so much as a by-your-leave,* he thought. *That must be the American. Be lucky if he gets out of here without a spear in his back.* The thought did not entirely displease Naismith.

Larke lengthened his stride and moved ahead of the others. Dressed in his whites, he almost snapped to a salute when he reached the DO.

"Keith Larke, sir."

"Good morning, Mr Larke." Naismith did not offer to shake hands. "Would you be so kind as to introduce . . ." Naismith stopped in mid-sentence as he got a clear view of Louise Birmingham. The thoughts and memories shot through his brain like an electric current. *The hair, eyes, shape of face. My God, it could be Amelia.*

"Mr and Mrs Birmingham," Larke said, "this is Mr Naismith, the district officer. Mr Webb, Mr Naismith."

Recovering quickly, Naismith removed his sun helmet, shook hands and murmured his greetings. "There is a small government guesthouse. Only a couple of rooms, I'm afraid, which you'll have to share. Quarters have been assigned for you, of course, Mr Larke."

"Can we get in out of the sun?" Birmingham growled. "I'm getting a headache."

Naismith snapped orders that Baekani, standing behind him, relayed to a team of islanders who walked along the wharf to where the Europeans' baggage was being piled. "I'd like to see you in my office in an hour, Mr Larke," Naismith said, "and perhaps Mr and Mrs Birmingham and Mr Webb could join me for dinner. Say at eight."

"That's a long time to wait for something to eat," Birmingham said.

Naismith turned away, trying not to let his anger show. "There's a cook at the guesthouse," he said.

Webb spoke in fairly rapid pidgin to the islander carrying his box, and the man replied. Naismith took his first good look at the anthropologist. *A hard case,* he decided. *Capable and nobody's fool.* He made Larke appear more youthful and uncertain than perhaps he was. On the surface, Webb would be a better candidate for the job. But then Naismith remembered the hard, calloused hand and the strength of the man's grip, and thought perhaps not; he didn't need any challenges to his authority just then. He could not bring himself to look at the woman but nodded curtly and marched off up the hill, followed by the detachment of police.

"Nice guy," Birmingham said. "Let's go, honey. My head is killing me."

Louise wanted to say that the headache was self-induced, but was reluctant to make her first words on the island critical ones. "I suppose he's got a tough job," she said. "Will you take a look at those hills, Tom! They'll give you something to write about."

A cloud had come across the sun, darkening the landscape and making the high hills around the small, grey beach looming and full of threat. The water darkened and more heavy clouds boiled up on the horizon beyond the lagoon opening.

"Cheers," Larke said. He set off after Baekani and a man carrying his box.

Webb shouldered his canvas holdall. "We'd better get to the guesthouse before the rain comes. I'm sorry to cramp you, but I don't expect to be staying here long."

Birmingham followed the three porters up a track towards a small building set up on two-metre stilts above the ground. Louise fell into step beside Webb. "I hope we won't be here long either, Mr Webb," she said. "Is it nicer where you're going?"

"I doubt it," Birmingham said. "Murdo isn't supposed to be nice."

"This compound's OK, though," Louise said. "I like the flowers." She slipped on the muddy track, and Webb instinctively gripped her arm to steady her. Birmingham was three paces ahead.

Sandwiches supplied at the Alma guesthouse — curried egg, tomato, corned beef with pickles — were surprisingly good. Tom Birmingham had drunk a bottle of beer with the food and taken a few nips of whisky on the sly, so he was feeling cheerful as he sat on the verandah with his wife and Webb.

"That's a fine gun," Webb said.

Birmingham was cleaning a disassembled double-barrelled Winchester shotgun, carefully applying oil to all the moving parts. "Yeah. It's a beauty. Gotta look after a gun in this climate. Neglect it for a day or so and you've got rust like you wouldn't believe. Well, Dick, how long you figure you're going to be here?"

"Hard to say. A year, perhaps longer."

Louise gasped. "A year!"

Birmingham squinted through the barrels. "Man's got a job to do, hon. You'll live in a village, sleep on a mat, eat the grub, that sort of thing?"

Webb smiled. "More or less."

Birmingham wiped away a drop of perspiration that had fallen from his face onto the gun. "And sleep with the women?"

Louise looked at Webb, whose smile faded somewhat but who displayed no other reaction. "That would be very unwise, I'm led to believe. The To'beili speared a missionary recently for some such offence."

"Heard about that," Birmingham said. "So you reckon that as long as you mind your manners, you'll be OK?"

"I expect so. I'm more worried about getting co-operation from this chap Naismith than anything else at the moment. I was going to come over in a few days' time with a friend of his to smooth the way. But the resident commissioner insisted I come today. Can't quite see why."

"Yes, I wondered about that," Louise said. "I guess I thought we should've had a few days to acclimatise and so on. But no, it was almost as if we came today or not at all."

Birmingham buffed the stock of the shotgun with a chamois cloth. "British are waking up at last. Getting off their butts and pushing things along."

"I wonder," Webb said. "I have a feeling it's to do with the killings on Hemisphere. I'm afraid we might have come at a bad time for Naismith."

"Maybe that's the idea," Louise said.

Webb and Louise were sitting a little apart on a cane settee; Birmingham, with his gun-cleaning equipment spread out around him, occupied a chair. Webb was suddenly aware of the woman's gaze directed at his face, and of her tension. "Why d'you say that?"

Louise shrugged and deliberately looked away into the dark, cloudy distance. "When my father wanted to get rid of someone, a salesman or an editor, he loaded him up with work and waited for him to break. He said it never failed."

Birmingham stopped polishing. "He's a tough guy, old Hiram. I just hope . . . "

"It's an interesting theory," Webb said. "But there's one thing against it."

Louise took up the challenge. "And what's that?"

"Price-Kane has assigned Keith Larke to work with Naismith. That should lighten his load, not increase it."

Louise was enjoying herself; this was the sort of conversation she was accustomed to have with some of her New York acquaintances, never with Tom.

"That's if Mr Larke's any good, surely. If not, then he might just make more work for the DO."

Webb said, "Good point. I think we have to give your theory serious consideration. Bring it up at the next briefing."

Louise laughed. "You sound like someone from a war movie."

Birmingham resumed cleaning but stopped whistling cheerfully through his teeth. "In the war, were you, Dick?"

"Yes," Webb said, "worse luck. Here comes the rain."

The rain thundering on the iron roof made it difficult for Keith Larke to hear Naismith as the DO outlined the duties of a cadet and the things expected of him. "I suppose you think this is romantic, this business?"

"Romantic, sir?"

Naismith waved his arm at the window, which was held open by a hinged prop. Water sheeted down from the gutterless roof and splashed into a channel around the house. Through the curtain of water the compound was mistily visible, a swirl of blue-grey shapes as the wind drove the rain about in gusts. "It's not exactly a South Pacific paradise, is it?"

"No, sir."

Naismith leaned forward in his chair and put his elbows on the desk. "It *can* be pleasant enough at times. The climate's better on the lee side, anyway. This is called the weather coast, as you might know."

Larke didn't know. He was rather bored and wanted a cigarette, but there was no sign in Naismith's meticulously clean and ordered office that anything so casual as cigarette smoking had ever happened there. He nodded, stifling a yawn.

"My rule of thumb is to regard the weather coast as the norm. Metaphorically, do you follow me?"

"Not exactly, sir."

Naismith sighed. "Prepare for the worst at all times. Now, I'm glad to have you here, and I hope we can work together well. Your main task will be to take the burden of the clerical work off my shoulders so that I can get on with patrolling, acting as magistrate and generally trying to get this place under control."

The words struck Larke like stones. "I'd rather hoped to get out and about myself, sir."

"You will, you will, after a time. There's a lot to learn first."

"I have done the admin college course, sir."

Naismith's laugh was a short bark. "Can you talk pidgin? Do you know enough not to let a native woman stand or sit with her head higher than a man? Can you judge the value of a piece of shell money? Can you tell a counterfeit shilling from a real one? Can you hit a man hard enough to knock him down?"

Larke said nothing.

"This is an odd place, Larke. You can be sitting in court and have two murderers brought in to face you. Say they've put their Sniders up against some poor devil's kidneys and pulled the triggers. And do you know what? These two fully grown men can stand there holding hands like a couple of lovers or schoolgirls. What do you think of that, eh?"

There and then, Larke decided that the DO was mad. He understood now the subtlety of the resident commissioner's brief. He was to collect evidence on Naismith's instability while excelling at his work in every other respect. And there could be only one appropriate reward. "Chaps promoted in the field often make the most inspiring leaders," his brother Jeffrey had said.

Naismith was unimpressed by Larke as he looked at him, awaiting a response. *A dreamer,* he thought, *and not a very bright one. Still, he'll be useful behind a desk.* "Larke?"

Larke was jerked back to the hot, damp reality. "Sir?"

"Think you'll be able to cope?"

"Yes, sir. Without a doubt. If I may say so, sir, your boy seems a little neglectful." Naismith's silence was ominous but Larke blundered on. "One of the other boys dropped my bag in the mud, and your chap didn't reprimand him. Had to do it myself."

"You'll find, Mr Larke, that Baekani is more than just 'my boy' as you put it."

"Sir?"

"He's my friend."

Mad, Larke was convinced. *Quite mad.*

The servant at the guesthouse pressed trousers and jackets for Birmingham and Webb and carefully ironed into its pleats a favourite linen dress of Louise's. Larke, likewise, presented himself at Naismith's bungalow in immaculate whites. The guests were embarrassed when Naismith greeted them in open-necked shirt and slacks. Far from being discomforted himself, Naismith was amused.

"You're all far too formal for me," he boomed. "I believe in dressing for the climate. Permission to take off your tie, Mr Larke."

"I'm quite comfortable, sir," Larke said.

Webb and Birmingham removed their ties.

"And the jackets, for goodness sake," Naismith said. "I'm sure Mrs Birmingham won't object."

"Not in the least. Being able to wear lighter clothes is one of the few advantages women enjoy over men."

"Quite possibly." Naismith had no intention of beginning a debate over women's rights, but he was still astonished by the resemblance between Louise and Amelia, and he found it difficult to behave naturally. "Well, come along. We'll sit out here until they have the food ready. Pretty ordinary fare, I'm afraid."

The party sat on the verandah; there was a long and awkward silence which Birmingham eventually broke by taking his pipe from his pocket. "I'll smoke a pipe, if no one objects." His irony was directed at Louise, who hadn't smoked for twenty-four hours and had announced her attention of giving up the habit.

Naismith frowned but waved his hand. Larke nervously extracted his Players and offered the tin to Webb and Louise, both of whom refused. Birmingham packed his pipe, lit it and puffed luxuriously. *Party's a bit slow to get going,* he thought. *But I guess a few drinks'll loosen it up.* "I guess you know why I'm here, Mr Naismith?"

"Yes, to write a book. I have to admit I don't know what you'll write about. Nothing much happens here."

"I'll make it up, then," Birmingham said cheerfully. He looked through the open door into the house. *Where's the boy with the drinks?*

Naismith looked alarmed; he stroked his big chin and wondered what this fine-looking woman saw in such an oaf. *But then, what did Amelia see in me?*

"I'd like to hear your views on the events at Wesley the other day, Mr Naismith," Webb said. "I noticed that the To'beili seemed pretty excited down at the wharf today. Some people seem to think there could be trouble."

"What people?" Naismith snapped.

"There was some talk in Patugi, and I had a word with a few sailors on the boat coming over."

"To'beili?"

"No, Kweili."

"Ah, well, there's always talk in Patugi, and very little else, in my experience. And you can't believe a word of what a Kweili'll say about the To'beili."

"Still," Webb persisted. "Three men dead. The shell money bounties're sure to be pretty big."

"You seem to know a great deal about things."

"I hope to learn more."

"Yes, well, there's lots of interesting things to study around the Alma lagoon. The canoe building . . ."

"I want to study the To'beili."

"That'll be impossible, I'm afraid, given the state of things."

Webb felt a vein throb in his forehead. His palms were suddenly sticky. At the LSE he had been told that colonial administrators could be difficult but no practical suggestions had been forthcoming. "I took you to mean, Mr Naismith, when you said that the Kweili exaggerate the belligerence of the To'beili, that there wouldn't be any . . . unusual degree of unrest on Murdo."

Naismith was saved from a reply by the dinner gong.

Soup was followed by fried fish with rice; dessert was bananas with desiccated coconut and custard. Naismith sat at the head of the table, with Louise on his right and Birmingham on his left. Webb sat next to Louise, with Larke at the other end of the table. Immediately on taking his place, Tom Birmingham seized one of the several glass pitchers on the table filled with an amber fluid, and poured.

"That's a sort of punch I've invented," Naismith said. "Lime juice is the secret. Very refreshing. I don't serve alcohol here, I'm afraid."

It had been many years since Birmingham had sat down to a substantial meal without a palate-preparing drink, and he almost choked on the semi-sweet punch. He tackled his soup listlessly, finding difficulty in concentrating on what was being said around him.

Not that much *was* being said. Webb was anxious to press his claim for permission to work in the To'beili district, but he sensed that the dinner table did not provide the time or place. Naismith attacked his food with gusto and showed little inclination to talk. Keith Larke was tired, but anxious to get back to his quarters to prepare his first report

on his superior. Several times, he noticed Naismith looking
at Louise Birmingham in a way that seemed odd to him.
He fancied that Naismith, as well as avowing friendship
for a native and being a rabid teetotaller, was a sex maniac.
Louise, acutely aware of Webb sitting quietly beside her,
found the food vile, but she didn't care. She had faced
curdled soup and rancid oyster patties in her time and had
been brought up to soldier on socially. She indicated a
glass-fronted cabinet in a corner, filled with mounted silver
cups and engraved plates. "You're a sportsman, Mr
Naismith."

Naismith paused and smiled as amiably as a mouthful
of fish would permit. Birmingham's interest was momentarily awakened. "Shoot?" he said.

Naismith shook his head. A bone had lodged under his
dental plate and was irking him. "No, I haven't done any
shooting since I was in the army. Those are for cricket and
golf, mostly."

"Saw some cricket in India," Birmingham said. "Couldn't
see anything in it. Now baseball, there's a game."

To annoy her husband Louise said, "You served in the
Great War, Mr Naismith?"

Naismith was about to excuse himself; he had to get rid
of the bone. "Boer War."

"How interesting."

Naismith stood. "Not really. A waste of time. Excuse
me for just a minute."

Larke made a mental note of Naismith's apparent lack
of enthusiasm for the Empire, while Webb wondered at
Naismith's sudden departure. He assumed it was a call of
nature, and smiled. He looked up to see Louise Birmingham returning the smile. Her blonde hair shone under the
light from the lanterns; a simple gold chain accentuated
the slimness of her neck and the shapeliness of her
shoulders. Webb felt again an urgent desire to touch her
breasts and kiss her wide, smiling mouth.

"Plan on doing any shooting, Keith?" Birmingham said.
He pulled out the flask he carried in his jacket pocket and
added a hefty slug of whisky to his punch. He grinned

conspiratorially, leaned forward and deftly spiked the guests' drinks. He suspended the flask over Naismith's glass.

Tom at his best, Louise thought. She laughed but shook her head. "Don't, Tom."

Birmingham tilted the flask but stopped as a volley of shots shattered the quiet of the evening. There was a scream and more shooting. A dull roar built into a deep, resounding explosion and night was turned into day by a billowing ball of fire.

10

Webb was the first to reach the verandah. He saw flashes from the rifles and dark, rushing shapes at the edge of the compound. One building was burning fiercely; sparks flew into the air and drifted out across the beach and water.

"What's happening?" Louise was beside him, staring at the fire, which was now sending clouds of smoke into the air and across the parade ground and lawn. Birmingham appeared at the doorway carrying a lantern, and Webb screamed at him, "Douse the light, you fool!"

As he did so, several shots rang out and bullets thumped into the wall above their heads. Webb pulled Louise down behind the flimsy barrier of the latticed balcony. He held her immobile with one arm as he swivelled to look back. Birmingham stumbled and fell, letting the lantern fall forward and down the steps, A bush burst into flame and Webb swore. He released Louise, rolled and went down the steps in a crouch. When he reached the bottom he yelled at Larke to throw down his jacket. The white garment fluttered through the air; Webb soaked it in the channel that caught the runoff water from the roof and beat at the flames. Another bush caught and Webb shouted for a bucket. He flailed at the fire, which licked at the painted lattice, caught and flared. Then two islanders were beside him, baling water from the channel and throwing it at the fire. Webb used the sodden jacket to beat out small outbreaks in the dry grass under the verandah.

Suddenly the shouting and shooting stopped. The night was quiet, apart from the crackling of the fire that entirely consumed the building on the edge of the compound. Webb and the islanders extinguished the last sparks near the house and, breathing heavily, Webb straightened up to look around. He saw policemen grouped hesitantly on the edge of the parade area, then Naismith appeared with Baekani beside him.

"The wharf!" Naismith shouted.

Half the police party ran towards the water, while Baekani led the remainder off to the nearest bush track. Webb mounted the steps for a clearer view and saw a fleet of canoes, paddlers bent low, working in a rapid, steady rhythm, sending the craft racing towards the reef. The police ran out to the end of the jetty and opened fire, but the canoes did not waver and were soon in the shadow of the hills. The *solodia* continued to fire raggedly, long after they ceased to have visible targets.

"Too late," Webb said. "Terrible guard work."

"I agree with you." Naismith appeared at the foot of the steps. "I want to thank you, Mr Webb, for saving my house."

"Are you all right?" Louise came down the steps and took the sopping, torn jacket from Webb's hand.

"Yes," Webb said. "Anyone hurt up there?"

"Tom fell and twisted his ankle. I'm fine. Mr Larke . . ."

"Where *is* Mr Larke?" Naismith said.

Louise held up the jacket and managed a shaky laugh. "Perhaps he's gone to get a new coat."

Naismith scowled at her. "This is no laughing matter, Mrs Birmingham. Dangerous prisoners have been released from the gaol. Two of my police have been killed."

"Oh, no," Louise said, "I'm sorry."

Naismith's shirt was bloodied; his neatly parted and combed hair was awry. He was pale and shaking as he climbed past Webb and went into the house. Louise and Webb followed him. They found Birmingham sitting on a cane chair with his shoe off. He was draining the last of his flask as Naismith stalked past him.

"Guess the party's over," Birmingham said. "Say, this is great stuff for my book."

"Tom, you're a fool," Louise said.

Webb went through to the dining room where Naismith was pouring himself a glass of water. "Will it be safe for Mrs Birmingham to go back to the guesthouse, Naismith?"

If the DO objected to the abrupt use of his surname he showed no sign of it. "Yes, quite safe. There'll be pickets out and so forth. But you were right, things were very slack."

"I didn't intend a criticism. It was just a reflex."

Naismith nodded. "They'll pay for this."

"Eglito, or the To'beili generally?"

"We'll see," Naismith muttered. "Where is that cadet?"

"Here, sir." Larke appeared in the doorway; jacketless and with his tie twisted to one side, he looked like a schoolboy. "I've been assessing the damage."

"Have you?"

"Yes, it appears to be minor, apart from . . ."

A loud, reverberating explosion blotted out all other sound. Louise Birmingham rushed into the room. "The ship," she gasped, "they've blown up the ship!"

"Jesus bloody Christ!" It was the first time Will Naismith had sworn in twenty-five years.

Baekani returned an hour later and reported to Naismith. The DO was alarmed to see tears streaming down the man's face.

"Baekani. What is your trouble? Are you injured?"

"Sir, I am not injured. We did not catch them, the To'beili."

"There's no shame in that. I should've sent you to the

water with your rifle. If I had done this, some would be dead now."

"My brother is dead, sir. He was on guard, and they killed him. I am sorry, sir."

Naismith moved forward and laid his hand on Baekani's shoulder. "It is I who am sorry, Baekani. Truly sorry."

"Thank you, sir. My brother did not suffer. My brother was asleep."

Naismith understood then. Baekani's reaction was a mixture of grief, shame at his brother's dereliction and a rage to exact immediate revenge. That revenge would be terrible. The DO made gruff attempts to comfort his servant, but Baekani's mind was set one only one thing.

"Sir, you will hang Eglito?"

"I will."

"And I will burn his gardens and shit in the shrines of his ancestors. His name will stink like fish guts in the sun. His name will not be spoken."

Naismith nodded. It was a terrible curse, more terrible than it sounded. "Eglito's name will not be spoken, Baekani." Naismith's command of the language enabled him to give the words weight and finality. He also spoke more loudly than was necessary. "But your vengeance must not extend to all To'beili, nor to all members of the nameless one's clan."

Baekani stood rigidly; the dried tears streaked his dark face, and his mouth was red from the betel he had chewed, as all the Jeremians did when under stress or facing danger. "His brother," he said.

A compromise was being offered. The death of Eglito alone would not recompense Baekani, but Naismith could not sanction a wholesale clan feud. "His brother's name will not be spoken," he said. "Go and do the things for your brother, Baekani. You have no work to do in this house for two days."

"Thank you, sir."

Baekani left and Naismith sat in his favourite chair near the window where there seemed to be a breeze, even on the hottest nights. He had raised his voice when stating terms to Baekani because he knew other servants in the house would be listening. They would convey to others around Alma and beyond that Baekani's vengeance would be limited. This would come as a great relief to To'beili servants, labourers, sailors, prisoners and police.

A servant appeared in the doorway and Naismith ordered tea. His throat was sore from shouting orders and he cleared it several times. He touched the scar on his neck and wondered whether a bullet or his ailments would do for him in the end. He cranked up the gramophone and put on a record, but failed to find solace in the music and shut it off.

He wanted to calm himself before deciding on his next move. Once he had decided, the action would have to be swift and effective. The assault on the compound and the release of To'beili prisoners constituted the most serious challenge to his authority he had yet faced; the greatest challenge to imperial power in the Jeremiahs since huge head-hunting expeditions had been suppressed forty years before. One part of Naismith was exultant — here was a chance to distinguish himself and, by a firm, well supported action, to bring Murdo under control. Another part of him doubted this was possible. He was aware of his rheumatism, occasional shortness of breath and vulnerability to bouts of malaria. A punitive expedition against the offender (Naismith fell easily into the Murdoan practice of avoiding the name of a seriously cursed individual), would be incredibly physically demanding. Perhaps he needed to take a subtler, more guileful tack? Experience had shown him that the Murdoans respected guile almost as much as courage and physical strength.

Naismith allowed his mind to wander. The Birmingham woman had held up pretty well, he considered. She still reminded him of Amelia, forceful and strong, but needing another's strength. Amelia had needed him for his strength, or so he thought. But in the end she had needed more: qualities he did not have, did not even understand, and she had found those things elsewhere. In his lowest, most self-pitying moments he entertained the thought that

Amelia might not have found what she wanted and that he might have her yet. But then he despised himself for wishing years of unhappiness on her and he brushed the thoughts aside. Amelia had said he was stubborn. He knew it, and knew what it had cost him and how it had served him.

Naismith pushed memories away and thought of the present. About Larke he couldn't be sure. He had kept on the move at least, not stood about goggling. But had he moved towards the trouble or away from it? About Birmingham there could be no doubt: a fool and a drunk. No latitude could be given to him; he would be kept close to Alma and shown canoes and butterflies until boredom drove him away.

But Mr Richard Webb, Naismith thought, *is a different kettle of fish altogether. And I am now considerably in his debt.* Naismith was not a devious man, but he was an experienced one. Life had taught him that it was wise to have more than one solution to a problem. Selecting the right shot was a major part of golf and cricket, and life was the same — except that in life you usually had more time to make your choice. *There must be some use I can make of Mr Webb.*

The tea arrived. Naismith poured and sipped it gratefully. He had changed out of the clothes stained with the blood from the wounded and dead policemen, but he still felt unclean. His anger rose then. *How dared they do this? He'd brought justice to this heathen plot, hadn't he?* Then he had an image of Ashley Price-Kane, dressed up as a gentleman yachter, going aboard the *Braidwood* when she was first put into service. Naismith almost smiled at the thought of the RC's discomfiture. But the matter had its serious side. The vessel was Price-Kane's pride and joy and his response to the crisis might very well be determined by the degree of damage to the ship. That was something for tomorrow, as well as many other things. Too many.

Keith Larke knew he was being foolish when he felt angry at the state of his jacket. After all, his tropical clothing allowance would certainly pay for a replacement. One of

Naismith's servants had brought the ruined garment to him, and Larke was sure he detected the hint of a smile in the man's manner.

"Throw it away," Larke had snarled, "or keep it for yourself."

He knew that Webb had acted swiftly and appropriately. He should have jumped down to help him, baled water, stripped off his shirt and beat out the flames. The missed opportunity for a display of valour nagged at him almost as much as the uncomfortable knowledge of what he *had* done, which was to put as much distance between himself and the shooting as possible. He comforted himself with the thought that no one knew, and that he hadn't actually run away. In fact he had gone outside at the back of the house and witnessed some of the action, at a distance. Everything had happened so quickly — one minute the centre of attention was the stockade, the next the wharf. If only he could have done something about that, alerted Naismith to the vulnerability of the ship . . . At least no blame could be attached to him. The blame was Naismith's, surely, and Naismith was not a gentleman.

Writing on a leaf torn from a notebook, Larke began his secret report to the resident commissioner.

Alma station,
13 February 1928, 1.05 a.m.
Dear Sir

The outrage which occurred at this station on the night of 12/2/28 must in part be attributed to the poor standard of the police guard. I have heard that one of the guards who was killed by the attackers was asleep at his post. This was the brother of Bikani, Mr Naismith's house servant. This slackness does not surprise me if the dead brother was in any way like Bikani. Bikani is arrogant and insubordinate, and I must say that he is encouraged in this attitude by the DO, who referred to him, in my presence, as 'my friend'.

No guard was mounted over the *Braidwood*, a fact which I intended to bring to Mr Naismith's attention as soon as the social occasion he had arranged was concluded. The attack on the station and the ship came before I could make this observation.

I have no reason to think that the DO did not act properly during the course of the emergency. I was occupied with fighting the fire at the front of his house and directing police activity and saw very little of him. Mrs and Mrs Birmingham and Mr Webb, the DO's guests, were not injured in the incident.

On a personal level, Mr Naismith exhibits a good many peculiarities. He is given to profanity and yet is a rabid teetotaller and anti-smoker. Most alarming is his apparent lack of regard for the traditions of the Empire. He referred to the Boer War as 'a bloody waste of time' and appears anxious to avoid the Great War as a topic of conversation. There are two possible explanations for this. The first is that he is in some way pro-German. I will endeavour to investigate this more thoroughly, perhaps by observing his behaviour towards some of the German commercials present in the group. It is also possible that Mr Naismith harbours pro-American sympathies. His behaviour towards the Birminghams is strange. He looks at Mrs Birmingham in a most peculiar way and appears to approve of her, although I fancy her opinions are somewhat radical. Mr Birmingham, altogether a more sympathetic person who speaks well of the British administration in India and is knowledgeable about sport, Mr Naismith appears to regard with contempt.

I noticed yesterday that the flag was not flying in the station compound. This may have something to do with the DO's nationality. Perhaps Mr Naismith is a republican.

Further reports will follow in due course.

I remain, sir, your most humble servant.

Larke signed the page with a flourish but he had not the slightest idea how to get the message to Price-Kane.

"Nightcap, Dick?" Birmingham suggested when the two men and Louise returned to the guesthouse. "You look as if you could use a pick-me-up."

"Thanks. I'm a bit done in, to tell the truth." Webb rubbed at the arm he had strained the day before. "A quick drink'd do me some good."

"Of course it will. Had a pow-wow with the barman

here so I can offer you Johnnie Walker — red or black label?"

"Either, thanks. Will you join us, Mrs Birmingham?"

"Please call me Louise. Are you usually called Dick?"

Webb shook his head and sat on one of the verandah chairs. "No, but if Tom wants to call me Dick it's fine with me. All we'd need then would be a Harry."

Louise laughed. "More water for me, Tom."

Birmingham had a long pull on the whisky bottle as he was mixing the drinks, downed his own stiff one in a gulp and prepared a slightly weaker version before bringing the glasses out to the verandah.

"Cheers," Louise said. "It's been quite a night."

Birmingham packed his pipe. "You said it. Wonder how it's gonna affect our work on the island? Will they bring in the troops, maybe?"

"I shouldn't think so," Webb said. "It'll be a police action at most, but it could get quite nasty. There've been some torrid conflicts in New Guinea, I'm told. Though it's quieter there now."

"Maybe that's where we should've gone," Birmingham said. "More civilised."

Louise looked at her husband in alarm. It was the first time she had heard him speak in favour of 'more civilised' parts, and contradicted his earlier endorsement of the Jeremiahs. Savagery was meant to be his stock-in-trade. She wondered if Tom was losing his grip. She'd noticed the unsteadiness of his hand and knew it wasn't due to simply consuming most of a flask in Naismith's bungalow. *A secret drinker,* she thought. *How pathetic.*

"Quiet would suit me better," Webb said. "I wanted to concentrate on kinship and land tenure, now I might have to switch to bounty hunting and conflict."

"Bounty hunting?" Birmingham said. "Like in the old West?"

Webb nodded. "Something like it. A man acquires a reputation as the most fearsome killer around by killing people other people want killed. They have shell money prices on their heads, bounties."

"The fastest gun?" Birmingham murmured. His voice was slowing and thickening as he lowered his drink.

"Why do they have prices on their heads?" Louise asked.

"For various reasons, mostly to do with clan feuding. The grievances can go back generations and surface anytime."

Louise sipped her drink. "It sounds as if life around here's pretty risky."

"Yes," Webb said, "it's one of the arguments for colonialism, generally — pacification."

"Colonialism's finished," Birmingham muttered.

Webb said, "I've got a feeling you're going to see it in full flood around here in a while. Perhaps its last surge, but still . . ."

He was interrupted by the crunch of heavy boots on the gravel path leading to the guesthouse. Webb and Louise became alert. "What's that?" Louise said.

Webb put his hand on her arm. "Don't worry, it's the police guard. If the feet you hear are wearing boots, you're probably safe."

Louise laughed softly; she was enjoying the feel of Webb's hard hand. "I'd feel safer in New York. Where are you from, Richard?"

"London. Why are you whispering?"

"Oh, the guard," Louise said. "He's standing just over there."

The Murdoan was immobile, massive in tunic jacket and long lavalava, a few feet from the balcony.

"You don't need to do that, Louise. He probably doesn't understand English quickly spoken, especially not with an American accent. And if he did, he probably wouldn't be interested."

"What do you mean?"

Webb moved his hand away. "Don't be offended. I don't mean what you say isn't interesting. It is to us, fascinating. But to him other things are much more important. It's a hard idea to grasp — that the locals don't especially care about us one way or the other, but I've read that it's true."

"They're *goin'* to care, and how," Birmingham said. " 'Nother drink?"

Webb shook his head.

"You've had enough, Tom," Louise said.

Birmingham stood unsteadily. "You're right, hon, an' when a man's had enough to drink, it's time to go to bed. G'night."

"Night," Webb said.

When Birmingham had gone inside the house, Louise said, "Tell me about London."

11

The resident commissioner, arriving at Alma aboard the *Equator*, was relieved to see the *Braidwood* tied up at the dock. His vessel, as he thought of it, had been severely damaged at the stern, but the main impact of the blast seemed to have been taken by the wharf itself. A section had collapsed, spilling stone blocks, coral and timber into the water. He walked gingerly along the wharf to the beach.

"The wharf's sound, sir," Naismith said.

The DO had the unhappy knack of irritating Price-Kane. He did so now by drawing attention to the RC's tentative approach.

"Good," Price-Kane said, "and the vessel?"

"She'll need a refit, but she'll see service again. The dynamite cartridge was very badly placed — wharf took most of the blast. A couple of barrels of tar and a fuel drum went up."

Price-Kane nodded. Why did it always seem so much hotter on Murdo than elsewhere in the group? "You'd better show me the rest of the damage."

An hour later, after a tour of the gaol, where a wall had been blown out and extensive fire damage had occurred, and the infirmary where two policemen were recovering from wounds, Price-Kane sat in Naismith's office. It was late in the afternoon and very hot; the fan blades hardly seemed to disturb the air, let alone create a cooling draught. The RC could have done with a beer but Naismith, true to form, had offered tea. And the tea was infernally strong stuff that needed so much milk to make it drinkable that it became tepid. Price-Kane pushed the cup away and lit a cigar.

"An ashtray, if you please, Naismith."

Naismith didn't have one in the office. He sent a native clerk to fetch one. "What do the clerks do when they want a smoke?" Price-Kane asked.

Naismith pointed to the door. "Outside."

A battered metal object arrived and Price-Kane tapped off an inch of ash. "Well, this is a bloody shambles. You never suspected that something like this could happen? Your reports certainly haven't suggested it."

"I've constantly said that I need more support. If I'd been able to get out and patrol more, I might have picked up useful intelligence."

It seemed like a weak reply to the RC, and he determined to let Naismith go on, perhaps to reveal that the situation was beyond his control. He drew on his cigar and said nothing.

"These things don't just happen overnight," Naismith said. "Eglito isn't simply a crazy murderer, or a rebel."

Price-Kane raised one eyebrow.

"His motives are probably political."

Price-Kane was alarmed. "Political?"

"In the local sense. Eglito probably wants to set up as a *lemo*, a war leader. He would have sacrificed pigs and read other signs before last night's attack. He escaped without one of his party being killed. That will bring him enormous prestige. It shows the power of his magic."

Price-Kane, relieved that the word 'political' hadn't carried any of the associations he gave it, yawned. "Absurd."

"To some," Naismith said.

"Don't be impertinent, Naismith. This is a serious situation that has nothing to do with sacrificing pigs, as I see it. Four members of the staff of the Protectorate have been killed, and government property has been damaged. What d'you propose to do about it?"

Naismith's tea, since he drank it black, was still hot. He finished his cup and resisted the impulse to wave away Price-Kane's cigar smoke. "Two things," he said quietly. "First, I'm going to despatch a police patrol into the To'beili district."

"Good. To arrest this murdering swine."

Naismith shook his head. "They won't manage that. The place Eglito comes from is virtually impenetrable. It would certainly be impossible to surprise him there. Eglito will stay on the move."

"What purpose will be served, then?"

"The patrol will burn his gardens and just might manage to get a crack at one of his supporters. As soon as he suffers some injury, however small, Eglito's enormous prestige will drop."

"I don't follow."

"It's like a motor car," Naismith explained patiently. "You buy one, and at that moment it's worth two hundred pounds. The second you drive it out onto the street its value drops to say, a hundred and fifty."

Price-Kane grunted. "It sounds rather roundabout to me. Why not just shell the village, like in the old days?"

"It's too far inland. I've been in the vicinity once or twice. It's damnable country."

Damnable, eh? Price-Kane thought. *First time I've heard Will Naismith swear, or almost swear. I wonder if his nerve's going.* He drew luxuriously on the cigar and looked at Naismith's tired, careworn face. "You're not leading this patrol yourself?"

"No, sir. Baekani will lead it."

"Why?"

"His brother was killed in the attack on the gaol, so he has a score to settle with Eglito. But he has a cool head;

I believe I can rely on him to harass Eglito effectively, but not let the patrol get out of hand."

"I meant, why aren't you leading the patrol?"

Naismith swung about in his chair to face the large map of the Jeremiahs pinned to the wall. Redowa, Quiros and the other scattered outliers lay far to the northwest; the central division was dominated by Hemisphere and its satellites, Pinto and Christopher Island. Murdo, across the strait that bore the same name, was approximately a hundred and sixty kilometres long and forty kilometres across at its widest point. It was shaped like a bird with a thick body, a curving, sharp-billed head and a long, plumed tail. In the north, tiny islands clustered under the bird's beak resembled the crop of a fowl, and more such islands and the treacherous southern reefs, coral atolls and sandbars formed the tail. Part of this coastline was indented and protected by a long reef. These waters, the Tau lagoon, also had artificial islands, built by migrants from the north in the distant past. To the east was the long, narrow shape of low-lying Santa Juliana.

Naismith picked up a ruler and tapped the map at three places. "Here's Alma, here's Eglito's mountain territory and here's Sunburi — it's the point on the coast where the bush To'beili pay their taxes. Or should. Not many have on the last two occasions. Eglito's a little unusual in that he's not exactly a bushman or a saltwater man. He has extensive kinship connections with both."

Price-Kane was weary and dry and in no mood for a diatribe. "I asked you what you planned to do to get hold of the bastard so we can hang him, not for an anthropology class."

"I propose to collect the tax right around Murdo, do a census and confiscate the guns."

"What will that achieve?"

"A great many things, sir. Above all it'll enable us to gauge the strength of support for Eglito. Every man who pays the tax will be declaring for the government. That's how they'll see it. The census will also help us to identify supporters and opponents."

"And the guns? You've resisted my instructions to confiscate them for some years now."

Naismith knew that the RC saw his duties as primarily ceremonial and diplomatic and that his ignorance of life on the beaches and in the bush was profound. As a consequence, he often fell into the habit of lecturing his superior. "The guns are harmless, or virtually so, as weapons of offence. The *lemos* used them until recently for close-work killing, but they're even getting past that. There's very little ammunition for the old Sniders, and the newer kinds of ammunition are harder to convert."

"Convert?"

"Oh, yes. The Murdoans are expert in adapting bullets to fit guns of a different calibre. They've done it for years."

"Remarkable," Price-Kane said.

"The point is that the guns are symbols only — symbols of authority and power. Some of the oldest ones are consecrated to certain powerful ancestors."

The RC sniffed and stubbed out his cigar. "Mumbo-jumbo. So why pick up the rifles now?"

"Every rifle collected represents a victory of my authority over the *lemos*. Even over the ancestor spirits."

"*Your* authority?"

"The authority of the Crown," Naismith said.

"That's better." Despite the antagonism he felt towards Naismith, Price-Kane could see the merits of the scheme. It would look well in his reports — a judicious, administratively sound action, leading to . . . what? With any luck, something more dramatic and decisive with Naismith out of the way. The RC had no faith in ameliorative action.

"How long would this tax collecting and so on take?"

"Hard to say. A couple of months, perhaps."

"And what of your duties here?"

"I have every confidence that Mr Larke will be able to keep house until I get back."

The statement contained a veiled insult for the desk-sitter, and Price-Kane did not miss it. He gazed across at Naismith's broad, determined face and could detect no signs of weakness in it, though he felt there was something missing, some doubt. Still, it all looked satisfactory. He could represent his posting of Larke to Murdo as necessary for carrying out Naismith's plan. In so doing he could imply to the Colonial Office that he was the architect of the scheme. But to do that, he would certainly need to know Naismith's ultimate solution. He got up, walked around the desk and looked closely at the map. He was playing for time, appearing to be considering the DO's proposal which, after all, he had the power to veto. He plucked at the grey bristles of his moustache.

"Of course," Naismith said, "there'll be consequences of this action which you'll approve of more than me, sir?"

"Oh?"

"Labour recruiting will pick up. There's no other way a lot of the people will be able to pay the tax except by signing on to avoid it or collecting the beach payment for their brothers and sons and using that."

Price-Kane nodded. He knew how much Naismith disliked the scene he was projecting.

"And a good number will go into the mission villages for much the same reason — to earn an exemption."

"The commercial and spiritual welfare of the Protectorate is a large part of our duty," Price-Kane said.

Naismith sighed. "Murdoans are unpredictable, especially the To'beili. All this could go wrong, but I don't think it will. I think I'll be able to isolate Eglito, harry him, cut him off from supplies and supporters and lead a strong patrol into the mountains to bring him out."

"You think he'll surrender?"

"It'll depend on the size and nature of his support. A leader in his position has a problem. Their warfare isn't like ours. If Eglito fights and some of his friends are killed, their kin will take vengeance on Eglito himself or *his* kin. Eglito has several sons. It could be braver to surrender than to fight."

"I see." Price-Kane moved away from the map and towards the door. "I'm in support of this plan, Naismith. Of course, it'll need some elaboration, allocation of resources and so on, but basically I approve. When would you plan to set off?"

"In two days, sir."

Typical Naismith, Price-Kane thought, *attack the pin at all times.* He brushed dust from his sun helmet. "By the way, how are the Birminghams and Webb settling in?"

"Birmingham's a fool and a drunk. He'll be on a short leash. Webb distinguished himself the other night. I'm inclined to let him do what he wants."

"Which is what exactly?"

"Live in and study a To'beili community."

"Would that be wise with this brouhaha on?"

"I'll choose the community. He could make a useful listening post."

Price-Kane nodded and looked at his watch. He could have his tea on the boat back to Patugi. What one of Naismith's teas might amount to he hated to think. He knew he should say something affirmative — the man was embarking on a major exercise, after all. But a look at Naismith, standing stolidly beside his desk with the map of Murdo, his dominion, apparently sitting on his shoulder, prevented him. He sketched a salute and walked out of the office.

The DO pushed the ashtray aside with an exclamation of distaste. He went to the door and watched Price-Kane walking, stiff-spined and straight-shouldered, towards the wharf. He noted with approval that two of his policemen, as instructed, discreetly took up positions on the right and left flanks as the RC advanced. He was about to return to his desk when he saw Keith Larke approach Price-Kane before he reached the wharf. The cadet handed something to Price-Kane. A newspaper? A letter? The RC scarcely acknowledged the gesture, but his hand moved to his pocket and Larke stepped back empty-handed. Naismith stepped quickly out of sight and watched Larke from a window. The cadet adopted an over-casual saunter as he approached Louise Birmingham and Richard Webb, who were standing on the grey sand beach, watching the activity on the wharf.

"Good afternoon," Larke said. "You've just missed the RC.
I thought you might be travelling back with him, Mrs
Birmingham."

"Why would you think that?"

"Well, after what happened."

"I have the feeling that Mr Naismith will soon get things
under control," Louise said.

The three watched as two wounded policemen were
carried on stretchers onto the wharf for removal to the
better hospital facilities at Patugi.

"What's their condition, Mr Larke, do you know?"
Webb said.

"Bad, I believe," Larke said indifferently.

"Are they To'beili?"

"I really couldn't say. Excuse me, I must see the DO."

Louise acknowledged Larke's nod. "Could you tell him
my husband would like to see him as soon as possible?"

"I'll see what I can do."

"I don't like that young man," Louise said when Larke
was out of earshot.

"Young's the operative word," Webb said. "I imagine
Naismith will lick him into shape."

"Do you realise we've both been singing Mr William
Naismith's praises? But he's such a cold fish. I don't quite
know *what* I think of him. Do you rate him so highly,
Richard?"

"The Murdoans respect him. Most of them, anyway."

"I keep forgetting the way your head's screwed on. You
see things from the natives' point of view, don't you?"

"I try," Webb said. As a rule, he found it difficult to talk
easily with women who attracted him sexually. French
whores during the war had constituted a notable exception.
But the problem had recurred at Oxford and subsequently.
In their brief talk the night before and again now, he found
Louise Birmingham more than just sexually interesting.
It was as if what they said to each other led somewhere
naturally, easily and interesting to them both.

"I've never met anyone with that attitude before," Louise said. "Tom just assumes he's superior — everyone else is there for local colour."

"People study the Indians in America."

"Never met one, nor an Indian for that matter. Closest I've been to Indians is looking at the collections in the Smithsonian."

"I'd like to see them," Webb said. *With you,* he thought.

"Maybe you will one day." Louise paused as she remembered the feel of his arms around her, wrestling her down as the bullets hit the wall above them. "Why did you come here, Richard? Africa would've been a darn sight closer to home for you. Say, why didn't you go to Arizona for the Indians?"

Webb laughed. "Or Australia, for the Aborigines?"

"Sure."

"Pull of the Pacific, I suppose — Stevenson and Melville, Captain Bligh and Fletcher Christian, Jack London, Malinowski now. Romanticism."

"I thought anthropology was supposed to be a science. The books on it we publish certainly look scientific — full of diagrams and charts."

"Oh, the thesis'll be scientific enough. Kinship systems and land tenure and so on. No romanticism there, but that's just a means to an end. I'm going to record stories and traditions, myths and legends. That's more my real interest. Mind you, don't tell anyone I said so."

"Won't you need to speak the language for that?"

"I'll pick it up. I've got a grammar for the main Murdoan tongues. Now that I've settled on the To'beili, I'll get down to a serious study of that. Excuse me, Louise, this chap seems to want something." A Murdoan, aged about thirty and dressed in a clean white shirt and khaki shorts with leather sandals, stood a few feet away, waiting for Webb to notice him. When Webb looked in his direction the man moved closer. "Excuse me sir, and miss, my name is Peter Mamuka. I believe my brother spoke to you about finding employment for me."

"Right," Webb said. "He's a sailor, on the *Equator*."

"Yes, sir. We are To'beili. Saltwater men, but I was born in Queensland. I came back to Murdo only ten years ago."

"Queensland, Australia?" Louise said.

"Yes, miss. My parents went there as labourers. A lot of people died, most returned, some stayed." Peter Mamuka's face was impassive. "I was born there so I could've stayed. I did for a time, then I left."

"You know why I'm here?" Webb asked.

"To study custom, sir."

"That's right."

"I worked for an American who was studying fish and for a Frenchman who was studying butterflies."

Louise laughed. "An Englishman studying customs sounds almost normal."

"It would be an honour, sir. Perhaps we should move to the shade. The lady looks very hot."

"Oh God, I'm sorry. Louise. D'you want to go back to the house? I can do this later."

"No, I'm interested. If you don't mind."

Peter Mamuka steered Webb and Louise into the shade of a stand of coconut trees. A hum of insects filled the air; heavily scented parasite flowers were twining around the trunks of the trees.

Louise sat on a rock and the men squatted. "You speak To'beili, Peter?" Webb said.

"Fluently, sir, and Kweili and some Maka Maka."

"There's your teacher," Louise said.

"I'd like to engage you," Webb said, "but I have to get permission from the DO to work in the To'beili district first."

"You will get the permission, sir."

An ant crawled up Louise's leg, and she smacked at it. "How do you know?"

Peter smiled widely, showing the reddened teeth of the betel chewer. "Another brother, this one in Mr Naismith's office."

Before Webb could respond, Tom Birmingham came, almost at a run, into the patch of shade. He was red in the face and panting. "You know what that bastard wants to do?" he gasped. "He wants to take away my goddamned guns!"

12

Being an experienced skeet shooter herself, Louise had no particular aversion to guns, but she disliked her husband's devotion to them. As a constitution-loving American, however, she was outraged. "He can't do that!"

"I'm afraid he can," Webb said. "His authority is pretty much absolute here, and as he's just been seeing the RC, I imagine he's got the go-ahead to do whatever he thinks best. Did he give you any reason, Tom?"

Birmingham sat on the rock beside his wife and shook his head. "No. He said something about collecting up all the guns on the island." He patted his pockets. "Have you got a cigarette, hon?"

"No," Louise said.

"You never do these days. Have you quit or something? Goddamn it, I need a smoke."

"Here." Webb held out a tin of Players. "I keep them to get people talking to me. Take a few."

Birmingham scrabbled three cigarettes from the tin, stuck one in his mouth and lit it with his petrol lighter. He put the other two away in a pocket with the lighter.

"Thanks." He puffed furiously; sweat continued to run from his flushed face into his crumpled shirt collar.

Louise reached out and touched Webb's wrist. "I need a cigarette, too." When she had one lit, she said, "You need the guns for protection, Tom. There are some dangerous places on this island, I'm sure."

"Maybe, but we ain't goin' to any of 'em. Tin god Naismith says we're confined to the precincts of the station here. Says he'll give us an escort if we want to go outside the compound. Mighty white of him."

"That's not much use to you, is it?" Webb said.

"Damn all." Birmingham looked up and glowered at Peter Mamuka, who had moved discreetly away but was still within earshot. "What's he want?"

"It's all right," Webb said. "I'm going to employ him if Naismith will . . ."

"Forgot to tell you, he wants to see you. Ask him for your own boat and a hundred pounds while you're about it. You're the blue-eyed boy."

Louise smoked quietly; Birmingham's bitterness was like a force field around him, and she wanted to withdraw from it. She looked up at Webb, who was thoughtfully tapping his fingers on the cigarette tin.

"I'm sorry, Tom," Webb said. "I'll see what I can do."

Birmingham took out a cigarette and lit it from the stub of the one he was smoking. "Don't do me any favours."

Webb nodded to Louise and turned away. Peter Mamuka fell in beside him as he walked up the track towards the DO's office.

"You're going to make yourself ill, Tom," Louise said. "You're sweating terribly, and your colour isn't good."

Birmingham smoked and said nothing.

Louise said the last words she wanted to say. "We're going to have to get out of here. Try somewhere else. Fiji perhaps, or Samoa."

"That's a laugh. You know how often the boats come? About once a goddamned month, that's how often. And my funds are low, real low. I'm waiting for a cable to authorise me to collect some dough in Patugi, but it hasn't come yet. I'm close to broke, and Naismith knows it."

"How could he know?"

"He knows. Probably put one of his pet niggers to looking through our things."

Louise was alarmed by everything she heard and by the manner of its delivery. The sweating, bleary-eyed hulk beside her bore little resemblance to laughing Tom Birmingham of the Manhattan cocktail circuit. But there was a sizable measure of comfort — she could stay for a time longer on the same island as Richard Webb.

Webb told Peter Mamuka to wait. He knocked on the architrave of Naismith's open office door.

"Yes?"

Webb stepped in and found Naismith working at his desk. The bird-shaped map of the island seemed to hover over his bent head. "Mr Naismith, you wanted to see me?"

"Ah, yes, Webb. Take a seat." Naismith looked up and pushed his chair back.

Webb sat where Ashley Price-Kane had been sitting. There was a light scattering of fine ash on the desktop but no ashtray. "I've just been talking to Tom Birmingham. I gather you were rather severe with him."

"Man deserves it. He's a fool. Came rampaging in here demanding this and that."

"For example, Mr Naismith?"

"A launch and a team of boys to go crocodile shooting. Absurd. I had a good mind to send him back to Patugi to drink and play golf until the next steamer."

"Why didn't you, if I may ask?"

"Well, the chap's a writer. No knowing what nonsense he could put about. And his wife's a decent sort. Couldn't just show her the door, could I?"

Webb was surprised by this endorsement, but he merely nodded in agreement. "What have you got a good mind to do with me?"

Naismith picked up his ruler and exerted pressure on it at both ends. The thick wood bent a little, and Webb could see the sinews standing out in the DO's powerful forearms.

"Just what exactly do you want, Mr Webb?"

"I want your permission to establish myself at Sunburi for six months." Webb pointed to the map. "An introduction to the headman, John Kaluae, a modest amount of support — mail delivery, some medical supplies. That's all."

Naismith was impressed with Webb's quick pinpointing of the Sunburi passage on the rugged, confusing coastline, and by his succinctness, but it was not his habit to pay compliments. "Why Sunburi?"

"It's a traditional settlement area, not a post-colonial one. There's an unusual amount of contact between the saltwater and bush people. Big recruiting point in the labour trade days. And there are no Christians in the vicinity."

"You've done your homework."

Webb nodded. "I've read the Spanish accounts, the beachcomber and whaler journals and the recruiting logs. And all the government Blue Book reports, of course."

"Did you select Sunburi before this business blew up, or after?"

"Before. I know it's Eglito's passage, though."

"That doesn't worry you?"

"My understanding was that Eglito's ambitions and hostilities were essentially local. I assume the attack on the station changes that?"

Naismith's respect for Webb mounted. It was the crucial question, and one Price-Kane had not had the insight to put. "It might represent a challenge to government authority or simply be a flamboyant, attention-getting act."

"Or it might be directed at you personally."

"Why do you say that?"

"You've gaoled a few of the *lemos*, your police have confiscated a good deal of shell bounty. There's a rumour that you put up a bounty yourself."

"That's absurd. Would you mind telling me how you came by all this?"

"Simply by talking to some To'beili around the place."

Naismith's methodical mind absorbed and processed the

information. He was confirmed in his view that Webb would be a useful ally; his concern now was that the anthropologist would make a dangerous enemy. "You're aware that I wouldn't be able to protect you at Sunburi, and that I'm not permitting weapons to be held by civilians?"

"I wouldn't expect to need protection. If Eglito's intentions are local and internal, they'd have nothing to do with me. If they go further . . ." Webb spread his hands. "I'm not associated with the government, or the planters, or the missions."

"I see," Naismith said. "I'm inclined to grant your request, Mr Webb. But first, let me tell you what I intend to do about Eglito." Naismith spoke for five minutes, using his ruler to indicate places on the map and occasionally speaking pidgin and using words in the Alma lagoon language to emphasise his points. His account was more detailed than the one he had given to the resident commissioner. Webb listened quietly, occasionally nodding and sometimes tempted to take notes. He was impressed by Naismith's detailed, almost obsessive, knowledge of the economy and politics of his island.

When the DO had finished, Webb said, "You'll be relying very heavily on Baekani to keep the police in check?"

"Yes."

"Has he the authority?"

Naismith worked his tongue against his plate. He was developing an ulcer where his gum had been irritated the previous night. Life seemed to be a series of small physical collapses these days; he envied Webb his youth. "Baekani's authority is sufficient and his judgment is good. What I want to know, Mr Webb, is whether you're willing to help me in this enterprise."

"I'm not sure I understand you. Are you asking me to spy for you?"

"Not at all. I'd simply like to know of any trouble that might be in the air before I get to Sunburi to collect the tax."

"Wouldn't John Kaluae tell you?"

"Yes. But I'd like you to tell me as well."

"Will I get the permission to go to Sunburi if I refuse?"
Naismith looked at Webb levelly and didn't answer.

Webb shrugged. "I can't see any harm in it."

"Good."

"There's something I'd like you to agree to in turn, Mr
Naismith."

Naismith was unused to being bargained with.

"And that is . . . ?"

"I want to employ Peter Mamuka as my field assistant.
I believe he's unusually well qualified."

"He's a troublemaker."

"In what way?"

"He's insubordinate."

"He's a civilian, Mr Naismith."

The DO snorted. "He certainly is. I booted him off the
police force."

"Was he incompetent?"

"No, undisciplined."

"I don't think I'm going to require much in the way
of discipline. I think he'll be a great help to me in my work.
I entertain the hope that my work will be of some help
to you, Mr Naismith. You seem to want to understand the
place, not just put your foot on it."

Naismith allowed himself a thin smile. "I appreciate
that. Peter Mamuka, eh? He's a rascal, you know. Well, I
won't oppose it."

"Thank you. I said I'd put in a word with you for
Birmingham. Perhaps you could let him him have one gun?
I think he feels about his guns the way the *lemo* do."

"Very likely, and all the more dangerous on that
account."

"Perhaps just one — loaded with birdshot or something?" Webb was aware that he was pleading more for
Louise Birmingham's sake than her husband's.

"Perhaps," Naismith said. "Now, about getting round to
Sunburi. There are two ways to do it. You could come with
me on my launch when I make the tax collecting trip, but

I'm starting down the other coast. It'd be a few weeks before you got there. Or you could walk across. It's a very hard walk for a newcomer, even for someone who looks as fit as you — a few days of the worst effort you ever made in your life. You'll toughen up fast at Sunburi and I wouldn't be surprised if you made the return trip on foot in half the time, but I'd advise the boat first off."

"I'm sure you're right on all counts, but Colin Clements is coming across at the end of the week with his company boat. He wants to do some curio collecting in the artificial islands, and I'm pretty sure he'd give me a ride to Sunburi. You remember that you invited him over? He says he hopes to see you but understands that you'll be busy. From what you say he'll miss out altogether."

"I'd forgotten about Clements. You and he are thick, are you?"

"Not really. We seem to get along, share a few interests."

"He's supposed to clear curio collecting with me."

"I got the impression that he had done so."

Naismith grunted. "How did you come by this message, if I may ask?"

"The RC brought it across on the *Equator*. He left it with the bosun who passed it on to me."

"I don't approve of this passing on of messages by the natives," Naismith said. "It could lead to trouble." His mind flicked to the image of Larke handing something to Price-Kane. "There's altogether too much message-passing, if you ask me."

"I beg your pardon?"

Naismith waved the image and Webb's question away. "Never mind. I'll write a note to John Kaluae for you. He can read after a fashion. See what I mean? More note passing. We need better radio communications on each coast, that's what we need."

Webb nodded.

Naismith got up, carefully disguising the creakiness in his bones from the younger man. He looked at the map. "I don't suppose you've seen those flying boats, by any chance?"

"Felixstowes and the like?" Webb said. "Yes, I've seen them."

"That's what I need here. Cover the whole place in a flash. I expect it'll happen, but not in my time. Well, Webb, I wish you luck."

The two men shook hands. Webb moved towards the door. "I wish you the same, Mr Naismith. You've got a difficult job."

"Makes it worthwhile," Naismith said. "By the way, how much are you paying that scoundrel Mamuka?"

"I thought ten bob a week."

Naismith suddenly raised his voice. "Watch out for him, he'll rob you blind." He smiled and turned away.

Webb found Mamuka listening intently, his ear only inches from the door. Mamuka grinned, and Webb did the same. He had not suspected a sense of humour in Will Naismith.

13

Over the next few days Naismith was busy making preparations for his voyage around the island. He organised the procurement and loading of fuel and supplies, current copies of the tax rolls, ordnance for the small contingent of police he would take with him, and his personal comforts — gramophone records, books and the Australian brand of tea he favoured. Much of his time was also spent in familiarising Keith Larke with the working of the station. Larke mastered the clerical duties easily enough, struggled with the technicalities of the radio and appeared to make no progress in learning pidgin.

Naismith had misgivings: Larke showed an interest in magisterial duties but the DO decreed that all judicial matters be held over until his return. Larke was extremely keen to drill and inspect the police, a routine task Naismith could hardly withhold from him, but he performed very badly in this role.

"Sir," Baekani reported, "Mister Larke kept the squad waiting in the sun for an hour. They are angry."

"I'll speak to him," Naismith said.

Larke was unrepentant. "They were slovenly. They needed to be taught a lesson."

"You listen to me," Naismith growled. "Those men are hand-picked by Baekani and me. They are good men, and respected men on this island."

"Two of them have been in prison themselves," Larke protested.

"That doesn't matter. When you understand this place a bit better, you'll see that." Naismith longed to ask Larke what he had handed to the resident commissioner that day, but he knew he could not. He was struggling against a growing dislike and disrespect for the cadet and suspected Larke would lie.

"I must say, sir, that you leave me in a very uncomfortable position. I can't tell whether my authority will be paramount here or that of your servant."

"Yours is," Naismith said. "Baekani will obey any order you give him." Naismith knew that he himself was lying and that Baekani would exercise his own judgment, in which he had faith. He had misgivings aplenty, but no real choice. The tax collection was a major stroke that could not be delayed; if things fell into disarray at Alma while he was gone it couldn't be helped. He would soon set them straight.

Larke seemed somewhat mollified. "What is to be done with Mr and Mrs Birmingham?"

"Colin Clements is coming over in a few days to take Webb around to the weather coast. I suggest the Birminghams go back to Hemisphere with him. I'll leave you to handle that."

Larke scribbled in a pocket-sized notebook he'd taken to carrying with him. "Right," he said. "What sort of a chap is this Clements?"

"Quiet," Naismith said. "Scholarly, I suppose you'd say. Remind him to leave any guns on board his boat. No guns ashore."

Larke made another note.

"Birdshot?" Tom Birmingham said. "That's a goddamned insult."

"It's better than nothing," Louise said. "At least you can clean it for hours the way you like to do and go out shooting at birds, though God knows why. Anyway, it's the best Richard could do."

"Richard," Birmingham said. "Well, it's fine for him. He can go off and study how these people wipe their asses and blow their noses and get to be a professor on the strength of it. I can't write a book about shooting goddamned birds."

The Birminghams were sitting on the porch of the guesthouse. Smoking his pipe and drinking a pre-lunch beer, Birmingham was uncomfortably aware of a sudden recent weight gain and accompanying loss of muscle tone. Ordinarily on his research trips he trekked hard, lived fairly rough and burned off his food and liquor intake by hunting animals and tracking down interesting characters. Having Louise along, he told himself, had slowed him down and softened him. He'd hardly walked a hundred yards since San Francisco. And he was drinking too much. Who wouldn't, with the worries he had? Still no cable from New York authorising funds. Accommodation was free at the Alma guesthouse, but food, drink and tobacco had to be paid for at steep prices, and the islanders who washed and ironed clothes, heated water for baths and cleaned the room all had to be paid, too. He was running low.

"What we should be doing," Birmingham said, "is going on this boat ride with Naismith. He'll see some action for sure. There's no chance he'd take us, I suppose?"

Louise shuddered at the thought of being trapped on a twenty-foot cutter with Naismith, Tom and the crocodiles for company. She poured herself a small glass of beer from her husband's bottle as Birmingham dropped the sinker of a pull-through down the barrel of his gun. "I guess I could ask Richard," she said. "But I think Mr Naismith wouldn't welcome tourists." She saw Birmingham stiffen at the word 'tourists' and hastened to repair the damage. "Anyway, Tom, things can't be so bad. I see you writing every day and at night sometimes. You must be getting inspiration from somewhere."

Birmingham grunted and began easing the pull-through along the barrel.

Louise stood and took two steps to the rail which ran around the porch. She was wearing a blue cotton blouse and loose white trousers with a narrow leather belt. In a Chinese store in Patugi she had found a pair of shoes with slightly built-up rubber heels and canvas uppers. One of the guesthouse servants had blancoed the uppers to a startling whiteness; the shoes left her toes bare and her feet comfortable. *Easily kicked off and these trousers come down . . .* Louise gripped the rail in an effort to control her fantasies. For the last wo days she had walked in the late afternoon with Richard Webb while Birmingham slept off his lunch and post-lunch drinks.

The gong sounded softly and Birmingham, forgetting his waistline, said, "Lunch. Just us, I guess. Where's Webb? Sure would like to ask him about our chances of making the boat trip."

Louise shrugged. "I don't know. Do you mind if I miss lunch, Tom? I'm not hungry. I think I'd rather have a nap."

Birmingham balanced the disagreeability of eating alone against the thought of being able to have a second bottle of beer without Louise's reproachful eye. The beer won. "Go ahead," he said. "Sure you're not sick or something? Take you right out of here, if you are."

Louise touched his flushed, puffy face. This was a note Birmingham had been striking often lately — the possibility of using Louise as an excuse to leave the Jeremiahs. "I'm fine," she said. "Enjoy your lunch."

Birmingham returned the gun to its case, put the cleaning gear in a soft leather bag and got to his feet. "I'll take that up," Louise said.

"Thanks, hon. Gun's worth a lotta money. Hope I don't have to hock it."

Louise was thoughtful as she climbed the stairs. Tom was sounding more and more negative, looking for excuses and outs and drinking like a camel. Why? She went into their room, put the gun case and bag on the dresser, took off her clothes and stretched out naked on the bed under the stiff sheet. The servants changed the sheets daily and put on fresh ones with too much starch in them. The room was hot, but a light breeze was coming in, stirring the mosquito netting piled up over the bed and making her clothes rustle softly on their wall hooks. She tried not to think about Richard Webb, and failed. *He won't do or say anything. He's an English gentleman, and English gentlemen don't do or say anything* . . . . But of course they did. There was H.G. Wells, whom she'd met in New York and who had made an unmistakable pass at her. But maybe Wells wasn't a gentleman. *Maybe Webb isn't either* . . . She fell asleep, hoping not.

When she awoke an hour later, aroused by Birmingham's loud snore from the other bed, she was sweating. He was lying on his back with his mouth open, and flies were buzzing around his chin, down which some liquid had dribbled. Louise closed her eyes and tried to sleep again, but the steady snoring prevented her. She got up and wrapped herself in the length of trade cloth she had chosen in the store with Webb. In the mirror she looked slender, dark and interesting, she thought. *Perhaps a bit yellow.* She'd heard that women went yellow in the tropics. She went closer to to the mirror to check on this possible deterioration, and her eye fell on the black notebook her husband had been writing in so industriously of late. The book lay on the floor near the bed, and Birmingham's uncapped fountain pen lay beside it.

Louise examined her face in the mirror. *Trick of the light*, she decided. *No yellowing there.* She picked up the pen and screwed the cap on. As one who had worked, however marginally, in publishing, Louise knew the protocol that governed writing and editing. You didn't read a manuscript unless you were asked to, and then only according to instructions. If a writer said, "Tear it apart, honey," as likely as not he meant, "Tell me it's wonderful." She was sure Tom would welcome criticism like syphilis. And as for reading uninvited . . .

A loud, bubbling snore decided her. Keeping a watchful
eye on her husband, she picked up the book, sat on the end
of her bed and opened it. She read:

> I was born in Twisted Bone, Montana, on 7 October 1883. Local
> lore has it that on the night of my birth a flight of ten huge native
> ducks passed over the house on their annual migration to the warm
> south. My mother said: "This boy will travel," and he has.
>
> My father had a small ranch but we were dirt poor, in debt to
> the bank and neighbours. My father worked as a timber cutter,
> cowboy, buffalo shooter and gambler, and if you think gambling
> for a living isn't working, try it, you'll find out different. I have
> followed all of these occupations myself and many more. Caspar
> Birmingham, my Dad, was the son of Joseph, who was the son of
> Wilbur. Wilbur was supposed to have some Sioux blood in him
> and that may be true. I remember when I was trapping in the
> Montana woods as a lad, old Charley Two Braids said, "Young Tom
> Birmingham, you move like an Indian."
>
> I have to admit that Caspar Birmingham spent some time in the
> penitentiary, mostly for crimes he couldn't avoid committing. He
> chased the bank men off his farm with a shotgun one time, and
> when his house was burned down by a jealous neighbour he rebuilt
> it with lumber that wasn't strictly his. I've followed Caspar there
> too, in seeing the inside of many a hoosegow.
>
> You might ask at this point: why was the neighbour jealous? Well
> sir, the answer is that Casper had married him the prettiest woman
> in Root River County, and that was Alberta May Robard. Abbie,
> as everyone called her, was part-French, and she was the best dancer,
> the best singer, the best needlewoman, the best cook, the best
> gardener, the best housekeeper in Montana. Plus, she was the best
> mother in the world.

My God, Louise thought, *this is terrible writing.* She was also
surprised to find that her husband was six years older than
she'd thought. She read on, through Tom's rebellious years
in the one-teacher rural school, to his prominence as a
football player at Twisted Bone high school. Young Tom
was always getting into scrapes, and out of them, with his
hide and honour intact. Caspar was an endless source of

sound manly advice, and his mother was an angel come to earth. Tom's two brothers, Clyde and Kenneth, somehow never quite inherited the full spirit of Caspar. But, Yvonne, his only sister, was Abbie reborn in all her perfect glory.

Louise read with mounting dismay. Birmingham had written more than a hundred pages in less than a week. The script at the beginning of each writing session was firm and rounded, but it degenerated, as the writer's alcohol level rose, to a messy scrawl.

She turned to the last entry, made presumably that afternoon.

2nd Lt Tom Birmingham was commissioned as an infantry officer on 2 September 1917, and he was the proudest man in the United States, unless, just maybe, Caspar was a little piece prouder still. He was, one of his officers later testified, 'a hell of a good soldier', and promotion to 1st lieutenant came quickly at Camp Sheridan. This was where the members of the ninth division were receiving their last training before being despatched to the front.

Camp Sheridan is near Montgomery, Alabama, and is one of the toughest posts in the army. The senior officers were tough, the NCOs were tough, the men were tough and the newly commissioned subalterns had to show that they were tough too. Birmingham showed tough on the parade ground, in field exercises in the Alabama swamps and in the boxing ring. He won the light heavyweight championship of Camp Sheridan and only narrowly lost in the southern command finals.

It should not be thought that training for war was toy soldier stuff. Birmingham's platoon actually saw action — against a band of desperate convicts who'd escaped from the chain gang of the Alabama state farm. There were six convicts in all, killers, lifers. They bashed a guard and took his shotgun before disappearing into the swamps. The sheriff called in the army, and Birmingham and his men spent three days and nights in the swamps tracking the desperadoes with dogs, aware that they could be ambushed at any moment.

Eventually, after being harassed unmercifully to the point of exhaustion, the convicts surrendered to the sheriff and his deputies.

Sheriff Everett P. Clanton personally commended Birmingham and his men for their role in putting down this threat to civil order.

The handwriting began to deteriorate at this point.

Readers may wonder why the sections detailing Birmingham's military experiences are written in the third person. The reason is simple. Tom Birmingham never went to war, and this is something he is deeply ashamed of and has regretted for almost ten years. He feels a need to put a barrier between himself and that eager young warrior who boarded the USS *Cannonball* for transshipment to the muddy, bloody trenches in France. When the news came that the war had ended and that he and his men had lost their chance for glory, Birmingham wept. It was the only time other men were to see him cry . . .

The page was damp from Birmingham's tears.

He snored loudly and flopped over on the bed like a stranded sea creature dying on a beach. Louise returned the notebook to its former position, dressed quickly and went off to meet Richard Webb for their afternoon walk.

The war changed everything, Webb thought as he waited by the breakwater at the north end of the small harbour. *Before the war you didn't go out walking with married women. Now, if you could, you did.* He'd known men, fellow officers, who boasted of their conquests after every leave. "An absolute poppet," Captain Harry Dangay would say, "nanny to take care of the kiddies, and all afternoon to redecorate the bedroom, if you see what I mean, old boy." The reasoning of the adulterers was simple — given the mortality rates among junior officers in France, the chances of any complications arising from brief liaisons, however passionate, were slight. That the philanderers themselves might be cuckolded by their wives likewise never seemed to occur to them. Webb doubted that many of them would have cared. 'Live for the moment' was the motto, and all but the terminally shy put it into practice. Webb had had his own adventures. He could not now remember the women's names.

The afternoon rain had passed, leaving the air clean and sweet smelling. Webb had got accustomed to the perspiration and wettings that were a part of the climate. You towelled down, changed your shirt and got on with it. It was the reverse of the situation in France. There, when you were at your filthiest, it was too cold to wash, and when you could wash there was no clean water. After France, Webb had fallen into the habit of treating each day as a bonus and each inconvenience and discomfort as a passing trifle. The attitude had made him a calm and methodical student, an efficient worker and an effective pursuer of his own advantage. Selfish, some might have said, and Webb might have smiled and agreed.

He watched as Louise Birmingham walked towards him along the beach. Would Harry Dangay have called her 'an absolute poppet'? Probably, but Harry had been blown to pieces by a mortar at Chateau Thierry. Webb watched the swing of her hips as she placed her feet very neatly and straight. No one else on Murdo Island could possibly leave tracks like that. He was smiling at the thought when she reached him.

"Hullo," she said, "what's funny?"

Webb told her.

"Let me see your footprints."

Webb, not long back from a walk to a nearby village with Peter Mamuka, was wearing his walking boots and shorts. He took three strides along the beach, stopped and turned. Louise stood and looked at the footprints, which were quite large. The left foot was slightly off line. "Know 'em anywhere," she said. She pointed to the left imprint. "If you were drunk, that'd make you wobble." She walked towards Webb, stretching her stride and treading exactly in his prints.

"I haven't been drunk for a long time," Webb said.

"Tom's hardly been sober since we got here."

"I suppose he's disappointed with the way things have turned out. Sorry I can't help."

Louise shrugged. They began to walk along the beach in the direction of the slipway, where the *Braidwood* was undergoing repairs. "He wants you to ask Naismith to let him go with him round the island."

Webb said, "I doubt the DO would agree to that. In any case, there wouldn't be room for you on Naismith's launch."

"I wouldn't go," Louise said. "Just Tom."

"What would you do?"

"I don't know. Go home, I suppose."

Webb stopped. They were standing in a patch of shade close to the boat, almost under it, as it sat high up out of the water on the slipway. The rear of the hull was stoved in and the engine screw was severely twisted. Webb put his hands on Louise's shoulders, drew her towards him and kissed her. Her arms went around him; she felt his ribs and spine. She pressed her body hard against him and leaned into the kiss with a fierceness that surprised her. Webb felt her tremble as their mouths parted; he was hungry for her, but she turned her head away. He kissed and stroked her hair as she clung to him.

He held her too hard and when she finally stepped back she was breathing hard and tears were in her eyes.

"Did I hurt you?" he said.

"No. Not yet."

"What does that mean?"

"What did the kiss mean?"

"I wanted to do it, that's all I know."

"And I wanted you to."

Webb reached for her hands and they stood close together under the damaged boat, not speaking. Suddenly the *Braidwood's* planks creaked loudly and Louise started. "Christ! I don't want to be crushed to death by a goddamned boat."

Webb laughed. "That would be a terrible waste."

They skirted around the slipway and moved up the beach towards the coconut tree fringe. Louise sat on the sand and began to trickle the large, grey grains through her fingers. "Could I have one of those cigarettes you carry, please?"

Webb squatted beside her and produced his Players tin. He lit Louise's cigarette. "Thanks," she said. "I've been thinking about you most of the time for the last few days."

"I've been thinking about you."

"About making love to me?"

Webb nodded. "Yes."

Louise blew smoke. "You'd like to?"

"Yes."

"So would I. I'd like to lock myself in a room with you and get on the bed and do everything we could think of, over and over again."

Webb's hand was on her arm, smoothing the fine hairs, gently caressing the firm flesh. "Yes," he said. "That would be wonderful."

"Then what would we do, Richard?"

Yes, Webb thought. *What would we do then?* It was the question Harry Dangay had never had to face. Suddenly, he wanted to tell Louise all about Harry Dangay and the women in London during the war, whose names he couldn't remember. He shook his head violently.

"What?" Louise said.

"Nothing, I . . ."

Peter Mamuka's sandals slapped the hard sand as he ran; he burst into sight from behind a clump of bushes and sprinted towards Webb and Louise. His shirt, normally tucked neatly into his shorts, was flapping wildly. "Mr Webb, Mrs Birmingham, come quickly," he gasped. "Mr Birmingham has shot himself."

14

As Louise ran back to the guesthouse her head was filled with one thought, one hope, almost a prayer. *Let him be dead. Let him be dead.* She tried to throw off the thought, but it clung to her. She ran, almost tripped as her heels dug into a soft patch of sand. Webb was ahead of her now, running awkwardly in his boots but moving quickly. Louise kicked the shoes off, picked them up and ran fast, easily catching Webb. Together, with Mamuka behind them, they raced up the steps to the guesthouse and the short flight of stairs inside that led to the hallway.

The door was open. Louise reached it first and stopped in the opening. Birmingham lay on his back on the bed; his left trouser leg was torn and soaked in blood, which had darkened the sheet in a wide, still-spreading stain. His eyes were closed and his face was chalk white. Webb pushed Louise aside roughly, strode into the room and felt for the injured man's pulse.

"Is he . . . ?" Louise leaned against the doorjamb, weak with fear and hope.

"He's alive," Webb said, "but he's still losing blood.

Needs a tourniquet." He felt in his pocket, took out a clasp knife and cut the trousers from crotch to cuff. The wound was a long, pulpy gouge down the inside of the leg to a point just above the knee. Blood was coming from it in small, spasmodic spurts. Webb tore a wide strip from the sheets and bound it tightly around the leg above the wound. Birmingham groaned and his eyelids fluttered.

Webb said, "Peter, you there?"

"Yes, Mr Webb."

"We need hot water and some clean cloths, also a blanket, two blankets. Who does the doctoring in Alma?"

"Pastor Stoltenberg at the Maryborough Mission. He has been summoned. I will get the water and the blankets."

Louise forced herself to react. "Blankets?"

"Shock's the next problem. He needs to be warm and comfortable. Please pull the curtain over the window. He won't want bright light when he wakes up."

Louise pulled the curtains across and took a towel from the dresser. She moistened a corner of it with water from the drinking carafe and gently wiped sweat from her husband's forehead. She was surprised to find her hand steady. She was unaffected by the welling blood. "You've done this before."

"Hundreds of times," Webb said. "Much worse."

"And it happened to you?"

Webb checked the tourniquet and waved away flies that were beginning to buzz around the wound. "Wound in the left arm. Not this bad."

Louise longed to touch Webb's arm, to see the scar. She forced herself to move to the end of the bed. "How long will the doctor take to get here? Where's this place?"

"The Maryborough Mission? It's at the head of the next bay. About an hour by water, bit more by land."

It was only then that Louise noticed the gun. It was lying on the floor, almost under the bed — a long-barrelled revolver which was one of Birmingham's prizes. "He said it belonged to Tom Horn."

"What? Who?"

She pointed. "This gun."

Webb reached down and slid the gun into view. "Double-action Colt," he said.

"You know about guns?"

"A bit. Who was Tom Horn?"

"I think he was an outlaw. Tom likes to make out he's been a bit of a desperado in his time."

"Has he?"

Louise shook her head. "I don't think so. God, listen to us. We're here chatting and he's bleeding to death."

Webb examined the wound. "No, he's not. The bleeding's almost stopped. There's nothing else we can do."

"No. Will it matter if I smoke?"

Webb said it wouldn't. Louise found Birmingham's cigarettes and lit up. Webb pulled a chair up beside the bed and sat where he could adjust the tourniquet if necessary. Louise leaned against the wall near the window and smoked vigorously.

The flies buzzed loudly. Mamuka appeared with the blankets and Webb laid them carefully over Birmingham, who stirred but remained unconscious. He unwrapped the mosquito net and let it drop down over the bed.

"Mr Naismith should be accurately informed," Mamuka said.

Webb nodded. "Would you do that, Peter, please?"

He moved to the window and watched the groups of people gathering in the compound. After a few moments Naismith appeared, striding towards the guesthouse. Mamuka approached him and the DO waved him aside angrily.

"Naismith's on his way," Webb said. "Are you all right?"

"I wanted him dead," Louise said. "I prayed he was dead."

"Shh, it's not so terrible. It's normal. We'll talk later."

Naismith's voice from the doorway was surprisingly gentle. "The maid says the water's boiling. D'you want it now, Webb?"

"When the doctor comes," Webb said.

Naismith spoke in rapid pidgin to the maid and then came into the room, taking off his hat as he did so. He nodded to Louise and looked at the net-shrouded figure on the bed. "How is he?"

"Fainted," Webb said. "Severe leg wound. He may be in shock."

Naismith bent and picked up the revolver. He looked at Louise. "His?"

"Of course."

"What happened?"

Louise stubbed her cigarette out in an ashtray on the dresser. "I don't know. I left him sleeping. I was out for a walk."

"Amateurs shouldn't play with guns," the DO said. He examined the Colt carefully. "I think this thing has a hair trigger."

"It was a memento of some kind, Mrs Birmingham tells me," Webb said. "It must have gone off accidentally."

Naismith put his hat on a chair and carefully laid the revolver down beside it. "All wounds are dangerous in this climate. Are you all right, Mrs Birmingham? I've asked for some tea."

"Tea," Louise said. She almost laughed but stopped herself. "I'm all right."

"Maybe Mrs Birmingham would prefer a whisky," Webb said. He looked around the room.

Louise shook her head. "It's all gone. Tom drank it all. Where's that doctor? Isn't there a hospital here?"

"No, he'll have to go over to Patugi." Naismith checked his watch. "I can have the launch ready in a couple of hours."

Louise struggled to focus her attention on Tom. She willed herself to imagine his pain. "Thank you," she whispered.

Pastor Karl Stoltenberg was a pale-eyed, pale-haired man around fifty years of age. A native of Silesia, he was a passionate puritan with a keen nose for sin. Migrating from Prussia before the war, he arrived in Queensland as a Lutheran-trained missionary who had failed in several African fields. Pastor Stoltenberg was intolerant of native

customs, which he saw as a barrier to conversion. In
Queensland he discovered thousands of Melanesians almost
totally detached from their traditional religion, unwelcome
in the established churches and desperately seeking
comfort. Very quickly, he married the wealthy widow of
a Maryborough sugar planter and established a mission to
the 'kanakas'. The Maryborough Evangelical South Sea
Islands Mission flourished until the repatriation of the
islanders in 1906, when its congregation was reduced in
a matter of months to one-tenth of its former size.

In Queensland, Stoltenberg experienced the only success he had ever known, and he was reluctant to surrender
it. He persuaded his wife to fund a shift of the mission back
to the 'kanaka' homeland, specifically to Murdo, whence
a large number of his adherents had come. He laboured in
this field for almost twenty years and established Christian
villages along the east coast of the island, in the face of
opposition from the pagans and scant encouragement from
Will Naismith.

Stoltenberg's ambition to lead a crusade had been almost
extinguished by disappointment. His followers were pious
and poverty-stricken, not welcome as plantation labourers,
exposed to the collection of 'the rate' and not skilled in
any of the traditional arts. Stoltenberg's medical skills were
adequate — he could amputate mangled limbs, set broken
ones and treat ulcers.

Now he bustled into the room in the guesthouse where
Tom Birmingham lay, ignored the Europeans present and
gestured for Mamuka to lift the mosquito net.

"Water," Stoltenberg said.

Naismith snapped his fingers; feet scurried in the hall
and two large tin basins of steaming water appeared within
a minute. Stoltenberg opened his case, removed instru-
ments and bottles and began cleaning the wound.

"How bad is it, doctor?" Louise said.

Stoltenberg's clipped, angry tone suggested he resented
using English rather than German, but he spoke the
language fluently. "The bullet remains. I must extract it.
The man looks strong. He should survive the operation."

"Do you need any help, Stoltenberg?" Naismith asked.

The missionary shook his head. "A boy to fetch and carry. The rest of you please leave the room."

There was no argument. Mamuka nodded at Webb's enquiring glance. Naismith, Webb and Louise filed out as Stoltenberg prepared a syringe.

Naismith stood in the hall holding his hat and the gun. Suddenly he appeared awkward, no longer in control of the situation. Louise, looking older and more serious than before, reminded him painfully of Amelia. "I'll have to make out a report," he said gruffly. "Accidental shooting, I should think."

"Yes," Louise said. "The gun must have misfired or something."

"Mm," Naismith fumbled with the catch to release the cylinder. "Practically an antique."

"Let me see it." Webb took the Colt, dropped the cylinder with a practised movement and let the spent cartridge and five more spill into his hand. He snapped the mechanism shut and put the revolver and the bullets in his pocket.

Naismith checked the impulse to protest, nodded, replaced his hat and stalked off towards the stairs. From inside the room came the sound of metal hitting metal.

"He's got the bullet out," Webb said. "That was quick. Must know what he's doing."

"I'd like a drink."

"I haven't got anything, I'm afraid. The houseboy has a few sly bottles, I'm told. We could probably persuade him to give us a drink, if that's all right."

Webb and Louise went down the stairs to the room that served as a sort of parlour-cum-smoking-and-reading room. Newspapers were thrown haphazardly into open wicker baskets and onto the seats of chairs; books were scattered about on two low tables. Webb called for the house servant and spoke to him in pidgin; Louise caught the words "whisky and water", but nothing more. They cleared two chairs of papers and waited in silence until the man appeared with a half-full bottle of Johnnie Walker

and a bottle that had once contained Booth's gin but now
held water.

"It's one hell of a situation," Louise said. "What would
we do if we were in New York or London?"

"And you had a husband?"

"Yes, there's no avoiding that."

The blood was thudding in Webb's head. He remembered the short, hectic leaves in London — the meetings
in Piccadilly, the taxi drives to Kensington hotels, the trains
to Brighton. "Be discreet, I suppose."

"No chance of that here."

"No."

"Are you thinking about affairs you've had?"

"Yes, sort of abstractly."

Louise laughed but smothered the sound by raising her
glass. "I'd love to hear about them all, every detail. And
where you grew up and went to school and about your
childhood sweetheart. My God, I'm babbling."

"It's all right."

"It's not!" Louise said fiercely. "It's not all right. I don't
want to go to Hemisphere and nurse Tom back to health.
To hell with him. Are you shocked?"

Webb shook his head. "If we'd met on the ship we
probably would have got off in Brisbane."

"Or cast ourselves adrift in a boat."

The houseboy hovered near the table, and Webb looked
up at him. "Yes?"

A folded slip of paper was extended. *Wailis bilong Missi.*

Louise stared uncomprehendingly. Webb took the paper
and nodded to the man. "*Tenkyu.* It's a wireless message."
He handed the paper to Louise, who read it quickly and
put it on the table. "What?" Webb said.

"It's from New York, from my . . . from Tom's publisher.
They tell him they're not sending any money and suggest
he call off the trip and the book."

"Can they do that?"

Louise finished her drink. She reached for the bottle and
poured more whisky. "Can I have a cigarette, please? Yes,
they can do it. You know the funny part? They're calling

off the rest of my honeymoon, but they're too late." Her
voice wavered on the edge of hysteria.

Webb gave her a cigarette and filled her glass with water.
"Whisky won't help. You've got to try . . ."

He broke off, as Pastor Stoltenberg was signalling from
the doorway. Webb beckoned, but the missionary shook
his head.

"Go and see what he wants," Louise said. "I'll be OK."

Ordinarily Webb would have carried his drink when he
crossed a room to talk to someone, but some instinct made
him put his scotch on the table before he approached the
missionary.

"I do not enter premises where ardent spirits are being
consumed," Stoltenberg said.

"I see. Your privilege, of course. Do you want to speak
to Mrs Birmingham? I'm afraid she's still rather upset."

Stoltenberg did not answer. He looked past Webb to
where Louise sat, smoking and sipping her drink.
Stoltenberg's thin mouth tightened. "Not necessary. You
appear to be in the woman's confidence."

"I don't like your tone, doctor."

"My title is Pastor, I minister more to souls than bodies."

"In this case it's your doctoring that's relevant. I don't
mean to be rude."

Stoltenberg shrugged. "You English put too much
importance on being polite at the expense of being honest.
No matter. I have extracted the bullet and clamped the
artery. It was not severed but the damage is considerable,
and Mr Birmingham is not in good physical condition."

"You said he looked strong."

"Outwardly. I suspect he has liver damage, probably
from excessive alcohol intake over time. Or possibly from
earlier bouts of malaria."

"Earlier?"

"I see signs of it. Has Mr Birmingham spent much time
in the tropics?"

"Some time, certainly. How much, I don't know."

"Alcohol and malaria, malaria and alcohol. They are
dynamite and fuse. So his removal to a better climate and

more civilised medical circumstances is advisable."

"Mr Naismith has made his launch available to take him to Patugi tonight."

The missionary shook his head. "Not tonight, not for several days. He should not be moved. He has a fever, rapid pulse and has lost much blood. I should advise keeping him here for a time. Then he should go to Patugi and leave the tropics as soon as possible."

"Any other treatment at the moment?"

"I have administered morphine but he will experience pain when its effects diminish. He will need water, sponging, light food and rest. Is Mrs Birmingham competent to nurse him?"

Stoltenberg's tone implied that she was not. Webb said, "She will be very grateful for your attention, doctor. Will you be available to look at Mr Birmingham again?"

The missionary put on his soft cloth hat, covering his lank, straw-coloured hair. "In two days. I understand that you have come to study the native customs, Mr Webb? That you are an anthropologist?"

"Yes."

"Not German science's most notable achievement, in my view. I exercise the privilege of my calling by presuming to advise you, Mr Webb. I fear you are about to become immersed in sin."

Webb was almost amused. "I think I would prefer to call it culture, Mr Stoltenberg, or tradition."

"I was not referring to the natives. Your behaviour has been observed."

Before Webb could react, the missionary had turned and left. Webb walked slowly back to his seat.

"What was all that about?" Louise said.

Webb sat down and took a gulp of his drink. "Being hanged for a sheep," he said.

15

Louise Birmingham had never nursed anybody, never having shared the passion for the idea of nursing current among fashionable young women during and after the war. Never seriously ill herself and blessed with healthy parents, she had seen sickness only at second hand — in the houses of friends and relatives, and there professionals had been hired or servants did the necessary tasks. Not that the role allotted to her in this case was taxing — she was not required to change her husband's dressings, or administer medicine. The missionary would do that himself. Hers was a watching brief — to sponge Birmingham's forehead, readjust the bedding if he moved it and give him water when required.

She took up her post immediately after dinner, which she had eaten alone. Webb had disappeared and she had politely refused Keith Larke's offer of company. She sat in a pool of lantern light with a book, beside the bed, and tried to read, but couldn't concentrate. She went out onto the balcony and smoked until she was sick of the sound of the sea and the taste of tobacco. Then she went to the

bathroom and washed herself, cleaned her teeth and
applied perfume. Back in the room, she wiped sweat from
her husband's flushed brow and attempted to measure his
pulse as she had seen nurses do in films. She lost the count
and gave up. She wanted a drink but was aware of the shock
waves that would have resultd had she put a request to the
servant.

"God damn you, Tom," she said aloud. "Why didn't you
kill yourself and be done with it?"

"Louise . . ."

"God, oh, Tom, I didn't mean . . ."

"Louise . . . marry Louise . . . marry Clementine . . .
marry . . . marry Louise . . ."

Birmingham was muttering in his drugged sleep and
twitching slightly. Louise lifted the mosquito net and
examined him almost clinically. His jaws were slack. *That's
good, isn't it?* she thought. *That he hasn't gone rigid? Or is
that only lockjaw, or rabies?* She almost giggled at the thought
of rabies. Then she remembered Webb saying that
Stoltenberg had mentioned malaria. *What are the symptoms?*
She recalled that Tom had a book on tropical diseases in
what he called his 'equatorial kit'. She dropped the net back
into place and began to hunt through the bags. She took
the book, Dr Kenneth Bruce's *Tropical Diseases — Their
Avoidance and Treatment,* over to the light and checked the
entry under 'malarial fever'.

'The febrile complaints so classed', Louise read, 'consist
of intermittent fever, or ague, remittent fever, and yellow
fever.' References to 'quotidian, tertian and quartum' forms
of the fever failed to enlighten her, and she skipped to the
warning that 'yellow fever is the most dangerous of the
varieties' and the sombre information that 'malarial fevers,
once contracted, typically recur throughout the remainder
of the sufferer's life and may result in gradual and
progressive debilitation'.

She was aware now that her own complexion had
undergone some yellowing which, Tom had told her, was
the result of taking the malarial-preventive quinine. She
put the book down and peered at Birmingham through

the netting. Was he more yellow than before? She couldn't tell. The words 'gradual and progressive debilitation' echoed inside her head. Not a happy prospect. Birmingham groaned and stirred. Suddenly, she felt intensely sorry for him. He had been kind to her, considerate when it mattered, and unfailingly generous. He had wanted her to share his life, and it was not his fault that the life had diminished to the point where he was a penniless invalid, without prospects and a long way from home. *Did he try to kill himself?* It seemed unlikely. He did not even know about Waldeck & Marsh's decision to cut off his money. On the other hand, he had taken several blows to his self-esteem and was well aware of trouble brewing in New York. Still, Louise could hardly believe that buoyant, blustering Tom Birmingham could be capable of suicidal despair. Then she remembered the diary. Self-pitying Tom Birmingham, self-doubting Tom Birmingham. And if he knew that his wife of ten weeks was in love with another man . . .

It was the first time she had allowed the thought to fully form in her mind. *In love.* What did it mean? What did it matter? Possibly everything to Birmingham, possibly a great deal to her. And what to Richard Webb?

The air in the room seemed to grow more stifling, as if the slight breeze had ceased altogether. She opened the door to the hallway in an attempt to create a cross-draught and went out onto the balcony. She peered at a strange shape near the guesthouse front steps and, having excellent vision, made out the figure of the police guard, squatting with his rifle across his knees.

Keith Larke appeared from the shadows. "You there! What d'you think you're doing?"

The policeman stood slowly and moved the rifle to his shoulder.

"You were sleeping on duty!"

"No, *masta*."

"Don't 'no, *masta*' me. You're on report. What's your name?"

Louise could not distinguish the Murdoan's muttered

response. Larke made an entry in a notebook and stalked away.

"God help us when he's in charge," Louise murmured to herself.

"Who?" Richard Webb said from the doorway.

Louise turned as Webb stepped into the room. He moved to the bed and looked down at Birmingham. A slight nod, and then he was standing beside her in the warm, still air. Louise smelled a faint but sharp aroma she couldn't identify. She saw him lick his lips and run his tongue over his teeth. He made a slight sucking sound. "Sorry," Webb said. "I've been chewing betel. It's dried my mouth out rather. Be all right in a minute. Who were you talking about?"

Louise pointed to where the guard was standing bolt upright by the steps. "A few minutes ago he was squatting down, nicely hidden, then our stupid Mr Larke came along and bawled him out. Accused him of sleeping on guard or something ridiculous. I don't know why the man didn't hit him."

"He'd have gone to the stockade if he had. Six months on the grass-cutting, wharf-mending gang, I shouldn't wonder. But you're right, young Larke has a hell of a lot to learn. How's Tom?"

"He seems to be all right, a bit restless. You've been with the natives, have you?"

Webb nodded. "Some To'beili. Very worried they are, too. I can't quite make it all out, but I don't think Eglito intends to let matters stand where they are."

"Does he know what Naismith's planning?"

Webb laughed. "The people I was talking to do, so you can bet Eglito does, down to the last detail. That's unless Naismith has a secret plan, something he hasn't spoken to anyone about."

"Is that likely?"

"It's what I'd do in his place."

"And if I were in Eglito's place, I'd have a secret plan too," Louise said.

"There's talk of a big swear."

"What's that?"

"I'm not sure. Something like a vow, but more than that. The dedication of an action to the ancestors." Webb shook his head. "I don't know enough, but it's a very traditional thing and involves witchcraft and violence."

"Against whom?"

"At its worst, against everybody." Webb gripped the balcony rail. Acutely aware of the woman beside him, stimulated by the betel and the talk of conflict, he was in the mood for an emotional engagement of some kind, for better or for worse. He reached into the pocket of his bush jacket and took out a flat bottle. "I thought you might like a drink. And we should have a talk. Come along to my room. Tom'll be all right for a while."

Louise almost ran from the room, scarcely glancing at her husband as she did so. Webb opened his door, and she brushed against him as she went into the room. They stood in the darkness close together, and Webb put his arms around her. They kissed hard and urgently; Webb was careful not to hold her too tightly. She pressed against him and felt him harden; as she moved her body against his growing erection, her own response ran through her like a convulsion. The sensation in Webb's lips and tongue was a little deadened by the betel, and Louise gasped as his mouth bruised hers. She broke the kiss, took his head in her hands and kissed him more softly, lightly brushing his mouth.

"Don't talk," Louise said. "I don't want to talk now."

They undressed quickly and touched and stroked each other eagerly, with tenderness and curiosity. Louise thrust up hard as he entered her; she put her hands around, joined them behind his back and drew him down with a strength she didn't know she had. Webb felt the bite of her hard bones, and then the softness of her and the warmth. He lifted himself to begin to pump the way he had with the French whores and the London wives, but she held him down, immobile.

"Don't move," she gasped. "I like you there. Just stay there."

He stayed. After a time she said, "All right," and he moved slowly and rhythmically, and she moved with him until he came in a long, shuddering spasm that he fought to hold off but finally surrendered to.

"I'm sorry," he whispered. "It's been a long time."

"Don't worry. It felt wonderful. I'll get there next time."

The bed was narrow and hard, and Webb's weight began to discomfort her; Louise wriggled, and he eased himself off. They lay side by side, their bodies touching and their hands exploring.

"You've made love to married women before," Louise said.

"Not with their husbands in the next room."

"Are we very terrible?"

"It depends who we hurt. There's no children involved for a start. That's good."

"You haven't got a wife, have you?"

Webb smiled in the darkness. She felt the movement and traced his lips with a fingertip. "No," he said. "No wife."

"Fiancee, sweetheart, mistress?"

He shook his head and didn't speak.

"So it comes down to Tom."

Webb said, "And ourselves. In the war you didn't have to think like this. Most likely you'd be dead soon, and both of you knew it."

Louise was almost angry. "The war's been over for almost ten years. You must have had other women since then."

"I stayed friendly with a few of the women I knew then. Just friendly and a bit more, you know. Not serious. In a way, you're the first since the war. Unconnected with the war, do you follow?"

Louise kissed him. "I didn't want to be connected with your war widows. I wanted to be something new for you."

"You are."

"But . . . "

"No buts." He kissed her.

"You taste funny."

"Must be the betel. You take it with a sort of lime paste

and it does strange things to your mouth. Would you rather taste whisky?"

"I'll try the betel with you sometime, but the whisky would be great right now."

Webb swung his legs off the bed, stood and moved across the room to where his jacket lay on the floor. Louise heard him grunt as he located the bottle, and then the chink of glasses. "Water?"

"Doesn't matter. Richard, I can't see a thing. How come you can see in the dark?"

Webb returned to the bed, picked up her hand and placed the glass of whisky in it. "There. Cheers. I can't exactly see in the dark, not really. It's something you got used to at the front. You had to know exactly where everything was — rifle, gas mask, whistle, that sort of thing. One minute the flares and bombardment made the place like a high street at midday, and the next it'd be pitch dark. Your life depended on knowing where things were. Became a habit."

Louise had struggled up to a sitting position; the hard back board on the bed bit into her shoulders and Webb pushed a pillow behind her. "Thanks. Maybe Tom's right."

Webb drank some whisky and didn't speak.

"Tom missed the war, and it seems to be the tragedy of his life. I think he believes there's something totally different about men who went."

"There is," Webb said. "A hell of a lot of them are dead. Tom's wrong — if you missed it, you were bloody lucky. There's a lot to live for, especially for him with . . ."

"You were going to say with a woman like me."

Webb nodded.

"That brings us back to where we were before."

"Yes."

"Do you think this is just sex, or loneliness or adventure or . . ."

"Or what?"

"I was going to say selfishness."

"Love is always selfishness, a sort of shared selfishness, if that makes any sense."

"You said love."

Webb finished his whisky, took her glass and put it on the bedside table. He put his arms around her and drew her down. "I did, didn't I? I did say that."

They made love again, more slowly. Louise climaxed and let out a long hiss of pleasure that was loud in the small, dark room. She fell asleep almost immediately; after a time, Webb disentangled himself, wrapped a towel around his waist and went out onto the balcony. He peered around the partition that divided the balcony off into sections for each room. He could detect no movement from the Birminghams' room. Over the noise of the sea and the soft murmurings of the jungle, he could hear Tom Birmingham's regular, adenoidal snore. Webb reached through the window and took Louise's half-drunk whisky. Her lipstick had smeared the edge and he could taste it as he sipped the drink.

Things are not going according to plan, he thought. *But when did things ever do that?* He hadn't planned on the war, or getting shot, or going to Oxford. Things happened. Maybe Eglito would launch a full-scale attack on Alma, and nobody would be going anywhere, not he, not Naismith, not Tom Birmingham. As he looked down at the flag hanging listlessly at the mast and the guards maintaining their watch in the dog hours, he thought the outpost seemed vulnerable; all the force appeared to lie with the sea and the bush-covered escarpment towering over everything. From those quarters drama could be expected.

Meantime, the drama for him was all in the two rooms of the guesthouse. Webb knew that he wanted to carry out his study, to understand the To'beili world, enter into it as far as he could. And he knew why: the war had made him impatient with European civilisation, mistrustful of it. He wanted to at least know about something else. He wondered if Louise would understand. He thought she would. He wanted to wake her up and tell her about it, and the thought made him laugh aloud.

"What? Richard?" Louise's voice from the room was startled and dislocated.

"Here," Webb said quietly. "Out here."

"What're you doing?"

Webb went back into the room. "I was drinking your drink and trying to work out how the hell we can stay together."

16

The day before he was due to set out on his demonstration of personal and symbolic power, Will Naismith sat as magistrate in a special court session at Alma. The court was convened for seven in the morning, before the heat made the police inattentive, prisoners irritable and witnesses sleepy. Naismith could not ignore the build-up of cases awaiting his judgment, nor entrust them to Keith Larke. He rationalised that attending the court would be the best possible instruction for the cadet.

As he sat at the table in the courtroom which adjoined his office, Larke, very correct in his whites and tense with anticipation beside him, Naismith reflected on the vagaries of life. He had twice been a prisoner in the dock himself: once, as a youth, accused of stealing a horse. He'd stoutly resisted the charge, provided an explanation of the circumstances that led to his being apprehended riding a horse which had undoubtedly been stolen, and was acquitted. It had taken Naismith two months to locate the actual thief who had misrepresented himself as the owner of the animal. It had taken him ten minutes to give the man a thrashing, in a fight much enjoyed by onlookers and blind-eyed by the police.

Naismith rapped the table with the heel of his hand and called the court to order. Larke ran his eye down the list of prisoners and charges (Fa'a Boa for assault; Batiana, theft; Tarunga, abusive language; Hatavi, absconding from indentured service) and made a mental note to try to secure a gavel for the day he would sit in judgment.

Naismith dealt with the cases swiftly and efficiently. He questioned the prisoner and witnesses, using the Alma language when possible, otherwise pidgin, and resorting to translation only in cases of real incomprehensibility. In a British court, his judgments would have seemed arbitrary and harsh; something very close to a presumption of guilt was operating and gaol sentences and fines were handed out in what looked like a capricious fashion.

"Surely he should have gone to gaol, sir," Larke whispered in Naismith's ear after the DO had sentenced Tobias Manu'loa to a fine of a hundred pieces of red shell money for destroying Siole's canoes.

"What good would that do Siole?" Naismith said. "This way Manu'loa will have to sell his canoes to get the shell money. His pride'll take a terrible knock and Siole'll consider himself even."

"What happens to the shell money? It's not worth anything, is it?"

"Not to us. But it'll buy information and co-operation. Baekani'll know what to do with it."

Baekani again, Larke thought. *It's always Baekani.* He almost drowsed through the next few cases but came sickeningly awake when he heard Naismith bellow at the top of his voice: "Liar!"

A six-foot Murdoan, wearing a police laplap but without the uniform shirt or cartridge belt, stood in front of Naismith's table staring defiantly at the DO. Two policemen, smaller in stature, stood nervously beside him holding him by the upper arms.

"No, *masta.*"

Larke searched the charge list in confusion and located the case: Corporal Usulia, rape.

Naismith spoke harshly in the Alma language. "You took this woman by force to shame her brother. If he had fought, you would have killed him."

"He is a coward. He did not fight. I did not take the woman."

"Liar," Naismith shouted. "You took her, then she climbed on the roof of your hut and shat over your head."

Usulia bellowed and sprang forward, throwing off the restraining arms of the police; he aimed a wild, scything blow at Naismith's head as if he had a *sarip* in his hand. Naismith swayed back and stood in one swift movement; his left hand shot out and gripped the man's hair; Usulia's head was travelling forward as Naismith's right fist landed with full force on his nose. Naismith kept his grip and punched again, landing solidly on Usulia's jaw. The islander slid to the floor unconscious.

"Guilty," Naismith said. "Ten years' hard labour."

Larke stared as the policemen dragged their former colleague from the court. Blood from Usulia's damaged nose splattered the scrubbed floorboards. Naismith rubbed his skinned knuckles and took a sip of water. "What are you gaping at, Mr Larke?"

"N . . . nothing, sir."

"Good. Would you mind asking one of the boys to get us some tea? This is thirsty work."

While Larke went to send for the tea, Naismith thought about his other court appearance as a defendant — in South Africa as a sergeant in the Light Horse, charged with insubordination. He was guilty and everyone knew it; it was also known that the officer who had laid the charge was a fool. Naismith's refusal of the order to set fire to a Boer farm after the occupants' resistance had been overcome was officially deplored by the field court martial. He was stripped of his rank and severely reprimanded. After the hearing the presiding officer took Naismith aside and offered him a cigarette, which was refused.

"A western district man, I understand, Sergeant Naismith?"

Naismith had saluted. "Private Naismith. Yes, sir."

"I'm from Gippsland myself. That whole valley was tinder dry — it would have gone up like a haystack."

"Yes, sir."

Naismith had his stripes back within a month and received his commission soon after.

Larke's voice jerked the DO out of his reverie. "I've ordered the tea, sir."

"Good. There was a lesson in that episode for you, Mr Larke. These people understand anger. They respect it."

Larke nodded. "Why wasn't the woman called to give evidence?"

Naismith initialled the sentencing order the clerk had placed before him. "She's dead. One of Usulia's clan killed her for the insult. We're still looking for him. Ah, here's the tea. Why don't you handle the next case?"

Larke's hand shook as he reached for his cup. "Sir?"

Naismith spooned in sugar. "Simple enough. Illegal possession of playing cards. He's guilty. Give him six months."

Larke sipped his tea and concentrated on forming his soft features into a sternness he did not feel. As he waited for the prisoner to be brought forward, his mind jumped to what he would write in his next report to the resident commissioner: *Mr Naismith is a violent and impulsive man who cares nothing for the forms and procedures of British justice. In court the other day he assaulted a prisoner, knocking him unconscious, because of an imagined threat to his own person. His servant Bikani is entrusted with suborning witnesses and otherwise manipulating the course of justice by using a fund of money built up from fines imposed by the DO . . .*

Richard Webb stared over the side of the Burns Philp cutter *Woodlark* at the still, translucent water of the Alma lagoon. It was late afternoon under a heavy sky, and small phosphorescent flashes appeared in the water. Tiny, silver fish darted under the boat, nibbled at the rope that held the dinghy and disappeared in a shadowy flutter as larger fish swam near. Webb emptied the dregs of his tea mug overboard and created havoc among the scooting fish.

"So that's how things stand," Webb said. "I'm sorry to burden you with all this, but I had to tell someone or go crazy."

"I'm glad you did," Clements said. He was sitting in a shaded section of the deck carefully cleaning crusted dirt from a hafted stone axe. The dirt was falling on a sheet of newspaper spread at Clements' feet. "For someone who lives life vicariously as I do, this is a treat. I don't mean I don't take your problem seriously, I do. I'm just saying I'm the right person to tell."

"Thank you."

"Damned tricky, this." Clements used an old toothbrush to clear dirt from the bindings that held the stone head to the handle. "If I'm not careful the whole thing could just fall apart. This is a hundred years old at least."

"What did you pay for it?"

"Top price. Five bob. Gently does it. Telling me about it's one thing, solving your problem's quite another."

"I don't think there is a solution." Webb let out a short laugh.

Clements glanced up, surprised. "I can't see the funny side, myself."

"I was thinking about a chap who went to Mexico to study the Aztec trade patterns. He fell in love with a Mexican whore and applied to change his dissertation topic to prostitution in Yucatan, or something such. Christ, adultery in the British Jeremiah Islands Protectorate, how does that sound?"

"There's not a lot of it," Clements said. "My opinion is that the heat weakens the sex drive. Of course, I wouldn't know much about that sort of thing. I'm speaking as an observer. Well, what can you do? Nothing. You go to Sunburi, she goes to Patugi with her husband. You write to each other. You finish your work, Birmingham gets back on his feet. You and Mrs B get together, or you don't. QED."

"That sounds so . . . tepid."

"D'you want to abandon your study? Chuck in anthropology?"

"No. I can't do that. I have to see things through. They told me that after the war."

Clements put down the toothbrush and gave Webb his full attention. "Who?"

"The doctors, the psychiatrists. When you live for a time not knowing when your last second's coming, you lose something — a sort of refusal to believe in tomorrow can set in. The cure's to complete things, finally and utterly, and move on to something else. They tell me you can rebuild the belief in tomorrow."

"Mm. Interesting, and very tricky for you, especially if Mrs Birmingham's the something else you want to move on to."

"She is. And you're right. The doctors warned me against wanting two things at once. I've been a one-thing-at-a-time man for years now."

"Have you told her any of this?"

"Tried to, but she thinks I'm being evasive."

"What's her solution?"

Webb shrugged. "She has more problems than I. She feels guilty about Birmingham, uncertain about me and unsure of herself."

"In what way?"

Webb was suddenly aware that he had been addressing most of his remarks to the fish. He turned and watched Clements resume his cautious cleaning of the axe head. "She's actually begun to like this place."

"Alma? She must be mad."

"We've walked to a few of the villages, spent some time in them. Her pidgin's come along well, she's taken some photographs which could be stunning."

Clements nodded. "I see, makes it worse. You could be a team."

"No chance of that. And I gather Birmingham's acting strangely."

"Stay here?" Louise said. "You can't stay here. You have to go to the hospital."

"No I don't, hon. The reverend doctor says I'm healing fine. I can get back on my feet right here." Tom Birmingham was sitting up in bed, propped by two pillows. He was pale but fresh-looking, as if he had had a long, restorative sleep. In fact the morphine had caused him to sleep for almost thirty-six hours and he had taken frequent naps over the next twenty-four. Now, shaved and bathed and a little leaner in the face, he looked better than he had for months. Louise, feeling slightly cruel, had judged him sufficiently recovered to be given the cable from Waldeck & Marsh. Birmingham had received it calmly.

"The reverend gentleman seems to be paying you a great deal of attention," Louise said.

Birmingham nodded. "He's a good man. Really been around and knows how things work. He's got his finger on the pulse here, I can tell you."

"What do you mean?"

Birmingham tapped the side of his nose. "Trouble. I can smell it."

Louise's patience, exercised for days as her attachment to Webb deepened and her concern for her husband persisted, snapped. "I'm not surprised you can smell goddamn trouble. That cable you got was nothing but trouble. No money, no book. That's trouble!"

Birmingham leaned back against the pillows. "Don't worry about that, Louie. Everything's going to be all right. We got enough money to stay here for a while. As long as it takes."

Louise detested the name Louie, which Birmingham seemed to be using more and more often. She clenched her fists below the level of the bed where he couldn't see them. She wanted to hit him. "As long as it takes for *what?*"

Birmingham's eyes, almost clear of their former blood-shot cloudiness, opened wide. "Why, for my leg to heal. What else?"

Louise looked at him uneasily. In some ways he was like

the old Tom, buoyant and optimistic, but there was something else, a secretiveness, she didn't like. She looked at her watch. An hour until it was time to meet Richard. She stood and moved towards the door. "I think there's some beer in the Coolgardie safe. Would you like one?"

"In the what?"

"Coolgardie safe. It's something the Aussies thought up. You put a wet burlap sack over a box and leave it in a breeze. The evaporation cools the goods inside. Clever, huh? Something for your book, maybe."

"There isn't going to be a book, and no, I don't want any beer."

"No book? Then why stay here?"

"There's other things, bigger things."

"I don't understand, Tom. Let me get you a drink and we can talk . . ."

"I told you I don't want a drink. I'm not drinking any more. The stuff was killing me. I don't want to talk either. Just wait and watch, Louie, wait and watch. But I could give you a word of advice."

Louise felt guilt rise to the surface at the tone of his voice. *Is this it?* she thought. She said nothing.

"You oughta be careful about the way you're dressing, hon. That laplap thing and the blouse and bare legs. You're going native."

"It's comfortable for walking around in."

"You're doing a bit of that, I hear."

"I've been going to the villages, taking pictures. I've got some great stuff. Come to think of it . . ." Louise moved over to the dresser and picked up her camera. Birmingham's camera and field glasses were there, also the new bushknife and kerosene lantern, but the gun cases were missing. "Where're your guns?"

Birmingham was studying a folding map of the island; he looked up as if surprised that Louise was still in the room. "I lent 'em to people who need 'em more than me."

"Who?"

Birmingham chuckled. "Naismith, maybe. If you're going walking, don't let me hold you up."

"Is there anything you want?"

"No. Dr Stoltenberg's stopping by soon. He's bringing me what I need."

"He's up to something, I know he is. He's like a bear with a honey jar."

Webb had read in the newspapers about the successful publication a few years before of *Winnie the Pooh*. He'd been amused by the illustrations. "Christopher Robin and Winnie the Pooh," he said. "I didn't think it'd catch on in America."

Louise was sitting on a log trying to weave coconut palm leaves into a tight pattern for basket making. A sharp edge cut her finger. "Goddamnit! What are you talking about, Richard?"

Webb explained about the children's story, but Louise scarcely listened. "You English haven't got a monopoly on bears and honey jars. I bet you haven't got any goddamn bears in England anyway. We've got millions of them."

Webb sat on the log, took out his handkerchief and wiped the blood from the cut finger. "It's not deep. Suck it for a bit."

"You just want to stop me talking."

"Why are we quarrelling?"

Louise looked at his dark, thin face, tight with strain he was trying not to show. To please him, she licked briefly at her finger. "I don't know," she said. "All those songs about being in love. They don't say anything about your lover going off into the jungle and your husband becoming a religious crazy."

"Tom?"

"He's as thick as thieves with that Stoltenberg character. I can't stand that guy."

Webb nodded. "I didn't exactly take to him, either. And I don't like what I hear about him."

"Tom's quit drinking. He's talking about . . . Christ, I can't do this!" Louise threw the half-plaited leaves on the sand.

Webb put his arm around her shoulders and drew her

close to him. They were on a rocky stretch of beach on
the north side of the lagoon. The land behind it was too
poor for gardening and the rocky foreshore was unsuitable
for fishing. Later, when the tide was out, women would
gather shellfish from the rocks and muddy pools, but now
the beach was deserted. However, it was still not private
enough. Webb and Louise had only had two nights of
intimacy. On awakening Tom Birmingham was demanding, and after his first long session with Pastor Stoltenberg
Louise had fancied that he was watchful. Frustrated
himself, Webb searched for words to comfort her in what
he recognised was her worse frustration. "It's good you're
staying on this island," he said.

"Why?"

"When I'm fit enough I can walk across in a day and
a half," Webb said. "*You* look fit enough to walk across it
now."

"If only I could."

"Look, Louise, we don't know what's going to happen.
Maybe Colin Clements could bring you for a visit soon,
be a sort of chaperone."

Louise stared at him. "You've told him?"

"Yes."

"What?"

"That I love you . . . and that there are difficulties."

Louise laughed. "And what was his advice?"

Webb shrugged.

"God, I wish there was someone I could tell." Louise
put her hand on his arm and felt the muscle under the
cotton shirt. "But I'm glad you've told someone you love
me. That helps."

Webb said, "I'm going tomorrow."

"I know."

"I'll have a field radio," Webb said. "There's a good basic
radio system in the Protectorate. It's for official use only,
of course, but . . . " Webb tore a sheet from his notebook,
scribbled on it and handed the paper to Louise. "This is
the call sign. We're conspiring to misuse government
property."

Louise folded the sheet until it was two inches square. "I like that," she said. "I'll send you a message. And you've got to promise me you'll come across and see me before I have to go."

Webb promised, and kissed her.

17

Will Naismith's steam launch was named *Loloburu*, which meant 'west wind' in the language of the lagoon people to the south of Alma. It was a nickname the islanders had applied to Naismith himself, dating from the days when he had patrolled in a whaleboat. Periodically, the west wind hit the offshore islands hard, damaging the fragile stone and coral structures, uprooting trees that clung to the thin soil and causing people to evacuate to the mainland until they could rebuild their homes. So Naismith had been seen in the early days — a fierce wind, punisher of criminals, rooter-out of troublemakers and destroyer of places where his enemies thought themselves safe. It was a piece of vanity on Naismith's part to attach the name to his launch, of which he was inordinately proud.

Now, a day out from Alma, he sat under a canopy at the rear of the deck and evaluated the situation. He did not expect trouble at his first port of call. In Murdoan terms, Maka Maka was a cosmopolitan place; at the boundary between the Kweili and Oremi language groups, it was a 'passage' for numerous bush communities in the interior, boasting a trade store and a substantial copra-loading wharf. It was a place where Naismith's writ ran strongly. He would, he expected, collect taxes here, confiscate Sniders and reinforce the authority of the headman he had appointed a few years previously. And he would get intelligence of the state of feeling about Eglito and his defiance of the *gafamanu*.

The *Loloburu* entered the deep channel that ran through the reef to the Maka Maka passage. Smoke rose from the village fires, and the activity on the wharf and beach appeared normal: a copra schooner was loading and three canoes that had taken a net beyond the reef were beached while the fishermen divided the catch. Naismith had the tax rolls prepared and had co-opted a Maka Maka man to advise him on the value of the strings of shell money that some of the bush people would tender as payment. Naismith would use his judgment, rejecting some offers and insisting on coin when he judged the islanders had the ability to pay, accepting shell money in other cases with a warning to produce shillings next time. He expected to complete the collection in two sessions, one that afternoon and the other the following morning.

The headman greeted him respectfully as Naismith stepped onto the wharf.

"*Gut dei, masta.*"

"*Gut dei, Timoti. Oketa stap gut long hia?*"

"*Yes, masta. Oketa busman, oketa salwata man him pei nau.*"[*]

Naismith nodded, signalled to two armed police constables to accompany him, and walked up the beach in the direction of the leaf hut which was designated the *haus bilong reit*.[**] The hut, sitting on stilts a few feet high, had an open front that could be enclosed by means of two large panels. At present these stood propped against the side of the hut. Naismith sat at a table at the top of the short stairs. He was thus, even when sitting, about thirty centimetres

---

[*] "Good day, Timothy. Is everyone here well?"
"Yes, master. All the bush and saltwater people will pay now."
[**] tax collection house

above the head of the taxpayer, who would stand beside a policeman stationed on the first step. This was an arrangement carefully constructed by Naismith to symbolise the supremacy of the authority he represented. A large group of islanders assembled under the cover of a stand of Moreton Bay fig trees. The trees, grown from seeds brought from Australia more than fifty years before, underlined Maka Maka's acceptance of a wider world.

The collection began at one in the afternoon. Naismith was intensely occupied, greeting some of the people who were known to him, questioning the identity of others, discussing the method of payment, granting and with-holding exceptions and using the tax rolls as a means of taking a census and registering deaths. Disputes were few and Naismith's word was final. He seldom raised his voice. He looked up, almost for the first time, at 3.45 and saw that the man standing on the step in front of him extending his money was the last in line. He said nothing, registered the payment and cut a notch in the taxpayer's numbered wooden disc, the notch representing his receipt. Naismith kept his eyes on the roll, aware that Timoti, the headman, was standing nervously by.

"Tea," Naismith said.

The tea arrived and Naismith drank it, looking out at the clearing in front of the tax house. Activity on the beach and wharf had ceased; the clusters of people who had gathered under the Moreton Bay figs had melted into the bush. Naismith turned to Timoti and spoke to him in Kweili, which the Maka Maka man understood but disliked hearing. Naismith's use of it was a veiled insult.

"You told me that everyone was ready to pay the rate."

"I hoped that it would be so, sir."

"You hoped."

"Sir, I thought that the power of the *gafamanu* would stop the people talking about not paying the rate."

"What people?"

"Many, sir. Many of the bushmen."

Naismith reflected. Most of the money he had collected had come from the saltwater people, but this was as he had expected. He had been inattentive and had not noticed that virtually no one from the bush villages had paid. He could not afford to lose face so he made no reference to this. "The bushmen will pay tomorrow," he said flatly.

Timoti's voice was without inflection or emphasis. "Yes, sir."

Naismith felt a surge of alarm. He knew that tone, and that the headman meant the opposite of what he had said. This was a very significant denial of his authority. His only strategem was to deflect the threat. "How many Sniders have you collected, Timoti?"

"One, sir."

"One?"

"*Bipo Eglito, him killim . . .* "

"Shut your mouth!" Naismith was incensed; by switching to pidgin and emphasising that no rifles had been collected since Eglito went on the rampage, Timoti was making a point. Naismith could hardly believe it: here, at his first port of call, scarcely a day's march from Alma, he was encountering resistance and insults from his own appointee. His mind raced; in the early days he had imposed shell money fines, summarily sentenced men to work on wharves and bridges and expropriated pigs as methods of bringing people under control. Twice he had shot to kill. He had imagined that those days were over, and in any case he had never encountered passive resistance on this scale before. He was at a loss.

"Timoti, Eglito is an outlaw. He will be hanged."

The headman nodded; he appeared to be well pleased by this prospect. "Yes, sir. He will be hanged. Sir, the people want a *klinik*. They say they pay the *takus* and they should have a *klinik*. I am telling you what the people say, sir."

"And what do you say?"

Timoti said nothing.

Naismith knew that he needed time to consider this situation. That the headman had merely relayed the information and not acted as spokesman for those demanding a *quid pro quo* for paying the rate was a small consolation. Also, a sizable number of people *had* paid; he would need time to analyse them in terms of their clan affiliations and influence. He would need the assistance of Baekani. Naismith stood so abruptly that Timoti stepped back in alarm. "Give the Snider to this constable," Naismith indicated the nearest policeman. "That is all."

Timoti did not move.

"That is all, Timoti!"

It was far from being all, and both men knew it. Timoti relied on receiving a proportion of the shell money paid in lieu of the tax to reward his supporters and prop up his authority. To be deprived of this was a considerable blow to him. In his turn, Naismith had left the headman something serious to think about.

Almost the first thing Tom Birmingham had seen on coming out of his drugged sleep had been the cable from New York. His muddled mind had difficulty concentrating on the words but, to his surprise, when he had decoded the message he experienced a feeling of relief. As if by revelation, he realised that he did not want to write another book about the exploits of 'Redwood' Adams. He was sick of him, his confidence, athleticism, resourcefulness. *What a great chapter it'll make in the autobiography,* he thought. *How an author killed off his best-selling character, his meal ticket.* There was a sobering side to that thought, of course. Adams wasn't a best-seller any more, and Birmingham himself was in financial trouble, with a cancelled contract and a lawsuit hanging over him.

But, possibly because the morphine was still working in his system, the feeling of liberation prevailed over the problems. It was while he was in this mood that Pastor Karl Stoltenberg paid his first visit to his patient as a conscious, communicating person.

"I am pleased to see you responding so well, Mr Birmingham," the missionary said.

Birmingham had no idea of who the tall, pale-eyed man was, but when Stoltenberg enlightened him he was loud in his praise. "I've been wounded before, doc. I have to say you've done a great job."

Stoltenberg was removing bandages. "The war. Ah yes, we were all wounded one way or another. Remarkable."

"What?"

"The wound is very clean. No sign of infection. You must have a remarkable constitution."

"I'd say you were a damn fine doctor."

"No profanity, please, Mr Birmingham. I am also a minister of religion."

Tom Birmingham had seen some strange things in his travels — Indian fakirs, snake-charmers and firewalkers, Tibetan holy men and Yaqui shamans. Though an adherent of no religion, he was not a spiritual sceptic, and he had a respect for those who claimed to be in touch with a higher power. As Stoltenberg ministered to him with gentleness and a sure touch, he was receptive, open to influence. He felt that his life was about to change, and if a German missionary with healing hands was an instrument of that change, he would not resist. He apologised for his language and was in a mood to confess. "To tell you the truth, reverend," he said, "I'm not sure what got into me when I was handling that gun. Scares me a little. Maybe I was trying to . . . you know."

An experienced exploiter of human frailty, Stoltenberg recognised the tone of a help-seeker. He smiled benignly and continued to treat the wound. When he had re-dressed the injury and checked Birmingham's pulse and temperature, he poured a glass of water and handed it to Birmingham. "This should be your drink from now on, Mr Birmingham, if you wish to give thanks for your escape."

Birmingham had a raging thirst and had begun to think about whisky; he downed the drink in a couple of gulps and found it refreshing. "It's been a long time since I drank straight water, doc."

"Your life would change if you drank nothing else."

"Believe you're right. You think I'm going to be OK, then?"

"It's largely in your hands. When I first saw you, I recommended that you should leave these parts as soon as possible. You have damaged your constitution severely."

Stoltenberg wrapped up the discarded dressings, cleaned his hands with surgical spirit and packed his medical bag. "But an abstemious man can live anywhere."

"I'm on the wagon, as of now."

"I'll call in tomorrow."

In fact, the missionary came twice the following day, choosing times when Louise was not present. Birmingham's recovery was rapid, and he responded to Stoltenberg's flattery. On the second meeting, when they were drinking tea, Stoltenberg remarked that Murdo was on the brink of a cataclysm.

"How d'you mean, doc?"

"The forces of darkness are powerful on this island. William Naismith has done nothing to curtail them. Now he may reap the whirlwind."

"You don't like Naismith? Can't say I took to him myself."

"He has encouraged the pagans to remain what they were. The civilising influences of honest labour, church attendance and the wearing of decent clothes have never been part of his policy."

"Seems to keep his police in order."

Stoltenberg sniffed. "That is one of the worst aspects of his regime. The police trade in shell money. Do you know what the main function of shell money is, Mr Birmingham?"

"No."

"Bride price — for use in the buying and selling of human beings. I have laboured for ten years to stamp out this barbarous custom. But, I regret to say, even some of the mission people still practise it."

"Sounds bad."

"It is. The women are bought and sold like pigs, and married off to old men in ceremonies that culminate in sexual orgies."

The words and images excited Birmingham, who felt the early stirrings of an idea. When he saw Stoltenberg the following morning, he said, "Are you really saying that

Murdo Island could rebel against the British, reverend?"

"I prefer the term 'pastor'."

"Pastor. Is that what you're saying?"

"Yes. The bush people are only nominally under control here. No one is quite sure how many there are, or precisely where they are. Apart from the Christian communities, and not all of them are truly saved, the coastal people pay taxes, work and obey government regulations because they are exposed to Naismith's police and courts and have no choice. If they thought they could get away with it, many of them would revert to the previous state of things. The state of nature, as some people call it, which is really the state of sin."

"Uh huh. That's very interesting. How's the wound looking?"

While the missionary dealt with the wound, Birmingham formed the idea in his mind. *The man on the spot thinks the place is ready to blow,* he thought. *What if it happened? What would the Hearst papers pay for a series of articles by a famous writer, written on the spot as the balloon went up? And the book he could write. And the chapter it'd make in the autobiography!* It seemed to Tom Birmingham almost as if there had been divine intervention in his personal affairs. Here was the chance he'd been denied in 1918 — to be a man of action in fact, not just in print. He questioned the missionary closely about the state of Murdo and found him a mine of information, not only about the disposition, as he saw it, of the islanders, but about Naismith's habits, his relationship with certain trusted servants, and how the DO was viewed in the Protectorate.

"The Catholics and Anglicans approve of him," Stoltenberg said.

"How so?"

"They approve of heathenism. Their own practices are primitive and ritualistic, and they imagine they can graft Jeremian paganism onto the doctrines of Rome and Canterbury."

Birmingham's grasp of theology was limited; he was better at sports. "Who's against?" he said.

"My mission, the Seventh-day Adventists, the Wesleyans. Some of the less decadent Anglicans could be called waverers."

"But you wouldn't want to see this Eglito actually win? I mean, take over the island?"

Stoltenberg's smile was infinitely patient. He found the American stupid and slow thinking, but to convert a celebrity would be a feather in his cap. And so far the auguries were good — there was no sign of his having resumed drinking, no smell of tobacco. There was also little sign of his presence of the wife, which was a strong card in Stoltenberg's hand. "There is no danger of that. But a serious outbreak would have to be put down seriously. A warship to fire on some of the coastal villages would be a salutary lesson. And a properly mounted punitive expedition could lift the curtain on the interior of this dark island once and for all. Much good could come of it."

"Yeah, I can see that." Birmingham was thinking that the shelling of villages and punitive expeditions to the cannibalistic, pagan interior was the sort of stuff that sold newspapers. And probably long overdue, too — this was 1928 after all. Hidden valleys of primitive people belonged in Rider Haggard, not the real world. Besides, they probably all needed medicine and dental care.

"The behaviour of the police here at Alma is the critical thing," Stoltenberg said. "If they obey their orders, do nothing rash, Naismith may ride out the storm. But many of the police are anxious to revenge themselves against Eglito and the To'beili. Some of my people feel defenceless. Some of them are To'beili originally, but as Queensland-born Christians they have broken their clan ties. Pagans seeking vengeance may not make any distinctions."

"Can't they defend themselves?"

"Naismith has confiscated their weapons — an easy enough thing to do on the coast."

Birmingham rubbed his chin. *Need a shave,* he thought, *and that maid does a damn fine job of it.* "A man can always get hold of a gun or two," he said.

18

London, 17 February 1928

Ernest Childers took two pages of the lined foolscap paper that bore the heading 'Foreign Office — Internal', unscrewed the cap on his fountain pen and began to write. A modern young man, a double first graduate of Oxford who had scored well in the Civil Service entrance exams, Childers would have preferred to type his memoranda. However, the minister, Sir Hugh Stafford, was not a modern man, far from it. He would not willingly read typed documents and absolutely forbade them in areas where he had control. Over the behaviour of clerks charged with commenting on wireless messages from outposts within the High Commission for the Western Pacific, Sir Hugh's control was absolute. Childers wrote:

> Major Price-Kane's report is less than clear. While on the one hand he appears to wish to give the impression that the island of Murdo in the BJIP is virtually ungovernable unless important changes in policy and execution are made, he stresses that he has the situation 'under control'.
>
> The blame for the unrest Major Price-Kane lays at the feet of

District Officer Naismith, whom he accuses of 'unorthodoxy'. The High Commissioner, however, in an enclosure, expresses confidence in Mr Naismith and some doubts about the RC's capacity to handle a crisis.

It would appear that there is a lack of administrative cohesion in the BJIP, possibly owing to the employment of colonials as well as British personnel. An evaluation of the true nature of the situation on Murdo is made difficult by this disunity, but it should be noted that the island has a long and bloody history and has been the site of massacres and punitive reprisals.

Discretion suggests that firm action should be taken in the BJIP to allow no opportunity for French pretensions in the Pacific to gain expression and to still the concern for security in the region manifested by the government of the Commonwealth of Australia. In addition, such a policy has the advantage of demonstrating to the Japanese government and Japanese nationals in the BJIP that the British writ still runs in the Western Pacific. Support from Washington is assured.

Nicely put, Childers thought. *Judicious.*

The report, much minuted upon and glossed by other hands, reached Sir Hugh Stafford at the end of a long session with the departmental first assistant secretary, Hubert Dalziel.

"These bloody specks in the ocean are more trouble than they're worth," Stafford grunted. "What does this place produce, for God's sake?"

"Copra," Dalziel said.

"What's that?"

"I believe it's used in the manufacture of soap."

Sir Hugh Stafford was tired and looking forward to slipping away to his club, where a few whiskies would restore his sense of his own importance, always eroded by the supercilious and over-informed Whitehall officials. "What's the name of that other stuff? Sounds like copra."

"Guano, Sir Hugh."

"That's it, bird droppings. Soap and bird droppings. Is that what the Empire's come to?"

Dalziel, immaculate at the end of the day in his uniform

of black coat, wing collar and striped trousers, gazed at the cigar ash on the baronet's waistcoat and said nothing.

"Well, well, Hubert, what's to be done?"

Dalziel rubbed his dry hands together, making a scraping sound calculated to get on Stafford's nerves. Dalziel had often done this to bring tiresome meetings — those involving the Minister's African obsessions — to an end. "The resources of the Protectorate are, of course, insignificant, but in strategic terms and in view of its possible role in a communications network, the place can be said to matter. A firm action there could, as . . . " Dalziel glanced at the file to refresh his memory, " . . . Childers, yes, Childers, recommends — deter the French and Japanese and reassure the Australians without attracting adverse comment in non-involved quarters."

Sir Hugh Stafford stubbed out his cigar and employed his walking stick to lever his huge bulk upright. "Tell this Kane-Price chap to come down hard," he said.

Dalziel nodded and stood respectfully as the minister lumbered towards the door.

"Diamonds," Stafford muttered, "diamonds and gold. That's the stuff. Guano . . ."

Back in his own office, Dalziel lit a Players Silk Cut and prepared to minute the slim BJIP file. He made a note of the time and date of his conference with the minister and wrote a one-paragraph summary of the discussion. In his small, precise hand he directed that a despatch be forwarded to the High Commissioner for the Western Pacific on the subject of disturbances on Murdo and Hemisphere islands. He wrote 'Action', underlined the word and deliberated. He finished his cigarette and entered, 'As per minute of EC, 17/3/28.' *Let young Childers try his hand*, he thought. *Promising young fellow, Childers. Balliol man of course. You can always put your faith in a Balliol man.*

Childers prepared himself for drafting the despatch by reading the Blue Books on the Jeremiahs and any other material he could lay his hands on, including the few anthropological studies. These were on the outlying Polynesian islets, where the climate tended to be more benign than on the larger islands in the group, and whose Polynesian inhabitants were more easily communicated with and more amenable. Childers emerged from the reading well informed about the history of the group and with some grasp of the complexities of native politics. He leaned back in his chair and heard, for the first time since he had begun working, the noise and bustle of the street outside. It was unusually mild for February in London, and Childers had opened the window a fraction.

Too much to hope for blue sky, he thought. He recalled a lecture given by Arthur Grimble some years before in which the former Gilbert and Ellice Islands RC had waxed lyrical about the pleasures of the Colonial Administrative Service — tropic isles, azure seas, exotic cultures, duty and responsibility. Childers had been tempted, but he was an ambitious man and the road to the top was via Whitehall desks, not sandy beaches. Still, he sometimes regretted the decision. He sighed and began to leaf through the recent papers on the BJIP: unimpressive taxation receipts, equally unimpressive expenditure on medical services, export figures for copra, timber and fish products. *Nothing much at stake here,* Childers thought. *Why couldn't Dalziel have given me Kenya?*

That thought led him to search the register for intelligence files on the Protectorate. Who knew? There could be some secret, some skulduggery long concealed that would require delicate handling, and earn kudos for the clerk who provided the delicate touch. But Childers' enquiries led to no such finds. He flicked through the lists of residents, deportees and people awaiting deportation. A telegraphed list of recent arrivals had been enclosed in a Western Pacific High Commission despatch, and Childers ran his eye down it. He noted Birmingham's name and was aware of his books but was uninterested, being a classicist who read little modern fiction and tended to despise it. Then a name brought him up short: 'Richard Webb, British, 29 years, anthropologist; destination Murdo Island.' *My God, Richard Webb!*

Childers recalled Webb from his Oxford years — tall

and thin, dark and intense. Older than himself and the rest of his fellow students, brighter than some, more hard-working than all. They had almost become friends, but not quite. Childers had been been unsure why and would have become resentful had not Webb explained it to him when both were drunk after securing their Firsts.

"Got out of the habit in the war," Webb had slurred. "Get close to a chap and bang, he's dead. Lose a comrade and a friend. Better to just lose a comrade."

"War's over," Childers said.

"So they tell me. I see it all around me here, still happening. Want to go somewhere it never happened. No trenches, no gas, no bodies. Tell you, Ernie, 'nother war comes, you go away — South Pole, North Pole, Himalayas. Don't have anything to do with it."

A week later Childers had gone on the obligatory trip to Europe to acquire a foreign language — German, in his case — and had taken his Civil Service exams. He heard that Webb was studying something in London, but they had not met. *Well, Richard,* he thought. *You've made it to a place the war didn't touch. I hope you've found the peace you wanted.* He made a mental note to write a personal letter to Webb, then he inserted a sheet of paper in the typewriter and tapped: 'CO to WPHC — Draft Despatch, 20/3/28. File CO/225.'

19

Uta'a, 20 February 1928

Uta'a, a passage thirty miles south of Maka Maka, was not one of Naismith's favourite places, though the people were all right, in his judgment — vigorous fishermen and canoe makers on the coast, expert gardeners and pig-raisers in the bush. The trouble was the Seventh-day Adventist mission, which existed — Naismith could not bring himself to say *thrived* — at the head of the deep bay.

It was mid-morning and very hot. Naismith's police escort, Corporal Moro and a constable from the Alma lagoon and one To'beili, together with the clerk, marched beside him along the rough, steep track to the clearing where the tax house was set. The march took them around a large rock and out of sight of the wharf. Naismith detected nervousness in the demeanour of the young To'beili. Speaking pidgin, the DO asked the constable what was troubling him. The constable replied that he saw nothing amiss, but had a bad feeling.

This could mean anything, as Naismith knew. He checked that his pistol holster was within reach and the policemen, taking their cue from him, fingered the safety catches on their carbines. They entered the clearing and saw a large group of mission saltwater people, the men decently clad in shorts and singlets and the women in Mother Hubbards, waiting patiently in a line outside the tax house. Naismith mounted the steps and waited while the police arranged the table and chairs. Naismith sat and gestured for the clerk to sit beside him.

He was disconcerted by the absence of the headman and addressed the mision people: *"Headman Malu'u, watpo i no stap?"**

There was no response from the Christians. Naismith shrugged and beckoned the first taxpayer forward. As he went through the procedures of collecting the taxes — many fewer exemptions and unorthodoxies here than at Mata Mata — Naismith was aware of the edginess of the police. He glanced up from time to time but saw nothing amiss except the absence of bush people. He had expected that after the experience at Maka Maka — here too, the bush was boycotting the rate. He would have to think of a strategy to overcome the problem. He cut a notch in a disc and handed it back with a nod to the owner. *Probably have to send some patrols in to spread the word,* he thought. *Baekani's patrol would be well under way by now. I wonder what effect that's having?* He'd get word at the next point of call, in the Tau lagoon to the south.

"Masta!"

The police sergeant's voice was just above a whisper, but full of alarm, even fear. Naismith looked up. There was not a singlet or Mother Hubbard in sight. The clearing was full of armed, war-painted bushmen. They stood in silence — stocky, dark figures, some wearing bright feather cloaks, others with feathers in their hair. All were hung around with amulets and chest decorations, many had bones through their septums, and all carried spears or bows. Arrows with red quills stuck up from quivers on their backs; the serrated, bone-headed spears looked like slivers of death. Naismith saw several old rifles cradled in the arms

* "Why isn't Headman Malu'u here?"

of proud, defiant men. His hand moved to his holster as he stood to face the silent group. The police slowly lifted their carbines. The sun was directly overhead, beating down into the open space in which not a breath of air stirred.

Naismith felt a weariness in his bones as he stood. He recognised several of the feather-cloaked men — bush *lemos*, inactive for many years but still carrying authority in their manner and murder in their hearts. He took the revolver from its holster and laid it on the table in front of him. The men in the front rank were a mere two strides from the tax house steps; if one of them mounted the steps, attempted to place himself physically on a level with the DO or above, Naismith would shoot him. It was a convention of Murdoan warfare that no attack would be launched from a lower level, a convention which usually brought death to the first attacker.

In loud, clear pidgin, using the dignified form, "People of Uta'a," Naismith began to address the crowd.

At a signal from one of the *lemos* the bushmen let out a resounding shout; none moved a step, but in a single, co-ordinated motion ten spears were thrown. They thudded into the closely bound wicker panels above the heads of the DO and the police. Naismith's hand swept down for his pistol and the police cocked their rifles, but the bushmen were faster — ten arrows whistled through the short space and embedded quivering into the posts which supported the verandah of the tax house. Again, the arrows lodged at points higher than the heads of Naismith and his men.

"Hold your fire," Naismith snapped.

The bushmen shook their spears and began a slow, rhythmic dance, moving in a circling line around the clearing. Insults were shouted — insults to the police, speculating about their parentage and sexual habits, insults to the *gafamanu*, too weak to protect itself from real warriors, insults to the Christians of the passage who were women with small pigs and small penises. The clerk Marius, a prize pupil of Father Bondil's, sat quietly, feigning a sophisticated indifference, but Naismith could sense the fury building in the young To'beili constable and his comrades. Much more of this and he would have difficulty in preventing them from firing on the dancing, spear-waving braggarts.

After several circuits of the clearing the dancers stopped; another shout echoed in the enclosed space and then a loud clicking started as the bushmen threw their tax discs into a pile in front of the hut. Four men leapt forward shouting imprecations which made even Marius react with an angry hiss of breath. When the four curse-sayers stepped back Naismith saw that they had shielded a fifth man who had squatted and defecated on the pile of discs. A last shout and the bushmen backed out of the clearing, still shaking their weapons, still almost dancing as they moved. Within seconds the clearing was empty. The grass was stamped down and dust swirled waist high. Flies buzzed noisily over the pile of shit.

20

Alma, 21 February 1928

Tom Birmingham was very adept with the crutches, which he had on loan from the mission hospital. "Used to be the stilts man at the Deer Lodge county fair," he boasted. "Walk on those damn things like they were my legs, even dance on 'em." His mobility and cheerfulness were remarkable, and he insisted on going down to the wharf to see Webb and Clements off on the *Woodlark* to Sunburi. His mobility was complemented by an alertness Louise had not seen in him before. She had not a minute alone with Webb, and their parting was utterly formal.

Showing off, Birmingham skipped ahead on the path leading from the wharf, which left Louise in the company of Pastor Stoltenberg.

"Temptation removed is less worthy than temptation resisted, Mrs Birmingham," the missionary said. "But far, far better than temptation yielded to. Would you not agree?"

Stoltenberg had a long stride but Louise, enjoying the freedom of her *sulu*, cotton blouse and bare feet, had no trouble keeping up. "No, I would not agree. In fact I would completely reverse the order."

"You are an adulteress."

"And you're a hypocrite."

"How do you arrive at that extraordinary untruth?"

"You work the natives like slaves on your plantations. You withhold their wages, you break up families to get more people under your control. You take away the things that make life meaningful for these people."

"And what, pray, are those things?"

"Rituals, ceremonies — sum it up as *kastom*."

"Call it barbarism, rather, paganism, benightedness, darkness."

"Rubbish. A bushman, raising pigs, tending his gardens, trading with the coast, nurturing his family, respecting his ancestors, would never work for you or sing those pathetic hymns."

Stoltenberg shook his head. "I fear you have been talking to the wrong people, Mrs Birmingham."

"I've been talking to the women in the villages, and to . . ."

"Richard Webb."

"Yes."

"Well, you won't be talking to him any longer, will you? You'll have to talk to your husband, who sees things very differently. And instead of walking miles to those pagan villages, you can come to the mission. We have several cows and fresh milk. I can give you an excellent cup of tea."

"I'd rather drink kava in the bush."

"I'm not surprised." They were nearing the guesthouse, and Birmingham was sitting triumphantly on the steps. Stoltenberg slowed his pace to allow them a few more words in private. "Aren't you pleased that Thomas has stopped drinking?"

"I have to admit that I am."

"Then you have to admit that I'm exerting a good influence on him."

"Not for a minute. You're manipulating him for some

purpose of your own, something sneaky and bound to cause harm."

"To whom?"

"To everyone. But let me tell you this, *reverend*. Tom Birmingham's no fool. He's seen a lot of the world, and a lot of the bastards in it. He can be a bit of a bastard himself. Have you given any thought to the idea that he might be manipulating *you?*"

"What're you two so goldarned intense about?" Birmingham called from the steps.

"Your husband is a deeply troubled man."

Louise glanced up at Birmingham, who was sitting on the top step with his crutches crossed in front of him. "He looks pretty happy to me."

"How happy would he be if he knew you were deceiving him?"

"You're out of your depth, reverend. Tom's been married three times; he knows a bit about life. But he's also very proud. You might find yourself rather unpopular as the bearer of that news."

Louise waved at her husband, stepped off the path and ran down the slope in the direction of the outhouse kitchen. Stoltenberg watched her, aware that he had been beaten on the significant points in their exchange. He forced a smile onto his face and climbed the steps. "You have made an amazing recovery, Thomas."

No one had ever called Birmingham 'Thomas'. He found he liked the dignity it conferred. "Thanks to you, doc. You could set up in New York and make a fortune."

"Are there many gunshot wounds in New York?"

Birmingham chuckled. "More than get reported. Those rich wives get liquored up, pull out those little gold-plated .22s, and watch out Henry. You don't want to stay here all your life, do you?"

Stoltenberg took off his hat and fanned himself. The heat and humidity were building to that point where they turned the skin clammy at the slightest exertion. To remain cool and dry was impossible, even sitting under a fan. Wave an arm at a mosquito and perspiration broke out. Relief

came in the afternoon with a downpour that cooled
everything off for several hours. Conditions could be
almost pleasant for a while in the evening if there was a
breeze. If not, the build-up of heat began again before
midnight.

Born and bred in the northern hemisphere, Stoltenberg
suffered in the heat. At times he hated the islands, the
islanders, the mission, his rich, fat wife, life itself. He
looked at Birmingham, sitting clear-eyed and firm-fleshed
above him. He looked purposeful. "I don't follow you,
Thomas."

"Great opportunities in New York, doctor," Birmingham said. "Medical and spiritual. Got a growing black
population there, only a generation away from slavery, like
these folks." Birmingham waved his arm to take in the
compound, Murdo, the BJIP. "A man with the right
credentials could make a big success of himself in Harlem."

"Harlem?"

"High hundreds on Manhattan. Greatest city in the
world."

"I thought you were interested in more ... remote
places."

"I've seen the light, doc. I'm making a change. No more
travelling in dugout canoes for me. I'm returning to
journalism."

"Returning?"

"I was a reporter, best training in the world for a writer.
The point is, I could be a big help to you in that capacity
if you decided to ... move on and up. Of course, it'd be
returning a favour."

Stoltenberg, though interested, was cautious. He had
seen few alcoholics cured of what he thought of as their
weakness and he instinctively distrusted *arrivistes*. "I was
simply doing my duty. To heal the sick, to advise a troubled
soul ... "

"I don't mean that. I'm grateful, but I'm talking about
something else. Listen, Louise tells me that the people on
this island aren't happy, that Naismith hasn't really got the

place under control. This Eglito could make big waves. How does that sound to you?"

"I think Mrs Birmingham has been carried away. A little learning is a dangerous thing."

"Right. How Christian are your Christians?"

The missionary thought of his disappointments — the schools deserted when the tuna were running, and the young men who were basically uninterested in the Christian message; he recalled the mocking eyes of the old men when a mission garden failed, or a devout adherent of Christianity fell sick and died. "They vary," he said.

Birmingham stuck out a crutch, wedged it on a step and leaned forward, using the crutch for support until his mouth was close to the missionary's ear. "I need a headline out of this place," he said. "A scoop on a big native rebellion against the British raj. A few dead men, the whiter the better."

"That's outrageous!"

"If it's going to happen anyway, what's the harm in someone making something out of it? You and me, for example?"

"Me?"

"I'll be controlling the information that gets out of here, at least initially. I can make sure you look good, very good. Like I say, the sky's the limit in New York for a man who can arrive with the right credentials."

Stoltenberg stroked his bony, smooth-shaven chin. "It's true that Murdo is a volatile island. It always has been, but District Officer Naismith . . . "

"Don't worry about him. I'm working on that."

"I can't see what use I can be to you."

"You're not a pacifist, are you, Pastor?"

"Indeed not. 'An eye for an eye and a tooth for a tooth', so the Bible says."

"Absolutely. So that if your people were threatened by a rampaging mob of pagans you'd arm them, and advise them to fight?"

"Indeed. But I can't see . . . "

"Don't worry. You don't have to see."

Stoltenberg's heart was pounding, and he discovered that what he was experiencing was excitement. He'd last experienced it when he realised that marrying the widow Bruce of Maryborough would make him a successful missionary at a stroke. Before that, in Africa sometime, when he had *almost* converted a whole village. Almost. He'd read enough hagiographies of soldiers of Christ to know that men of destiny seized their opportunities. "I'll admit, Thomas, that I have ambitions that run beyond this narrow field. But I won't be a party to wrongdoing, and I repeat that Naismith is a formidable man, albeit an unenlightened one."

Birmingham nodded solemnly. He'd summed his man up right. "And I'll repeat that I can deal with Naismith."

The new firmness in Birmingham almost alarmed the missionary; then he remembered that he had a card to play against him, if need be. He raised one eyebrow sceptically. "How?"

"The man has enemies," Birmingham said.

Keith Larke was puzzled because he had received no word from Price-Kane on his first report about Naismith. As instructed by the DO, he called the capital on the radio three times a day to gather information about weather, shipping and other matters affecting the administration of Murdo. He expected some signal from the RC but nothing came. His second despatch, sent over that morning to Hemisphere on a copra boat with other routine mail, he had heavily sealed and directed personally to Price-Kane. In it he had gone into considerable detail on the DO's court demeanour and concept of justice.

One paragraph in particular he considered a model of intelligence-gathering.

Mr Naismith has despatched his servant Bikani into the bush at the head of a team of the most desperate-looking fellows I have ever seen. Bikani holds no commission of any kind; at least two of his party were serving gaol sentences until given parole for this mission, and a third appears to be simple-minded. I have also ascertained that Bikani drew a considerable amount of ammunition from the stores. I fear he is up to no good.

Alone in his quarters after a taxing day of paper shuffling and supervising of public works, Larke was considering a second whisky before dinner when he heard a curious noise outside his door. His hand reached for the old BSA .45 automatic he had found in a drawer in Naismith's office. Another odd sound, and then a firm knock came on the door.

"Who's there?" Larke said.

"Tom Birmingham. Want to talk to you a minute."

Larke put the pistol on the floor beside his chair and got up to open the door, realising as he did so that the alarming sound must have been made by Birmingham's crutches. Larke threw the door open with an exaggerated vigour. "Mr Birmingham. Let me help you."

"I can manage fine, son. Can I take that chair over there?" He pointed with one crutch at the chair Larke had occupied. Without waiting for an answer, he hopped across the room and dropped into the chair. He picked up the .45. "Fine weapon. Yours, Mr Larke?"

Larke nodded, the lie coming without any premeditation. "Well, it is now. It was among my brother's effects. He was killed in France."

Birmingham's face set in solid, understanding lines. He put the pistol back on the floor and rubbed his hands together. "How are you finding it? Being the man in charge?"

Larke flushed, closed the door and walked over to where another chair was set against the wall. He picked it up and carried it close to where the American was sitting. This took him past the bottle set on a low table, and he waved at the whisky. "Care for a drink?"

Birmingham shook his head. "Off it. Doctor's orders. But you go right ahead."

Larke hesitated, then recovered his glass and poured a

small measure. He sat down opposite Birmingham and took out his cigarette. "Players?"

Again, Birmingham declined. Larke lit up and took a sip of his whisky. He felt uncomfortable, as if he was performing in a play and didn't know his lines. He drew on the cigarette. "Well, there's not much to it, actually. I . . . "

"That's where you're wrong, son. There's a lot to it. A hell of a lot. This place is headed for big trouble."

Larke had the conventional Englishman's habit of thinking that colonials and others always exaggerated and shouldn't interfere in the business of the British Empire anyway. He managed a cool smile. "Why d'you say that?"

"Because it's true. This place is a powder keg."

"I hardly think so. I can't say that I think it's been well administered, but . . . "

"You could make a name for yourself here, Keith. Wouldn't you like to prove that the good ol' British Empire pulse still throbs? All that?"

Larke sipped his whisky. "Of course. It still does, very much so."

"Could be you're going to get a chance to display some initiative. What d'you think of Naismith?"

"It wouldn't be proper for me to discuss my senior officer with a . . . civilian."

"What would you say if I told you that the man is sick, very sick? His teeth are rotten, he gets rheumatism, lumbago and sciatica, and terrible blinding headaches, his liver's shot and probably his kidneys, too."

"How could you possibly know all that?"

Birmingham winked. "I never saw a house with servants yet where all the servants thought everything was hunky-dory. I found a guy who hates Baekani like an orphan hates Christmas. He's my source."

Larke was already thinking how well this information would look in his next report. *Of course it'll have to be checked in every detail.* "That's very interesting," he said. "But administrative officers have a thorough medical check every two years."

Birmingham snapped, "Naismith hasn't had one for five."

"I see. Why are you telling me this?"

"Murdo's headed for trouble. Naismith's not the man to control it. Pastor Stoltenberg's the man to enlist the support of the missions and planters. Maybe you're the man to co-ordinate the resistance to the rebels."

"What rebels?"

Birmingham had not missed Larke's instinctive reaction to Baekani's name. In his new, clear-headed, strategy-making state of mind he saw an opportunity and capitalised on it quickly. "Eglito," he said, "and Baekani."

Larke sneered. "He's Naismith's slave."

"Not for long. When this thing gets out of hand, when they start killing each other for revenge and God knows what other reasons, Baekani's going to have to choose between being Naismith's lapdog and being a big man himself. I've talked to a few people about this guy. He'll go for broke, especially if Naismith's out of action."

Keith Larke had intoxicating visions of himself holding the Alma outpost against hordes of savages. A few gallant planters by his side; the missionaries stiffening the resolve of the loyal Christian natives; the weary garrison rationing water and ammunition; the relief gunboat coming into the bay, the boom of its two-pound guns . . .

He shook his head and finished his whisky. The cigarette had burned down to a stub, neglected in his fingers. He put it in the ashtray. "And what would your part be in all this, Mr Birmingham?"

"Good question," Birmingham said, "I was in the military myself and I can handle a gun. This goddam leg's no help but I can be useful when it comes to a fight. More important though, long-term and short-term, I'm the man to write about what's happening here and I need your help to send wireless messages to the world press."

Larke shook his head. "Out of the question."

"Listen, son. You know how slowly things move in places like this. Two weeks to get a despatch to the big boss in Fiji. What d'you call him?"

"The High Commissioner for the Western Pacific," Larke said.

"Yeah. Him. Six weeks for him to contact London. Bit of radio traffic then, if you're lucky. They can't do anything pronto! Only the men on the spot can act. Now what do you want to be — one of the poor devils who gets repatriated to Hemisphere with his tail between his legs when the RC finally sees it's time to send for the gunboats, or the man who alerts the world to what's happening, takes firm action and brings the place under control with a minimum of blood being shed?"

"You'll have to convince me that things are as bad as you say first. You'll forgive me, Mr Birmingham, but your recent actions don't exactly stamp you as the most stable person in the world."

Birmingham touched his thigh and winced as he did so. "You mean this?"

"Exactly."

"What do you think happened? How d'you think I got shot?"

"Well, I . . . "

"I'll tell you what happened. I disturbed one of Baekani's thugs going through my things in my room. Baekani's orders or Naismith's, I don't know. I pulled the gun on him, he jumped me and we fought. The gun went off. Christ, son, I've been handling firearms for thirty years, d'you think I could shoot myself like some amateur duck hunter?"

"Why didn't you report this?"

"One, I didn't want to alarm my wife. Second, report to who? Naismith? I don't trust him. When I heard he was going on tour, that was just fine with me. Meant I could deal with more reasonable people. Then I just thought it was part of the guy's nuttiness. Now I think there's a lot more to it."

Larke was struggling to accommodate this rush of information. "More?" he said.

"I've seen types like Naismith before. White rajahs, they call them, northwest of here."

"White rajahs?"

"I can't say any more, Keith, not until I know whether you're with me or against me."

21

The *Loloburu* disappeared around the long landspit that marked the entrance to the Alma lagoon. Baekani watched until the only sign of the boat was the wake washing back against the jetty, then raised his hand and signalled for his patrol to follow him into the bush. The six men were Sergeant Bitamae, Constable Bellua and Luku — Kweili, like Baekani himself; Senior Constable Bacca, a To'beili, and Samsu, a man from the outer islands reputed to be able to catch bullets. Samsu was a roly-poly figure, part Polynesian and with a weakness for beer. He worked mostly as a maker of nets and shell money, and it was only on condition that he be co-opted that Bacca consented to join the patrol. Bacca was something of a renegade; hounded from To'beili territory by accusations of sorcery, he welcomed the opportunity to exact some revenge. But he was deeply convinced of the malevolent power of certain spirits and equally convinced of Samsu's supernatural abilities. A reading of the bones had told him that a bullet intended for his heart would be stopped by Samsu's hand.

The patrol entered the bush to the north of the outpost

and immediately encountered steep grades and wet, slippery tracks on the climb towards the central plateau. There the going would be easier for a time, until they began the descents and climbs that would take them through a succession of valleys surrounding the To'beili fastnesses. Of these, Bacca had some knowledge and some fear. The others had curiosity or sought profit.

In the narrow, little-changing world of the Jeremiahs, any experience a man could gather and translate into story was valuable. Bellua, who fancied himself as a storyteller, imagined passing on the story of the patrol to his grandchildren — the incredible physical feats of endurance, the dark, forbidding, spirit-haunted valleys, the threat of death from poison-tipped arrows held against taut bowstrings. Sketching out the story in advance in his mind, Bellua almost felt the fear he would attempt to communicate. But his telling would not go into detail about the superior firepower of the patrol, armed as they were with Lee Enfield carbines, Webley revolvers and as much ammunition as they could carry. Mention would inevitably be made of one thing in their favour — the ability of their leader, Baekani, to put a bullet through the eye of a pigeon at a hundred yards.

Sergeant Bitamae hated all To'beili and kept as much distance between Bacca and himself as possible. Like Baekani, he had personal reasons for action against Eglito. His brother had been severely wounded in the attack on Alma and was now in the Patugi hospital, poised between life and death. Bitamae was convinced that if he could spill the blood of one of Eglito's followers, the balance would be shifted in his brother's favour.

"*Yu tomas slo, Samsu.*" Bitamae growled as the light-skinned man struggled up the slope, "*tomas fat.*"*

Bellua said, "He is carrying his own weight in betel. He will move more quickly when he has chewed an arm and a leg."

Baekani smiled and spoke quietly in Kweili. "Samsu will

---

* "You're much too slow, Samsu, much too fat."

get thin on this patrol, thinner than Luku. By the end he will skip ahead of us like a piglet."

The men laughed, including Samsu who could understand most of the dialects of Murdo and enjoyed a good joke. Luku laughed less heartily and more briefly than the others. Luku seldom laughed. Keith Larke was wrong in reporting that two of Baekani's patrol had been released from prison; only Luku was in that category. Luku had been serving seven years for manslaughter, and Baekani wanted him because Luku was a killer.

February nights are cold and damp in the Murdo mountains. The patrol, tired after a hard day's trekking, bivouacked the first night on the site of an abandoned garden where there was an abundance of timber for their fire. Baekani allotted tasks which were accepted and performed without protest. The men ate rice and tinned fish and drank hot, sweet tea. They spoke little and spent the time after the meal attending to the cuts and abrasions suffered on the track, and cleaning and maintaining their weapons. Baekani carefully cleaned and oiled the Mannlicher rifle, working over it inch by inch to ensure that it had suffered no damage, that nothing would interfere with its smooth, deadly action. Baekani had had an intricately carved piece of shell inlaid in the rifle's oiled walnut stock. He had never told anyone what the significance of this ornament was and had even treated Naismith's query non-committally.

"*Kastom?*" the DO had asked.

Baekani had nodded, and Naismith knew better than to persist. In fact the whorls and striations on the dark red shell marked generations of Baekani's kin. Bright specks of gold represented famous *lemos* and sorcerers. The weapon was dedicated to the spirits of two particular ancestors, famous fighting men in the time before the arrival of the Europeans, and Baekani had taken a vow to equal them in fame, as far as was possible in these quieter, more peaceable times. He made a last check of the delicate sights, peering along them at the moon which was briefly visible through the clouds.

"Would you kill the moon, Baekani?" said Samsu, who was struggling to get his blanket to cover his shoulders.

"If I had to," Baekani said.

Bellua knocked ash out of his clay pipe and put it away in his pack. He made a mental note to remember Baekani's words — they would sound well in his story.

On the second day out the patrol encountered people from several bush villages located on the plateau in places where gardens were possible. As they were still in Kweili territory, Baekani's reputation and Sergeant Bitamae's authority were formidable, though the people denied all knowledge of the passage through their country of Eglito's raiding party. This was no more than Baekani had expected. No Murdoan would admit to such a violation since it constituted a pollution of sacred sites, an insult to the ancestors. Questions had to be framed carefully.

"If a party had passed through here," Baekani asked a bushman, who continued to work in his garden, "would it have moved to the east or west of that hill?"

The bushman did not look along the line of Baekani's pointing finger. He hacked at a tough root with his bushknife. "West," he said.

"Why?"

"The climb is easier on the west."

"And quicker?"

"No." The bushman gave the appearance of ignoring his questioner. The knife thwacked down fifteen centimetres from Baekani's foot. Baekani stood still.

"Would not such a party wish to move quickly?"

Thwack! "If there were wounded men in such a party it might not be possible for it to move quickly."

The patrol took the west track. Baekani had no thought of catching up with the raiders before they reached To'beili territory, but it was symbolically important to follow the enemy's trail, and there was always the chance of learning something useful: the condition of a camp site could indicate the state of health and morale of the occupants, a discarded weapon might be found, even a grave. Furthermore, as they came closer to the To'beili domain, it would be possible to gauge the strength of support for Eglito and the amount of fear he generated.

The second night was a bleak, cold one, spent on the edge of the plateau where the cloud settled like a freezing blanket. Bellua attempted a joke about Samsu's fat insulating him from the cold, but the joke fell flat. Bacca was nervous; they would encounter the first To'beili clans tomorrow, and he would see again the contempt on people's faces, the turning away from him, hear the muttered slurs. He oiled his rifle and hoped he would get the chance to fire it into one of the mocking faces. Luku sat apart from the rest, honing a bayonet to a razor edge. Baekani had told him that he might be required to deal with sentries quickly and silently. It was dishonourable to kill a man from behind, but Luku did not care. Honour had no part in his scheme of things.

Sergeant Bitamae had taken care to arrange a supply of wood around the fire, which would dry out and provide him with warmth and light when he burned it during his watch. Bitamae preferred the first watch; he liked to fight off sleep and then succumb and sleep the longest and deepest of all. Luku, a fitful sleeper, would take the second watch, and Baekani the third. The men tapped out their pipes, rolled themselves in their blankets and slept. Bitamae chewed on a piece of roasted yam; he tucked a section of tough skin into the corner of his mouth with his tongue and sucked on it, extracting the salt and flavour. Luku tossed uneasily in his blankets and snored softly. Bitamae was glad of the sound and happy with the thought that Luku would be easy to wake. The first watch was the best.

It was after midnight when Baekani came suddenly and starkly awake. He was aware of neither sound nor movement, but he accepted that there was a reason for him to be awake and did not bother to ask what had alerted him. The fire had died down very low, which did not surprise him; Luku cared nothing for warmth and light and would do no more than keep the fire alive. A loud snore came from Luku; Bellua turned over in his sleep and farted softly. Baekani grinned. *That's enough to keep the ghosts away.*

Then his mind lurched. *Luku is still in his blankets!* He leapt
to his feet and stepped over Bellua and Samsu to where
Bitamae sat with his back to a tree. The sergeant's head
lolled forward and the blanket around his shoulders was
black with blood. His throat had been cut from ear to ear.

The *Woodlark* chugged into Birdbeak Bay, the large
expanse of water sheltered by the long, thin, curved
peninsula at the north end of Murdo that accounted for the
name. There were three artificial islands in the bay, many
fewer and less impressive than those to the south, but of
great interest to Clements. The Birdbeak people were great
carvers and makers of decorated string bags. Because
protocol demanded that the visitor pay his respects to the
main onshore village before venturing out to the islands,
the *Woodlark* dropped anchor a hundred yards out.

   The sailors rolled cigarettes and prepared to fish. Two
men were assigned the task of rowing Clements, Webb and
Peter Mamuka ashore. They grumbled and joked about the
crazy white man who collected old *bilums*, which were so
frayed and weak that nothing could be carried in them.
They spoke in a mixture of pidgin and Kweili. Webb
scarcely caught more than a word; Mamuka grinned at the
jokes. If Clements understood he showed no sign of
annoyance.

   "No jetties here," Clements said. "The sand shifts too
much. The bay's pretty calm but the currents are fierce.
I'm sorry, Richard. Am I boring you?"

   "What? Sorry, Colin. I was miles away."

   "Thinking of Louise Birmingham. Look around you.
This is an interesting spot. Much more so than some dirty
little To'beili bush village. If you can't take an interest in
things here, God knows how you're going to manage in
the bush."

   Webb shook his head and adjusted his hat brim against
the angle of the sun. "You're right. I must pull myself
together. Yes, it's a marvellous spot."

   The yellow beach was wide and gently sloping back up
to thick undergrowth that almost seemed to form a hedge

where the sand began. A gap in the thick bush which marked the beginning of a track was arched over with tangled vines, giving the appearance of an elaborate gateway.

"Wonderful people here," Clements said.

It was not the first time Clements had praised the affability of the Birdbeakers, and Webb had prepared himself for a throng of happy saltwater people, paddling out to the boat, offering fruit, fish and yams and shouting jokes and insults to the sailors. He gazed at the beach, waiting for people to come through the arched gate. The beach remained deserted. Mamuka and the boatman jumped into the shallow water and grounded the dinghy on the beach. The boatman turned to look at Clements.

"*Trabel, masta, plenti trabel.*"

Clements nodded. "That's the way it looks." He jumped onto the sand and turned to help Webb, but Webb's jump carried him several feet further.

"Didn't know you were an Olympian," Clements laughed nervously.

Webb looked along the beach; some distance away he saw a shape he could not distinguish — a group of canoes perhaps, but with something odd about them. "What can have happened?" he said. "Some sickness, d'you think? An epidemic?"

The explanation seemed to encourage Clements, who shouldered his bag and took a few steps up the beach. "Only one way to find out."

The boatman hung back.

"*Wonem?*"* Webb said.

The boatman shrugged. "*Mi laik casim gan.*"**

"Nonsense," Clements said. "Wait here. We'll take a look. Come on, Richard. Peter, you please yourself."

Mamuka grinned and reached into the boat. He picked up his bushknife, bent down for a handful of sand and polished the blade. A sixth sense told Webb that the

---

* "What's wrong?"
** "I'd like to get a gun."

boatman was right, that there was serious trouble in this place. Automatically, from long training and bitter experience, his mind flicked to the revolver he had taken from Naismith. Somehow it had got into his traps, and it was with his things on the *Woodlark*. He wished it was in his pocket instead of the clasp knife and tin of Players cigarettes. He shrugged and followed Clements and Mamuka up the beach to the track. No one had been on the beach since the last tide, and the thin crust of dried sand broke under their feet. Clements stumbled as soon as he passed under the archway and Webb, whose eyes adjusted immediately to the dim light, steadied him.

"I tripped over something," Clements said. "A bundle . . ."

Webb was on his knees examing the obstruction. He straightened up and gave Clements a gentle shove, moving him away a little. "It's a child," he said. "With an arrow in his back. He's dead."

"Christ. What's going *on* here?"

"How far's the village?"

"Just at the end of the track, about a hundred yards."

"Wait here. I'm going to take a look."

Clements said, "I'll go." But Webb and Mamuka had already disappeared into the bush by the side of the track. Clements strained his eyes in the gloom, but he could detect no sign of movement beside the path.

Webb's military training had made him expert at moving through cover, and he had advanced many times into perilous situations with cover much sparser than he now had. Mamuka moved silently behind him. There were no other bodies on the path, no evidence of unrest. The path ended in a clearing cut by a deep drainage ditch. The huts were grouped in a tight circle on the other side of the ditch. There was no smoke from cooking fires, no animal noises, no sound of work being done, although it was late morning, normally a busy time of day.

Cautiously, bending low, Webb and Mamuka scuttled across the clearing to the log bridge over the ditch. One glance to the left as they crossed the logs showed them another body — a man lying half submerged in the shallow water.

They approached the rear of the men's house — a long, low structure set aside from the circle of huts. Usually old men could be found inside at any time of day, and there was constant coming and going as clan and village business was conducted. The two men stepped from the shadows into the bright light in front of the building and climbed the three steps to its open door. The men's house was empty. Webb glanced around to make sure he was unobserved; Mamuka nodded and stationed himself by the door. Webb took two steps into the dim, smoky interior. The smoke-blackened walls and uprights and the thatch carried the scents of scores of years and thousands of bodies. From his reading Webb knew that sacred objects would be lodged on racks at the end of the building — weapons, skulls, tools, pig tusks, strings of shell money. A few rays of light from chinks in the walls fell on the floor beneath the racks. The area was covered with broken bone, wood and shell. Webb could see something light-coloured hanging from the racks. He moved closer and saw that it was a woman's dress, a vast Mother Hubbard, stained with what was either actually or symbolically menstrual blood. The garment was suspended over the smashed objects, polluting and dishonouring them forever. Despite his bitter experience of life, his agnosticism and scientific training, Webb felt the enormity of the act — it was desecration.

When he came out of the men's house he found Mamuka squatting beside a cold fire smoking a cigarette. A pot had overturned and spilled taro and water onto the ground. Insects were devouring the taro, which gave off a rotting, sickly smell.

"What happened here, Peter?" Webb said.

Mamuka traced patterns in the dirt with the hooked point of his bushknife. "Raid. Like in the old days. Did you see the canoes along the beach?"

Webb shook his head. "I saw something. I couldn't tell what."

"Smashed canoes. This is a terrible thing for saltwater people."

"Where *are* the people?"

Mamuka shrugged. "Some dead. Most of them have run away into the bush."

Eglito slept fitfully in the small bush village just inside the boundary of the To'beili language group. He and his followers were safe here for the time being. Much depended on the recovery of those wounded in the attack on Alma. If one of the men, particularly a well-connected warrior, should die, Eglito's authority would be diminished. He had exuded confidence, but his sleep betrayed him. He tossed and dreamed of mud slides, cascades of mud flowing down slopes and burying houses and gardens until the land was a sea of mud that no man could cross.

He awoke, sweating and with his eyes staring at the fire embers and the thin wisps of smoke that rose towards the blackened roof of the men's house. A mud slide of the kind he had dreamed about would sweep these structures, shrines and graves away like children's playthings. The smoke-darkened objects of veneration — the weapons, ritual masks, bones and ornaments — would be buried forever and their power forever lost.

As he came fully awake, Eglito shook off the phantasms. His men lay sound asleep around him, tired after the forced marches from Alma and unburdened by the cares of leadership. Eglito filled and lit his pipe, purposeful again. He pulled the blanket around his shoulders and smoked until the pipe was finished. The action calmed his mind and allowed him to enjoy the memory of the burning lockup and the great sound as the explosion rocked the wharf and, so he hoped, tore apart the government boat. These things would be talked about for years to come. Famous victories. His one fear, that Baekani would be sent with his terrible rifle to shoot before they had cleared the headland, had not come to pass. Baekani had been humiliated like the white man he served.

But still Eglito was troubled. Perhaps the victory had been won too easily because the *solodia* had been asleep. He dismissed the thought; there had been fighting and he had not been afraid. He had heard news of other disturbances on the island and rejoiced. Certain allies would be welcome although, in the nature of things on Murdo, they would inevitably become enemies in time. But something nagged at him, something he could locate and deal with.

He thrust his hand into the pigskin pouch he carried at all times and felt his fingers close over the two circular metal objects, the English shillings. He pulled them out and stared at them in the flickering firelight. The shillings were blackened by age and handling. Eglito had had the coins consecrated, he had preserved them carefully, never allowing a woman to see them or unworthy persons to touch them. He could feel the power flowing in them but he could not be sure that the direction of the power was towards him.

22

New York, 20 February 1928

Hiram Waldeck was signing royalty cheques when William Cavendish knocked on his office door. Waldeck, glad of an interruption, barked, "Come in," and put down his pen. The tradition of the proprietor signing royalty cheques had started in Waldeck's father's time and continued to the present.

"They write the books, you write the cheques," old Wyatt Waldeck had told his son. "Remember that it takes them a lot longer, and you're just filling in numbers and signing your own name. Any fool can do that."

That wasn't quite the way Hiram Waldeck saw the author-publisher relationship, but he went along with the tradition because he hadn't thought of a good excuse to stop it. Yet.

"Yes, William?" Waldeck wasn't sure about Cavendish. He approved of his clothes and his smooth confidence, but suspected him of scruples.

Cavendish laid a piece of paper on Waldeck's huge, bare, highly polished desk. "We've had this extraordinary message from the *Chicago Daily News*. Hearst paper. I don't know quite what to make of it."

Waldeck took from a velvet-lined leather case the gold-rimmed spectacles he hated wearing and only put on when he had to read, which wasn't often. He hooked the thin gold wires over his ears and adjusted the spectacles on the bridge of his bony nose. Hiram Waldeck knew that his lips moved when he read and that this trait, enormously embarrassing in a second-generation publisher, was mocked by people he considered smart-asses. Consequently, whenever he read in the presence of others he read aloud. " 'We have received a wireless message via Sydney, Australia from your author Tom Birmingham. He is offering us exclusive, syndicatable rights to his firsthand account of the native rebellion on Murdo Island, British Jeremiah Islands Protectorate. He claims the British authorities are covering up the rebellion but that quote it will flare up like the sun any day now.' " Birmingham glanced up at Cavendish. "That sounds like Birmingham."

Cavendish was staring out the window at the sluggish East River. Snow was falling, but it appeared to melt as soon as it touched the tops of the taller buildings and bridges. Cavendish, a frustrated poet, had the familiar feeling of lines half-forming in his mind. They would never fully form. "It does," he said.

Waldeck read on, " 'Our enquiries reveal some evidence of recent unrest in the islands but its degree is difficult to gauge. An unconfirmed report mentions the wounding of an American writer some days back. Could you provide information on Birmingham's current whereabouts and assignment? Should the story and Birmingham's ability to report on it check out, what contractual arrangments between you and Birmingham might be relevant? I would respectfully ask you to keep this matter confidential as competition for overseas news stories is intense. British Jeremiah Islands Protectorate is believed to be of some interest to the State Department on account of the presence of Japanese nationals, Japanese and French activity in the area and as a possible site for US communications and

aviation facilities.' Signed ... Benjamin Clancy ...
Managing Editor, Chicago Daily News."

Waldeck finished with a flourish that made Cavendish
feel he should let out a cheer.

Waldeck read parts of the memo again, his lips moving.
Then he said, "What kind of a damn fool stunt is this
Birmingham bastard trying to pull?"

Cavendish gave up on the never-to-be poem. He turned
around and faced his employer. "Mr Waldeck, Hiram, I
should have thought that your first ... "

"Never mind what you thought. Did you send those
cables to this goddamn place, Jeremiah whatever it is?"

"Yes. And got no reply. Don't you think ... "

"I think Birmingham's trying to put over a fast one. Have
you been in touch with his agent?"

"Yes. I didn't want to be too specific in view of what
Clancy says about confidentiality, but I'm pretty sure
Barney Fitzgerald doesn't know a thing about this."

Waldeck pulled the glasses off, almost breaking them as
he did so. "The bastard! Trying to cut everybody out and
deal directly with Hearst! That's unethical. He's under
contract to us, isn't he?"

Cavendish spread his hands. "Well ... "

"Is he or isn't he?"

"The contract was to be cancelled, remember?"

"Uncancel it! I want Birmingham tied up tighter than
a Christmas turkey. He doesn't publish a word without our
say-so. We financed his trip out there, right?"

"Up to a point."

"What the hell does that mean?"

"We stopped his funds. He might argue that he's
covering this story under his own steam."

"I can keep lawyers longer in court over that than he
can. Get moving, William, get moving."

Cavendish recovered the memo and strolled to the door,
concealing his dislike and feeling for a strategy. "Ah, Valerie
Benson did a lot of the research on the Jeremiahs for Tom.
We're going to need that material if anything comes of
this."

Waldeck hated backing down, but he knew when there was no alternative. He nodded. "Talk to her."

Cavendish tapped the memo. "This says Birmingham may be wounded."

"Probably self-dramatisation, all these writers go in for it. Anyway, wounded isn't dead. He can write in bed, that's where most writers spend most of their time anyway, seems to me."

"I wasn't thinking so much of that."

"Time's money, William. Spit it out."

"I was wondering about Louise."

"What about her?"

"Hiram, this is about a native rebellion on some God-forsaken cannibal island. Your daughter's out there. A white woman. Her husband might have been wounded."

Waldeck straightened the bent arm of his spectacles and folded them carefully before putting them back in their case. "Louise can take care of herself," he said quietly. "Always has, always will. Like her mother that way."

23

Birdbeak Bay, 22 February 1928

Two hours after their landing at Birdbeak Bay, Clements and Webb were back on board the *Woodlark*. Webb and Mamuka had found three more corpses, evidence of fighting and a flight by the villagers into the bush. The raiders had destroyed eight canoes, desecrated the men's house and other shrines and looted the main village yam pit. A hut set a little apart from the others, where the deacon from the Anglican mission on Hemisphere visited and performed occasional services, had been burned to the ground.

The two men watched as Mamuka returned in a canoe from the nearest of the artificial islands. These structures, the largest of which was about an acre in size, were normally occupied by old people, those recovering from illness and by people of cantankerous disposition who welcomed the chance to get away from the intimacy of village life. Several times a year the islands were the scene of intense activity — in December when ceremonial offerings were made to the sharks by those clans that embraced the shark as their totem and in July when a large fleet of canoes set out from the major island, It'ia, to intercept the huge school of migrating tuna.

Mamuka tied the canoe to the stern of the cutter and climbed a rope up to the deck with the ease of a European walking up stairs. He took his bushknife from his belt and placed it on a pile of rope. The knife was bloodstained.

"Pig," Manuka said. "I found it on It'ia, wounded by the raiders. They killed the other pigs. We can eat this one tonight."

"Never mind about the pigs," Clements said, "what about the people?"

Mamuka held up two fingers. "Dead. Don't know about the others. Hard to tell how many people on the islands at any time. If there were more they must have gone in the canoes." He jerked his head to starboard. "Out to sea most likely."

"You mean they could still be out there?" Webb said.

Mamuka shrugged. "I don't know, sir. This happened about two days ago. If they had something to collect water in, they'd be all right for a few days on the sea. The weather has been good. Perhaps they came back and went into the bush, but they'd be very afraid for some time to do that."

"I don't understand this," Clements said. "Why would Eglito attack these people? They couldn't have done him any harm."

Mamuka tapped ash from the cigarette into his palm. "Eglite had nothing to do with this, Mr Clements. Not directly."

Clements raised his eyebrows. "Who, then?"

"These people are not popular on Murdo." Mamuka stilled Clements' protest with an upraised hand, like a schoolmaster. "I know *you* like them, sir. That's the trouble — all the white men liked the Birdbeak Bay people. But in the early days they raided around the coast and sold people to the plantations. Then they taxed the bush people who *wanted* to go to Queensland and Fiji and the plantations on the other islands. This is the best place on the coast for ships for many miles and the easiest to get to from the bush. The Birdbeak people made much money and many enemies. I do not like them myself."

Webb digested the information methodically. "Do you mean, Peter, that the village was raided by old enemies of the Birdbeak people? Maybe in revenge for something that happened a long time ago?"

Mamuka nodded. "Many shell money rewards have been put up. Some as long as thirty years ago or more. Some people remember these things, keep track of them."

"What people?" Clements said.

Mamuka shrugged. "Bush people, maybe, from the south and west of here."

Webb said, "To'beili?"

Mamuka shook his head. "Too far south. They have their own enemies to take care of. And To'beili mostly fight among themselves, anyway."

"That's what I thought," Webb said.

Clements stared at him. "You don't mean you still want to go down to Sunburi?"

"I do."

"You're crazy. The island's going up in flames, and you want to sit around tracing fathers' brothers' sisters?"

"We don't know that the whole island's going up in flames. This is just one incident. It may be isolated . . . Peter, why are you doing that?"

Mamuka was shaking his head and nervously plucking hairs from his short beard. "The boatmen are talking. They pick up things we don't hear. Perhaps from a canoe at night."

"What things?" Webb said.

"Trouble in some other part of the island. On the other side maybe."

"How could anyone know anything about that? It's days away."

Mamuka examined a short, bristly hair. "I am only telling you what they say, sir."

"No need to get huffy," Webb said.

"It confirms what I'm saying, Richard," said Clements. "It'd be madness to go to Sunburi. We'd better get back to Alma."

"You've got a plantation down the coast to visit."

"It may be ashes by now."

Webb laughed. "You're speculating that the rule of law has been destroyed on Murdo. That Naismith's kingdom has returned to savagery. That every man's hand is turned against his neighbour."

"Well," Clements said, "put like that."

"Sorry," Webb said. "That was uncalled for. Look, I don't want to come the old soldier and I know I haven't been here very long, but in a situation like this the lie of the land guides the thinking. Sunburi is just the place we should go. Hang on." He went below and returned with a map of Murdo, which he spread out on the deck. "Look, the island's almost at its narrowest at Sunburi; there's bound to be news there of anything happening on the other coast. Right, Peter?"

Mamuka nodded.

"You can make Alma overland in a day and a bit if you have to from Sunburi," Webb said.

Clements grimaced. "I couldn't."

Webb's finger traced south to the scattering of islands that formed the tail of the island. "You could reach Alma in a couple of days going this way about, *and* you're likely to run into Naismith. Between you Murdo would have been circumnavigated, and you could pool information. It's the logical thing to do."

Clements grunted. "And what you want."

Webb smiled. "Maybe everything will be quiet and peaceful there and I'll be able to ask people about their mothers' brothers' fathers."

Baekani was jolted by Sergeant Bitamae's assassination. The word for the act in the Alma language carried the implications of a quiet death, a symbolic death, a calculatedly restrained action. Baekani knew that the killer or killers could have accounted for most of the members of his patrol, if not all. He also knew what this signified. First, that the killers were local people who saw themselves as protecting their own territory. Second, that their message was, non-negotiably, that the patrol should quit their lands immediately. It was the third aspect of the message that most concerned Baekani. Although the members of the patrol knew that he, Baekani, was in command, to the bush people things would seem otherwise. Sergeant Bitamae was the oldest member of the party. He had served two DOs before Naismith and was officially the senior Murdoan representative of the police arm of British authority. By killing him, the Murdoans of the plateau were announcing their contempt for that authority.

Little of this would have been apparent to the others; Bellua perhaps would have the subtlety of mind to grasp it. Samsu and Bacca were simply afraid, and Luku thirsted for revenge, although he had no love for Bitamae. Baekani's method of compelling Samsu and Bacca to continue was simple. First, he made them more afraid of him than of hostile villagers. He did this by tongue-lashing them, forcing them to do the bulk of the work in preparing a grave for their dead comrade. When they were exhausted by this labour and close to tears from his abuse, he produced a bottle of rum and the patrol conducted a form of wake for Bitamae that included the swearing of many vows of revenge and other bloodthirsty oaths. Baekani scarcely drank.

"We will go back to Alma, Baekani," Bellua said. "And get more men and guns. Is it so?"

"No," Baekani said. "We go on, now."

Bellua gaped. "Now? We are drunk."

"Then you will not feel the arrows when they divide your ribs."

Baekani touched Bacca's ribs with his boot. "Get up, To'beili, we're heading for your gardens and ancestral shrines."

Bacca shook his head. "We will die."

Baekani kicked him. Bacca looked up; the front sight of the Mannlicher was only a couple of centimetres from his right eye. He scrambled to his feet and picked up his pack.

Baekani marched the patrol for six hours straight. They

camped without a fire, ate tinned beef and ship's biscuit, drank water and did not smoke. They were on the very edge of the To'beili uplands. Baekani chewed betel to stay awake through the night. He stimulated himself with visions of his triumphs against Eglito, with the shell money he would accumulate; Bellua would make him the hero of his story and Samsu would carry his fame to the outer islands. His mind, agitated by the danger and fired by the betel, constructed elaborate patterns of power and prestige with himself at the centre. When he fell into imagining William Naismith deferring to him, relaying his instructions, he jerked his mind back onto safer tracks.

Baekani awakened the patrol at first light. After a hasty conference with Bacca, he ordered a weapons check and gave the men time to shit, urinate, clear their throats and spit. The climb to one of the To'beili fortresses likely to be used by Eglito and his supporters would be silent. When the moment came he would want his men to make as much noise as possible: bottling them up beforehand would facilitate this.

Baekani's object was simple — to kill as many identifiable members of Eglito's clan as possible, and retire without incurring casualties. Baekani concurred in Naismith's judgment that this would dent Eglito's reputation. He would have the problem of explaining away Bitamae's death, but perhaps some action could be taken on the return trek to neutralise that damage.

The patrol climbed the steep, root-broken jungle track. Bacca, attempting at all times to keep Samsu between himself and danger, made hand signals to indicate directions and distances. They reached the first of the leafy fortresses mid-morning as the sun was heating up the jungle, turning the air moist and steamy. Baekani and his men watched the place — a cave with a clearing in front of it — for half an hour before cautiously advancing. A quick inspection showed that the site had been occupied by a number of people within the last twenty-four hours. It was now quite abandoned. Baekani permitted a rest with tobacco and tea before pressing on.

The next fortress yielded a similar reading of signs, although the occupation looked more recent, perhaps twelve hours before. A garden near the camp had been worked and some tools left behind. Baekani broke the tools and left them insultingly in the middle of the garden. They reached the next place mid-afternoon as the clouds gathered thick and dark overhead. On the last stages of the climb Baekani was aware of a tension in Bacca that was communicating itself to the other men. He peered through the thick bush on either side of the narrow path and strained to hear the telltale sounds of animals moving in the undergrowth, birds leaving cover or the murmur of voices that could carry long distances in the thin mountain air. Once Baekani thought he caught a flash of movement through the trees. He had the Mannlicher unshipped and ready in a split second, but saw nothing more.

A hiss from Bacca and Baekani waved the patrol to a halt. He crouched, staring ahead, seeing nothing. He looked enquiringly at Bacca, who stood and lifted his arm to point. There was a short whistling rush of sound, and Bellua screamed as an arrow penetrated his right eye. Bacca slipped behind Samsu as Baekani brought his rifle up. Before Baekani could fire, three quick shots sounded and Bellua died as a bullet severed his carotid artery, spraying blood all around him. The blood drenched Bacca, but he never knew it — another bullet passed through Samsu's fleshy neck and struck Bacca in the heart.

Luku and Baekani were firing now, shooting blindly in the direction from which the attack had come. Baekani was tasting the bitterness of defeat in this, his first major battle. He cursed Naismith and the foolish plan; he cursed himself for his arrogance, and all To'beili. As he pumped shots at the trees and rocks in front of him he felt his mind locking into sympathy with those of the defenders. *What arrogance to think that he could defy a thousand years of To'beili spirits. What did one generation of white men count for, or two or three? Nothing.* A bullet struck a rock beside his head and showered him with sharp slivers of stone; they flicked across his face, slicing the skin and causing blood to spring out from a dozen cuts. Baekani wiped the blood away and fired at a light shape above him. He heard a scream and smiled. Then a grunt came from behind him and Luku slumped to the ground with an arrow in his back. *His back! They are behind me!* Baekani wheeled around and fired two shots wildly into the bush. A crack sounded, a report from a heavy calibre rifle and Baekani felt the Mannlicher almost torn from his grasp. The bullet had struck the stock, splintering the wood and shattering the shell inlay. Baekani yelled in fear and bolted down the track, clutching the ruined rifle in one hand and his Webley pistol in the other. A man rose from the bush beside the track and threw back his arm to launch a spear; Baekani emptied the Webley in his face, threw the pistol aside, jumped the body and ran, slithering and falling back the way the patrol had come.

24

Patugi, 22 February 1928

Ashley Price-Kane signed his name with a flourish and pushed the paper aside. A permission to cut timber. *Why not? Level the place. Who was that chap who said it'd cut down the rainfall? Probably mad. Everyone goes mad in the tropics sooner or later.* A knock came on the door and he barked "Come in," while pulling the next paper towards him.

"Excuse me, sir." The tall, sandy-haired young man who entered was Cameron Somerville, a radio engineer who had installed the network in the BJIP over the past eighteen months. His enthusiasm for his job was boundless: he visited every outpost personally to set up the radio transmitters and receivers and to decide on the most appropriate power sources — in some cases wind power sufficed, in others auxiliary generators were required. The best of the islanders he had trained were capable of maintaining the equipment, even adapting it to cope with changed demands. Although his period of contract had almost finished and the network was functioning well, Somerville still liked to man the Patugi station regularly, fine-tuning the system. He was twenty-six and Price-Kane could scarcely understand a word he said.

"Somerville?" the RC said, without looking up.

"Picked up something rather odd on the bands, sir."

Price-Kane sighed and waved at a chair. "Sit down, Somerville, and talk English, for God's sake. Your gibberish is as bad as this bloody pidgin."

Somerville, who had acquired a fluent if not altogether accurate pidgin and delighted in using it over the air to native operators, tried not to let his dislike of Price-Kane's attitude show. Privately, he thought the old Raj style of administration was on the way out. He hoped that rapid communications would deliver the *coup de grâce*. He sat with his long legs tucked up awkwardly and looked at a scribbling block he held in his hand. "Some sort of private messages have been going out from Murdo."

"Private? That's a government installation."

"Not very expertly handled. Clearly not Will Naismith's work or Baekani's."

"Who?"

"Baekani, Naismith's right-hand man. He's a damn good radio operator. The messages are signed 'Birmingham'. He's that writer chap, isn't he? The one who was wounded?"

"Yes. Damn fool shot himself when he was drunk. How can he be sending messages?"

"Well, I hardly think he could. He'd have to be given the call signs, frequencies and so on. That would be a pretty severe breach of regulations."

"Really? But not for Naismith to give them to a native?"

Somerville ignored the remark. "I think Keith Larke must have sent them and signed them in Birmingham's name."

"God. I suppose that violates regulations, too?"

"Very much so. The messages were brief, and I only personally picked up a bit of one. Another operator heard some more but couldn't get it down because there was bad static, and Larke, if it was Larke, isn't much of an operator. The calls were to the *Daily Sun* newspaper in Sydney to be relayed to the *Chicago Daily News*."

"What? I can't believe it. What do they say?"

Somerville looked at his notes. "Bit hard to be sure, but they seem to be about a native rebellion on Murdo. Birmingham seems to be trying to sell the story to the American press."

"*What* bloody story? There *is* no rebellion on Murdo!"

Somerville stood. "I think you should have a talk with Larke, sir. Do you want me to try to jam any traffic out of Murdo?"

"Can you do that?"

"Mmm, but it might make it difficult to communicate with them from here. Best done after you get through."

Price-Kane was aware of the gentle pressure to act. "Yes, yes, thanks, Somerville. I'll collect my thoughts and be along shortly. Open the channel or whatever it is you do."

"Right. Oh, one more thing, sir. Telegraphic advice from Suva of an important despatch coming from London. The WPHC wanted to alert you. Twenty minutes, then?"

Price-Kane didn't answer. Somerville left and shut the door firmly. The RC sat back in his chair and felt the strong and urgent need for a whisky. His stiff knee, a legacy of Verdun, was paining him as it always did when he felt outflanked. Military training had predisposed Price-Kane in favour of dealing with one thing at a time. The High Command didn't order a chap to take a hill and blow up a bridge at the same time, and Price-Kane distrusted people, like Cameron Somerville, who appeared to be able to handle two or more matters simultaneously. Consequently, when demands were made on his judgment from two different quarters he felt the pressure.

Price-Kane worried, thirsted and thought militarily. *Two attacks — one from Murdo, one from Suva — it was like a pincer movement.* What the hell was happening on Murdo? And what was the important despatch from London? He could recall several previous advance notices of despatches, but not their contents. Nothing earth-shattering. And Larke. Bloody Larke. Price-Kane had read Larke's two despatches several times without being able to make any sense of them. *Naismith a republican? Naismith taking an unseemly interest in a young woman? Ridiculous.* Still, there was the matter of the native, Baekani, obviously a focus of Larke's antagonism and now reported to be a skilled radio operator.

Uninterested as he was in the texture of life in the BJIP, Price-Kane had learned that the waterfront was the listening post of the islands, the communications hub that Cameron Somerville's radio network might one day complement but would never supersede. He needed information about Murdo, and he needed it quickly. He took up his hat and walked to the outer office.

"Dr Herbert to see you in five minutes, sir," his secretary said.

"Tell him to wait. I'm talking to the harbourmaster, then using the radio. Back in an hour or so."

"Yes, sir."

The RC winced as the high, bright sun hit him. He used his stick to ease the pressure on his knee as he crunched along the gravel path towards the harbour. *Straight back. Chin up. A curt nod to whites, ignore natives and Orientals. The only way.*

Half an hour later, walking towards the radio room, his back was less straight and his chin drooped somewhat. Although he seldom smoked in the open, Price-Kane was puffing on a cheroot as an aid to thought. The harbourmaster had called in the skippers of several ships that had been around Murdo in the last few days. Their information had been wild native gossip, canoe talk, coconut chatter, but it had been consistent. There was trouble on Murdo, and it wasn't confined to one place. An exaggerated account of the demonstration at Uta'a was going the rounds occasioning mirth among the Murdoans and disquiet among others.

Mulling the news over, Price-Kane fastened his ire on the figure of Larke. *Naismith should never have left him in charge.* He did not extend the thought to take in his own compliance with the plan. *Larke ought to have reported on these events by radio. Instead of . . .*

By the time he reached the radio room, situated at the

back of the Secretariat with ventilation, insulation and availability of natural light carefully designed by Somerville, the RC had worked himself up into a fury. He stormed into the quiet, bright room, ignoring warning lights and notices requesting silence and no smoking.

"Put me through to Larke on Murdo," he bellowed to the operator.

The islander, seated and wearing earphones, did not look up. Price-Kane banged his fist on the desk, causing needles on dials to jump and the earphones to fill with static. The operator tore the earphones off and prepared to shout in reply when he recognised the RC. He scrambled to his feet.

"Your Excellency, I . . . "

"Murdo! I want to speak to Murdo *now*!"

Somerville strolled into the room and gave the operator a reassuring smile. "I'm afraid that won't be possible, sir."

"Why the devil not?"

The operator half-bowed and left the room quickly. Somerville bent over the de Forrest receiving and transmitting unit, inspecting it for damage. The needles were at rest in the proper place and the clock showed the correct time. "The station's not receiving. My guess is that your Mr Larke has let the batteries run down. Either that or he's flipped the switch to close off the circuits and doesn't know what he's done."

"Hell and damnation!"

"Would you mind giving me the cigar, sir? We can't permit smoking in here." Somerville took the cheroot from Price-Kane's fingers, crossed the room and dropped it out the window.

"Are you telling me Murdo's out of radio contact?"

"Not exactly, sir. There's a station in the Tau lagoon. We got through to Headman Tefu, but couldn't make a lot of sense of what he had to say. Sounded rather panicked. Will Naismith's due there pretty soon, and we managed to get it through to the headman that the DO should call us as soon as possible."

Price-Kane slumped into a chair. "Good, good. That's good work, Somerville. Thank you. What in the name of all that's holy can be happening at Alma?"

Somerville shrugged. "Search me, sir. A message to the station has been picked up. We weren't tuned in for it here, but they got it at Quiros. I called around asking if people had picked up Alma signals, you see."

Price-Kane nodded respectfully at yet another show of initiative. *Why wasn't this bright chap in the service instead of fiddling with dials?* Then he remembered the despatches he'd seen with their references to the Americans' interest in establishing a communications base in the Protectorate. *Is this the diplomacy of the future? God help us.* "To Alma, from where?" he said.

"Sydney, sir. It was repeated a few times. Sydney was relaying a message from Chicago, apparently. The message read: 'Chicago very interested. Send more soonest.'"

"Soonest? Soonest? What the hell does that mean?"

"It's telegraphic jargon, used by the press. He could have begun sending already, for all we know."

The RC heaved himself to his feet and ignored the twinges from his knee. A course of action was clear. "Don't know much about this radio business. Can we do anything about telegraph messages coming out of Murdo?"

Somerville shook his head. "Pick them up, that's all. Do you want me to arrange that?"

"Yes, Somerville. I do."

"You don't want to wait until Naismith gets to the Tau lagoon? Be useful to speak to him, I should think. He'll be able to sort this out, surely."

"I'm beginning to wonder," Price-Kane said. "It'll take me an hour or two to get ready. Keep trying to get through to the Tau lagoon. That's a mouthful, isn't there any other name for it?"

Somerville turned to look at a map on the wall. "The station's on an island called . . ." he squinted at the red dot, " . . . Tefu. So the call sign is SMT 1 — south, Murdo, Tefu — and of course it's the only station in the area, so it's number one."

Price-Kane searched his memory. "I've heard that word

before. From Naismith I think. Tefu, I believe that's the name of the headman."

Somerville raised an eyebrow. "He must really be important."

"Keep calling. I'd like to talk to Naismith if I can. Otherwise I'm going to have to go over and have a look at his bloody island for myself."

25

South-west coast of Murdo, 22 February 1928

The *Loloburu* developed engine trouble on the run from the Uta'a passage to the Tau lagoon. Will Naismith fumed as the launch drifted on the current — south, certainly, but much too slowly for the DO's liking. After the humiliation at Uta'a he was anxious to demonstrate that his writ still ran, and the Tau lagoon would be a perfect place to do it. He had information that Lagailemo, his one remaining murderer at large (apart from Eglito) was in the bush above the lagoon. Headman Tefu, though old, was still a staunch *man bilong gafamanu*. He would co-operate to the hilt in Naismith's plan, which was to send a party to the east as a feint while the real strike was made at Kwanasila, the bush stronghold where Lagailemo was boasting of his defiance of the government and his intention of collecting more shell money bounties.

Like the DO, the police aboard the launch were thirsty for action, especially Marius, the Catholic convert and clerk. In some way the insult at Uta'a had loosened the bonds of civilisation so carefully tied by Father Bondil. Naismith, missing Baekani and feeling the loneliness of power, found himself confiding in Marius as the mechanic seated over the engine.

"Will you collect the rate at Tau, sir?" the clerk asked. "The rolls are very good for the artificial islands and the beach people, also for the bush villages to the east."

"Baekani and I were there two years ago," Naismith said. "One of the most peaceful places on Murdo, which is why Lagailemo chooses to hide there. There, he is a big man."

Marius was unused to this degree of volubility from Naismith. He was inexperienced in direct conversation with Europeans apart from Father Bondil, but he decided to risk persisting with his questions. "The tax, sir?"

"I'll collect the tax *after* I've collected Lagailemo."

This Marius understood — revenge, a show of strength. The only question was: how far would such a demonstration go? The district officer and the clerk were sitting on canvas chairs under a canopy across the rear section of the *Loloburu's* deck. The launch drifted sluggishly a hundred metres offshore. The coastline here was rugged — sheer cliffs interspersed with thickly wooded promontories ending in clusters of dark mangroves. As he looked at the gnarled, forbidding mangrove swamps, Naismith reflected that he was growing careless — one of his predecessors had been shot dead in just such a situation. The officer, whose name Naismith could not at that minute recall, had been in a whaleboat, sitting erect, shaving, and a single bullet from a mangrove swamp had passed through the back of his head and shattered the mirror he was holding in his hand. Naismith had toured in whaleboats too and had always taken care to keep well offshore. And here he was now, twice humiliated on his own island, and drifting along within rifle shot. *Getting careless and soft,* he thought. *No, by God. Not soft!*

Marius ventured his question, framed as a statement: "Lagailemo will have supporters. They may not shoot above our heads."

"Then we will blows theirs off," Naismith said. As he spoke the engine roared into life, and a shout of triumph came from below the engine hatch.

At six feet and two inches, Headman Tefu was a giant among Jeremians, and he owed some of his authority to his physical size. Nor had that prestige been reduced twenty years before when he had lost half of his right leg to a shark. Tefu was of the clan that had the shark as its minor totem, and he freely admitted that he had been neglectful in his duties to his shark totem ancestors. He had favoured the crocodile totem and had paid the penalty. Tefu reasoned that he had been lucky — the crocodile would not have been so lenient in its punishment. Now, supported by a long stick carved at its top into the form of a crutch and much carved and ornamented along its whole length, he stood on the stone jetty which jutted out into the waters of the Tau lagoon and watched the *Loloburu* draw near.

Tefu's father had acquired the name, and the headman's chest plate, from an early DO who had asked a tall saltwater man his name and had been told, instead and uncomprehendingly, that of the largest of the artificial islands. The DO, impressed by the man's height, bearing and apparent understanding of the wishes of the British government, had appointed him headman. Tefu the elder immediately assassinated the old *lemo* who held sway on the coast and used the firepower of a police patrol to subdue several local clans and earn some shell money bounties. Hated, but more importantly, feared by the bushmen, he did everything the government asked of him. He dragooned people into public works projects, assisted in compiling of the tax rolls, informed on murderers and absconders from plantations and offered his full support to the Anglican, Catholic and Seventh-day Adventist missions in turn.

The extension of government control, the end of the colonial labour recruiting and faster communications gave Tefu the younger less room to manoeuvre. But he had inherited the name, office and style of his father, and they had served him well. Now, however, as he saw the launch cut its engines and drift towards the jetty, he felt that they was time to consider his position.

"*Masta*." Tefu stood very straight and tall as Naismith stepped ashore.

"Tefu, good day." Naismith noticed the tension in the headman and decided to assert himself from the start. He ordered the police ashore and directed the sergeant to drill them for an hour. He ordered tea to be brewed by the launch's cook and brought to him; then he marched towards the tax house, conveniently located close to the beach and a freshwater stream. Although Tefu could move with great speed when he chose, he expressed his doubts by lagging far behind. Naismith was seated on the verandah with a map spread out in front of him when the headman limped up.

"Tefu, you are slow. I think you must be getting old."

"No, *masta*. There is much trouble in this place." Then the words poured out: Tefu told the DO about the rumours that had been coming out of the bush, rumours of feuding, raiding of plantations and missions and, most distressing of all, the killing of government appointees. Tefu knew that most of the rumours were false, but he was concerned. He had heard of the demonstration at Uta'a but made no reference to it. His own people, he said, were *'plenti poreit'*, very frightened.

"Frightened?" Naismith said. "Of what?"

The headman hesitated. The Tau people were more frightened of their neighbours and of rampant *lemos* than of the DO, but Tefu knew better than to tell Naismith this. He opted to change the subject. "There is much talking on the wireless, *masta*. Would you care to talk on the wireless to his honour, the resident commissioner?" Tefu framed the proposal carefully, knowing that Naismith disliked using the radio except for emergencies.

"Why the hell didn't you say so?"

Naismith folded the map and began to retrace his steps to the beach, again followed by Tefu. The headman was very confused, never having heard Naismith swear before. On the way they met the cook's assistant, who was carrying a tray with a pot of tea on it. Naismith beckoned him to pour the tea as he walked. The servant attempted to do it, but he dropped the pot; it broke, and the tea splashed over the DO's trousers. He bellowed and took a swipe at the servant with his rolled-up map. The man ducked away and stood trembling, holding the tray and juggling the sugar bowl. The cubes rattled loudly. Naismith looked at him, threw back his head and howled with laughter. "Never mind," he said, "never mind the tea. Quick and lively now, where's the canoe?"

The headman had a large canoe launched and sat proudly behind Naismith as two sturdy Tau men paddled to Tefu Island. Naismith continued to chuckle and Tefu continued to worry. He had never seen the DO in such a mood before, and the sight of the police patrol drilling tightly and determinedly at the far end of the beach did nothing to allay his fears. And something else worried him — why had Naismith been looking at a map rather than the tax rolls? For a conservative traditionalist like Tefu, all these signs of change were disturbing.

The large island of Tefu had been built for the same reason as all the other artificial islands around Murdo — to escape from the debilitating sickness brought by the mosquitoes which had been seasonally in plague proportions on the coast in earlier times. Unlike the islands in the north, those at Tau were permanently occupied by clans whose lineages stretched back to the time of the mosquito plagues and beyond. Why the mosquitoes had ceased to swarm in millions no one knew; the Tefuans had a legend about seven winds blowing them away. These people had welcomed the installation of the radio on their island because with it went a small house with a tin roof from which the water could be collected in a tank. Tefuans were spared the daily trips to the mainland to bring water laboriously back in hollowed-out bamboos. Tefu was consecrated to the shark and turtle totems, and the headman himself had composed the songs that would placate the shark and turtle totems for the violation of their shrines.

Much of this history was known to Naismith and normally something of it would pass through his mind

when he set foot on Tefu. But today he had thoughts only
for the radio and his responsibilities. He greeted the Tefuans
perfunctorily and waited with ill-concealed impatience
while Tefu unlocked the door to the radio shed. The
installation was wind-powered with a generator as back-up.
Naismith checked the battery levels and, as regulations
required sub-stations to call the station next above them
before contacting the Hemisphere base, he put through a
routine call to Alma. He got no response.

"Wailis himi no tok tok long Alma," Tefu said, *"Alma, himi
die pinis."**

Naismith called Patugi and got an instant response from
Cameron Somerville: "AC 1 receiving, SMT 1. Somerville
here, Mr Naismith. How's the reception?"

"Reception's fine, AC 1. Hullo, Mr Somerville. I was told
the RC wanted to speak to me."

"You've just missed him, I'm afraid. He's on the way to
Murdo. He left about . . ."

"What the devil for?"

"There appears to be a good deal of unrest on the island
from what we're picking up here."

"It's nothing to be concerned about. I tried to call Alma
but couldn't contact the station. Is it out of order?"

"Alma's not transmitting or receiving. That's one of the
things Major Price-Kane's gone across to look into."

Naismith was stunned and did not reply. Somerville,
fearing he had lost the signal, spoke urgently. "AC 1 to
SMT 1, are you receiving?"

"SMT 1. Yes, I hear you. That's madness! The RC
worried about a radio station? I can't believe it."

"There's more to it than that, Mr Naismith. I'm afraid
I can't discuss it on air like this. It's . . . sensitive, I suppose
you'd say."

"Talk sense, man."

"I'm under orders to that effect, Mr Naismith. I'm sorry.
Can I help you in any way? Are you in good health?"

---

* "We can't make wireless contact with Alma. The Alma station
doesn't answer."

Naismith fought for control. "Of course I'm in good health. Let me get this straight, Somerville. You say the RC left Hemisphere quite recently?"

"Within the hour. Perhaps you should arrange to rendezvous with him there."

"No fear. If he wants to waste his time fixing radios, let him. I'll be here a few days, and I'll call Alma from time to time. If I don't get through I can use Richard Webb's field radio from Sunburi. It'd get through to Patugi, wouldn't it?"

"Yes, if it's been properly maintained. Can you let me know what action you're taking about unrest on the island? I should put something in the log."

Naismith clenched the microphone in his fist. "Put that I'm going into the bush to catch Lagailemo, bring him back and hang him on the beach. I'm ending this transmission, AC 1. SMT 1 out."

Naismith flipped the 'off' switch and let out a sigh made up of tension and relief. When he looked up he saw Tefu staring at him with wide, terrified eyes.

The headman stammered, *"Masta, masta . . ."*

"Yes?"

"Lagailemo stap long bus."

"I know," Naismith said impatiently. "What of it?"

"He is now with Eglito, *masta."*

Naismith suddenly felt old. The pain from the ailments which dogged him, aching joints, sore teeth and gums, headaches, all seemed to hit him at once. He felt his face flush and didn't know whether it was humiliation or the sudden outbreak of a fever. He clutched the arms of the cane chair and his vision clouded over, making him feel panicked and almost frail. Deprived by self-discipline of the comforts of drink and tobacco and with Baekani far away, Naismith felt beseiged. He levered himself upright and moved slowly to the door. Tefu's crutches scraped the floor behind him.

"You are sick, sir?"

Naismith stood on the narrow plank porch that ran along the front of the radio building. He looked out over the lagoon past the nearest island to the sea beyond the reef. At first the scene was like something from one of those French painters he'd seen in art galleries in Paris — the sorts of things Amelia had liked and he had once dreamed of buying for her. *What had she called them? Impressionists, that was it.* Then his vision cleared, and he saw the white water thrown up as the waves hit the reef and the grey, level flatness of the lagoon as it lay under the heavy afternoon clouds waiting for rain. As he watched the light died; a black cloud blotted out the sun and the breeze shifted direction and stiffened. He heard Tefu move uneasily on his stick. "No, Tefu, I'm not sick. I was thinking about Lagailemo and Eglito. That's all."

"*Yu hangimap, masta?*"

Naismith nodded.

"*Yu hangimap long Sunburi, masta?*"

Naismith's face remained grim, but he smiled inwardly. It was typical of Tefu to think of his own skin first. A clash between renegades and the police at Sunburi could do him nothing but good. It would inevitably lower To'beili prestige and raise his own. The Tau lagoon, under the leadership of headman Tefu, was a safe place to be. "You're a rogue, Tefu," Naismith said. "Take me back to the *Loloburu.*"

26

Alma, 20 February 1928

Tom Birmingham carefully cleaned rust from around the firing pin of a .38 Luger automatic. "This is goin' to be big, Louise. Really big. The hostiles're leavin' the reservation. And I reckon I'm goin' to see some action at last."

Louise was grinding a piece of pearlshell, using a mortar and pestle method she had observed in the villages. It was slow, painstaking work, but she was gratified to see the grinding bringing out the colour in the shell and the disc shape slowly forming. "I don't see why you say that," she said. "Everything looks perfectly normal around here to me."

"That's what you think." Birmingham cocked and fired the pistol. The pin clicked satisfactorily.

"It *is* what I think, and it's what I hear, too. Unlike you, I can actually talk to these people now."

"I hear all I need to hear from the reverend, and I hear different."

"Just what do you hear, Tom?"

"Place is on the brink of rebellion."

"Rubbish. I wish you wouldn't play with that thing. It looks so old it could blow up in your hand. Where did you get it?"

"Bought it off a Jap down on the beach — a sort of travelling man, he was. Those Japs've got plenty of guns. 'Course," Birmingham smiled as he worked the Luger's mechanism, "most of 'em are like this one was and would jam first time you fired it, but they're ready."

Louise had noticed a certain nervousness on the part of the Chinese proprietor in one of the two Alma trade stores, but she had put it down to commercial problems. Business in the store had seemed very slow of late. She was unaware of any Japanese in the islands and the information, even though she discounted Tom's delusions, unsettled her. She worked on the shell, grinding evenly so as not to cause a break. Since what he called his 'accident', Birmingham had made no sexual demands, spent most of his time with Keith Larke and Pastor Stoltenberg and left Louise to visit the villages, talk to the women and take photographs. She swam in a freshwater rock pool a couple of kilometres from Alma, and her body was firm and strong from the walking and occasional work in the gardens. She slept soundly. If she hadn't been feeling a fierce longing for Richard Webb, she would have been content.

Birmingham began to work on the rust on the Luger's barrel. "This is a piece of shit," he said. "But I've gotta have a weapon, and that bastard Webb ran off with my Colt."

Louise forced herself not to react, aware that Birmingham was watching her closely. She held the disc of shell between thumb and forefinger; it caught the sun and reflected it dazzlingly into Birmingham's eyes. He winced. "Sorry," Louise said. "This is coming along nicely."

Birmingham wrapped the pistol in a cloth and put it into the pocket of his bush shirt. He stood up, using the stick he had adopted in place of the crutch, and put on his sun helmet. "I've got to see the reverend," he said. "You're invited to the mission for lunch."

"No, thanks," Louise said. "I'm going to the village."

"It's not safe."

Louise laughed. "It's a lot safer than eating that tinned junk at the mission. Give the reverend my regards and tell him I'd like to take a photograph of him."

Birmingham had taken two steps away; he stopped and turned back. "I thought you didn't like him."

"I don't."

"Then why?"

"I want to put him in my book."

"What book?"

"I'm going to do a book about the Jeremiahs, a book of photographs."

Birmingham grunted, saluted his wife with a waggle of his stick and set off towards the mission. Walking had never been one of his favourite occupations, and he considered that he'd done ten times as much of it in his lifetime as a normal man. The stick helped; it gave him, to his own mind, an air of authority and purposefulness. And the weight of the Luger in his pocket was comforting. He looked suspiciously at the Murdoans he encountered along the track. Unlike Louise, he did not instinctively distinguish the pagans from the Christians. Grubby cotton trousers, shorts and singlets signified 'native' to Birmingham just as much as bare chests, bone necklaces, broad belts and lavalavas. The only distinction Birmingham made was between members of the police force, government employees and the others. He saw very few of the first about and considered this worth reporting to Stoltenberg. Perhaps the rats had begun to desert the sinking ship.

When he reached the mission, around one in the afternoon, he found Stoltenberg and Larke deep into an argument that seemed to be sending shock waves out from the large, open-sided thatch hut that was used as the mission's meeting centre. Normally the mission people hung about the hut awaiting prayer sessions, work instructions or just killing time. Today no one was close to the building; Stoltenberg's flock was keeping well clear of the shepherd.

"That is simply not possible, Dr Stoltenberg," Birmingham heard Larke almost shout. "I have no such authority."

"You must assume the authority. No one else can."

Birmingham approached quietly and stood unobserved outside the hut. He wanted to witness the scene in order the gauge the personalities of the men with whom he had cast his lot. "Ridiculous," Larke snapped. He reached for his cigarette tin.

"Please do not smoke in here," Stoltenberg said. "This is the house of God."

"God!" Larke exclaimed. "I wish to God I knew what you were up to. Naismith . . ."

"The district officer is dead, I have told you that. He was killed at Uta'a — at the very least he was seriously injured."

"There's no evidence of that."

"I believe my informants. News travels incredibly quickly along the coast."

Birmingham could not play the observer any longer. He stepped forward, letting his stick rap on the cement slab that formed the floor of the hut. "What's this? Did you say Naismith's dead, reverend?"

Stoltenberg inclined his head gravely. Larke turned almost guiltily but relaxed when he saw Birmingham. "Dr Stoltenberg wants me to assume command here. To call for a punitive expedition at Uta'a and punish some of the bush people he claims are harassing the mission. I don't have the authority. I tried to call the Tefu station and Patugi but the radio seems to be out of order."

"Goddamnit! Sorry, reverend, no offence." Birmingham advanced, exaggerating his limp, and sat down in a canvas-backed chair beside Larke.

Stoltenberg sat opposite, stiff-spined and austere in a high-backed Victorian chair that resembled a throne. It was his favourite piece of furniture, polished by a youth from the mission every day. "This unfortunate radio failure only makes it more imperative for Mr Larke to act."

Larke turned to Birmingham, his face a picture of

confusion and indecision. "I'm sorry, Birmingham. I know the radio was important to you."

"Don't you pay it no mind," Birmingham said. "I know a little about that equipment. I'll take a look at it." Birmingham had one of the radio's smaller valves in his pocket as he spoke, having removed it a few hours before. "What's this about Naismith?"

Larke opened his mouth, but Stoltenberg spoke first. He gave Birmingham a highly flavoured coloured of an attack on Naismith, his clerk and two policemen by the bush people above the Uta'a passage. The police were dead, the story went, and Naismith either dead or close to it. Birmingham listened carefully, trying to judge whether the missionary believed the story himself or not. He couldn't tell. "Where's Naismith or his body now?" he asked.

Stoltenberg took off his wire-framed glasses and massaged the bridge of his beaky nose. "I don't know. It's unclear whether or not the launch was attacked."

"I don't believe a word of it," said Larke.

"It's consistent with what we've been hearing," Birmingham said. "Naismith thought he had this place under his thumb, but he was wrong, dead wrong. Sorry, gentlemen, no joke intended."

"The plan was to go on to the Tau lagoon," Larke said. "He'd have reached there by now. If I could just get a call through . . . "

Birmingham could hear the desperation in Larke's voice. The boy was in a fine state to be manipulated, but the question was, in which direction? Control of communications he'd considered his ace in the hole. *But Naismith massacred at Uta'a is from left field,* he thought. *Some headline, if it's the McCoy. I need a private word with the reverend.* Birmingham punched Larke's upper arm lightly. "I'll take a look-see at the radio, Keith, but first I wonder if I could have a private confab with the reverend? Married man talk, you understand."

Larke blushed and stood. "Of course. I'll have a cigarette outside."

"You do that."

Birmingham and Stoltenberg sat in silence until Larke disappeared into the shade of the stunted pine trees the missionary had had planted. The trees had failed to thrive in the unsuitable soil and climate.

"Well, reverend," Birmingham said, "things seem to be moving ahead pretty fast."

"Yes, indeed."

"Is this story about Naismith true? I've gotta get it on the wire, if it is."

"It's hard to tell. The people here are inveterate liars. Something certainly happened immediately to the south, at Maka Maka, and something more serious again at the next passage. I think a massacre is quite likely, quite likely."

"Likely won't cut it with the *Chicago News Tribune*, doctor."

Before Stoltenberg could answer, the light in the hut suddenly dropped as if a lantern had been extinguished. Birmingham checked himself before he swore. "What's that?"

"A storm," Stoltenberg said. "I heard that a severe one was coming."

"How bad?"

"They can be very bad in these islands. Absolute cyclones — hurricanes, I think you Americans call them."

"A hurricane, eh? Great copy. I'd better get on the air. This is enough to kick off with. A good newsman can do a lot with a rumour and a hurricane."

The interior of the hut was now almost dark, and Birmingham could not see Stoltenberg's smile. "I thought the radio was out of action?"

"Well, I'm sure I can put it right."

"I'm sure you can. I think we understand each other, Mr Birmingham."

Birmingham drew a deep breath. "I think we do. You sure something happened to Naismith?"

"Something, yes."

"The people around're frisky?"

"I'm sorry."

"Restless?"

"Yes, very."

"Good. What're we going to do about Larke?"

At that moment Larke dashed up the steps and into the hut. "My God," he said. "You should see the sky. It's absolutely purple. I've just been thinking, they'll send someone across from Patugi if I don't make radio contact today."

Birmingham walked to the door and looked out towards the escarpment. A huge black cloud appeared to sit on the top of the trees like a black, swollen airship. A puff of wind lifted dust on the clearing in front of the hut, then a spiral of dust rose and filled the space momentarily before the air became still again. The tops of the trees waved briefly and subsided. "If I read the signs right," Birmingham said, "and I've been down Florida way enough to know, there's one hell of a hurricane brewing. Ain't no one coming over the water from Patugi today."

27

The rain lashed Baekani as he slithered, hobbled and ran down the jungle tracks heading east, back to Alma, away from the scene of the massacre of his patrol and the death of his ambitious hopes. He clutched the shattered stock of his rifle, ignoring the splinters that deeply penetrated his hand. Blood also flowed freely from the stone cuts to his face, but the pounding rain washed the blood away.

Nothing had happened as he had imagined.

"I am disgraced," he raved aloud. "My ancestors are disgraced, my clan is disgraced. The spirits are shitting on my head. I feel it through the rain. I hear their laughter above the wind."

He fell heavily, hitting his head on a tree trunk and twisting the arm that clung to the Mannlicher, whatever stress came on it from whatever direction. The fall dazed him further but seemed to give him extra strength. He pulled himself upright and staggered on, only vaguely aware of the direction he took, heedless of his injuries and exhaustion.

The wind roared above, flattening the tops of the trees,

breaking off branches and sending them crashing down the slopes. Lightning split the sky and the flashes cast a ghastly blue-yellow light over the swaying, thrashing trees and the track which was a moving, flowing path of mud and rocks. Baekani waded, fell, floundered and fought his way on. The surrounding jungle protected him from the fierceness of the howling wind which was uprooting everything in cleared spaces and tearing out immature trees by the roots.

Baekani sobbed as he swam across a creek and dragged himself up the muddy bank opposite. Suddenly the rain stopped and the wind died. Baekani looked up and gave a terrified shriek as a huge bolt of forked lightning danced across the dark sky. The thunderclap that followed had physical force. Baekani was flung to the ground. He lay with his face in the mud and had visions of the arrow piercing Bellua's eye. He heard Bellua's scream and then felt Samsu's blood spraying all over him. But it wasn't blood; the rain had begun again, heavier than before, and the wind pressed Baekani deeper into the mud so he had to turn and lift his head and gasp for air.

"Oh, Kitai'i, wind spirit, spare me," he babbled. "Oh, Tamburu, lightning spirit, spare me. Spare me, Jesus, spare me, God. Mr Naismith, help me. I was only doing what you bade me. I will make atonement for Bellua and Samsu, and Bacca . . . I will do the things for them and make payment to their clans."

The wind seemed to mock him, and he fought to stand upright and shake his rifle high above his head in the air. "I am Baekani," he shouted. "The *lemo* above all others. Mock me at your peril. I will kill you all."

He threw himself forward, pushing against the wind, stumbling until his numbed, bruised feet found the track. He laughed as a tree fell across his path. Then another fell at right angles, forming a perfect cross on the ground. Baekani saluted with his rifle. "Thank you," he shouted. "Thank you, Jesus, for saving my life!"

He plunged on, walking and wading for hours until the wind dropped and the rain eased to a steady downpour. He walked until his muscles refused to function; his legs buckled and he fell. He crawled under a bush and slept with his cheek resting against the cold, hard steel of the rifle.

Richard Webb's field radio was inoperative. It had been left uncovered on the deck of the *Woodlark* and had stayed so when the storm hit. Mamuka attempted to shoulder the blame, but Webb cursed himself for his own carelessness. The cutter was hove to in the most sheltered part of Birdbeak Bay.

"Consider yourself lucky you didn't lose it altogether," Clements shouted over the noise of the wind. "Most of the other stuff on the deck went over when that swell hit."

The swell had been like a minor tidal wave, arriving suddenly at the moment the sky had darkened and the wind had swung around. Then came the sheeting rain. The cutter's crew had worked frantically to get her to safe anchor, and Clements had congratulated them and authorised a rum ration. Now he and Webb huddled in the saloon cabin.

"Isn't this the wrong time of year for this sort of thing?" Webb bellowed.

Clements nodded. "Bit early, but they can hit any time. This seems to be a particularly bad one, though. It'll cause a lot of damage. People will starve, and there'll be a lot of fighting over crops and land."

"As if the place didn't have enough troubles," Webb said. "I wish I could call Alma." When he saw that Clements couldn't hear him, he cupped his hands and shouted into the other man's ear, "I wish we could get through to Alma."

Clements dug a pencil and a notebook from his pocket and scribbled. Webb read, "It'll be all right. Alma's built to take these things." Webb smiled and nodded. He wondered if the same applied to the villages, where Louise was most likely to be. For the first time he felt a weakening of his resolve to complete his study, write his thesis and advance his career. The fates seemed to be against him: love and the elements, at least. He took the pencil and wrote, "Sunburi?"

Clements wrote "Sheltered", followed by, "Naismith?"

A swell hit the *Woodlark*'s hull, lifting and holding her aloft for a nerve-wrenching moment and then dropping her back with a grinding thud. Webb's mind drifted to the thought of the refugees from Birdbeak Bay who might still be out on the water. He peered from the porthole at the black, swirling sky. *No chance for them out there,* he thought, *and little joy for any hiding in the bush.* The boat swung around several degrees, allowing Webb to see the beach. It was littered with fallen trees and branches, and leaves and other debris bumped against the sides of the cutter. By the lantern light in the cabin Webb could see from his watch that it was late in the afternoon, though outside it was almost as dark as night.

A fist pounded on the cabin door, and Clements reached across to allow Mamuka to creep into the confined space. He was wearing an oilskin from which the water streamed. Already wet through, Webb and Clements did not complain.

"Everyone safe?" Webb shouted. "We didn't lose anyone?"

Mamuka shook his head. He reached under the oilskin and pulled out a canvas pouch. "Spare batteries," he said. "For the radio. Dry."

Webb grabbed the pouch and kissed it. Then he pumped Mamuka's hand. "You're a genius, Peter."

Mamuka smiled. *"Tru,"* he said. *"Tru nau."*

Louise crowded into the cave with about ten women and a dozen or more children from Polosila, the small non-Christian village east of Alma. The women lit kerosene lanterns and set about accounting for all the children. Once they had done this they were unconcerned about the storm, which seemed remote, apart from an occasional roar at the mouth of the deep cave.

Louise was drenched, her thin clothes clinging to her. Her hair lay flat on her skull, and she shook her head to clear her ears of water. The storm had hit without warning, and she had felt as if she had taken a plunge off a cliff into a deep pool. The children sat quietly and Louise was reluctant to complain or request a fire. Suddenly, an old woman had addressed her in a queer, cracked voice in English, which was flavoured by Victorian expressions.

"I am Rumae," the woman said. "But you may call me Nanni if you wish, young lady."

"Nanni?"

"Nanni. Many white children have called me Nanni. They will light a fire soon so that you may get warm. Are you hungry, child?"

Louise shook her head. Her teeth were chattering.

Nanni's quiet voice was suddenly raised and in a piercing stream of sound she issued instructions of unmistakable urgency. "The fire will be ready in a minute."

"Thank you . . . Nanni."

"And some tea. It is so pleasant to have someone to talk to. You must tell me all about yourself. Have you been to Brisbane?"

Louise nodded.

"Suva?"

"Yes."

"Wonderful places. I was in Queensland for twenty years and then in Fiji and Tonga. I did not like Tonga." A sly smile came over Nanni's face, and Louise controlled her shivering sufficiently to ask, "Why not?"

The old woman glanced around and then put her sunken, wrinkled mouth close to Louise's ear. "I am a small woman. The men in Tonga are too big." This was followed by a shrill cackle of laughter that brought knowing smiles from the other women.

"Are we safe here?" Louise asked.

"Goodness me, yes. Polosila women have been using this cave to shelter from storms since time began. The men use another one. It's a hundred yards or so away, but it's not connected." Again the cackle. "More's the pity."

Wood and dry grass had been dragged from a dark recess of the cave and the women soon had a fire blazing. Nanni secured a place near it for Louise and helped her remove her blouse and *sulu*. "They'll be dry before you can say Jack

Robinson. Here's a cloth. Rub your hair dry. You don't want
to catch a chill."

Louise did as she was told, feeling like a child. She
recognised the authority in Nanni's voice — it was the
same as that of the servants who had looked after her from
the cradle to puberty. Her former life seemed a long way
off — Manhattan, the house on Long Island, the
horse-riding and weekend parties, college — and very long
ago.

After a while tea was brewed and the women lit pipes
and rolled cigarettes of twist tobacco in newspaper. Louise
sucked tentatively at the thick paper tube and nearly
choked on the harsh, pungent smoke. Nanni drew on her
cigarette until it glowed; she sucked the smoke deep into
her lungs and expelled it with satisfaction.

Louise burned her mouth on the scalding tea. Tears came
to her eyes, and she brushed them away angrily. Nanni laid
a hard, intensely wrinkled hand on her arm. "This is a
rough place for a lady, Mrs Birmingham."

"I'm not sure that I'm much of a lady, Nanni."

"Ah, you're in an owning up mood, are you? I used to
love it when the children owned up."

"Owned up? I'm not sure I know what you mean."

"I mean when they told me what they'd done that would
get them into trouble if I told anybody. Which they knew
I wouldn't. What would you call it in America?"

Louise smiled. "We called it ''fessing up'."

"Then you 'fess up to Nanni. You'll feel a lot better if
you do."

To her surprise, Louise found herself pouring out
everything to the old woman, who made soothing sounds,
touched her hand sympathetically from time to time and
eventually produced a bone comb and began drawing it
through Louise's matted hair. "I don't hate my husband,
but I don't trust him."

"And you do love and trust the other man."

"Yes," Louise whispered.

"Then that's where you belong. With him. Don't let
anything stop you. I know what I'm talking about."

Louise looked at the old, folded face. Nanni had no teeth, and her eyes were buried in a thousand wrinkles. The firelight gave her the look of an ancient statue carved by a sculptor who wanted to capture wisdom and experience in stone. "Tell me about your life, Nanni."

"My goodness, child. I don't think this little blow'll last long enough for that. I was born here, and I'll die here, I know that much."

"It's what's in between that's interesting."

"Do you think so? I'm not sure that we Murdoans agree with you. I've been to more churches in more towns and cities than I can count. All the white people were looking for comfort, but I can tell you that it's looking into the fire in this cave, where my people have been for so long and where the spirits still are, that comforts me. Your people are too loose, nothing ties them together."

"You may be right."

"I *am* right, my dear. Put your blouse on. It's dry now. I left here when I was about fourteen years old, I can't be sure. I went to Queensland and worked harder than I imagined a person could ever work. I almost died. But I saw that for the kanakas, the rules were the same as for the white people — those who went to school and worked inside lived a lot better than those who didn't."

"So you . . . ?"

"Went to school and looked after white children and taught them. When the children turned nine or ten they were taken away from me. No one thought a nigger woman could teach a white child anything useful after that age. But I kept a white man's roof over my head always."

Louise looked into the fire and sipped the cooling tea. She wished she had a drink and a real cigarette and that Richard Webb was with her. She almost dropped the tea mug when the thought hit her: *Richard! He could have been drowned in that terrible storm.*

The old woman sensed the young woman's distress. She reached out and straightened the collar of her blouse. "What's the matter?"

Louise told her. Nanni smiled and shook her head. "The

men on the boat would have known the storm was coming. They know all the safe places around Murdo. I don't think you need have any fear for him."

"How old are you, Nanni?"

"About ninety, child."

"How many children have you had?"

"Many, many. Most of them died when they were little. Many different men and places. I have no regrets about the men I have had, but I do have regrets about one I did not have."

"Can you tell me?"

"It is still painful. It was in Fiji and he was beautiful, a man from Tikopia. I did nothing and he went away."

"What are you telling me?"

"If you want Mr Webb, go after him. Do not wait. Where is he going?"

"Sunburi. What's wrong?"

A shadow had passed across the old face, making it look tired and doubtful. Nanni glanced around at the women and children, some of them sleeping now and others apparently settling down to spend the night in the cave. She reached out, took a branch and stirred the fire. Sparks leapt up, and the smoke curled away into a corner of the cave where it escaped into the open. Louise grasped Nanni's arm and was amazed at its thinness. There was almost no flesh around the bone, and she relaxed her grip, fearing to snap the arm.

"Nanni, tell me!"

"Sunburi is a bad place," Nanni murmured. "It has always been a bad place. Unlucky. Many bad swears, many curses."

"I think Richard is interested in those things. Will he be in danger?"

"In normal times, no. But these are not normal times. Everyone is is in danger now."

"Why do you say that?"

"I hear people talking." Nanni turned her head to make sure the nearest woman was asleep. "I hear the men. They think I am old and stupid and do not matter. They talk

in front of me, but they forget that I have lived so long
and understand so much."

"What do you mean?"

"I have heard much about Eglito."

"Yes."

"Eglito is a strange man. He has many faces. Sometimes
he is a crazy man." Nanni touched the side of her head and
rolled her eyes in an instant miming of bedlam. Louise
almost recoiled at the sight of the ancient eyes moving in
the folded, puckered flesh.

"A crazy man? A lunatic?"

"Yes, so some people think. But he is more than that."
Nannit told Louise about the execution of Eglito's father
and Eglito's subsequent violent career. "He is also a man
of tradition, of the old ways. I am worried about that. I
think a lot about the old ways myself and I value them.
I am not sure that Eglito values them in the same way."

Louise shook her head. "I still don't understand."

'Nor do I, not exactly. But I know this. Eglito is planning
to do something very dramatic, to make a big swear, at
Sunburi."

28

Eglito was dry and warm inside the hut. His followers had used heavy vines to lash the building down before the storm hit — something done only for very important structures housing very important people. Eglito was now the most important man in the To'beili language area and beyond it. His name was on the lips of every fighting man on Murdo. Eglito knew this and rejoiced. He sucked on his pipe and stared into the fire, almost inducing a trance, so intense were his memories, dreams and ambitions. He had had two wives, both chosen for political reasons, who had borne him two sons and a daughter. Eglito was a stern parent. His children would marry advantageously and he would provide generously for them when the time came. But his dreams and ambitions, he had increasingly come to realise, did not project far in the future.

Eglito sat in front of the fire in a hut deep in the To'beili bush, higher even than the strongholds reached by Baekani's patrol. He was naked except for a broad cartridge belt that crossed his chest, and a leather pouch, made of pigskin, enclosing his genitals. The best of the police rifles, looted when he attacked the Alma lockup, rested across his thighs.

Three other men sat smoking in the hut — his cousin, Meilai, Nalai'u, leader of a major To'beili clan and Lagailemo, the renegade from the Maka Maka passage. Lagailemo had been admitted to the company of the To'beili after a long recitation of names had established a common ancestry between him and Eglito, which both knew to be fictitious. If Lagailemo was nervous about being here at Sutamae, a sanctified place, almost a To'beili shrine to the memory of past warriors, he showed no sign of it.

"My brother will live," Meilai said. He was speaking of the man who had been wounded in the Alma attack. He had to be carried most of the way back across the island and his life had been feared for. But now he was safe, and Eglito's reputation stood untarnished by any deaths among his followers. All present knew that, if events continued on their present course, this could not be maintained, but for now the wounded man's recovery was yet another good omen.

Eglito nodded and tapped ash from his pipe. "The signs were very favourable before we went to Alma. They were the same as when my grandfather took the *Swift Maid.*" This was a reference to a famous episode in To'beili history, when the warriors had attacked a recruiting ship. They had killed every member of its crew, looted the vessel down to its last length of rope and burned it to the waterline. Unlike other such attacks, this one had not brought a response from the British, caught in a period of indecision over policy in the Pacific. Eglito's grandfather had become the most feared *lemo* on the island, as well as the richest. His party had suffered no casualties so he had avoided the usual payment of compensation to the kin of fallen comrades that often took the gloss from a major victory.

"When will you kill the pigs and read the signs again, Eglito?" Lagailemo asked. He used the language of the people to the south, which was understood by To'beili and Maka Maka people alike.

As a leader who had spilled blood and been favoured by

the ancestors, spirits and totems, Eglito was not obliged to answer any question put to him about his plans and intentions. He exercised that right now and continued to stare into the fire. This discomfited Nalai'u, who had entered into an uneasy alliance with Eglito after his success at Alma. Nalai'u had led the attack against Baekani's patrol and so shared in his success. Only partly, though — the kin of the man Baekani had shot on the path after he fled the attack were demanding compensation, and Nalai'u had failed to take the greatest prize of all, the object that had made him agree to ambush the patrol — Baekani's famous, magically consecrated rifle. The patrol had carried valuable shell money strings, which had fallen to Nalai'u, as well as rifles and ammunition. Nalai'u wondered whether he should withdraw at this point and not risk his gains. But he could think of no way of putting the thought into words.

Eglito's face slowly turned from the fire. He looked at Nalai'u with eyes that seemed to carry the light of the fire in them. His jaw thrust out and his hands caressed the stock of his rifle. "Baekani lives," he said.

Nalai'u had reported that Baekani was so badly wounded he could not possibly have lived for long in the storm-blasted jungle. Nalai'u dared not contradict Eglito, and he had a suspicion that the new lemo was right. It would be no easy matter to kill Baekani. In fact, all killing would become more difficult from now on, with the Christian communities and everyone else on the alert. The easy killing was over and Nalai'u was afraid, but he was older than Eglito and used to power. He could not submit to another's will without a fight. "How do you know this?" he said.

This was a different kind of question, and it demanded an answer. "I have spoken to my grandfather," Eglito said slowly. "He has told me that Baekani is alive, and that he will soon be with the white men at Alma."

None present interpreted this statement as the literal truth. Eglito had spent the past twenty-four hours chewing betel, smoking and fasting. He had drunk only enough water to keep him from falling ill, and he had not slept at all.

This was a purifying process Murdoan leaders traditionally went through before battle, and the visions they experienced formed an important part of their strategy. There was always an ambiguity about pronouncements made after purification. If Baekani had in fact died in the jungle, he could still have been alive at the time Eglito had spoken. If his body were taken to Alma, Eglito's statement would also be true. If his body were never found it would be impossible to perform the rites that would return his ghost to its home, and his unpacified spirit could be thought to be seeking comfort with the Europeans. Such errant shades were considered very dangerous.

Eglito spat into the ashes at the edge of the fire. He put his left finger into the spittle and withdrew it. He daubed the wet ash on his forehead and the back of his right hand. Among Murdoans, left-handed people were considered particularly potent in both spiritual and temporal matters. Eglito began a low chant as he continued to dab ash on other parts of his body. The other men got slowly and quietly to their feet and left the hut. They knew that the *lemo* was entering a new phase of his preparation, one that would bring to him many confusing visions they would be invited to hear and interpret. It was an exhaustive process, only undertaken before a major action. The result was likely to be a big swear — a taking of oaths and a giving of pledges that would bind them and their kin to a certain course of action on penalty of death and worse.

Lagailemo glanced back as he left the hut. Eglito's left hand appeared to be in the fire, being held steady and without apparent inconvenience. He shivered and stepped out into the blinding light of the clear day that had followed the storm. Eglito had not claimed credit for the storm, but no one who followed the old ways on Murdo doubted that he had thrown the thunder and lightning at his enemies.

Will Naismith usually enjoyed the violent storms that periodically hit the Jeremiahs. They reminded him that the

islands had a history of their own, independent of
Europeans and their desires. Although he fully accepted
that Murdo and the other islands had to be brought under
the sway of civilisation and that there would be many
casualties in the process, the storms indicated that
everything that had been introduced — the buildings,
roads, bridges, Christianity — was on the surface and could
be swept away. Not that he formulated these thoughts
coherently or ever set them down on paper (except once,
in a letter to Amelia that she had utterly failed to
comprehend). It was simply that when he saw a section
of gravel road reduced to yellow mud and a coconut tree
bent almost double in the wind but then springing back,
he experienced a release from his usual feelings of intense
personal responsibility. The place would get on all right
without him.

But no such easeful thoughts came to his mind as he
weathered this storm aboard the *Loloburu*, riding the tide
at Tefu island in the Tau lagoon. At low tide the launch
sat on the sandy bottom of the lagoon and at high tide she
floated flimsily in the swirling water. The sailors were kept
constantly busy adjusting the moorings; the bosun supervised them and kept well clear of the DO as he brooded
over the turn of events. Marius the clerk alternately studied
the handbook of administrative regulations issued to native
government officers who aspired to advance in the service
and wondered at the feelings of outrage inside him at the
insults offered at Maka Maka. *Bush kanakas, why do I care?*
But he did care, and it was not something he could have
explained to Father Bondil, only to his pagan uncle in the
home village.

The storm raged all through the later part of the day
and into the night. Eventually Naismith fell into a light
sleep plagued by dreams of western district pastures filled
with sheep being hunted by paint-daubed Jeremians. He
awoke with pain in his bowels and spent an agonised hour
crouched in the ship's lavatory. Tension aggravated his
haemorrhoids and tendency to constipation. With the pain
came decisions. He would attempt to make radio contact

with the Catholic mission at Sulu'u on the weather coast, with Webb, whom he calculated would be at Birdbeak Bay, and with the headman Kaluae at Sunburi. If there was still no response from Alma, he would urge the despatch of a vessel from Patugi to appraise the situation there. When he had all the information from these quarters he would decide on his course of action. He tried to keep an open mind, but he was already forming plans to put together two strong patrols with Baekani and himself at their heads. Pushing north and south respectively from Sunburi, they could harry the renegades the length and breadth of Murdo Island.

Soon after first light, Naismith bathed and shaved, ate a breakfast of tea, ship's biscuit and jam and went on deck. The sky was intensely light after the storm, and the air carried fresh scents of whipped-up seaspray and shattered coconut trees. The launch had weathered the storm well — its decks were sticky with salt from the water that had flowed over them and the ropes and other fittings were dark and sodden. But Naismith could see no serious damage. The beach was strewn with debris, and the water was silty from the sand stirred up by the violent waves. As always, the artificial island showed signs of the battering it had endured; parts of the bulwarks of coral and rock had slid into the sea, and some soil and vegetation with it. The weather side of the island, though, had been built up by trapped branches and other flotsam, and the Tefuans would soon be at work reinforcing and consolidating these gains.

Naismith climbed stiffly over the side of the launch and lowered himself down onto the heavy planks of the jetty. Steam was rising from the wet wood, which was slick, and the DO trod warily, keeping his eyes down until he was standing on solid rock. When he looked up, his stomach lurched.

"My God! Oh, my God."

The radio shed with its proud iron roof was a flattened ruin. The mast, necessary to receive the signal from outside the high rim of land that enclosed the lagoon, had collapsed and touched the ground a few feet from where

Naismith stood. The wind apparatus was a crumpled ruin. Naismith closed his eyes and felt dizziness coming over him. He lurched forward and grabbed the wet trunk of a tree for support. His fingers sank sickeningly into the pulpy bark and he snatched his hand away.

"I don't believe it," Naismith said.

The tall, spindly figure of Tefu came limping towards him, his stick slipping on the thick carpet of wet leaves. *"Wailis bagerup,"* he said, *"himi go pinis."*

"I can see that, you idiot!" Naismith's fist shot out and caught the old man on the jaw. Tefu's eyes rolled back, and he fell heavily and awkwardly, tangling his sound leg with the stick as he went down. Naismith stood over him, panting and feeling the blood pound in his head. His mind went blank for an instant and he fell himself, tumbling across Tefu's inert body and throwing out his hands to break his fall. His hands hit the sharp coral and the skin was scraped and torn from both palms up to the wrists. Pain shot up Naismith's arms, and he felt the bite of tiny pieces of coral embedded deep in the wounds.

His breath was short and gasping and his hands dripped blood as he helped the half-conscious headman to his feet. *"Mi sorri tomas, Tefu. Mi sorri . . ."* Naismith bent and picked up the stick. Tefu took it and supported himself, staring at the DO. Naismith wiped sweat from his eyes and left a thick smear of blood across his face, which was pale instead of its usual tan. The headman recoiled and muttered harshly in the Tau language. Slowly, exhibiting great dignity and contempt, he made a sign with his thumb and little finger, turned his back and limped away.

Naismith stood impotently, reproaching himself for having struck an old, crippled man. *What is happening to me?* he thought. *I must be going mad.* He turned back towards the launch and found Marius standing hesitantly a pace away.

"You are hurt, sir," the clerk said. "You must clean the cuts or they will become infected."

"Never mind that," Naismith gasped. "What did he say?"

"I do not understand the Tau language, sir."

"You understand the sign. What did it mean?"

"He has put a curse on you, sir. He will go to his ancestor shrine and make a very bad swear."

Cameron Somerville swore in the Gaelic taught him by his Scots mother as he surveyed the damage around Patugi. The storm had been the most severe he had experienced since coming to the islands, even dwarfing the violence of some he had seen in the Outer Hebrides when holidaying with his grandparents. But there the rocks had seemed able to take the battering, and so little stuck up more than a few feet from the ground that the winds had little to shake. The stone houses with tightly lashed down thatch roofs usually survived unscathed. Here the storm seemed to clear a path before it in certain directions, levelling huts, capsizing boats, snapping tree trunks.

He swore again, a rural obscenity concerning the anatomy of sheep, and began to walk quickly towards the Secretariat. He had designed the radio control centre to withstand heavy rain and high wind, but he was not sure that his calculations had allowed for yesterday's elemental energy. The building, however, was undamaged, and the gardeners had already begun a clean-up. The Secretariat was on high ground but sheltered on the weather side by a hill that was the beginning of the island's escarpment. The storm had virtually swept over the administration centre and released its force on the structures below. From his vantage point Somerville could see that Parkinson's Hotel had been partly unroofed, the police barracks had suffered extensive damage and a section of the wharf listed badly. One of the Chinese trade stores had been flattened, and the outbuildings to several others were spilling a tangle of cane, cloth and wet straw. The town's meagre gravel roads had been washed away in many places, and the bridge over the creek, a neat, smartly painted structure, had disappeared. People were crossing on a makeshift bridge of logs and sheet iron. Two horses grazed unconcernedly on the grassy slope behind the Secretariat. Elsewhere carefully cultivated lawns were waterlogged and dark.

Somerville entered the Secretariat and negotiated buckets set to catch drips, clerks tutting over wet documents, and ruined carpets. He was relieved to find the radio room dry and unscathed. He had already verified from outside that the mast, stoutly supported by guy wires lashing down a heavy stanchion bolted into concrete blocks, was undamaged. He sat down, ran tests on the equipment and found everything functioning normally. One of his assistants entered the room and handed Somerville a note. Somerville glanced at it.

"Damn," he said, "when?"

"In thirty minutes, sir. The Resident's secretary says he is very busy."

"*He's* busy! All right, thank you. Tell them I'll be there."

Somerville turned back to the control panel and began to work fast, calling receiving and transmitting stations throughout the area his signal could reach. He acknowledged signs, rapped out brief messages, closed channels with a practised snap of the switches and scribbled notes. He glanced frequently at his watch, and after twenty-eight minutes' work, he pulled off his headphones and left the room.

"Well, Somerville?" Ashley Price-Kane's face was tired and drawn. He drew on a cigar as if he hoped the tobacco would give him strength.

"Extensive damage through the group, sir. As you would expect. Loss of life. Damage to the government station at Quiros's pretty bad."

"Damn it, man, I mean what news is there from Murdo?"

"None sir."

"None? *None?*"

"Must have been hit pretty badly. Still no response from Alma, nothing from the Tau lagoon. A weak signal from the Catholic mission on the weather coast, but too much static to hear. That sometimes happens after a violent electrical storm. And I almost picked up something that sounded like a field radio signal, but it faded out."

"Naismith?"

Somerville shrugged. "Possible, but it'd be out of the ordinary — he usually calls from the stations around the island. Will you be going over, sir? As you said before the storm hit?"

Price-Kane drew on his cigar and sucked the smoke down, something he rarely did. Inhaled smoke made him cough; he wondered whether he'd got a touch of gas in France, although the doctors said not. "I can't." He coughed several times and cleared his throat. "Too much to do here. Two people were killed in the hotel, a lot of other casualties, and a devil of a lot of damage to property. Most of it the government's. I'm up to my ears in paperwork. You'll have to go."

"Me, sir?"

"It's a radio matter, isn't it? Stations on the blink. You go over and set it right."

"What about the . . . political situation on the island?"

"With any luck the storm will have taken care of that. I'll scribble you a note telling Naismith to forget about the tax and get everyone working on the clean-up. Bit of public spirit might be just what the bloody place needs."

Somerville almost saluted. Travelling around the islands to set up the stations had been the aspect of his work he had most enjoyed. A trip around Murdo would be a nice finale to his tour of duty. "What about a boat, sir?"

The RC had dropped his eyes to the papers on his desk and seemed to have forgotten Somerville's presence. "Yes, yes," he said distractedly, "you'll need one."

29

The time they spent together sheltering from the storm gave the Reverend Stoltenberg and Tom Birmingham ample opportunity to hatch some plans. There were anxious moments during the 'blow', as when a section of the roof of the meeting house vanished like smoke up a chimney. The rest of the roof held but the danger, plus enforced intimacies such as having to relieve themselves in the far corner of the building, permitted the two men to lower their guards somewhat. Stoltenberg admitted to impatience at the slow pace of proselytisation in the Jeremiahs and to feelings of frustration that his powers were being underused. Birmingham acknowledged that his career was in decline and needed a sudden, sharp stimulus. Although not codified as such, these confessions amounted to an agreement to profit from the situation in the islands to the maximum. And if that meant some manipulation, even misrepresentation of the situation, so be it.

But old habits die hard, and the missionary asked the

conventional question when the two stepped for the first time into the open air. "Your wife?"

"She was going to the heathen village across the way. I guess they know how to keep out of the wind?"

Stoltenberg nodded. "The caves," he said. He surveyed the damage to the mission compound. Apart from the partial unroofing of the meeting house, there were collapsed huts, shattered windows and fallen trees. The destruction represented many hours of reluctant work by the converts. The missionary turned away, thinking that perhaps he need not bother himself with the endless building and repairing any longer, nor with the 'rice Christians' and backsliders.

"I've got to get to the radio shack and put out a bulletin. We've got a rebellion here, and a terrible cyclone. The readers'll lap it up. I can quote you that the natives see these things as visitations from the spirits and such?"

Stoltenberg nodded. "Christians and pagans alike. You can operate the radio?"

Birmingham drew the valve from his pocket. "Sometimes you have to take steps. What are you going to do now, doctor?"

"I think I should assemble my congregation, give thanks for surviving the storm, commiserate with those who have lost people and suggest that no more taxes be paid to the government until it protects us from the pagans."

"I don't follow you."

"As I said, my people will blame the storm on the pagans, who will blame them."

"Will it come to fighting?"

Stoltenberg shrugged. "If God so wills it."

Tom Birmingham did not consider himself a hypocrite, and the missionary's response would normally have curled his lip. But these were not ordinary times. Birmingham hesitated, then put the question that had been simmering in his mind for days. "Doctor, before you go — has my wife been sleeping with Richard Webb?"

Stoltenberg, too, hesitated. He needed Birmingham if he was to derive some personal enhancement from developments, but he recognised that the man was under pressure and his behaviour unpredictable. What answer would be most likely to keep him on the present path?

He decided. "Yes," he said, "she has."

"How do you know?"

"She admitted it to me."

Birmingham's face was grey with stubble and haggard from sleeplessness and stress. He juggled the valve in his hand and spoke quietly. "You'll have to tell me about it in detail some time."

"Very well."

Birmingham turned and limped away, picking his path carefully among the debris and puddles. His bush shirt, which had become wet when the roof gave way, was damp, itchy and stiff in places with dried perspiration. His wound throbbed and he felt feverish as sweat broke out on his face. The path was rough and steep and he struggled to retain his balance. His shoes and socks quickly became sodden and heavy. Murdoans went about their business, cleaning ditches and raking branches, fallen coconuts and broken timber into piles. They ignored Birmingham, and he saw no police or other officials. He was breathing heavily and feeling dazed and light-headed when he reached the administrative building that housed the radio room. A tree outside the building had been uprooted and Birmingham sat on the trunk, which lay along the ground. He mopped his face with his handkerchief and surveyed the scene.

To Birmingham's eye, practised from witnessing the aftermath of Florida hurricanes, the Alma harbour seemed to have sustained a great deal of damage. He saw single-hulled canoes and other larger craft smashed and beached. Railings around the jetty had disappeared and the water was dark with debris and a large, glistening oil slick.

His mind already checking on details to include in his report, he shifted his gaze to the compound. The solidly built guesthouse had survived intact, as had the DO's house and the trade store. The flagpole had been snapped off cleanly about two metres from the ground. The shaft of the pole to which, presumably, the flag was still attached, was nowhere to be seen.

"Jesus Christ," he said aloud. "Some storm." He found himself speculating about the fate of vessels at sea, and that led to consideration of Richard Webb and Louise. Tom Birmingham had been mostly faithful to his wives. Never predatory about women, he had loved and neglected those he had married, and had never pretended to love the few he had slept with and not married. He considered that he had done relatively little harm sexually and that relatively little had been done to him. He had readily forgiven the wives who strayed, and passed easily on to another woman, another bottle, another book. But this was different. He was stone cold sober and the only women around were stocky, dark creatures with averted heads and broad, splayed feet, who smelled of tobacco and coconut oil. There was no easy rebound relationship here. And no easy book. He knew that he was in a crisis as a writer and a man, and Louise's desertion was an affront that had less to do with sex than with questions of character. He saw Richard Webb's lean, dark face tense with decision and command after the fire. In his mind's eye Webb wore a smartly tailored uniform, ablaze with medals and ribbons. He passed the handkerchief vigorously across his face and stood. "I hope the bastard went to the bottom."

He entered the building, ignored the puzzled clerk who was using a mop on the floor of the main office, and stalked through to the radio room. He seated himself in front of the panel and began flipping the switches. He breathed a sigh of relief as the circuits closed and the transmitter signal cut in. *Guy who installed this stuff knew his onions,* he thought. *Here's hoping we haven't got static from here to Sydney.* He took a notebook from his pocket and checked the few pages he'd written by lantern light while the storm had howled. "Not bad," he said.

"*Masta?*" The clerk stood anxiously in the doorway.

To Birmingham, accustomed to black menials, the mop he carried seemed appropriate. "Yes?"

"*Yu tok long wailis?*"

Birmingham took the valve from his pocket and plugged it into the socket. "That's right. If you don't like it, buster, go see Mr Larke. Savvy?" He adjusted the carbon microphone, held one of the earphone pieces to his right ear, opened the channel and radioed Sydney. As he had feared, the static was intense, distorting the bands. Birmingham struggled to find a clear path.

"This is Alma, AC 1 calling Sydney, KX 2997. Come in Sydney, come in Sydney. Over."

A faint, static-filled response. Birmingham fine-tuned the frequency setting and boosted the transmitting power.

"This is Alma, AC 1 calling Sydney, KX 2997 . . ."

"What the hell d'you think you're doing?" Keith Larke burst into the room. He was unshaven, tousle-haired, and his eyes were red. His clothes were mud-smeared, and there was a long, bloody graze on his right cheek. In his hand he held a pistol.

Birmingham turned away from the radio. He put down the earphone and set the radio to receive. "Hey, hey, Keith. Careful with the six-shooter. Put it away."

Larke shoved the pistol into his pocket and waved away the clerk who stood nervously at the door. He shut the door and leaned back against it, facing Birmingham. "I asked you what you were doing here."

"Radioing Sydney, like we agreed. I've gotta get the story out."

"The radio's not working."

"I fixed it. I'll get through. Why don't you try to organise us some coffee? I could really do with some, and you look all tuckered out."

Larke moved slowly across the room and slumped into a chair. "I've been trying to keep things together. It's hopeless. Most of the police went back home. Nothing's guarded. The prison stockade half blew away, and only the prisoners who were in cells are still there. The rest just walked out. There's scarcely a window left intact."

Birmingham surveyed the radio room. "This place is OK."

Larke's hands shook as he took out his cigarette tin. He

lit the cigarette awkwardly, so that it burned unevenly down one side. "Yes, yes, it is. These idiot natives tell me some genius from Hemisphere came across and fixed it up like this. Pity he couldn't have done the same for my quarters. They're awash."

"That's tough," Birmingham said. He made a note on the pad in front of him. "Bad about the prisoners too. Any tough ones among 'em?"

"God knows. They all look like cannibals to me. You know what they say to me when I try to get them to do something? 'Wait for Baekani, wait for Baekani.' It seems Baekani's the only man who can organise anything around here."

Birmingham scribbled another note and picked up the earphone. "How do you spell that — B . . . y . . . ?"

Larke exploded from his chair. "Why do you *want* to spell it? Christ Almighty, I thought I could rely on the white men in the place to be behave like human beings. I'll ask you again — what are you doing here? This is government property, and I . . ."

"You are the officer in charge. The gallant young subaltern, Keith Larke, who single-handledly organised the relief operation in the hurricane-battered town of Alma. But for this officer's efforts, the loss of life would have been much greater, and residents of the far-flung specks of empire can have confidence that Larke's energy, when turned to the political situation on the savage island of Murdo, will bring results." Birmingham rapped with a pencil on the desk to accentuate certain words. "That's you, Keith. Leastways, that's how I'm telling it."

Larke subsided into his chair. "That's remarkable."

"It will be if I can get through to Sydney. Like I say, some coffee would help."

"Well, I'll see what I can do. That chap who brought me over here seems to have some sense. Maybe he can do something about coffee. Yes, that's it."

"You should get some sleep, Keith."

"Yes. I say, I'll have to call Patugi. Will you be long? Sending your despatch, I mean?"

Birmingham shook his head. "Patugi's station's damaged. Not receiving. I think we're cut off here. We're just going to have to do what we think best. I think a pow-wow with Doctor Stoltenberg and maybe that planter down the coast'd be in order. What's his name?"

"Anderson."

"We'll try him. If he's still alive."

"What? Why shouldn't he be?"

"You think Eglito'll be just sitting on his ass? This is his big chance to wipe us out. Wanted action, didn't you, Keith?"

Larke dropped his cigarette end onto the rush mat and stood on it. "Yes. I'd better look lively. I take it you're in touch with Dr Stoltenberg? I'll send a message to Anderson."

"You do that. And don't forget the coffee." Larke moved to the door but stopped when Birmingham spoke again in a softer tone, "Haven't seem my wife, have you, Larke?"

"No. My God! I thought she was with you."

"Went to some village. Be grateful if you could locate her, see that she's all right."

"Of course."

Larke left the room and Birmingham put on the earphones in time to hear the crackly, Australian-accented voice. "This is Sydney, KX 2997, calling Alma, AC 1. Over."

30

New York, 25 February 1928

"Have you seen this?" Maxwell Peters dumped a slightly soggy copy of the *Chicago Daily News*, open at the international news page, on William Cavendish's desk. The paper had got wet during his dash from a taxi to the office building. The rain had not improved Peters' mood.

Cavendish laid aside the manuscript he had been reading and glanced at the paper. A large headline read: 'Report of Uprising in Jeremiahs — Islands hit by Storm and Strife.' "Yes, I've seen it. They got Tom's age wrong. He's forty-seven, not forty-four."

"Who the hell cares what age he is? He probably lopped off a few years himself. The point is, this stuff is hot. Listen — 'The Jeremiah Islands, a strategically important and exotically beautiful British possession, are in the grip of natural and manmade disasters. Many deaths have been reported from the effects of a hurricane which battered the islands mercilessly for forty-eight hours, but there have been other, more sinister deaths. A native uprising is said to be in progress. A government official is rumoured to have been massacred, and unrest among the islands, divided between Christians and pagans, is rising to fever pitch. The Jeremiahs, where the US government has expressed interest in establishing a communications base, are of vital concern to Britain owing to their closeness to Australia and New Zealand. The presence of French missionaries, Chinese traders and Japanese immigrants contribute to the unsettled state of the islands. Our correspondent, the noted author Mr Tom Birmingham, has radioed graphic reports of the violence. "I have seen the mangled bodies of policemen, and smoke rising in the air from fire-bombed prison stockades and government vessels. I have seen . . ." '

"I read it," Cavendish said wearily, "I read it. What's your point?"

Peters paced around the room. His usually slick hair was ruffled, and several buttons at the top of his vest were undone. His silk tie, normally a flat-sitting adornment to his hand-stitched shirt and collar, was buckled and coffee-stained. "We've got this guy, one of our writers, sitting on this hot subject, and he's not even getting in touch with us. We haven't got any control over this material at all."

"May I remind you that it was you who wanted to relinquish control over Tom and his material? When we first got an inkling of these developments, Mr Waldeck instructed me to . . . 'tie Birmingham up like a Christmas turkey' . . . I believe they were his words."

"And did you?"

Cavendish blinked as a shaft of light suddenly pierced the window and bounced off his polished desk. "Lacava's working on it. It's by no means clear. Perhaps you'd like to talk to him?"

"Me? Why?"

"You should be well briefed, Maxwell. Mr Waldeck was impressed by the firmness of your advocacy at the meeting. You know he rescinded some of the decisions, though?"

"What decisions?"

"Valerie Benson has been offered a contract to research background on the Jeremiahs."

"Christ. No one told me."

"Are you feeling somewhat sidelined, Maxwell?"

Peters stopped by the desk and picked up the paper. "When you take a real close look at it, there's nothing much very solid here."

"There never was in Tom's books. That didn't stop him turning out a string of best-sellers."

Peters grunted. "Times change. Communications are much faster now. He'll have to come up with some facts if Hearst's going to run with this."

"What were the facts before San Juan Hill?"

"Still, the war happened, didn't it? Christ, I wish I *knew* what was going on out there!"

"I imagine a lot of people will share your interest, and they'll have the *Daily News* to keep them informed." Cavendish picked up a pencil and scribbled a note on a pad. "That reminds me to check on whether sales of Tom's books pick up. *Adams in Assam* was very sluggish, but a little stimulus like this could get it moving."

"We should cable Birmingham an advance."

"We may not be the first. By the way, did you hear the report that he was wounded?"

"No! Wounded? God, that's good!"

Cavendish, not usually a vindictive man, began to enjoy himself. In his view publishing was, and should be, a profession in which gentlemen could function as gentlemen and in which hucksters like Peters should not thrive. He leaned back in his chair. "We've also had another piece of news. Very sad from one point of view, of course, but commercially very advantageous. Life is a rich tapestry."

"Spit it out."

"Nigel Burton died yesterday. He was run down by a trolley car on 38th Street and died in hospital. He hadn't signed the papers relating to our . . . arrangement in respect of Tom's indiscretion. And, as you may or may not know, the dead can't be libelled under British law."

"The lucky stiff," Peters said.

Cavendish smiled. "I take it you aren't talking about Mr Burton. With the threat of that action removed, and the possiblity that this publicity could boost Tom's stocks somewhat, things could return to normal around here. It was a regrettable lapse on Birmingham's part and very unprofessional of Miss Benson, but there's no reason they should be pilloried for it."

"What's the strategy as of now?"

"I don't know that there is one, particularly. As I say, I think it should be business as usual. If something comes of all this Jeremiah high jinks, and we get a book out of it, well and good. If not, the firm will survive. Business as usual, although that's never good news for your type."

"What's my type?"

"You thrive on discord, you flourish amid dissension." Cavendish wondered whether there might be a poem struggling to get out in this assessment. He sighed. *Probably not.*

Peters put the newspaper under his arm and walked towards the door. "You think you've got me summed up, William. But I may have a few surprises for you."

Cavendish's impressive eyebrows rose. "Oh?"

"Yeah. I'm betting that guinea lawyer hasn't given any thought to how we can get a handle on Birmingham except through pieces of paper."

"What do you mean?"

"Birmingham's got a wife, hasn't he? Where does she fit into the picture? Maybe she's got a story to tell. Maybe a *different* story. That could be an angle."

"It certainly could. I'm sure you'd enjoy playing in muddy waters like that. By the way, how are your negotiations going with Hemingway's agent?"

Peters' hand was on the door. He flushed as he gave the handle a savage jerk. "Lousy," he said.

In London on the same day, Ernest Childers read over the final draft of his despatch to the High Commissioner for the Western Pacific on 'Disturbances in the Jeremiah Islands'. He nodded with approval at some of his elegant turns of phrase – 'enlightened authority', 'tacking with the winds of change', 'integration of British behaviour with the indigenous code of conduct', 'accommodation of

American interests'. They looked particularly well in type, he thought, and would look even better printed in the Blue Books. He believed that his chief recommendation, the appointment of more youthful officers to senior and sensitive positions in native administration, had been subtly insinuated. He ran his finger down the margins of the relevant pages. *Yes, four mentions of this proposal. Sufficient.*

Childers attached the list of officials to whom the despatch should be sent for comment, headed by the departmental first assistant secretary, Hubert Dalziel, and modestly initialled the bottom of the list. He rang for the runner and handed the document over with a sigh of relief and a smile of satisfaction for a job well done. *A spot of lunch at the Oxford Club,* he thought. *That's the ticket.* He put on his hat and coat, picked up his umbrella and left the office. As he walked down Whitehall towards Regent Street in the fine rain, he felt happy: a man serving a great cause and serving it well. He enjoyed the club. He always gave it as his address when he wrote to fellows he'd known at Balliol who were now out in the wider world — in Africa mostly, but some in India and even China. It was one of the pleasures of his life to read his mail over a drink in the club. He had written to Richard Webb care of the Club a few days before. He looked forward to the reply and for reaction on the spot to some of his recommendations. A network of friends in the right places, he was convinced, was the key to success.

Two hours later, with a Dover sole, a bottle of hock and a very good brandy under his waistcoat, he should have been comfortable, but he was not.

"I take it, from a reading of your exemplary despatch, Childers, that you haven't seen this?" Hubert Dalziel slid a newspaper clipping across his desk. Keeping his spine unnaturally straight, Childers bent forward to take it.

"Let me summarise it for you," Dalziel said. "There is a rebellion in the BJIP. People have been slaughtered in a religious civil war. There has also been a cyclone."

Childers' reactions were slow and his eyesight rather blurred. He took his spectacles from his handkerchief pocket and dropped both spectacles and handkerchief to the floor. "Damn. Excuse me, sir. That's preposterous."

"Pick up your things, man. Do you mean that cyclones are not a climatic feature in the area?"

"No, sir, of course not. I mean about the rebellion. It's not possible."

"So I gather from your despatch. You appear to think that the appointment of men under thirty to certain posts will set things right."

"I . . . I wouldn't quite put it like that, sir."

"I should hope not. Now, we can tear this despatch up," Dalziel gestured at the pages which represented many hours of Childers' work, "and get down to some serious business. The important thing seems to be radio. My God, it was easier in the old days when news travelled at a respectable speed. Radio. We're trying to get hold of some solid facts via the Australians. God help us. It seems this place Pluto . . ."

"Murdo, sir."

"Huh. This place is temporarily out of radio contact. Storm or strife, as this writer chappie says, we don't really know which. As soon as we get something solid, I want it whipped up into an answer. You follow?"

"Er . . . no, sir."

Dalziel spoke slowly, as if to a hard-of-hearing child. "An American national is involved, hmm? Washington still whispering about a western Pacific base. There's bound to be a question asked in the House. The minister will need an answer. Yes?"

"Yes, sir."

"Right. Well, get cracking."

Childers stood unsteadily, his handkerchief and his glasses, which he suspected were broken, clutched in his hand. "Do you mean, sir, that you want me to prepare the answer?"

"Good God, no. I'll prepare the answer. I want you to get the texts of the radio messages and any telegrams involved. You're a runner, Childers, nothing more. Is that clear? Off you go."

"Sir, can you tell me where to go to collect the . . . messages?"

"I haven't the faintest idea. Somewhere in the Foreign Office, I suppose. Contact your opposite number over there and ask around. Don't you know how the system works, man?"

For the first time Ernest Childers realised that he did *not* know how the system worked. He almost bowed and spoiled the gesture by dropping his handkerchief and spectacles. Glass crunched in his hand as he picked them up.

"And Childers." Dalziel was critically examining the point of a pencil.

"Sir?"

"The Australians want to send a warship to the Jeremiahs."

"They *want* to?"

"Oh, yes. Everyone is very keen on this little sideshow. That's what's going to make the job of writing an answer so challenging. A denial that there's any trouble would be a terrible disappointment to some."

"I see, sir. Well, I'll do all I . . ."

"I'm sure you will. Just find out if the Australians have got a ship to send, will you? Better get its name while you're at it."

"Ah, if this is to be taken so seriously, wouldn't a British vessel be . . . "

"British, Australian, in this context, there's no difference."

"No difference?"

Dalziel's nod was directed at the pencil point. "The essential thing is, Childers, that the ship isn't American or, God help us, French."

31

Alma, 27 February 1928

For his second bulletin, Tom Birmingham had some real news. The death toll from the storm in and around Alma was an unusually high twenty-nine, due to a mud slide that had killed twenty-three people in a small Christian settlement, an offshoot from the main body of the Maryborough mission. These people had adjusted certain aspects of the evangelical message to their own ways; in particular they had rejected passivist texts such as, "Resist not evil: but whosoever shall smite thee on the right cheek, turn to him the other also." The survivors, convinced that the presence of the pagans nearby had brought this disaster upon them, and encouraged in this belief by Stoltenberg, had attacked a small pagan settlement with two old rifles, bushknives and a ceremonial axe. Six 'pagans' were killed and three seriously hurt.

The bush telegraph brought no hard news of Naismith, but disturbing rumours of a massacre at Birdbeak Bay had begun to filter through, and Birmingham expanded them into a 'crisis in the north'. He thought it was safe to assume that the escaped prisoners were 'on the rampage, terrorising Christians and pagans alike'.

But the centrepiece of his report was the news that Lagailemo had joined forces with Eglito. This intelligence had travelled up the coast quite detached from any news of Naismith or the happenings at Maka Maka or Tau. One of the houseboys who harboured a hatred for Baekani had passed it on to Birmingham, who seized on it rapturously. Lagailemo became 'a notorious bandit' and Eglito the 'rebel leader', and the strength of their combined forces was set at 'five hundred armed, trained and warlike warriors thirsting for blood'.

True to his promise, Birmingham had included glowing references to the leadership qualities of Keith Larke and the Christian fortitude of Dr Karl Stoltenberg. A party of natives whose gardens had been destroyed by the storm had attempted to barter with food from the mission. Stoltenberg had led a party of Christians to send them packing, and for this action Birmingham likened him to Gordon at Khartoum.

"Pity about that German name, doc," Birmingham said. "Not so popular these days."

The two men were drinking tea in the radio room, which Birmingham had made his headquarters despite the protests of the native clerks. "My mother was Danish," Stoltenberg said. "Her name was Hansen. I could perhaps adopt that."

"Better," Birmingham said, "much better. We need something new quick. Something about Naismith. Nothing coming in?"

Stoltenberg shook his head. "By the way, have you heard anything from your wife?"

"Larke tells me she's still in the village, nursing the sick or something. I can't make a hell of a lot out of that."

As a matter of habit, Stoltenberg frowned at the strong language. "I could send some men to fetch her back."

"That's not a bad idea. Let me think about that."

"You don't have to think about it, Tom." Louise

Birmingham stood in the doorway. Nanni, standing beside her, barely reached to her shoulder.

Stoltenberg was so surprised that he forgot his manners and remained seated. He recognised Nanni as one of the most recalcitrant pagans in the district.

"Why, honey," Birmingham said. "It's great to see you." He stood and walked, accentuating the limp, across the room towards his wife.

Louise held him off with an upraised hand. Her hair was curled tightly around her head; her face was tanned and her clothes were creased and stained. Her feet were bare and dirty. The old bent woman beside her had a look of amusement on her face, but Louise was staring at the radio and the litter of Birmingham's pencils and notes. "I heard a bit of what you said, Tom. What mischief are you up to?"

Birmingham felt himself becoming excited at Louise's exotic appearance, then he remembered his grievance and thought instead of the possibilities of a photograph of her in this rig to accompany one of his articles. *Author's wife mucks in . . .*

"Just reporting the facts to the world, hon."

"What facts? Have you been in radio contact with Mr Naismith, or . . ."

"Webb?" Birmingham turned sharply and returned to his chair. "This is the only radio on the island that's working. This is where the news comes from."

Louise leaned wearily against the architrave. "Sit down over there, Nanni." She waved at a chair. "I'll see if we can get some tea."

"You can't . . ." Stoltenberg drew his legs up although Nanni, a stick-thin figure wrapped in a threadbare flannel shirt and a tattered *sulu*, passing to her chair, was three metres from him.

"Invite an old nigger woman to tea?" Louise said. "Sure I can. If a quack medicine man and a hack writer can take over the radio station, anything can happen."

"Louise!" Birmingham snapped the pencil he was fiddling with.

"What, Tom? You're not reporting news here, you're making it up. Well, I can give you some real news, if it's worth a cup of tea. What are you doing here, doctor? Don't you know there's a lot of injured and sick people out there? I think some kind of fever's starting up."

"Fever?" Stoltenberg could scarcely conceal his revulsion at Louise's appearance and manner.

"Sure, among the children. What's it called, Nanni?"

"*Bangu*, or bad water fever," Nanni said. "The floods put rotting vegetable matter into the drinking water and huddling wet and cold people together for days on end doesn't help."

Birmingham gaped as he heard Nanni speak. "Say, who is this? She talks like a schoolteacher."

"She was," Louise said.

"She is an irredeemable heathen," Stoltenberg said, "and I don't need to be told my duty by the likes of her. My people keep themselves clean and healthy, whatever the circumstances."

"There are two children dying in the mission as we speak, doctor," Nanni said, "and there'll be more unless you can persuade them to stop praying and do something practical about the water. They won't listen to me."

Stoltenberg jerked from his chair and hurried out of the room. Birmingham picked up a fresh pencil and prepared to write. "That your news, Lou? This fever?"

"No," Louise said. "Eglito . . ." The first of a series of shots echoed across the compound, silencing her.

Baekani recalled nothing of the last stages of his walk back to Alma. His mind seethed with images of death and retribution. A confused, intermingled procession of totems, ancestors, biblical figures and real persons wove through his brain, now dancing, now walking slowly, now standing accusingly in line. His mouth was dry and remained so, no matter how many times he stopped to drink. And a fever burned his head, no matter how often he bathed it in the cool water of the hill streams. His limbs trembled and he fell often but he kept going, clutching his damaged rifle.

The ammunition belt that crossed his chest chafed him and caught on the undergrowth as he pushed through fallen trees and trailing vines that had been torn loose by the storm, but he did not discard it.

The rock splinter cuts were open and suppurating. They bled too, and he frequently had to rub blood from his eyes. As a consequence, his face was smeared and daubed with mud and dirt to which leaves and dead insects stuck. For much of the time he was in a dream, lost in a hazy land of pain and shame. But he had long periods of clarity in which he felt filled with a sense of purpose. Everything he had learned from Naismith fell away. The bloodletting and the storm and his fever constructed a new reality for him. There were new imperatives, new directions. He must wipe out the failure and shame with a tremendous act, an act so vast it would lift the weight from his shoulders and draw the poison from his blood.

There was only one such act. He must kill Naismith.

The first person to see him as he staggered into the Alma compound was a woman carrying a bundle on her head. The huge figure, wild-eyed, blood-smeared, with leaves and twigs in its hair and sticking to its face, loomed up before her like a nightmare spirit, a *togu*. She screamed. Baekani gripped the Mannlicher around the barrel and trigger guard and shot her in the face. He stumbled on towards a group of children playing in a drainage ditch. They scrambled up to see where the sound had come from and saw the *togu*. Baekani shot them all. The three shots fired rapidly boomed out across the open space and echoed from the escarpment behind. A man who had been raking leaves near the fallen flagpole threw down his rake and ran. Baekani scarcely paused in his progress. He lifted the rifle, ignored the splinters tearing his cheek, sighted and shot the running man through the chest.

The screams started then, from the woman who ran towards the ditch and from the gardener, whose wound was not fatal. Figures appeared around the edges of the compound but retreated as Baekani fired a second shot into the wounded man and began to advance, almost marching,

towards the administrative building and the European
officers quarters.

"*Stap! Lusim gun!*"

A policeman, struggling to work the action on his rifle,
stepped into Baekani's path. Baekani stopped and watched
the man chamber a round. He brought the Mannlicher up
slowly.

"*Stap!*"

When he pulled the trigger, the policeman's rifle was
inches from Baekani's face, but the weapon and its
ammunition had been soaked in the storm and the hammer
clicked uselessly. Baekani put the muzzle of his rifle under
the policeman's chin and blew half his head away.

"My God, he's heading for Naismith's house." Louise
watched in horror as Baekani moved forward, slightly
crouching now, like a hunter stalking its prey. Birmingham
stood behind her; the hair on his head prickled, and he felt
his bowels beginning to loosen. *I haven't got the guts to do
anything,* he thought. *Even if there was something I could do.*

Nanni shuffled to the door and looked out. "Baekani,"
she said softly. "He's lost his mind. Have you got a gun,
Mr Birmingham?"

Birmingham sucked in breath to keep his bowels from
letting go. "In the guesthouse. Not here."

"Better get it," Nanni said.

Birmingham didn't move. Louise looked away from the
menacing sight of Baekani, weaving, crouched, retreating
and advancing, stalking Naismith's imposing bungalow.
He was less than sixty yards away, an easy target. She saw
that Birmingham was rigid with fear. "I'll go," she said.

Nanni tugged at her arm. "Use the side door, child, and
don't let him see you. He is possessed."

Louise nodded and darted away.

"Christ," Birmingham said. "He's going closer. What
does he want?"

Nanni stifled a cough. The wails of the woman cradling
the bodies of her dead children were audible all over the
compound, but it still seemed dangerous to make a sound
while Baekani, almost dancing now, was within hearing

range. "He does not know himself," Nanni whispered. "He is quite mad."

"Larke's in there," Birmingham said.

"God help him, then."

The woman stopped wailing and a silence fell over the compound. Then a loud whistle, repeated three times, signalled the arrival of a boat. A government launch came into view around the point. At that moment Keith Larke stepped out of Naismith's bungalow onto the verandah. He was carrying a revolver which he raised and levelled at Baekani, who had turned away and was staring at the launch. Larke's hand shook violently; he fired and the bullet kicked up grass and mud three metres from where Baekani stood. Larke fired again and the shot missed by an equal margin. Baekani stepped forward; he was standing now almost at the steps to the verandah, near where the fire had singed the lattice work and reduced the large ornamental bush to blackened twigs. Baekani lifted the Mannlicher and fired rapidly, emptying the remainder of the magazine into Larke's chest.

The force of the bullets threw Larke back against the door jamb. His twitching body seemed to bounce from the wood; he pitched forward and tumbled down the steps until he lay at Baekani's feet. Baekani stared down at the dead man whose soiled white shirt was now turning dark as blood ran from the massive wound. He threw back his head and shouted. A succession of high-pitched, hysterical words, that rose and fell like a chant, tumbled from his mouth. He reloaded the rifle from the ammunition belt as he shouted.

"My God," Birmingham said, "he's not through."

"He is for now," Nanni said.

She was right. His reloading completed, Baekani turned abruptly and walked away from Larke's body. He glanced once towards the water and could have seen the white mast of the government launch as it neared the jetty, but he displayed no interest. He retraced his steps, going past the corpses of the policeman and the gardener. The woman whose children had been killed sat in Baekani's path with the bodies around her. She stared fearlessly at the *togu* and shouted at him, daring him to kill her too. Later she would say that the feet and legs of the *togu* passed through her body like wind through grass. Baekani walked on.

Louise Birmingham pushed her husband aside and cocked the Sharps rifle. "Where is he?"

Nanni pointed. "There."

"That's too far. I'd never hit him."

They watched as Baekani stepped over the body of his first victim, the woman who had carried the bundle, and disappeared into the bush.

32

"We'll have to get them into the ground pretty quickly," Cameron Somerville said. "This climate ... you know."

Louise Birmingham nodded. "One of the clerks here seems to have some organising ability. I think he could get that done. He's the one who objected to my husband using the radio. George Roko, I think you trained him?"

"That's right. Yes, he's a bright fellow. I suppose there's no legitimate authority here now? With Naismith gone and Larke dead?"

"There's a police sergeant, but he went back to his village to help clean up. Things have really fallen apart. I guess you're the nearest thing to an official we've got."

"I'm just a contract officer. I've got no real standing. But in an emergency, I suppose ... "

"This *is* an emergency," Louise said fiercely. They were standing outside the guesthouse, where Tom Birmingham had retired pleading pain from his wound. Nanni had gone off to comfort the woman whose children Baekani had shot, and other people were cautiously emerging from hiding, talking in distressed and frightened groups.

Somerville gave Louise a cigarette and asked her to wait
for him. He hurried away calling for the bosun of the
government launch. Louise sat in the shade on the steps
of the guesthouse and watched, impressed, while Somerville
instructed George Roko and the bosun. She could hear
snatches of his fast, idiomatic pidgin, and his air of
authority combined with politeness reminded her painfully of Richard Webb. When Somerville rejoined her,
there was an air in the compound of things being done.
A party of women carried the children's bodies away; some
sailors from the launch wrapped the bodies of the
policeman, the gardener and Larke in blankets and removed
them.

"I'd better try to get the radio working first off,"
Somerville said. "Get some instructions from Patugi."

"The radio's working perfectly," Louise said. She told
him in outline about her husband's connivance with Larke
and Stoltenberg to manipulate the situation on Murdo to
their own advantage.

"My God," Somerville said. "This is complicated. And
who did you say made this bloodbath?"

"Baekani. District Officer Naismith's personal servant.
He'd been on patrol after Eglito, and he returned alone and
apparently demented."

"I'll have to collect my thoughts and contact Patugi. Can
you come with me and fill me in as I go along? I'm glad
you're here, Mrs Birmingham. You seem to have a pretty
cool head."

Louise looked down at the Sharps rifle lying on the step.
"It's a surprise to me. I don't know whether I could have
shot him, though."

"Someone will," Somerville said grimly. "I've been here
for nearly two years, and do you know, up to now, it's been
such a peaceful place."

Louise smiled. "There's hardly been a minute's peace
since I arrived. Do you want to use the radio now?"

They set off across the compound. Louise automatically
passed her arm through the sling and carried the rifle on

her shoulder. *If my father could see me now,* she thought. *And if only I could see Richard.*

Somerville swept aside Tom Birmingham's paraphernalia and called the Tulagi station. When he had made contact, he gave the operator a brief account of the recent events at Alma, reported the situation to be 'calm' and requested instructions. He sighed and laid the headphones aside. "The RC's out in the field somewhere. They'll try to get on to him, but if not I'll have to deal with the number two man. And he's a fool, a real idiot. Have to wait for a call. Cigarette?"

Louise shook her head. "There's more," she said.

"More? We've got a mass murderer, a missing DO, a plot against the government. There's going to be a hell of a stink about young Larke's death. A hell of a stink. How can there be more?"

Louise told Somerville about Nanni's certainty that Eglito planned a violent action at Sunburi, which was where Naismith was going. She did not mention Webb, but Somerville was shrewd enough to see that her concern extended beyond a regard for peace on Murdo and the well-being of the district officer. He took some notes as she talked. "Anything else?"

"Yes, but we'll have to talk to Nanni. I don't properly understand it yet."

Somerville attempted to call the Tau lagoon station and the Catholic mission at Sulu'u without success. He picked up a faint signal from another location, but couldn't lock onto it. "Sounds like a field radio."

"Richard!" Louise exclaimed.

"Who's Richard?"

"Richard Webb. He's an anthropologist. He's going to be working at Sunburi."

"Ah," Somerville said. He had his answer and several more questions, but he busied himself with the switches and dials. "Wet batteries interrupting the signal, probably. I suppose he took spares?"

Louise shook her head. "I don't know."

"Have to wait and see. I blame myself for this, you know."

"For what?"

"Those stations must be damaged — should've built 'em stronger."

"It was an extraordinarily bad storm, Nanni says."

"Where is this Nanni? You said I should hear what she has to say?"

Louise, flustered by her reaction to the possibility of contacting Webb, was glad of a chance to leave. "I'll see if I can find her. Also some tea."

Somerville lit another cigarette. "Goodoh," he said. "They'll make it on the launch if you can't find any other way."

Half an hour later Louise returned with Nanni and a pot of tea, milk, sugar and cups on a tray. Louise introduced Nanni to Somerville, who instinctively lifted himself an inch from his chair. He watched the old woman settle in a cane chair and wait to be served. The sight surprised him but he made no comment.

"Thank you, child," Nanni said as she received her cup. She put three heaped spoons of sugar into the brew and stirred vigorously.

"Nanni," Louise said after she had poured tea for Somerville and herself and again refused a cigarette, "please tell us what Baekani said after he shot Mr Larke."

Nanni sipped her tea. "Could I trouble you for a cigarette, Mr Somerville?"

Somerville bounded from his chair and proferred his tin. Nanni extracted a cigarette and waited for it to be lit. "Thank you. You have to understand that poor Baekani was in a state of shock."

Somerville almost choked on his tea. "*Poor Baekani?*"

"Yes, indeed. He is a remarkable man who has evidently undergone a terrible experience. I suspect that all the members of his patrol are dead."

"So are seven people in this compound."

"Six," Nanni said. "One of the children will survive. But I am not trying to put Baekani in a good light. I just want you to understand his state of mind."

Louise spoke more sharply than she intended. "What did he say, Nanni?"

"He said he would go to Sunburi. He swore to kill Mr Naismith."

"God," Somerville said. "Why?"

Nanni tapped ash into her saucer. "It's very complicated — to do with his totems and ancestors and with his feeling that all the good spirits have deserted him."

"Will killing Naismith bring him back into favour?" Louise said.

Nanni suddenly looked ancient, an embodiment of tradition. She put out her cigarette and brushed away the ash. The gesture looked like a ritual cleansing. "He would believe so, most passionately. With Eglito gathering his followers and making a big swear and Baekani so desperate, Mr Naismith, all the British and the Asians and many others are in terrible danger."

"Why, Nanni?" Louise said quietly.

"If Mr Naismith was killed, it would release enormous energy in the people of Murdo."

"In what way?" Somerville said.

"There is no love for peace and order on this island," Nanni said. "Some of the Christians may profess to love it, but that is only for what they can get out of it. Most people prefer the old ways — to take revenge against those who injure them, to kill witches, to accumulate blood money. At present a thousand old scores lie unsettled, with hundreds of people itching to settle them. Only the fear of the rope and the sicknesses in prison hold them back."

"What about this massacre?" Somerville said. "Will it release energy as well?"

Nanni accepted Louise's offer of more tea. "Yes, it is very lucky that your boat arrived, Mr Somerville. Without some show of British power, I believe that payback killing would start here in earnest. Baekani's kin will be in fear of their lives. The policeman he killed was a member of a very powerful clan, pagans. They will post a large bounty for Baekani."

"Dr Stoltenberg will love that," Louise said.

Somerville's tea had grown cold while he was listening to the old woman. He drank it anyway. "It sounds as if that gentleman should be arrested. And . . ."

"My husband with him?" Louise said.

Nanni shook her head. "It would not be a good time for you to fall out among yourselves. I don't believe that the people of the Jeremiahs have ever seen one white man arrest another. The shock would be very great."

"I don't follow," Somerville said.

Nanni leaned forward. "No, you don't. When I said that energy would be released on Murdo, I was not only talking about feuds and killings and revenge amongst my people. Every man hanged by Mr Naismith and his predecessors is a death unatoned for. The same for every man who has died in prison. There is a fortune in shell money posted as bounty for Mr Naismith. If Eglito kills him, he will earn it, but some of Eglito's people will be killed too. I cannot imagine Mr Naismith dying without a fight. Can you?"

Somerville shook his head.

"Those people will have to be avenged and in the right way. Do you see?"

"No," Louise said.

"Your Mr Webb would see. A white man would have to die, any white man. And so on."

"My God," Somerville said. "You mean that if Naismith is killed and takes a few with him, there wouldn't be a white person safe on Murdo?"

"That is exactly what I mean," Nanni said.

"That is damned tricky," Somerville murmured.

Louise stood and grabbed his cigarette tin. "Tricky! Don't be so bloody British! We have to get to Sunburi. We have to warn him, them, everybody."

Louise took out a cigarette and bent to the flame of Somerville's lighter. She paced the room, puffing smoke. She stopped in front of a map of Murdo pinned to a board at shoulder height. She jabbed the cigarette at a point on the west coast. "That's Sunburi. In your launch we could make it in, how long?"

"Thirty-six hours," Nanni said, "perhaps less, depending
on the weather."

"The weather's just great," Louise exclaimed. "Not a
cloud in the sky, not a breath of wind. What do you say?"
Before Somerville could reply the headphones crackled.
Somerville put them on and listened. He said, "Alma
receiving, over."

"What is it?" Louise said.

Somerville listened for a few minutes, then he said,
"Sydney, this is Alma, stand by, Sydney, over." He took off
the headphones and turned back to the two women in the
room. "It's a radio station in Sydney calling on behalf of
a newspaper. They want the latest bulletin."

"From Tom," Louise said. "To hell with them."

Somerville thought: *She means to hell with him. Lucky
Webb.* He sat undecided for a few seconds, wishing he had
instructions from Patugi. He sensed Nanni's eyes meas-
uring him and suddenly felt as if he represented all British
manhood, and that this category of humankind was up for
assessment. He wavered, then found solid ground.
Birmingham was unauthorised to use the radio. He put on the
headphones and spoke crisply: "This is Alma, AC 1 calling
Sydney. AC 1 to Sydney station monitoring. There will
no further bulletins. Repeat, no further bulletins. AC 1
out."

Nanni nodded approvingly. Louise smiled. Suddenly
exhausted, she leaned against the wall.

"I'll try Patugi again." Somerville lit a cigarette, balanced
it on the edge of the table and went through the procedures.
He held the earphones to his head with one hand and used
the other for the dials and to smoke. Nanni sat in the chair
with her eyes closed. Eventually Somerville switched off
and expelled a long breath. He took a last puff on the
cigarette and dropped the butt into the dregs of his tea.

"Well?" Louise said.

"No joy. The RC's still not available, and his deputy,
Barnett Campbell, hasn't a clue what to do."

"The field radio?"

Somerville shook his head.

"Looks like you're going to have the next move, Mr Somerville."

"Yes, it does," Somerville said slowly. "It's funny, I was all set to go back to Islington with my photographs and curios and write up a report for the government which no one would read except perhaps some American. Sorry, didn't mean to be rude."

"What *did* you mean?" Louise said.

"This place is ideally located to form part of a communications system — radio, telephone and so on. You Americans look to the future."

"*Do* we?"

Louise snorted her amusement. Her nose twitched at a smell of burning and she stood away quickly from the wall. Her cigarette had burned a hole through the laminated paper of the map. The dark hole obliterated the indentation on the coast of Murdo named Sunburi.

33

East coast of Murdo, 24 February 1928

Naismith spread the map on the engine hatch of the
Loloburu and examined it closely. The launch was steaming
sturdily up the east coast into a head wind and battling a
cross current. The choppy sea and brisk wind had
stimulated Naismith and helped to dispel his depression
after the confrontation with Tefu. His assault on the old
man had been witnessed by several of the sailors, who
remained impassive as the DO moved about the boat, but
he could feel their antagonism.

His plan was to call briefly at the Catholic mission at
Sulu'u to check on the welfare of the community and the
mood of the normally quiescent Murdoans in the district.
He would also send a message to Baekani to join him in
Sunburi. His plan, to collect the rate there and harry Eglito
and Lagailemo the length and breadth of the island, was
unchanged.

He heard the change in the engine's note and looked
towards the land. Naismith was familiar with the Sulu'u
coast from his whaleboat trips. Clouds piled up high and
white over the interior hills, and the long, yellow beach

beyond the reefs was clean — a sign that the tides had removed the storm's rubbish. Naismith was heartened by this evidence that his island was returning to normal. Birds wheeled over the reef and Naismith prepared himself for one of the sights that most pleased him — the spectacle of a screeching flock of birds escorting the *Loloburu* to a mooring point in the bay, then banking and streaming back to their reef fishery.

Suddenly the engines went into reverse and Naismith lurched and stumbled across the deck. Marius, sitting nearby, scrambled to prevent him from hitting the rail.

"Are we on the reef?" Naismith gasped.

"No, sir, but look." Marius pointed and Naismith saw that the birds that normally swirled chaotically and plunged individually towards the water after the darting fish were in a tight formation over the passage through the reef. He shaded his eyes against the bright sun and squinted. A long, light shape was visible in the water across the narrow gap, and something protruded from it above the surface of the water.

Marius' voice was full of sadness. "It's the *Jeanne d'Arc*, sir. The mission ship. She has sunk at the entrance to the passage. Pray God Father Simon and the brothers are safe."

Naismith's feeling of optimism had gone, and he was again feeling the aches and pains of age. His ankle was numb where he had knocked it on the hatch. The map he had clutched as he lost balance was crumpled and a little torn. He smoothed it out. "Tell the bosun to prepare the dinghy. I'll go ashore with two policemen and see what's been happening."

"I would like to accompany you, sir, I have friends at this place."

Naismith nodded. He fell into a brown study as he gazed at the water and the reef. He only dimly heard voices raised in dispute and was unprepared for the diffident arrival of Corporal Moro. He glanced up as the policeman shuffled his bare feet on the deck. To DO extended two fingers, signifying that he wished two policeman to go ashore.

The hapless Moro shook his head. Naismith's eyebrows shot up.

Marius appeared on deck equipped for a trip ashore. He nodded to Moro and stepped forward between him and Naismith. "The other policeman refuses to go, sir. Also the boatmen."

Naismith's roar was full-throated. "*What*! Refuse? I'll put them all in gaol!"

"They would rather be in gaol than land at Sulu'u. They are afraid."

"Afraid? Afraid of what?"

"They do not know, sir. That's the problem. They are superstitious men. They think a spell has been cast over this place. That a demon has destroyed the mission ship."

"That's absurd. She hit the reef."

"For them, this must be explained."

"The storm."

"The storm must be explained."

Naismith struggled to regain the self-control for which he was renowned, and which he prided himself on. He also believed that he understood Murdoans and their ways. There was no point in directly opposing fear so strong that it had caused policemen to mutiny. Another way had to be found. Marius spoke as if he read the DO's thoughts.

"Corporal Moro is willing to swim ashore, sir. He can secure a canoe and paddle back. When he returns safely, the others will be made easy in their minds."

Naismith stared shorewards. The waves lapped gently at the beach; smoke drifted up from huts beyond the fringing trees. "It looks peaceful enough."

"Yes, sir."

Naismith glanced at Moro, a slender, tough-faced man in his late twenties. He still looked hesitant, but Naismith judged that this was related to his loss of command over his men rather than to going ashore. He favoured the corporal with a sharp nod. Moro looked relieved, saluted and about-turned smartly. He marched to the bow of the launch, removed his shirt, belt and *sulu* and dived overboard.

Naismith and Marius moved to the bow and watched Moro swimming strongly towards the reef. The birds screeched overhead and the flag attached to the mast of the *Jeanne d'Arc* fluttered just above the waterline.

"Corporal Moro will be a useful man in the fight against Eglito and Lagailemo," Naismith said.

Marius said, "He is a good Catholic. He is unaffected by the fears that haunt the pagans."

"Like yourself. Like Baekani. Do you hate the pagans, Marius?"

"It is un-Christian to hate, sir. Oh, God! Oh, no!"

Naismith and Marius stared in horror as a silver-grey shape slid through the water, following the line of froth thrown up by Moro's rhythmic kick.

Naismith felt for the pistol holster he usually wore at his belt when on patrol. His pistol was below, on his bunk. "A gun, Marius! Quick!"

"Too late, sir."

The shark, a huge hammerhead, struck Moro on the right side, tearing away half his chest. The policeman screamed, and the water around him turned red. His hands flew up as if reaching for a non-existent ladder that would lift him up and away from the monster. The shark came at him again, hitting low, and the desperately seeking hands and head of Moro disappeared beneath the foaming red surface.

"My God," Naismith said. "My God, my God." Beside him he heard Marius mumbling prayers mixed with traditional incantations and supplications to the ancestor spirits. Moro's single anguished cry had brought the two constables and a couple of the sailors on deck. They had witnessed nothing of the death, but the spreading red patch in the water was as terrible. They muttered uneasily among themselves and looked fearfully towards Naismith who stood, gripping the rail, as if he was about to tear it loose. The bosun and other crew members came on deck. All watched as the red turned to pink and was finally diluted away to nothing.

The young To'beili constable pointed. *"Lukim!"*

A thin, brown arm, mangled at one end, trailing torn flesh, floated on the surface of the water. One of the sailors reached for a boathook. Will Naismith, veteran of war, riot, flogging and execution, vomited violently into the sea. He coughed, fought the nausea, lost the fight and vomited again. The spasms racked him, causing him to sink to his knees. He coughed and spluttered, thrust his head forward and spat. His hat fell into the water. The sailor with the boathook abandoned the task of snaring the arm and went after the hat.

"No!" Naismith said. "No, no, no."

Marius assisted him to a chair. Naismith turned away as Moro's arm was lifted aboard. He had never fainted in his life and never felt as close to doing it as then. The sun beat on his bare head and the birds screeched overhead. His mouth tasted foul and he mimed the action of drinking, unable to speak. Minutes passed. The faintness faded and strength returned to his limbs, but he shivered and felt cold before he became aware of Marius holding a glass to his mouth. He drank and felt the hot, charged fluid burn his gullet and spread inside his guts, warming him instantly. He gulped again. "What's that?"

"Brandy, sir," Marius said. "I thought . . ."

"You thought all white men drank it," Naismith croaked, "especially when they're in a funk."

"Sir?"

"Never mind. Thank you." He drank the rest of the brandy and handed Marius the glass. He coughed and drew a deep breath. "Would you get them to make some tea? Strong. They will do the things for Moro?"

"Yes, sir."

Naismith sat in his chair until he became conscious of the heat of the sun. He stood up slowly and pulled the chair into the shade. *Getting old,* he thought. *And soft. Not fit to command. But there's no one else.* He belched loudly and smiled as the taste of the brandy returned to his mouth. He had not drunk alcohol for more than thirty years, not since he had got blind drunk on beer after a cricket match in Port Fairy. He was seventeen, playing in the Warrnambool first eleven, and he'd scored a fast, opposition-wrecking century. Then he'd taken three catches in the field, or was it four? He couldn't remember. But he remembered the men slapping his back and pouring the drinks and urging him to get it down. And the sickness and remorse afterwards. Then the pledge, a personal thing. a promise to himself, renewed in South Africa and kept ever since.

"Sir." Marius held out a steaming mug of tea with a spoon in it. Naismith took it and added three spoons of brown sugar from a tin at his feet. He stirred vigorously and drank the liquid, which had scarcely gone off the boil; its heat did not bother him. There were better memories associated with tea — Amelia in the garden of her parents' house at Portland; his mother's seventy-fifth birthday; the christening of his brother Ted's eldest son, William, named for him and a promsing lad now at ten years of age. He sipped and remembered his first trip to the Jeremiahs on the recruiting schooner. *A wild place then,* he thought. The recollection brought him back abruptly to the present. *Still is, and dreaming like this is no way to tame it.*

He pondered the problem as he drank his tea. Authority was slipping away from him, an authority he had grown so used to that he had forgotten its source. Naismith's success on Murdo derived from his willingness to use the native structures and procedures to his own ends. The Murdoans, he had learned, had no concept of the impossible. Partly, this was a matter of not setting themselves insuperable tasks, but it was more than that. To a Murdoan, anything that could be thought of could be done. There was always a path through the jungle.

"Marius," Naismith said, "what totem was Moro?"

"Turtle, sir."

"And Solifu?" Naismith was referring to the other Alma lagoon constable.

"Shark. He is also a Catholic."

"Tell him I want to see him. Now."

Constable Solifu had served in the police for six years without any particular distinction. Naismith scarcely knew him, a measure of his insignificance. He was short and

stocky and wore a cross on a silver chain around his neck.
He stamped his feet as he stood at attention and snapped
a smart salute.

"Corporal Solifu, you are a good policeman." Naismith
spoke in the Alma language, choosing his words carefully.

"Thank you, sir."

"Would you wish to be promoted to sergeant?"

"Yes, sir."

"Would you wish to trade in shell money with the
taxpayers at Sunburi?"

"I would wish it, sir."

"You are of the shark totem. The sharks will not harm
you. You can swim to the beach and report on what has
happened at Sulu'u."

Solifu, for all his mediocrity, was no fool. He sensed that
Naismith would be partial to a compromise. "I am of the
shark totem, sir. I am also a Catholic. I believe I could take
the dinghy through the reef when the tide is high. Would
that be satisfactory, sir?"

"It would, constable," Naismith said.

In two hours Solifu returned to report that the mission
had been badly hit by the storm. Several people had been
killed, much of the mission garden destroyed and many of
the pigs lost in the bush. Father Simon Montcalm, the head
of the mission, had suffered concussion when a tree branch
fell on him, but he was recovering. The radio was out of
action because of a damaged generator, but the brother who
operated and maintained it was hopeful of making repairs.
There was an urgent request for supplies of flour, sugar,
soap and kerosene. No lives had been lost when the *Jeanne
d'Arc* hit the reef, but the loss of the vessel and extensive
damage to the chapel had weakened the faith of the
mission's adherents.

"A brother has deserted and joined the pagans, sir," Solifu
said. "Many of the people are wavering."

"Is there any news of Lagailemo and the one whose name
will not be spoken?" Naismith used the formula to express
his contempt for Eglito and to emphasise his outcast status.
This was difficult for Solifu. Eglito was being spoken

of with fear in the mission, but the sort of fear that hung around a powerful *lemo* like a cloak. A protective fear, and fear that acted as a weapon. He was not sure that Naismith would understand this. As part of his slender armed force, Solifu wanted the DO to recognise the strength of the power levelled against him, but, on the other hand, his own self-interest dictated that there should be a major tax collection at Sunburi. From this, if Naismith kept to his bargain, Solifu would profit mightily. The prospect made his mind uncharacteristically nimble. "They also speak of Baekani," he said.

"Ah, yes, Baekani. He will be with us at Sunburi. Thank you, sergeant. You have done well."

"Thank you, sir."

34

Near Sunburi, 27 February 1928

"I'm getting something," Webb said. "But the reception's lousy. The connections must still be a bit wet." He put his hands over the earphones to press them closer to his head, and his face became a mask of tense concentration.

"You'll burst a blood vessel," Clements said. "Relax. We'll be at Sunburi in a few hours, and you can get the equipment properly dried out and serviced there."

"I expect you're right." Webb took off the headphones and shook his head, sending his dark hair, now rather long and shaggy, flying out around his lean face. "It's maddening, though. I thought I could hear Alma calling Patugi. Maybe it was just what I *wanted* to hear. There was something about Larke, but I couldn't make out what it was."

"Probably putting in an order for cocoa," Clements said. He tapped ash from his pipe into his hand and blew it off, over the rail and into the sea. The *Woodlark* was making good progress down the east coast. "Can't get to sleep without it."

Webb smiled. "He did seem a bit wet, but you can never

tell. I saw some pretty unpromising types fight like lions in France."

"And the reverse, I'll wager — warriors turn to weaklings."

"Oh, yes. Plenty of that."

Clements sucked on his pipe. "Wonder which I would have been. Well, not to worry, I've been spared the test. I must say everything seems bloody quiet."

Webb looked landwards. The central spine of the island's rugged hills veered nearer the coast at this point than elsewhere, and he could see the high, light clouds hanging around the topmost reaches. Smoke rose from villages in the hills and on the narrow coastal plain, but the *Woodlark* was too far offshore for them to see human activity. "What would you expect?" Webb said.

Clements shrugged. "I don't know. It's more a feeling. I'd like to see a few fishing canoes, or people collecting driftwood from the reef. Anything."

The almost unnatural peace remained the dominant feature of the Murdo coastline for the rest of the voyage to Sunburi. It was late in the afternoon when the *Woodlark* entered the vast, almost landlocked bay. The heads, two narrow promontories, actually ran parallel to each other, so that the entrance to the bay was a deep, wide channel between them. From the sea it looked as if there was no entrance at all, but the experienced Burns Philp boatmen had no trouble locating and negotiating it.

Webb had read descriptions of the bay, but they had not prepared him for its grandeur. In the fading light, with the sun dipping towards the mountains, it was like a lake, nearly circular, with a large, rocky island set almost dead centre. Unlike the rugged coastline they had been following, the shores of Sunburi Bay sloped gently up to a wide, level stretch before the steep hills began. As the launch inched through the long channel, changing course frequently to avoid sandbars and shoals, Webb was able to take in most of the 360 degrees of scenery. He could see where tracks led out of the jungle, following natural watercourses and folds in the earth, down to the coast.

Sunburi was a 'passage' for a great many of the people of the interior.

The harbour reminded him of a phrase frequently used by a discoverer in the Pacific. 'A thousand ships of the line could ride at anchor in perfect safety.' *Easily that many,* he thought. *Probably more.* A short, narrow jetty was a feature of a slightly flattened section of the shore over to the east. Its shortness indicated the presence of deep water. Indeed, once through the channel, Webb was amazed at the colour of the water — a profound green, almost black, indicating great depth and abundant vegetation on the bottom. Which in turn meant abundant life, for Sunburi was famous for the quantity and quality of its fish. As he looked around Webb was aware, above all, of a sombreness. Again unlike much other coastline, the narrow strips of beach here were dark grey and the central island appeared to be wholly enveloped in a green-grey shadow of its own making.

Webb shivered despite the warm, moist air. "It looks as if the sun never shines here."

"It shines all right," Clements said. "Wait till midday. The place becomes a cauldron. It completely changes. All these blacks turn to yellow and red. Look, you can get some idea of it now in this last little flash of daylight."

A bright ray of intense light, emitted before the sun sank behind the tops of the looming mountains, spread across the treetops, beach and water to reach far out into the harbour, almost to the island. Webb saw colours glow briefly and eerily — in the water, amid the trees, in the air itself. The illusion that the place was charged with life and colour died almost instantly, to be replaced by a brooding, dark blankness.

"I've never seen anything like it," Webb said.

"Trick of the light," Clements said. "But of course there are other opinions."

"I've seen photographs of the place, but they don't do it justice. And I've read a couple of missionary accounts of life here, but they didn't prepare me for any of this . . . strangeness."

"Strangeness?" Clements asked.

"It's true. This must be one of the strangest places on earth."

"The missionary accounts don't do it justice."

Clements cleared his throat nervously. "This is no place for missionaries."

The bosun came back to where the two men sat, and Clements instructed him to tie up at the jetty and send a To'beili crewman to request the presence of headman Kaluae. He then asked Peter Mamuka to bring a box from his cabin. When the large wooden box was opened, Clements asked Mamuka's advice about gifts for the headman.

"I think he would like these and these." Mamuka selected a pair of straight razors and a matching set of silver-backed hairbrushes. Clements added a packet of fine grade pipe tobacco and several boxes of matches.

"Not a place to arrive empty-handed," Clements said. "The To'beili are generous people, and they expect the same. You'll get on well here as long as you give as good as you get."

Webb nodded. Since he had made the decision to work at Sunburi, he had been studying a simple To'beili grammar, the product of an abortive attempt by the Melanesian mission to win converts at the passage. He had also practised the language assiduously with Mamuka and felt he was making some headway. He spoke now, slowly, enunciating carefully. "Peter, my friend, what sort of man is Kaluae?"

Clements' look of surprise changed to one of admiration when Mamuka replied.

"Like no other."

"Are you showing off, Richard, or did you understand what he said?"

"I believe he said Kaluae is not a usual sort of man."

Clements laughed. "Well, you may be guessing, but that's certainly true. Do you really speak To'beili?"

"Picking it up," Webb said. "Is this him?"

Walking along the jetty beside the sailor was a man of

about fifty years of age, to judge from his silvery hair and
deeply lined face. Being about a hundred and sixty
centimetres tall, he was of average height for a Murdoan,
but there all commonplaces ended. Kaluae's shoulders were
extraordinarily broad and thick, and his chest, Webb
guessed, would have measured one and a half metres
around. His torso was cylindrical, without a waist, and his
arms and legs were constructed on the same massive lines.
He gave an impression of immense strength, deep dignity
and endless resolve. He wore a blue cotton shirt that failed
to meet across his chest and a *sulu* made from a piece of
cloth twice the normal length. A broad leather belt around
his middle was in fact two belts riveted together.

Clements packed his pipe and tried to appear casual as
the headman swept an imperious look over the launch and
then suddenly jumped, landing light as a cat, from the jetty
to the deck.

"*Gut dei, Mist Kalemen.*"

"*Gut dei, Kaluae. Yu stap gut?*"

The headman nodded, then turned to look at Webb who
stepped forward with his hand held out.

"I am honoured, Kaluae, to greet you and be greeted by
you," he said in slow, precise To'beili.

Kaluae's stern face relaxed. "Mamuka, you have taught
this white man our tongue?"

"He knew something of it, Kaluae, before I came to work
for him."

Kaluae gripped Webb's hand and shook it vigorously.
"You are welcome, sir, although these are very bad days."

Webb understod the welcome but not the last part of
the sentence. He arranged his face in a serious expression.
"Thank you, Kaluae. With your permission I would like
to live among you for a little time, to study custom. Mr
Naismith sends his greetings." This speech, carefully
researched and stretching Webb's grasp of the language to
the limit, found favour with the headman until the mention
of Naismith. At that, his face became troubled and a shade
less confident.

"There is much to talk about," he said.

A few curious people visited the jetty and talked with the crew, but Sunburi exuded wariness bordering on hostility. As night fell, fires winked along the beach and in the hill settlements around the huge bay. Kaluae was the guest of Clements and Webb for the evening meal, which they ate on board the *Woodlark*. The headman devoured huge quantities of fish and rice, followed by fried bananas. He refused beer, drank only strong, sweet tea and belched hugely and appreciatively when he finished eating. Over the meal, the white men told him what they had seen at Birdbeak Bay and of the peculiar passive feeling of the coast. The headman nodded and spoke of the damage caused by the storm. Sunburi harbour, peculiarly sheltered, had largely escaped unscathed but Kaluae had heard stories of widespread devastation.

Webb recognised the To'beili habit of approaching an important subject crabwise, speaking first of things not strictly relevant; he had seen the trait in Mamuka. It was a delicate matter to judge the moment at which to introduce the item at the head of the agenda. After Kaluae had received his gifts and had lit the pipe packed with sweet-smelling tobacco, Webb judged that the moment had come.

"Have you news of Eglito, Kaluae?" Webb asked, speaking To'beili.

"I have news of Baekani."

Webb translated for Clements, who held up his hand. "Just talk. Give me the gist afterwards."

Webb and the headman talked for several minutes, frequently switching to pidgin when Webb's comprehension failed him. Towards the end of their discussion Mamuka, who had gone on shore to visit relatives and friends, returned and sat quietly at a distance, drinking tea and working on a small wooden carving with a sharp knife. Eventually the headman heaved his massive body upright. "Tomorrow there will be a house for you, sir," he said, "and it will be called the house in which the talk is of custom."

"I am honoured," Webb said. "Thank you. And I hope the *wailis* will bring us good news of Mr Naismith."

Kaluae smiled bleakly, signalled to Clements and Mamuka, and left the boat, trailing honey-cured tobacco smoke from his clay pipe.

"Feels like a royal visit, doesn't it?" Clements said. "Well, Dick, the gist, if you please."

Webb beckoned for Mamuka to join them. "The island's alive with rumours," he said. "Baekani's patrol was attacked and wiped out."

Clements' jaw dropped. "Baekani's dead?"

Webb shook his head. "Possibly not. The information comes from supporters of Eglito, and Kaluae doesn't altogether believe them, not on every detail. But something pretty drastic's happened. Naismith has had trouble all down the coast — protests, demonstrations — call them what you like."

"Will wouldn't take kindly to that. What's he done?"

"Nothing."

"Nothing? That's impossible. Naismith would be a holy terror with that sort of thing."

"Kaluae is puzzled himself. He feels Naismith may be ill or he may be . . . cursed. There's a lot of talk about curses, most of which I didn't understand."

"May I speak?" Mamuka said.

Webb poured the last of a bottle of beer into his glass. "Of course, Peter."

"People tell me that Eglito has been joined by a man named Lagailemo. He is an escaped murderer. A Maka Maka man."

"I've heard of him," Clements said. "Will was very keen to get him back in prison."

Mamuka nodded. "He is a very bad man, and if he had some success in war he would attract many followers. Things are very unsettled on Murdo. The Christians are blaming the pagans for the storm, and vice versa. Many people feel that British power is about to end."

"That's ridiculous," Clements exclaimed. "Even if Will Naismith's lost his grip . . ."

"To many here, Mr Clements, Mr Naismith's grip, as you call it, and British power are the same thing."

"Eglito's not far away, is he, Peter?" Webb said.

"Not far. Lagailemo and others are with him."

"I don't know. It will depend, the people say, on how Eglito reads the signs. It will also depend on what Mr Naismith does."

"Where is he?" Clements said.

"Kaluae says he is somewhere to the south. I had trouble following this. There's a Catholic mission, Peter?"

Mamuka nodded. "At Sulu'u. A day to the south by launch."

"It seems the storm hit hard there, and a boat was sunk. At first I thought he meant Naismith's boat, but I gather not."

"The mission has a boat named after the Frenchwoman who was burnt," Mamuka said. "I have heard the story, but I could never believe it. Do French people burn each other?"

"The *Jeanne d'Arc*," Clements said. "Joan of Arc."

"Yes. That one. You must explain it to me. I do not understand what it has to do with Noah and the ark, but it is a very powerful boat, given magical power by the people there. If it has sunk, the mission at Sulu'u ..." Mamuka shook his head.

"So Will's at Sulu'u?"

Webb and Mamuka exchanged looks. "Perhaps," Mamuka said, "or he may be coming here. If he does, Eglito will act. Sunburi is a special place for him and all the clans he has ties with. And it will be a very big tax collection at this passage."

"I don't suppose you have any news from Alma?" Webb said.

"No, sir." Mamuka picked up his carving of a wooden bird and peeled a long, narrow strip from the back.

"I've got to get that radio working in the morning."

Webb picked up the strip of wood and examined it.
"Where do Kaluae's loyalties lie?"

Mamuka did not look up from his work. "With Kaluae,"
he said.

35

Alma, 28 February 1928

"You can't do that, Lou," Tom Birmingham said. "I forbid it."

Louise Birmingham laughed. "Forbid all you like, I'm going to Sunburi. And as soon as Mr Somerville can get organised."

Pastor Stoltenberg pointed his finger at her. " 'Let the woman learn in silence in all subjection,' " he intoned. " 'But I suffer not a woman to teach, nor to usurp authority over the man, but to be in silence.' "

"Hogwash," Louise said. "Try that on the jury in your trial."

"Trial?" Stoltenberg had pledged not to even speak to Louise Birmingham, and he was incensed to find himself almost in debate with her.

Louise pointed with the Sharps rifle across the compound. "When Mr Somerville gets back from using that radio, my guess is he'll be placing you two under arrest."

"That's absurd," Stoltenberg said.

"You conspired to ... how did you put it? Usurp

authority around here. That has to be some kind of criminal offence."

"You're out of your depth, Lou." Tom Birmingham was almost enjoying the confrontation. He was weighing the odds. Now that control of events had slipped from him, he was considering ways of sustaining a story. A trial wasn't such a bad idea. "We were working through the proper authority, which was Mr Larke."

"Who's dead and can't say any different. I figure there's one or two people around here can tell another story."

Birmingham smirked. "Not white people."

"You're disgusting," said Louise.

Birmingham's wound was throbbing. One moment he felt confused and feverish and the next coldly lucid. Confusion seized him. "And you're a nigger lover."

"No one will listen to you," Stoltenberg cut in. "You're deserting your husband. You're an adulteress."

Louise looked at her husband and felt the stirring of compassion. He was pale and looked scrawny around the neck. His mouth had collapsed over his big, strong teeth, giving him almost a buck-toothed, white trash look. She remembered his many kindnesses. "Tom," she said, "tell this mealy-mouthed hypocrite to take a running jump. This isn't you, all this sneaky stuff. He's exercising some sort of influence over you. You need some rest and proper food."

The alarm Stoltenberg had felt as soon as Somerville arrived mounted steeply. Birmingham had seemed to be in charge — the puppet master, manipulating Larke and the flow of information. He had seemed to be shaping events. Now things were different, and this woman was attempting to form a solid front against him. His own confidence was deserting him. He could sense opposition among his flock, resistance to his authority. Two of Baekani's victims had been mission adherents. Why, their kin were asking, had God not provided protection? Perhaps it was time for one of his trips to Queensland. A return to headquarters while events at the front sorted themselves out, as they had a way of doing. He remained silent, observing the clash of wills between Tom and Louise.

His lucidity returning, Birmingham sensed the missionary's uncertainty. *No allies,* he thought. *A cuckold is a laughing stock. No story in a laughing stock. Have to act. Got to regain the initiative.*

The solution came to him like a revelation. He favoured his wife with as warm a smile as he could muster. "Do what you feel you have to do, hon. Just be careful of that Sharps. It makes an awful big hole." He turned to Stoltenberg and took his arm. "We've got things to talk about, doc."

The two men walked down the steps and began to stroll along one of the compound paths. It was the path where the policeman who had challenged Baekani had died. Overnight rain had removed all traces of the blood-letting. The compound had been considerably cleared up; only the flagpole, with the long shaft lying clear of the splintered base, testified to the violence of the storm.

"You see the way the wind's shifted?" Birmingham said.

Stoltenberg fanned flies away with his hat. "Not exactly."

"That radio guy was a wild card. He could make trouble for us. Put us under a restraint order or whatever the hell they call it around here."

"Deportation's the more usual thing," the missionary said. "I can't help thinking a period of self-imposed leave might be in order."

"You're pulling out? Before the game's over?"

Stoltenberg stopped dead. "I cannot understand how the talk can be of games at a time like this. I was wrong to listen to you. I should have examined my conscience more . . ."

"No. You should take a good close look at things as they are. You get put in the hoosegow now or kicked out of the Jeremiahs and you lose everything. Right?"

Stoltenberg nodded. "It would be a considerable setback."

"So, double or nothing. And it's a good play because you've got nothing to lose."

"You're talking in riddles, Mr Birmingham."

"The mission's got a boat, right?"

"Yes, a schooner. The *Shining Light*."

"Auxiliary engine?"

"Yes."

"Tell you what we've got to do, doc. We've got to get to Sunburi before anyone else. Warn Naismith if we can, be in on the dust-up if that's the way it works out, and sing God save the goddamn king. We can come out of this smelling like roses. I get a great story. You helped smite the heathen."

Hesitation thickened Stoltenberg's accent. "I see many problems."

Ignoring this, Birmingham said, "Webb's got a radio. We can find out what's going on and I can get my stuff off to Sydney."

"Webb won't let you do that."

"I'll take care of Webb."

"I don't want to be part of any violence. I'm a man of God."

"You can be a man of God in New York City if you stick with me. We can still get it all."

"You really believe that, I can see you do. Tell me, what did you mean when you said I couldn't lose?"

Birmingham grinned. "If all this doesn't work out quite right, we run across to Australia in your schooner and see what we can do from there. We'll be out of reach of the Jeremiah authorities. It could be very interesting."

Eglito bent over the blue-grey pig entrails that lay in slimy clumps on the beaten earth. He examined minutely the twists and turns of the guts, the discolorations and the viscosity of the fluid that leaked from them. He touched the flaccid sack of tissue that had been the pig's stomach and rubbed thumb and forefinger together, testing the stickiness. His father had taught him how to read the signs and to compose his mind so that the messages came through clearly and fully. It was a matter of chanting for several hours before the pig was killed, approaching with eyes shut, breathing shallowly and then letting the steaming heap of entrails assault the senses — sight, smell and touch.

This had been a good reading. Eglito grunted with satisfaction. The messages he had received were consistent with his visions in the night. He had opened his bowels mightily that morning — another good sign — and he felt great strength within him. More importantly, he felt a field of strength around him. It would empower the others, the weaker ones. It would convince the waverers. It would frustrate his enemies. It would bring victory. He rose and left the secluded clearing where the reading had been made and returned to his camp.

"Was it good?" Meilai asked.

The leader had the option of replying or not, and it was always a question whether to do so. Much depended on the signs, but there could be no debate about their meaning. "It was good," Eglito said. "It was a fine pig." This was a compliment — Meilai had supplied the animal and would share in the glory.

Lagailemo, who had spent time on the white man's plantations, on his boats and in his prison, was less concerned about traditional auguries than his To'beili allies, but he knew better than to show any scepticism. He nodded at Eglito's news and continued cleaning his rifle. His head was full of numbers — the number of warriors they could count on, the number of guns, and the numbers of police and guns against them. His silence did not disturb the To'beili — taciturnity was entirely appropriate for a warrior.

One question was burning in Nalai'u's mind: *When?* He was chafing under Eglito's pretensions. A powerful clan leader himself, with aspirations to *lemo* status, he was irked by the way Eglito, apparently effortlessly, held the loyalty of his followers and even the allegiance of some of the men pledged primarily to himself. Nalai'u was a prolific feast-giver and bride-price broker, rather than a man of action. His fear was that he was seen as one who bought support rather than earned it. He was anxious to perform deeds. The anxiety made him both reckless and nervous and prompted the question: *when?* But to speak the question would be a sign of weakness.

In his visions, Eglito had seen a great crowd in a clearing close to the water. The sky was black and being split by forked lighting, and strong winds bent the trees and fluttered the headdresses of the warriors. But there was no rain. He did not see the white man's face, but he knew the white man was there, sitting on his chair, raised above the people. Eglito moved forward, and the crowd parted around him, but still he could not see the white man. The thunder cracked and the people looked up at the black sky. Eglito moved forward, filled with power but puzzling how he could get above the white man. How to strike down at him. The vision ended before he got an answer to this question. But he was given a clue — his *bokuru.*

The most sacred object Eglito possessed, of far greater value than his two blackened shillings, was the barrel of a Snider rifle. The weapon, then a shiny new thing, brassbound and with a gleaming walnut stock and stiff leather sling, had been brought back from Queensland in the 1870s. The man who brought it had left Murdo in the recruiting boat to escape punishment for a sexual offence committed against a woman belonging to the clan of Eglito's grandfather. This man, a *lemo* of ferocious reputation, had sworn to kill the recruit if he ever returned and, although he was an old man when that day arrived and possessed a very inferior weapon, he shot his enemy dead and took possession of the new Snider, which had never been fired.

Eglito's grandfather had used the Snider many times — to eliminate rivals, avenge slights and collect bounties. The weapon, although carefully maintained, had fallen into disuse in the early years of the twentieth century, when ammunition for it became unavailable. The stock had decayed, and for more than twenty years the Snider had lain in the rafters of the men's house, being 'smoked', periodically reconsecrated and brought out on ceremonial occasions by Eglito's father and Eglito himself. It carried the ritual name *bokuru*, which meant 'thunder' in the

To'beili language, and it possessed great power.

In his visions, Eglito had seen himself reaching back over his shoulder into the long pigskin pouch he wore at his back. The *bokuru* was sheathed in the pouch and Eglito awoke from the vision with the feel of his fingers gripping the cold steel of the barrel. Somehow, he knew, that sensation would provide him with the answer to his dilemma when the time came. He filled his pipe and lifted a coal from the fire with his hard, horny fingers. Meilai's eyes narrowed as he watched his cousin puff at the pipe. His own role in the events to be unfolded, he felt, was in the balance.

"Meilai, my kinsman," Eglito said, "would you send your son to the men's house to fetch the *bokuru* and to ask my son to return here with him?"

Meilai let out a quiet breath of satisfaction. He shot a glance at Lagailemo and saw that the leader's request had made an impact there. Nalai'u was impassive but undoubtedly impressed as well. Meilai was satisfied; his own stocks had risen, and he was encouraged enough to put one question to Eglito.

"It will be done, Eglito," he said. "And when will the thunder sound?"

Eglito smiled at the expression. "The thunder will sound as it always does. It will sound louder than ever before, louder even than in my father's time and his father's time. It will sound before the lighting strikes."

Baekani plundered gardens of bananas, pineapples and coconuts as he trekked east over the range, taking the shortest way across the island to Sunburi. He climbed hard, slid down tracks at a frantic pace and hurled himself along the short stretches of flat, easy going. He ate frequently and as frequently was seized by cramps and pains that he could only ease by emptying his bowels. He did this, ate and drank again, walked and suffered. He clung to the rifle and fired several shots at moving shapes he glimpsed in the bush. Whether the shapes were human or not he could not tell, but the mere suspicion was enough. In his heated, damaged brain, Baekani was convinced that every living human being, black and white, adult and child, was his mortal enemy.

Despite his injuries, which throbbed, bled and closed up only to open and pain him again, his body was tireless; he half-slept sometimes as he moved, but he never deviated from the path that would take him to the huge harbour. It was a place where he had often strutted his authority as Naismith's assistant, almost his deputy. He had a few friends there and many enemies. He had traded vast amounts of shell money with the taxpayers and driven hard bargains. He had been present, carrying his Mannlicher and ready to shoot the eye out of any To'beili would-be hero, when Naismith had arrested Eglito. The man Eglito had shot was a bounty killer himself and a witness testified that Eglito had been provoked. Eglito had looked bored while this defence was being offered and Naismith had not believed it. Still, the law was clear and the charge against the To'beili *lemo* was manslaughter, not murder. Baekani's advice to Naismith had not been heeded.

"He has killed many men, sir," Baekani had said, "and women. He deserves to die."

Naismith shook his head. "It is the law. He will serve ten years in prison. That is a long time."

Baekani struggled to understand the white man's law. Here was a dangerous enemy, captured, dishonoured, helpless, and the proposal was to feed, clothe and house him for ten years. To make him cut grass and build roads. Prisoners ate rice and had medical treatment; they grew fat in prison. Baekani had seen it, and it made no sense. There was no honour in the white man's world, no certainty. Foul and filthy things said, horrible curses uttered, brought no punishment, while things written on pieces of paper had the force of lightning and thunder. Once Baekani had thought he could understand this strange system but now in the face of Eglito's defiance and his own disgrace he knew he did not understand it.

The killings at Alma had eased Baekani's pain some-what, but he knew that he still had a big thing to do. A very big thing in this world which had turned inside out, bottom side up. He must destroy what he had protected, even if it meant destroying himself. He no longer mattered.

SUNBURI

36

"This is childish," Louise Birmingham said. "Very childish. You're turning this into a boat race like a bunch of college boys."

Somerville clenched his teeth around the stem of a pipe. "I know. But it's important we get there first."

"I've told you — Richard and Colin Clements will be there already, if they haven't ... "

"I mean, be the first to talk to Naismith."

"Yes, well, it looks as if you're going to win."

Somerville turned to look astern. The government launch was doing a steady twelve knots with a following breeze, and handling the choppy seas well. The mission schooner *Shining Light* was well behind. Somerville nodded with satisfaction. The schooner had left Alma an hour or more ahead, and not until they had rounded the north end of the island and left Birdbeak Bay behind had he become optimistic. The launch handled the conditions better and its crew were better watermen. They passed the *Shining Light* on the coastward side and had maintained a useful lead ever since. Still, there was no possibility of relaxing. Any mechanical faltering or navigational slip could turn the tables, and there were treacherous shoals aplenty off this coast.

Louise Birmingham had proved an excellent sailor, as Somerville expected she would. He looked at her now as she stood with her hair being ruffled by the wind. She was very tanned, in a way that would be thought unbecoming in London. But they weren't in London. She wore a red blouse and a *sulu* with large yellow sunbursts on a red background. Somerville was aware that he was doing more than racing to be the first to talk to Naismith. He was racing Louise's husband, and that was foolish because he was carrying her towards another man. Somerville had a nose for irony and a highly developed sense of humour — the present situation called for both.

"How's Nanni?" he said.

"In the pink. She's helping in the galley. You understand that she has to stay below."

"Why's that?"

"The Murdoans won't let a woman be placed physically above them."

"What about you? You're up here."

"I don't count. It's something I've come to understand. We really don't count to these people at all. Guns, boats, cameras, radios don't make any difference. We have no ancestor spirits, no totems, no sacred places. We don't count."

Somerville shrugged and turned to look at the coast off the starboard side. He saw nothing unusual in the stillness, the absence of canoes or activity on the reef. He had done a lot of boating around inhospitable parts of the coast of Scotland, and he was accustomed to traces of smoke from the hinterland as the only sign of human occupation.

"Look!" Louise exclaimed. "Oh, aren't they wonderful!"

A school of dolphins had began to gambol in the water — they raced along beside the launch, veering in and out of the wake, leaping the foam, twisting in midair and plunging into the smooth green water untouched by the

engine's screw. They played energetically for a couple of
minutes as Louise and Somerville watched, rapt. Then, as
if in response to an order, they all made a final graceful
leap, dived deep and were gone.

"Wonderful," Somerville said. "I saw some whales up in
the northern islands once. They . . . "

"What's that?" Louise pointed dead ahead.

Somerville shaded his eyes under the rim of his hat. He
squinted. "It's a boat."

The bosun appeared on deck and approached them
diffidently. He pointed. "*Sunburi, masta. Closeup.*"

Somerville nodded. "Thank you. Can you make out that
boat?"

The bosun, bare-headed, untroubled by the high, hot
sun, glanced casually across the shining stretch of water.
"*Loloburu,*" he said. "*Bot bilong Mista Naismith.*"

"Looks like we're going to be neck and neck," Somerville
said.

Louise felt her anxiety mount. She spoke more sharply
than she intended. "Just like Oxford and Cambridge."

"I didn't go to either, Mrs Birmingham," Somerville
said. "Your Mr Webb's the Oxford man."

"I'm sorry," Louise said. "I didn't mean to chew you out.
I'm nervous, I guess. Why are you smiling?"

Somerville laughed. "Fact is, I went to Birmingham
university."

Louise joined him in the laugh. They stood at the rail
and watched the distance beween the two steam launches
diminish. Somerville had heard about the peculiar entrance
to the Sunburi harbour; he wondered if it was possible for
two vessels to enter simultaneously. As they drew nearer,
he could see that it was not. The *Loloburu* and his boat
would reach the opening to the transverse channel at the
same time if they both kept on course.

"Hey," Louise said, "we're going to collide."

"I imagine the skippers know what they're doing."

"You English."

The launch bucked slightly as its engines slowed; the

Loloburu surged forward and made the slow, wide turn into the channel.

"Told you," Somerville said. He gazed across the water at the rear of Naismith's boat. An arm was raised in greeting.

"Naismith?" Louise asked.

"Yes, I think so."

"Thank God. If anyone can sort this mess out, he can."

The launch described an arc and followed the *Loloburu* into the narrow stretch of turbulent water between the two arms of land.

"You think so highly of him?"

Louise didn't reply. Instead she spun around to watch the mission schooner approach the channel. She could see movement on the deck but couldn't distinguish the figures. She sighed heavily.

"What?" Somerville said.

"I guess I was hoping they'd slope off someplace else."

Somerville sucked on his pipe but it had gone out, and the dead tobacco tasted sour. "No such luck. But here's something to brighten you up. Look."

Louise felt Europeans' usual awe on entering Sunburi harbour. The sheer size of the place and the almost perfect symmetry of its shape, with the island as an arresting pivotal point, seemed momentarily to dwarf human beings and their problems. "It's magnificent," she said.

Somerville jabbed his finger in the direction. "Not what I meant. Look there."

Louise saw a boat tied up at the jetty towards which the *Loloburu* was heading.

"That's the *Woodlark*," Somerville said. "BP boat. Colin Clements' tub."

"Ah," Louise said. "What a beautiful boat."

Naismith was somewhat surprised to see the government boat approach the channel. When it had yielded the right of way and when the two vessels were closest, his keen eyes identified Cameron Somerville. That was understandable — a radio matter. *Good,* he thought, *just what we need, a thorough check of the system right round.* Then he remembered that there was no radio at Sunburi, and puzzlement returned. It deepened when he failed to identify the smaller figure standing next to Somerville. A sudden lurch as the *Loloburu* negotiated the rip at the entrance to the channel distracted him. When he looked again the figure was gone.

"*Shining Light*," Marius said.

"What?"

The clerk pointed towards the north. "The mission ship, sir. She's approaching the channel too."

Naismith's surprise almost became alarm. He detested Pastor Stoltenberg at the best of times, even when the missionary was operating within his legitimate sphere of influence. As far as the DO knew, he had absolutely no business on the To'beili coast.

Turning away, he saw the *Woodlark* at the jetty. This was more of a pleasure; he was relieved that Clements had survived the storm. He had expected him to simply drop Webb off, but it would be agreeable to see him.

"Place looks set for a dashed regatta," he grumbled.

Marius nodded. The note of pleasure in Naismith's remark was the first he'd heard from the DO in days. He was heartened. Then he looked around the harbour and felt the encouragement dissipate.

The curious red and yellow colours that seemed to leak from the hills and spill down over the rocky beaches and outcrops of reef had a threatening effect. In the To'beili tongue there were many names for the harbour. *Sunburi* merely described one of its features — the central island — and the name had been adopted by European cartographers as an easy one to reproduce. As Marius knew, other names emphasised the deepness of the water, the sharpness of the rocks and the numbers of alligators inhabiting the mangrove-choked creeks that emptied into the harbour. Marius was glad of the presence of the other boats — against the spirits and warriors of Sunburi, the more white men and guns, the better.

"We'll be last home," Birmingham said. "I thought you said these guys were good boatmen."

Stoltenberg had hoped to be the first to talk to Naismith, to take the highest possible moral ground. The prospect of being second in line didn't appeal to him at all. Not that they could be sure the DO was aboard the launch. "It's the *Loloburu* all right," he said. "But that doesn't mean Naismith's aboard. He might be dead, as the rumours have it."

"I get the feeling he's alive," Birmingham growled. "And that we're in for a tough time."

"Perhaps we should . . ."

"Say, look. There seems to be no way in, but they're making it."

From the position the schooner occupied, the coastline appeared unbroken, and the sudden departures of the *Loloburu* and the government launch looked like unaccountable disappearances.

Stoltenberg shivered. "I don't like this."

"I gotta see it," Birmingham said. "Hey, you, captain. How d'they do that?"

The sailor standing nearby placed his hands in a parallel position in front of his chest a few inches apart. Then he indicated with his finger how the entrance was effected.

"That's great."

"It looks dangerous," the missionary said. "I've never been to this place. They are all pagans, every man, woman and child. They are also cannibals."

"C'mon, doc. You don't believe that."

The ship's bosun approached and invited the missionary's orders. Stoltenberg stared at the frothing water outside the channel. He felt the solid, threatening presence of the American beside him and knew he had no choice. "I don't know what I believe." He nodded; the bosun barked an order and the schooner began to turn.

Eglito's kinsman stood on a rock high above the harbour at a point where a track led back into the furthest reaches of the range in To'beili territory. He had been on watch for many hours and was tired, despite his consumption of tobacco and betel nut. Had he not been in a part of the country controlled by a clan distinctly unfriendly to his own, he might have been tempted to sleep. But he was alert enough to see the specks off the coast materialise into boats. At first he was puzzled; he had been advised to watch for the *Loloburu*, and here indeed it was, but what were these other vessels? He watched impassively as the two leading boats passed through the channel and entered the harbour.

A bushman who seldom ventured to the coast and knew nothing of the ships that plied around Murdo, he filed mental descriptions of the other two craft. He did not speculate on what effect their presence would have on Eglito's plans. He knew nothing of those plans. He was a scout, a watcher, a man with keen eyes and no imagination. Eglito knew all this and knew he would be able to rely on the information the man brought back. It was a talent of Eglito's to appoint the right man to the right job.

On the last stages of his journey Baekani had moved into a state of possession removed from rational thought, memory or sensory impulse. He was exhausted, but full of power and totally focussed. His stomach and bowels were empty but his brain was full. He was ready, and it felt right to him that he should be at Sunburi where the creeks ran into the sea and the alligators—his totems— basked in the mud.

He looked down on the water that shone blue-grey, like the barrel of his rifle. He noted with satisfaction that the *Loloburu* headed the procession to the jetty. How often he had stood on the deck, knowing that these fierce, proud To'beili would have to chew their lips while Naismith issued orders and told them how their lives would be. But he felt no sense of loss because he no longer shared in that power.

37

"I'm going to collect the rate," Naismith said. "Tomorrow."

Louise gasped. "After everything you've heard? You can't. That's madness."

Naismith's grey eyes rested on her. "Nevertheless," he said.

"You've no obligation to do so, of course," Clements said. "But would you mind telling us why?"

Will Naismith, Cameron Somerville, Colin Clements and Louise Birmingham were sitting in the Sunburi *haus takus*. This was of the usual design — panels of woven leaves lashed to a solid wooden structure, with a thatched roof and a rough verandah running the width of the building. It sat in a clearing to the east of the spit of land extended out to form the jetty. Several paths from the interior led down to the clearing, which had the name of Fitua, meaning 'dead leaves'. A carpet of leaves from the several varieties of tree that grew around the clearing covered the ground at most times of the year.

Naismith ignored the pains in his joints and gums. The information relayed by Webb, Clements and Somerville had cauterised his wounds. As he half-realised himself, he had not taken it all in — the murderous attack at Birdbeak Bay, the elimination of Baekani's patrol, the madness of Baekani, the death of Larke and the mischief caused by Stoltenberg and Birmingham.

"Mischief?" Louise had said after delivering a rapid summary of events to the DO. "Is that all you call it?"

"I'm a practical man, Mrs Birmingham," Naismith said. "I'll deal with Baekani and Eglito and Lagailemo and any others as practical problems. I can see the harm they've done. By comparison, yes, I'd call your husband's behaviour and that of Mr Stoltenberg mischievous."

"And how will you deal with that?"

Somerville, who had stood aside and let Louise have her say after making his own report, was apprehensive as to how Naismith would react to Louise's aggressiveness, but the DO's tone remained mild. "I will continue to refuse to see them and, as soon as possible, I'll issue deportation orders against them both. Will that inconvenience you, Mrs Birmingham?"

Was there sarcasm in Naismith's voice or irony in his expression? Louise didn't know. She shook her head and allowed Clements to speak. Then Naismith made the statement that Clements called on him to explain.

Naismith was obviously uncomfortable talking about such matters in the presence of a woman. Louise could feel his diffidence and embarrassment like a glass wall between her and the events that would be shaped by him. They would concern her, but she could have no direct bearing on them. She looked through the door and saw Nanni beckoning to her. Without a word, she stood and left the hut.

"Come and have some tea," Nanni said. "And bathe. Men are such fools."

Louise nodded. "Some men," she said. Webb, she had learned to her disappointment, was visiting a village a few hours' march away on the other side of the harbour. With her husband sulking aboard the *Shining Light* and Naismith planning reckless folly, she felt tired of the world of men.

Somerville watched Louise meet Nanni at the water's edge and walk towards the jetty. "She had a Sharps rifle loaded and cocked," he said. "If Baekani hadn't sloped off, I believe she would have shot him."

"What was her husband doing?" Naismith said.

"Nothing."

"I'm not surprised. Well, I never doubted she was a woman of spirit. Where's the Sharps now?"

"She still has it."

"Speaking of rifles," Naismith said slowly, "do you know what kind of a weapon Baekani used?"

Somerville shook his head. "Does it matter?"

"Yes indeed. Larke died bravely, she says?"

"Mm."

"You don't sound so sure."

"I found a whisky bottle in your quarters where he'd been. Tidied it away, of course. He took a few shots. He certainly wasn't hiding under the bed."

Naismith nodded. "Good. We're going to have a hard job making anything useful out of all this. Some severe lessons will have to be taught, and stories about white men's cowardice aren't going to help."

"How many armed men can you put together for the tax gathering, Will?" Clements said.

Naismith positioned his chair so that when he leaned back, it rested against a solid upright rather than a panel of leaves. "I'll have a pistol myself. I've got two constables on the *Loloburu*, and Marius the clerk looks a likely type. Peter Mamuka and Kaluae of course. Probably find a couple of ex-police in Kaluae's village and rustle up a few rifles. Say eight. Should be enough."

Somerville and Clements looked at each other. "You're forgetting us," Clements said. "And Webb."

Naismith shook his head. "I'm the only white man who's going to be involved in this. It's important that my authority is completely restored and seen to be restored. I'm sorry, gentlemen. No other Europeans involved."

"This is very unwise, Will," Clements said.

Amelia used the exact same phrase, Naismith thought, *when*

I told her that it was my duty to complete the task here. She had told him he'd done enough and he'd said there was more to do. Then she called him blind stubborn and turned away. He could see the set of her shoulders and the tilt of her head on her slender neck, and he'd wanted so much to be able to say he'd stay. But he knew it was impossible. He didn't know how or why, but the islands owned him, body, heart and soul.

"Stubborn ... " Naismith said.

"I beg your pardon, Will."

"It's my decision and I have the authority to take it. Look, there'll be hell to pay when Price-Kane and the high commissioner hear about Larke. It could be the end of me, because Baekani was my man. I'll fight if they try to get rid of me, but I'll need plenty to fight with. If I can show here that the government writ still runs, that'll help."

"What about Eglito and the others?" Somerville said. "The old woman, Nanni, is convinced that they plan to attack you."

Naismith smiled. "I'm not about to start making decisions on the basis of the fears of old women."

Clements packed his pipe although he knew better than to light it indoors with the DO present. "What about Baekani?"

"Kaluae's got men out looking for him. If he got across the range he must be exhausted."

"You want him captured?" Clements said.

Naismith did not reply.

Clements tamped down the tobacco. "Killed?"

"You'll have to let me organise these things as I see best," Naismith said. "You know a little about this, Colin, but not enough. I'm not sure I do myself. There are vast amounts of shell money posted as bounties along the coast and into the bush as a result of Eglito's actions. If all the members of Baekani's patrol were killed, that boosts it still further. It's all very delicate, a matter of which clans come out on top. With Kaluae's help, I'm hoping to get a good result. None of this ever gets into the official reports, of course, but it's the way this island's governed."

Clements got to his feet. "I'm going outside for a smoke. Let me know if there's any way I can help."

"Get the radio working," Naismith said. "That'd be a start."

"What radio?" Somerville said.

Clements said, "Webb's got a field radio. It got wet or something."

Somerville clicked his tongue. "Louise mentioned it. I forgot. Where is it? I'll get it working."

Louise looked across the water to the point at the furthest reach of the harbour, where she had been told Webb had gone. By canoe. He had seized the chance to talk to a nonagenarian whose memory extended back almost to the first significant European contacts on Murdo.

"He had to go," Clements told her. "This chap could pop off any day. Besides, he didn't know you were coming. If he had . . ."

"What?"

"I was going to say, if he'd known you were coming he would have stayed here, but I'm not entirely sure. He didn't talk much about you. I know he cares for you."

"I understand," Louise said. "I've never expected people to have second sight about my wants and needs, the way some women do."

Clements' admiration was manifest. "You've observed that, have you?"

Louise nodded. "Yes. Did you think I was stupid because I'm an adulteress?"

"I wasn't sure you *were* an adulteress. I told you, Webb's not a loose-mouthed sort of chap."

"I'm sorry," Louise said. "He's wonderful, isn't he?"

Clements had laughed. "You mightn't have thought so if you'd seen his first few paddle strokes. I suppose he's got the hang of it by now. He'll be back by dark."

"I have to see my husband," Louise said to Nanni, who was smoothing out one of several cigarettes she had accepted from Somerville.

"Is that wise, child?"

"Necessary." Louise walked along the jetty, which was somewhat decrepit, owing to the reluctance of the To'beili to carry out public works. A section had collapsed and there was now proper provision for only three vessels, so the *Shining Light* was moored to a pile detached from the rest of the structure. A series of rickety planks had been put down to allow access from deck to jetty.

Tom'd have to be stone sober to cross those, she thought. She called his name, and Birmingham appeared at the rail. He looked pale and tired; his hair was unkempt, and he was smoking a native cigarette — twist tobacco wrapped in newspaper.

"Louise," Birmingham said. "Queen of the jungle."

"You look like hell, Tom."

"I feel like hell. What's happening?"

Louise considered the question and the motives behind it. She had hardly exchanged two words with her husband since arriving at Sunburi. The hateful presence of Stoltenberg partly accounted for this. She doubted she would understand his motives, but Birmingham's were clear — he needed a story. "Nothing's happening," she lied. "They're going to starve the rebels out. Nothing's going to happen here."

"Shit!" Birmingham said. "What's Naismith doing?"

"Waiting for the radio to be repaired. Then he's going to send some messages before heading back to Alma."

"What about Baekani?"

Louise wondered how far to push it. *All the way!* "The rumour is he died in the bush from wounds. Tom, there's one more thing."

"Yeah?"

"The government's issuing deportation orders against you and Stoltenberg. I think you'd better take off."

Birmingham did not notice that Stoltenberg had come on deck. The missionary stood behind him. "Come with me," Birmingham said.

Louise's dislike of the pale, still figure in the background sharpened her reply more than she'd intended. "No chance of that."

Stoltenberg pointed at her; his long, bony finger waved in the air like a schoolmaster's cane. "We will go," he shouted, "and leave you and the other heathens to your sinning."

Birmingham buried his head in his hands. His shoulders heaved. Louise turned and walked back along the jetty to the beach. As she reached the sand, she heard the sound of the mission ship's engines starting up. She took Nanni's arm, and they walked in the direction of a group of huts where the women would cautiously welcome them. She did not look towards the water until they had almost reached the huts. By that time the *Shining Light* was almost out of sight in the shadow of the island in the centre of the harbour.

Richard Webb and Peter Mamuka had sat in the dark, smoky hut listening to the old man telling his tales of *kastom long taim bipo* for four hours. Webb's purpose was to decide at what point of the harbour to locate himself, and he had asked Mamuka to probe the questions of clan strength and history, the degree to which tradition was intact. Webb's knee joints were locked solidly and he staggered when he was finally told by Mamuka that it was time to stand, hand over more tobacco and take his leave. He had understood little of the ancient's speech, not only because of the thinness of the voice but because the inflections and words themselves were unfamiliar.

"He's a very old man," Mamuka said when they stood outside in the afternoon sun. "The language has changed since he was a boy. He remembers the old language and he says there are others who do, too. This may be a good place for you. He remembers things that happened sixty years ago better than what happened yesterday."

"Mm," Webb said. "That's common among very old people."

"You mean white people too? They become ... " Mamuka made fluttering movements with his hands.

Webb laughed. "Some of them become as silly as children."

"Ah. I did not know that."

A small boy about six years old rushed along the track towards the spot where Webb and Mamuka stood. The old man's hut was set at a distance from the rest of the settlement at his own request. He considered much of the ground occupied by the younger people to be polluted. The boy stopped about three metres from Webb, thrust out his hand and spoke in rapid, high-pitched To'beili.

"What?" Webb said.

"If you give him a cigarette he'll give you some information."

"He's too young to smoke."

"He won't smoke it. He'll trade it."

Webb grinned and produced a crumpled Players from his jacket pocket. The boy snatched it and spoke in pidgin so high-pitched and rapid that Webb could barely follow it. But he gathered that there were three ships at Sunburi now, filled with white men.

"Woman?" Webb said. "*Meri?*"

The boy nodded and held up one finger. Webb gave him another cigarette, and he and Mamuka hurried back to where they had beached the canoe. Rusa, the man whom Kaluae had deputed to accompany them, was standing guard over the canoe. His Winchester rifle gleamed in the sun. Webb noted the footprints in the sand — Rusa had had a good many visitors.

"*Yu lukim sips, Rusa?*" Webb said.

"*Mi lukim. Fofela sip kam, trifela stap, wanfela go.*"

The three men pushed the canoe into the shallows, held it steady, boarded and began the long paddle to the other side of the harbour. As they worked, swapping the paddles from side to side in a steady rhythm to cope with currents, Mamuka interrogated Rusa about the ships and his conversations on the beach.

"Mr Naismith has arrived," Mamuka informed Webb, "also another government boat. The woman was on this boat. The *Shining Light* came too but did not stay very long."

"The mission ship?"

"Yes."

"Well, we can do without that. What else does Rusa have to say?"

"He says there is going to be a big fight."

"Between who?"

A rip had to be traversed, and Mamuka gave his attention to his paddling for several minutes. "Eglito is not far away."

"Does he have much support?"

"It's very difficult to say, sir. He is a persuasive man."

"Does he have any . . . I don't know what to call it. Policy . . . political ideas?"

Mamuka laughed. "He wants to be the most famous *lemo* of all time. That is enough. Mr Naismith is stopping him."

Webb paddled steadily for a while before he spoke. "I thought the *lemo*s avoided fighting each other. I thought they threatened and shouted, but did not fight."

"Yes, that's true. But does Mr Naismith know this? The old *lemo* always avoided the final insult, the thing that would lead to the big swear and the big fight."

"I thought Baekani would tell him of these things."

"There is a rumour that Baekani is dead. If this is true, I am very afraid."

"What would it be — the action that would force a fight?"

"I don't know enough about these matters to say."

"What does Rusa make of all this? This talk of fighting?"

"He is looking forward to it."

38

London, 25 February 1928

Ernest Childers was confused. He had slept very little in the past two days and seemed to have lived at Whitehall. Cleaners saw him, haggard and wide-eyed, waiting outside offices hours before the occupants were due to arrive. His desk was littered with reports and files and memos, most of which bore only a tenuous relation to his problem.

He had almost sobbed out his request after locating what Dalziel had called his "opposite number in the FO" — copies of all communications with the BJIP.

"Simply can't be done quickly, old boy," the officer had said. "Leave it with me, and I'll get back to you."

"When? When?"

"Oh, say, this time next week."

"I can't wait that long! Don't you understand? Something is blowing up over there. Actually happening! And we need to know. My minister has to prepare an answer."

"You're obviously not aware of recent changes in regulations governing radio and telegraphic communications."

"What regulations? What changes?"

"Security regulations. The BJIP falls within one of the areas these regulations apply to. Strict security."

"Why, for God's sake? Nothing's happened there for thirty years."

"Doesn't mean things have to stay that way. Weren't you ever a Scout, Childers? 'Be prepared' and all that?"

"We need to know what's going on, now!"

The officer had sniffed and turned away. "You sound like a bloody American, Childers."

Childers so far forgot himself as to grab the man's sleeve. "What?"

"I've told you. We work through channels here. I have to go through the under-secretary, clear it with the Australian office and then advise the WPHC. After that, it's over to the intelligence wallahs. It takes time!"

"No, I meant, what was it you said about . . . Americans! That's it! Americans!" Childers ran down the corridor leaving the FO man scratching his head.

After frantic activity and innumerable telephone calls to Fleet Street, Childers was finally put in touch with one Evan Arkwright, a foreign news reporter on the *Express,* in touch with the Hearst paper in Chicago that had printed the news item from Birmingham. They arranged to meet in a Baker Street pub. Childers shook the snow off his coat and hat and downed two whiskies in rapid succession before Arkwright arrived, twenty minutes after the appointed time. Arkwright, a middle-sized man with a heavy moustache, shrewd eyes and the trace of a northern accent, accepted Childers' offer of a drink.

"A pint of bitter," he said.

Childers fetched the beer and another whisky for himself. "I need to know quickly and reliably what's going on in the BJIP."

"Do you? Why?"

"I don't think I should tell you that."

"You're new at this, aren't you, Mr Childers? You don't know how the game works."

Childers groaned. "Not *another* game! I've been playing Whitehall games for two days."

"Very frustrating, that, I know. Believe me, it's even harder trying to find out something from Whitehall if you're an outsider."

Childers drank some whisky. "I find that hard to believe."

"It's true. Now, I *can* help you. I know what you need to know, or more than you know already, at least. But I won't tell you unless you give me your side of the story."

"Story?"

"To you it's a report, to me it's a story."

"Then something *is* going on?"

"Ah, you've got some brains, I see. Look, it works like this — I tell you what I know, and you tell me what you know. Then we agree not to do certain things."

"Like what?"

"I agree not to reveal the source of my information when and if I publish a story."

Childers looked around the seedy pub and shuddered to think of what Dalziel, with his starched handkerchiefs and precise tie knots, would think of such a place as this and of one of his officers horse-trading in it. Arkwright's promise of confidentiality was of the first importance. "I see," he said. "And what do I agree to?"

"You agree to help me with information, if you can, next time I ask you."

Childers was sufficiently intelligent to see that he was embarking on a long road; he also knew that he had no choice. "Agreed," he said.

Arkwright drained his glass. "I'll have another pint."

When Childers returned with the drinks, Arkwright was spreading sheets of paper covered with typed and handwritten notes on the table in front of him. The edges of some of the sheets became soggy as they encountered beer puddles. "What've you got there?"

"Copies of radio traffic in the islands," Arkwright said. "Seems there was some sort of banana boat in the area with a decent radio. The *Chicago Daily News* got the lot."

"D'you mean the official traffic as well as . . . ?"

"My word." Arkwright drank some beer and assembled

a thin sheaf of papers. "Here you are. Doesn't amount to much — the gist is that the high commissioner wants the resident to use firm measures. The resident's passing that on to the district officer, if he's still alive."

Childers gaped. "Is there doubt about that?"

"There's doubt about everything, chum. A storm seems to have knocked communications for six. The most recent thing we've got," Arkwright detached a half-sheet, "is ambiguous."

"What d'you mean?"

"It's from a field radio, and the signal was weak. The boat didn't pick it all up. It *could* be the DO reporting that he's on the job, but it's hard to say."

"What about the American writer — Manchester?"

Arkwright grinned. "Birmingham. Nothing from him for a while. My guess is that the government's going to act, probably do something tough. Show the flag. Show anyone who's interested that a red dot on the map still means something." Arkwright patted the papers together and passed them across. "Now it's your turn. Why are you interested?"

"The minister's expecting a question in the House. He needs facts for an answer."

Arkwright laughed. "Facts? Since when? Anything else?"

Childers wracked his brains for interesting but innocuous information. He could think of nothing, and the only knowledge his own researches had produced popped into his head. He spoke impulsively. "Australia wants to send a warship," he said.

Awkwright produced a pencil and notebook like a conjurer. "Now that's interesting. Has Australia *got* a warship?"

The whisky had reached Childers. He giggled. "That's what my boss asked me."

"And?"

"Yes. There is one. The *Port Augusta,* a thousand-tonner."

"Excellent," Awkwright scribbled in his notebook. "Well, Mr Childers, have you got what you need?"

Childers tried to focus his whisky-clouded mind. "Think so. I c'n make a report. Tell me, how does the *Chicago Daily News* feel about, what's his name — Liverpool?"

"Birmingham," Arkwright said. "I gather they're not very happy. He seems to have disappeared. Now there's where you could help me, Mr Childers. You've got my number. Give me a ring if you hear anything about him."

"Who?" Childers said.

Arkwright finished his beer and went off to find coffee for Ernest Childers.

That night, Sir Hugh Stafford rose in the House of Commons to a question from a member on the opposition benches. As was his habit, Sir Hugh had scarcely bothered to listen to the question in detail; he knew the subject was coming up, and he had prepared his answer. That was all the scruffy fellow required or could expect, surely. "His Majesty's government," Sir Hugh intoned, "is fully aware of the situation in the British Jeremiah Islands Protectorate. Events that amount to disturbances have occurred. The resident commissioner is confident that order can be maintained."

Sir Hugh sat down and was astonished to see the Speaker give the questioner the call once more.

"Is it true that the Australian government is standing by to send a warship to the BJIP?"

Sir Hugh had had more than one brandy after dinner and was ill-prepared for this ungentlemanly harrying. He shuffled his papers and caught sight of a neatly typed memo. He stood. "HMAS *Port Augusta* is prepared to sail to the Protectorate on three hours' notice."

The "Hear! Hears!" from his own side of the House were quickly drowned out. The uproar around him took the minister completely by surprise. He clenched his fists and glared at the members opposite. He caught only fragments of their interjections: "disturbances", "cracking walnuts with a steamroller", "gunboat diplomacy".

"Well, well?" he bellowed. "What does it matter? It's

not Africa, is it? Is it?"

"I have Mr Clancy on the line, Mr Peters."

"Put him through," Maxwell Peters said. "Ben? Good to talk to you. I'm calling about our writer, Tom Birmingham. You made an approach . . . Sure, it was a while ago. But these things . . . "

Peters tapped nervously on his desk with a pencil while he listened. Outside the sky was dark, although it was only mid-afternoon; down on 10th Street a newsboy was shouting that RCA stock had risen above the magical 400 mark. Mavis Graeme, Peters' secretary, left her office and walked down a corridor to the room occupied by Valerie Benson. She knocked, opened the door and beckoned. A minute later Valerie Benson was listening on Miss Graeme's extension to the conversation between Peters and Benjamin Clancy of the *Chicago Daily News*.

"A little misunderstanding, Ben," Peters said. "We've got him locked up tight, but we don't want to be dog-in-the-manger about it. There could be enough in this for everyone."

"In what?" Clancy barked.

"Come on, Ben. In this rebellion-in-paradise stuff. This particular paradise has Frogs, Chinks and Japs in it and the State Department likes it for a communications base. Now, you're in touch with Tom. If you could just get him to cable us, I'm sure we can work something out."

Valerie Benson's strong face set in even more determined lines as she heard Clancy's reply.

"We haven't heard a thing from him in days. Dead silence."

"What do you mean?" Peters said.

"Just that. For a while the radio was out all over the goddamned place, then transmission began again. The boys in charge got busy telling each other what to do, but there was nothing from Birmingham."

"Nothing?"

"Not a peep. Hell of a lot of storms around there. Maybe he got sunk. Could be we're out a story, and you're out a writer. Anything else I can do for you, Peters? I gotta paper to get out here."

"No," Peters said. "I guess not."

"We've got a guy in Fiji asking around. Maybe he can pick up something. Birmingham's wife was with him, right?"

"Yes. She's the daughter of Hiram Waldeck."

"That so? Too bad. Well, I guess I'd better get the obituary guy to brush up his piece on Birmingham. You sell a few books after a writer croaks, don't you?"

Valerie Benson was suddenly aware that her jaw was locked and her teeth were grinding.

"Yes, we do. A lot, sometimes. It depends on the backlist and the circumstances of the death."

Clancy's short, barking laugh came over the line again. "Well, this is tailor-made, I'd say. So look on the bright side. You know what they say in the newspaper game?"

"No."

"Bad writers are a dime a dozen, good writers cost two bits."

"Shit!"

Valerie Benson burst into harsh laughter as Peters angrily slammed down the receiver.

39

Sunburi, 1 March 1928

Louise Birmingham and Richard Webb had been almost shy on meeting again at Sunburi. Their behaviour was constrained by the presence of Naismith and Clements and by the amount of information each had to impart. They had had only a few minutes alone before Webb was drawn into a long, argumentative session in which he tried to persuade Naismith not to hold the tax gathering, and the DO repeated his stubborn determination that it was time to assert his authority. Cameron Somerville had restored Webb's radio to working order and communicated with Patugi. He relayed the RC's message of support to Naismith.

"I think that should conclude our discussion, Mr Webb," the DO said. "I'm grateful for your advice, of course."

Webb looked sourly at Somerville and left the deck of the *Loloburu* where Naismith had conducted the meeting. Somerville hurried after him.

"Don't blame me, old chap," the technician said. "Just doing my job."

"Right," Webb grunted.

"Well, I'm off tonight," Somerville said. "Down south to take a look at the Tau lagoon. If you'll permit me to say so, you're a very lucky man."

Webb stepped off the jetty onto the dark sand and looked back up at the intense, intelligent face of Somerville. He respected good technicians and he was glad to have the radio operating. There was no point in taking out his frustration on this man. "How's that?" he said, attempting a friendly tone.

"Louise is a wonderful girl, and she's very stuck on you. Half your luck."

Webb smiled. "Thanks." He went in search of Louise but found her occupied with Nanni and some of the Sunburi women. Then Kaluae buttonholed him for a discussion on where Webb intended to take up residence — with his people or on the other side of the harbour. Webb became involved in a half-hour exercise in diplomacy. After a period spent with Mamuka, recording in his notebook the information they had acquired during the day, he was too tired to respond to Clements' call to have a farewell drink with Somerville.

"Mr Naismith has asked me to form part of his guard tomorrow," Mamuka said.

"You don't have to if you don't want to, Peter."

"There will be a fight."

"Mr Naismith doesn't think so."

"He is wrong, Mr Webb. I hear things."

"Kaluae hears things too. He is advising Mr Naismith." Mamuka shook his head. "We cannot both be right."

"Perhaps Mr Naismith is right. There are three boats in the harbour, and . . ."

"Two, sir. Mr Somerville is leaving tonight."

"Yes, but . . ."

"And Mr Naismith fell over on the beach today. Did you know that? His head hit the sand. Do you know what sort of a sign Eglito could take that for?"

Webb sighed. "I can guess. You're sure he's nearby? Kaluae has men watching."

"How loyal are they? And to whom?"

"I don't know, of course. Mr Naismith has made up his mind, and I can't do anything about it. You must decide for yourself what you want to do."

Mamuka stared up at the hills above the harbour, which were darkening as the light dropped. "It would be wise for you and Mrs Birmingham and Mr Clements to stay on the boat."

Webb nodded. "And you?"

Mamuka smiled. "I heard a saying in Queensland I liked very much. Here is a good chance to use it. I'll sleep on it."

Clements came back slightly tipsy from Somerville's send-off.

"Was she there?" Webb asked.

"Yep. But she's sleeping ashore. Said she'd see you at breakfast."

"Good. I'm bushed. Good night, Colin."

"What about some dinner?"

"Too tired to eat."

"That's your story. I'm not a big eater myself. I daresay if I was in love I'd be skin and bones."

Breakfast was a rather sedate affair, with Clements suffering from a mild hangover and Webb and Louise exhibiting excessive politeness. Webb suddenly realised that he hadn't seen Peter Mamuka that morning, which was unusual. "Seen Peter?" he asked Clements.

Clements took a tentative serving of fried bacon, a radical hangover cure. He glanced ashore and pointed.

The troop assembled at eight a.m. on the Sunburi jetty — Sergeant Solifu, two constables, Peter Mamuka, Marius, and Solomon and Kwainuna, two ex-policemen and close associates of the headman, Kaluae. All seven men were armed with police issue Lee Enfield rifles and wore bayonets in scabbards on their webbing belts. For the occasion they wore blue shirts and lava-lavas, police helmets and fully packed ammunition belts, crosswise from shoulder to waist. The brass on the weapons and bullets gleamed in the sun; the webbing was freshly cleaned and the newly appointed sergeant Solifu had a red feather in a band around the crown of his helmet. They made a brave showing.

Naismith was in freshly starched whites — shirt, shorts, long socks — and highly polished black shoes. His Webley was in a holster worn high on his left hip. A clasp knife, used for notching the tax disc, hung from a lanyard around his neck. He was shaved and barbered, and his face had regained some of its tanned vigour. He inspected his troops and had them about-turn smartly and march towards the *haus takus*. Several of the policemen carried bags of shell money for trading with the taxpayers. Under his arm Naismith carried the tax rolls and a small, lockable strongbox. Marius also carried documents and his rifle.

Richard Webb, Louise Birmingham and Colin Clements watched the proceedings from the deck of the *Woodlark*. They saw Naismith halt his party in the clearing and station Solifu and a constable outside the hut. A large crowd had already assembled, and more could be seen on the tracks leading down to the clearing. The people moved quietly and soberly. Webb scrutinised the scene through fieldglasses. He saw no women or children. The DO then mounted the steps to the verandah and supervised the arrangement of the table and chairs for Marius and himself. He directed Solomon to stand a little to one side of him and sent the other constable with Mamuka and Kwainuna into the hut.

"My God," Clements said, "why's he putting them *inside?*"

"He can't afford to display too much strength," Webb said. "It would indicate fear."

"That's insane," Louise said.

Webb smiled. "Men are, especially when it comes to war."

"Is this war?"

"Let's hope not."

"There must be a hundred people there already," Clements said. "It's going to be a long day."

Webb shook his head. "Naismith's not stupid. He'll call a halt when he feels he's made his point."

"That's a relief," Louise said, "I can feel a sort of tension in the air, a threat. A whole day of it would be unendurable. I want to watch for a while, though."

They watched as the ritual began. The taxpayers formed a long line leading to the tables. They stood two and three abreast but formed a single column when close to the verandah. At the end of the line the men stood in bunches, smoking, chewing betel and conducting last-minute hagglings over shell money and shillings. The sun climbed and the air heated up quickly; Louise looked out into the harbour and thought longingly of a swim. But there were no inviting beaches around Sunburi. She watched Webb as he raised the glasses. The dark hairs on the back of his hands, the firm skin stretched over his jawbone, everything about him excited her. She wanted this day to be over so that they could talk and make plans.

"See any weapons?" Clements said.

Webb nodded. "A few. Bows, axes, no guns."

"As you say, Naismith's no fool. He didn't mention the gun-collecting on this occasion. Wouldn't be wise to invite these chaps down with their Sniders."

"I'm worried, though," Webb said. "There's too many of them. The police on the ground are getting hemmed in. And there's more coming. Look at them on the tracks."

Men were streaming down the paths towards the clearing.

"Real bushmen, those," Clements said. "I wouldn't mind a couple of those headdresses for my collection."

"I don't like this," Webb said. "Louise, where's that Sharps you had back at Alma?"

"It's below. Richard, what you are going to do?"

"Get it, please. Colin, any guns on the *Loloburu*?"

"Could be a couple," Clements said. He took the binoculars and focussed them. "I see what you mean. The men who've paid shouldn't be hanging around like that. They usually go back home more or less straight off."

"They're edging this way," Webb said. He turned and beckoned one of the *Woodlark* crew. Speaking in pidgin, he told the man to alert the bosun of the *Loloburu* to the possibility of danger. The man leaped the rail and ran across the jetty to where the DO's boat was moored.

"They noticed that," Clement said. "We're getting some dirty looks."

Louise returned with the heavy rifle. She handed it to Webb, who checked it expertly. "Any ammunition?"

"Just what's in it," Louise said. "What's happening up at the tax hut?"

Eglito, Lagailemo, and Meila were in the clearing half an hour after the tax collecting began. At the last minute, Nalai'u had withdrawn his support, unconvinced by Eglito's reading of the signs, unsure that his own advancement would be served by an attack on the *gafamanu*. A plotter and intriguer by nature, he did not believe that Eglito's motives were as stated. There must be some deeper purpose, some devious design that would advance Eglito and harm all others. So he withdrew, to stand back from the action, but not to betray Eglito or to lift a hand against him. A survivor, Nalai'u, and many of his kinsmen, who had seen the power of the white men in bigger ports than at Alma and on wider roads than those of Patugi, were relieved.

Still, Eglito had passionate followers and Lagailemo likewise — adherents, adventurers, ambitious men, revenge- and glory-seekers, scorners of the new ways. They joined the trickle of bush people who went down to Sunburi to pay their taxes. Nearly all were aware of the simmering violence in Eglito's heart, and expected it. *Lemos* were known for their rages, which came over the horizon like storms, threw everything into confusion and departed, usually leaving things much as they were before. To be sure, Eglito's actions were extreme — he had killed on Hemisphere Island and attacked the *gafamanu* at Alma, but Murdoans had raided other islands before and attacked ships. Was not Baekani rumoured to be still alive and seeking vengeance? Were not all the old balances still in place? So people came to pay their taxes, curious to see whether Eglito would appear, curious about how the DO, humiliated at Maka Maka as everyone knew, would react — curious about Baekani.

Eglito and his followers easily eluded Kaluae's lookouts. No one could watch all paths to Fitua, the place of dead leaves, and when they arrived there, armed with rifles concealed in bundles of yams that the bush people traditionally traded for fish on the coast, and carrying bushknives, hunting knives and axes, their presence was unremarked by any whose business it was to communicate with the DO or his police. They mingled with the crowd, thirty desperadoes among an equal number of sympathisers, and at least three times that many who were either unaware of them or indifferent to their intentions.

Eglito had found the answer to his dilemma during the night and conferred briefly with his henchmen before he joined the tax line, to give them their instructions. Lagailemo nodded and smiled to show that he liked the scheme. Dour as ever, Meila listened intently to Eglito's words to fix them in his mind.

"As he cuts the disc of the man two places in front of me," Eglito said. "Then and not before."

Meila repeated the words. "Then, *bokuru*," he said.

Eglito's hand snaked back over his shoulder to touch the rifle barrel. "Yes. *Bokuru*." He stepped into line; the men around shrank back, but he gripped the nearest arm and jerked the man into place. Fear held him there; he shuffled forward. The man in front of him and the one behind Eglito did likewise. Eglito smiled. The power of the *lemo* could control three men as easily as a sow controlled her piglets.

"I can't see the policemen at all," Webb said. "I wouldn't have believed that clearing could hold so many people."

"Where's Peter?" Louise said.

Webb lowered the glasses. "Inside the hut. This has gone far enough. Naismith should bring them out and start clearing a few people off. Where's Kaluae?"

Clements shrugged. "Haven't seen him for a while. D'you think he's up to something?"

Webb was aware of a restlessness among the crew on the *Woodlark*. He glanced across at the *Loloburu* and saw signs of the same reaction there — the sailors stood about uneasily on the deck, looking towards the crowded clearing. He saw sunlight gleam on the barrel of a shotgun. He spun around when a shout came from behind him. The bosun of the vessel was struggling with one of his crew, a large man whom the bosun was having trouble controlling. Webb stepped forward and jabbed the sailor in the ribs with the rifle. His tone was harsh, with none of the usual lilt of pidgin. "Fools, why do you fight?"

The wrestlers fell apart. Clements said, "This chap wanted to cast off. The bosun wouldn't let him. I thought you might want this." He handed Webb the long-barrelled pistol that had belonged to Birmingham. Webb took it and presented the weapon to the bosun. The meaning of the gesture was clear — the sailors muttered but stayed clear of the mooring ropes.

"Do you have a firearm, Colin?" Webb said. "Anything at all?"

Clements shook his head. "There's a flare pistol in the supplies locker, I think. That's all."

"Get it, please. The clouds're coming in, and the light's dropping. A flare might show if it gets any darker."

Clements went below, and Louise looked at the sky. Heavy clouds were moving in from the sea. They passed across the face of the sun, casting a gloom over the harbour and the milling crowd in the clearing. Away in the distance, thunder growled.

"Could help," Webb said. "But I think I'm going to have to go up there and create some kind of diversion from behind." He checked the rifle and prepared to step over the rail onto the jetty. "Tell Colin . . ."

"Too late," Louise said. "Look!"

Three places back in the line, Eglito watched approvingly as his men took up their positions. The *solodia*, the policemen posted in the clearing, were as good as dead. Each one was covered by two men armed with hunting knives. The crowd was too tightly packed around them to allow use of their rifles. Those rifles would soon be in the hands of Eglito's followers. Marius made an entry in the roll, the man nodded and stepped away. Eglito drew a deep breath. The sky darkened suddenly and the DO looked up. For a chilling moment Eglito thought that Naismith would look down and see him. But the DO merely glanced at the sky, checked his watch and returned to his work. The next man, two in front of him, moved up to stand on the bottom step leading to the verandah. He was a tallish man, but his head was still at a level below that of the sitting Naismith. The man pushed his coin across the table. Naismith bent his bare head over the tax disc and notched it with his knife.

Wild, piercing screams sounded as Solifu and the constable were hacked to death. At the same moment Meila and his men cut through the bindings that attached the planks of the porch to the rest of the structure. The porch subsided instantly; screaming his defiance Eglito leapt onto the steps; he pullled the *koburu* from its pouch and swung it high. Naismith's hands flew up in surprise as he felt the porch sag under him. He began to rise, struggling for a foothold, but he was below the level of Eglito's eyes when the old rifle barrel crashed down onto his head with the full force of Eglito's arms, body and mind behind it. Naismith's skull cracked with a sound like a football being kicked; his brains splattered over Marius and the table and the tax rolls as he slumped forward.

Eglito's men cut through the panels that formed the walls of the hut and attacked the stunned Kwainuna and the constable in numbers at close quarters. They hacked and slashed with bushknives and severed hands and arms. Peter Mamuka, standing a little apart and holding his rifle at the ready, fought off two attackers and blew the head off a third. He clubbed down several knife thrusts and burst out of the hut.

Outside, Eglito swung the *koburu* at Marius who had snatched up Naismith's revolver. Eglito's blow missed as the broken porch subsided. Marius scrambled up and fired wildly. He missed Eglito, but hit the man beside him, the man who hadn't moved since the DO cut his tax disc. Lagailemo appeared from the hut with one of the police rifles; he shot Marius through the back of the head, whooped and fired three times into the air.

"Mamuka, Mamuka!" yelled Eglito.

Lagailemo saw Mamuka running towards the water. He sighted quickly and fired but missed. Solomon, who had fallen when the porch gave way and dropped his weapon, had sustained terrible wounds to his head and shoulders but managed to struggle free of the wildly excited attackers, who were snatching at rifles and the bundles of shell money the police had brought to trade with, and hobbled towards the beach. Meila, his bushknife dripping blood, strode after him. Lagailemo followed; he fumbled with a bayonet, trying to attach it to his rifle. Eglito jerked the lanyard from around Naismith's neck and held up the clasp knife. He looked for the pistol but could not find it. The knife and the brain pulp that spattered his chest were enough. He pushed aside shouting, whooping supporters, as well as people who had merely stood and watched as Naismith and the *solodia* were cut down, and caught up with Lagailemo. The three fanned out and advanced on the two men. Mamuka shouted to the wounded man to hurry and delayed his own retreat. He raised the rifle, sighted on Lagailemo's chest and fired. The weapon jammed. Mamuka changed his grip on it to hold it like a club. He waited while Solomon stumbled back. Meila made a rushing advance that deflected Mamuka away from the jetty. He was retreating towards the water itself, where no safety lay.

Richard Webb swung his legs over the rail onto the jetty and moved swiftly towards the sand, holding the heavy rifle at half port. The noise from the clearing, the shouts, shots and stirrings had died away. All eyes were focussed on the five men moving towards the water's edge. Mamuka jerked his bayonet from its scabbard and passed it to the wounded Solomon. They stepped back until the sand was soft under their feet. Lagailemo threw down the bayonet and raised his rifle. Richard Webb stopped and brought the Sharps up to his shoulder.

Three shots rang out so quickly that the sound they made seemed like one explosion. Eglito, Meila and Lagailemo fell almost at the same moment. Lagailemo and Meila did not move; Eglito twitched and his hands clawed at the sand before his body convulsed once and lay still.

Baekani had sat on the grassy knoll above the clearing and watched the crowd assemble. In his exhausted, almost hallucinating state, he had not interpreted the movements in the crowd as threatening. He had not seen Eglito until the last moment, when the *koburu* was raised and it was too late. At that moment, Baekani had had Naismith in his sights and had been about to end his life. He froze as Eglito's attack took place, watched in amazement as his master died, and the policemen were killed. Understanding nothing, his mind almost a blank and now without purpose, he had seen the three leaders emerge from the throng and advance with deadly intent on the two survivors.

In the instant before he squeezed the trigger, Baekani had a surge of feeling that was almost sympathy with the To'beili *lemo*. He understood what Eglito had done; he had made himself the last true lemo. He had used the old ways to bring those old ways to an end on Murdo. After this the bush people would be harried by the whites and the saltwater men; To'beili would be turned against To'beili; clan vengeance would explode and with it retribution from the *gufamanu*. Shrines would be desecrated, men's houses destroyed and the young people would turn against their elders and leave to work for the white men. It was the end of something. Baekani understood and approved. He fired three times and the expanding bullets blew apart the heads of Eglito and his comrades.

Tears were running down Baekani's face as he worked the bolt of the rifle. He recognised Mamuka and Solomon, and he saw no reason why they should not die as well. He chambered the next round and sighted. Then his head filled with a roaring like a giant wave; he felt the ground beneath him dissolve and he knew that his pain and shame were over, and that he too was part of the great ending of things.

Webb's first shot blew away most of Baekani's head. The next and the next were fired over the heads of the confused To'beili, attackers and onlookers alike, who stood in the clearing. The heavy rifle's boom was louder than all previous reports, and it echoed back from the mountain wall. Webb fired again, spacing the shots. Then the Very flare arced across the dark sky and burst into a brilliant, glaring cascade over the clearing. The To'beili wavered, clustered together, broke into groups and fled to the paths, trampling the bodies of Sergeant Solifu and his dead comrade, scrambling and pushing their way past the ruined tax house. Thunder rolled in the sky, lightning flickered over the sea and the rain began to fall.

40

Webb and Mamuka assisted Solomon to the *Woodlark*, but he died from shock and loss of blood within minutes of reaching the boat. Clements and Louise, together with Nanni and other women from Sunburi, offered help to the men and youths who had been injured in the fighting or the panic that had followed the shootings. The rain fell for half an hour, making the leaf-strewn clearing muddy and slippery. When Webb and Mamuka reached the place, they found Kaluae standing where Sergeant Solifu had died. The ground was soggy from the rain and the policeman's blood.

"Nailu'u told me there would be no attack," Kaluae said to Mamuka.

Webb caught the name but not the meaning of the comment. "Who is Nailu'u?" he said.

Mamuka grimaced. "He is an associate of Eglito's."

"He tricked me," Kaluae said.

This Webb understood. He said, "I see," and he looked steadily into the headman's eyes, trying to judge his sincerity. He was unable to do so and turned away.

"We will have to arrange the burials, sir," Mamuka said. He gestured to the beach where the bodies of Eglito, Meila and Lagailemo lay. "The kin of Eglito and Meila will collect them. Kwainuna and Solomon's people will do the things for them."

"What of Lagailemo?"

"They will probably feed him it to the sharks, or the crocodiles."

"That leaves Mr Naismith and Baekani," Webb said.

"Baekani killed the men who killed his master. They should be buried together."

Webb could see sense in this, but he knew that the gesture would outrage officialdom, which would see Baekani as the murderer of Keith Larke and nothing more. "We can't do that, Peter," he said. "We can bury them where they died — Baekani on the hill, and Mr Naismith by the *haus takus*."

"With Marius," Mamuka said.

Webb nodded. "He was a courageous man. He fought well. And you, Peter, you fought well and protected Solomon. That was also brave."

"It doesn't matter," Mamuka said. "Eglito's people will sing it one way, Baekani's another, and the white men will tell their own story. We don't know what happened here, not really."

Webb and Mamuka walked to the wrecked tax hut. Clements joined them, and they looked at Naismith's body, which had been laid on the ground, protected from the rain by one of the detached wall panels. The head was a ruin, and there was a deep gash in the right shoulder which had almost severed the arm.

"A waste," Clements said, "he was a good man. He tried to be fair."

"He made a mistake," Webb said, "and he paid for it. The pity is that a lot of others will pay for it too."

Clements had located Naismith's sun helmet under the collapsed porch. He bent and placed it over the shattered head. "What d'you mean?"

"This is a disaster for the To'beili," Webb said.

"Vengeance will be required for everyone who died here. Eglito's kin will be punished. You can multiply the number of dead by three or four."

"This is true," Mamuka said.

"At least there's no need for a punitive expedition," Clements said. "The ringleaders are dead. I couldn't bear the sight of the planters and commercials, armed to the teeth, panting through the bush looking for something to shoot."

"No, that's a mercy," Webb said. "But bounties will be out for revenge for the people Baekani killed. Murdo is going to be a very disturbed place for some time."

"A dangerous place," Clement said. "Will you be staying?"

"If they'll let me."

"They'll let you all right. You're the white man who took charge and held up the . . . imperial end of things, as it were."

Webb shook his head and turned away from the tax hut. The rain had cleared, and the sun was causing steam to lift from the wet ground. He saw two men climbing the hill to where Baekani's body lay. One bent, and when he straightened up he had the Mannlicher rifle in his hand. Webb looked towards the beach where people had gathered around the three corpses. The tide was coming in, threatening to sweep the beach clean. He could not see Eglito's rifle barrel, and he wondered what had happened to it. A man left the group on the beach and walked across the clearing. He handed Naismith's clasp knife to Webb and spoke in a choked voice to Mamuka.

"They want to take the bodies," Mamuka said. "They ask your permission."

Webb nodded, and the man turned away. "This is no good," Webb said. "I didn't come here to represent the bloody British Empire. I won't be able to do the work I want to do."

Clements' hand clasped his shoulder. "Maybe you can do something else."

Louise Birmingham and Nanni joined the men. "Nanni

says we should all go to the boats," Louise said, "except her and Peter. We have no business here now."

"I'm going to bury poor Will," Clements said. "Then I'll leave gladly. This is an awful place."

"Fitua," Mamuka said. "Dead leaves."

Webb radioed Patugi with a report on events at Sunburi at two p.m. Ashley Price-Kane spoke to him personally, ordering him to bring whatever documents or other evidence he could secure to the capital with the greatest despatch.

"Are there any prisoners?" the RC asked.

"Two," Webb said. "One identified as the killer of one of the policemen, and another as the man who mutilated Naismith's dead body."

"Bring them," Price-Kane said, "along with the witnesses. Anything further to report?"

"No," Webb said.

"Get back here as quickly as you can. And Mr Webb . . ."

"Yes, sir?"

"I understand you were a serving officer in the war. Infantry."

"Yes, sir."

"As I would have expected. Well done, Mr Webb."

The *Woodlark* sailed shortly before sunset. Aboard were Webb, Clements, Louise Birmingham, Peter Mamuka and Nanni. The prisoners Webb had referred to, and two To'beili witnesses, along with the headman Kaluae, were aboard the *Loloburu*, which departed shortly after the BP boat. The Europeans stood on the deck and gazed towards the land as the boat neared the central island. A sheet of flame shot up from the clearing, illuminating the rock wall behind it and the hill where Baekani had dealt death and died.

Louise gripped Webb's hand. "The tax hut's on fire."

"These people won't ever go in it again after so much death," Webb said. "They might as well burn it down."

EPILOGUE

The two To'beili taken to Patugi aboard the *Woodlark* were tried for murder, although there was no evidence that one of them had done more than strike at a man already dead. Both were found guilty and hanged. A further eleven attackers were arrested, tried and sentenced to terms of imprisonment; eight of these died in a typhoid fever epidemic that swept through the overcrowded Patugi gaol. And so the British avenged their dead, as the Murdoans also did many times over in the months that followed — by surprise attack, midnight raid and ambush. Webb's prediction that the number of dead on the island would multiply by a factor of three or four was an underestimate.

Ashley Price-Kane burned the two strange communications he had had from Keith Larke. They would not have fitted well with the perception of the cadet as a young idealist, performing his duties bravely as he was cut down by a deranged rebel. The resident commissioner retired a year after the events on Murdo, was knighted and went to live quietly in Surrey.

Richard Webb received official thanks for his handling

of what came to be called the 'Murdoan emergency'. His field research at Sunburi resulted in a dissertation entitled 'Conflict and resolution among the To'beili of Murdo' and the award of a doctorate from Oxford. The published version contained many criticisms of British colonial policy and practice, including a detailed critique of the trial verdicts. It became a prohibited import in the BJIP.

Louise Birmingham's Murdo photographs of the life and work of the islanders, including several of the fallen hero Naismith, the rebel Baekani and the aftermath of the attack at Sunburi, were published by Duckworth, along with an essay by the photographer, under the title *Jeremiah Journey.* The book was a modest success. Louise visited Webb at Sunburi during the course of his fieldwork, but they found that their hectic passion at the time of 'the emergency' had passed. However, they continued to meet and correspond. Louise's reputation was enhanced by further photographic studies of Melanesians, Polynesians and Amerindians. Webb was appointed to a lectureship and subsequently a chair at Cambridge, and Louise became curator of historical and ethnological photography at the Smithsonian Institute.

The firm of Waldeck & Marsh was a casualty of the stock market crash of 1929, although Hiram Waldeck did not live to see the disaster. He died in May of that year. Maxwell Peters embarked on a long period of unemployment; William Cavendish survived on dividends from a series of cautious, ultra-safe investments. Valerie Benson found congenial work as a researcher and as a fact-checker for the *New Yorker.* Her efforts as unpaid agent for Tom Birmingham bore no fruit.

Birmingham and Pastor Karl Stoltenberg reached Queensland in the *Shining Light* after a rough passage some weeks after interest in the 'Murdoan emergency' had abated. Stoltenberg, his nerve shaken by the voyage and the news of Naismith's fate, repaired quietly to Maryborough, there to continue his mission work under the critical eye of his wife.

Birmingham was unsuccessful in securing a contract

from American and British publishers for his account of events in the BJIP. Somewhat fraudulently, since his American agent had already disposed of them, he sold the film rights to his Adams series for a sufficient sum to live economically in Brisbane while he completed his memoirs. The book was rejected by publishers in New York, London and Sydney. Birmingham returned to the US, using borrowed funds, and secured the position of editor of a pulp fiction magazine, *Adventures Unlimited*, published in Philadelphia. He and Louise were divorced in 1933.

Ernest Childers continued to cultivate contacts among the press, domestic and foreign, so that eventually he became known in the Colonial Office as 'the man to see when the doors don't open'. This reputation, however, failed to advance him in the service. Reports by his superiors used expressions such as 'unorthodox methods' and 'dubious sources'. In 1939, on the eve of the outbreak of war, friends of Childers noticed a new confidence in his manner and a new cheerfulness in his disposition. They assumed he had been promoted; in fact, he had been seconded to MI6.

Colin Clements resigned his post with Burns Philp, leased land in the west of the Jeremiahs, failed again as a planter and joined W.R. Carpenter & Co. as a trading agent. He became a BJIP 'old hand', an expert on Naismith, Eglito and Baekani, much sought after by journalists and travellers for his account of the 'troubles'. His assembly of Jeremian artefacts formed the basis of the now-famous collection at the University of the Pacific.

Peter Mamuka became headman at Alma. During the war he assisted American and Australian coastwatchers in their resistance to the occupying Japanese forces. He represented the Kweili district on the advisory council on Murdo after the war.

The three To'beili attackers who eluded the hangman and survived the typhoid escaped from prison when the Japanese bombed Patugi and returned to Murdo where they remained in hiding for many years. Nanni lived to see the establishment of the advisory council and wrote to Louise

Birmingham in Washington D.C. to tell her of her pleasure. She died in 1949 at an age she described in a letter to Louise as 'safely over the century'.

The *koburu* sits in the rafters of a To'beili men's house; Baekani's Mannlicher is similarly smoked and consecrated by his descendants. Even though the kin of Eglito and Baekani paid dearly in blood and shell money for their deeds, time has made heroes of the pair. Eglito is sometimes referred to by the To'beili as the 'last *lemo*' and Baekani as the most fearsome *togu* ever to walk the land.

Four feet beneath the blackened earth where the blazing frame of the *haus takus* fell and burned for hours, the bones of the district officer rest, white and brittle in the acidic soil. He was laid on his back and the empty eye sockets point up at the sky that arches over what appears on all post-1928 maps as Naismith Bay.